D1079932

In

umfries and Galloway Libraries, Information and Archives

This item is to be returned on or before the last date shown below.

2 0 SEP 2013 Mt

.OCT 2013 Mt

1 8 DEC 2013 EW

9 JAN 2014 EW

1 3 MAR 2014 EW

1 8 APR 2018   1 1 MAY 2018

1 1 SEP 2018

RF

Awarded for excellence in public service
Dumfries and Galloway
Libraries, Information and Archives

Central Support Unit: Catherine Street Dumfries DG1 1JB
tel: 01387 253820   fax: 01387 260294   e-mail: libs&i@dumgal.gov.uk

24 HOUR LOAN RENEWAL BY PHONE AT LO-CALL RATE - 0845 2748080
OR ON OUR WEBSITE - WWW.DUMGAL.GOV.UK/LIA

All the characters in this book have no existence outside the imagination of the auth..e name or nam..own or unkn...

All Rig..a....reproduction in whole or in part in..published........arrangement with.....lequin Enterpr.................................for this publication........not....the.....of may not be re..onic or mechan...........................photocopying, recording.........................mation retrieva.............................without the written permission of the......lisher.

This bo...ade or otherwi..e prior consent...other.....wise.....of cover other.....that in which i..............................and without a sim....................including this.....ndition being in.................on the subsequent pur.....r

® and TM............are trademarks owned and.....ed by the trademark owner.....d/or its licensee............Trademarks marked with ® are registered with the United.....ngdom Patent...ket and in other countries.

DUMFRIES &
GALLOWAY
LIBRARIES

AS226893	
Askews & Holts	Jul-2013
AF	£5.99

Published in Great Britain 2013
by Mills & Boon, an imprint of Harlequin (UK) Limited,
Eton House, 18-24 Paradise Road, Richmond, Surrey TW9 1SR

THE HUDSONS: MAX, BELLA AND DEVLIN
© by Harlequin Enterprises II B.V./S.à.r.l 2013

Special thanks and acknowledgements to Emilie Rose, Catherine Mann
and Maureen Child for their contribution to THE HUDSONS: MAX, BELLA
AND DEVLIN.

Bargained Into Her Boss's Bed, Propositioned Into a Foreign Affair and
Seduced Into a Paper Marriage were first published in Great Britain by
Harlequin (UK) Limited.

Bargained Into Her Boss's Bed © Harlequin Books S.A. 2009
Propositioned Into a Foreign Affair © Harlequin Books S.A. 2009
Seduced Into a Paper Marriage © Harlequin Books S.A. 2009

ISBN: 978 0 263 90558 8
ebook ISBN: 978 1 472 00131 3

05-0713

Harlequin (UK) policy is to use papers that are natural, renewable and
recyclable products and made from wood grown in sustainable forests. The
logging and manufacturing processes conform to the legal environmental
regulations of the country of origin.

Printed and bound in Spain by Blackprint CPI, Barcelona

BARGAINED INTO HER BOSS'S BED

BY
EMILIE ROSE

Bestselling Desire™ author and RITA® Award finalist **Emilie Rose** lives in her native North Carolina with her four sons and two adopted mutts. Writing is her third (and hopefully her last) career. She's managed a medical office and run a home day care, neither of which offers half as much satisfaction as plotting happy endings. Her hobbies include gardening and cooking (especially cheesecake). She's a rabid country music fan because she can find an entire book in almost any song. She is currently working her way through her own "bucket list" which includes learning to ride a Harley. Visit her website at www.emilierose.com or e-mail EmilieRoseC@aol.com. Letters can be mailed to PO Box 20145, Raleigh, NC 27619, USA.

To LaShawn, a woman who truly embodies the phrase
"dance like nobody's watching." You go girl!

One

"What is this?"

Dana Fallon flinched at the irritation and impatience in Max Hudson's voice. She couldn't blame him. Hudson Pictures was up against an immovable deadline in shooting their current project, and her leaving now wasn't the nicest thing she could do to them.

But she had her reasons. Good ones.

Stand by your decision. Execute your plan. Her big brother's booming "coach" voice echoed in her head even though he was on the other side of the Atlantic Ocean.

She reined in her retreating courage, brushed the dark curtain of overgrown bangs out of her lashes and tucked the ends behind her ear. Her gaze bounced off the disbelief in Max's vivid blue eyes and focused instead on the V of tanned, muscled chest revealed by the three unfastened buttons of his white Joseph Abboud shirt. Dangerous territory.

"It's my resignation. I'm quitting, Max. You'll need to advertise for my replacement as soon as we return to the States. I've already drafted the ad for your approval."

"You can't quit." He wadded the paper one-handed and pitched it toward the trash can in the corner of the hotel suite he'd been using as a temporary office for the past several months. He missed. In the five years she'd worked for him, Dana didn't think he'd ever managed to hit a wastebasket with a paper ball regardless of which continent they were on. Max might be a creatively brilliant producer and film editor, but despite his killer body he had no athletic talents of the team sports variety.

She loved him anyway, and didn't that make her an idiot since her attachment was completely one-sided and unlikely to ever be returned? It was time she admitted Max would love his deceased wife until he joined her in the grave and move on.

He went back to shuffling papers as if his pronouncement settled everything, and she was tempted to scuffle back to her hotel room with her metaphorical tail between her legs. But she couldn't. Not this time.

When a job offer from a friend had coincided with the anniversary of her brother's accident, Dana had realized she was no closer to attaining her goals today than she'd been when she'd taken this job. Her brother had never quit pursuing his dream despite setbacks and staggering odds, and she owed it to him to find the same courage.

That morning she'd promised herself that as soon as she left France behind and returned to California with the rest of Hudson Pictures' cast and crew she'd seize control of her life and go after the career and family she wanted.

"I have to go, Max. I want to produce my own films, and you're never going to let me do that here at Hudson.

Like my letter says, I have an opportunity with an indie film company—"

"You misunderstood me. You *can't* quit—not to work for another filmmaker." His inflexible tone warned her not to argue.

She'd known this wouldn't be easy. That was the main reason it had taken her weeks—until the day before her departure from France—to work up the courage for this conversation. "I'm not asking your opinion."

"Because you already know what I'll say. It's a stupid decision and a step backward to leave a major player like Hudson to go to a fly-by-night independent studio. That aside, read your contract. You're forbidden to work for another film company for two years after you leave us."

Surprise snapped her shoulders back. She didn't remember signing a noncompete clause, but she'd been so thrilled to be offered a position at Hudson that she hadn't read the contract as carefully as she should have. The document in question was in her file cabinet at home. She couldn't verify or disprove his words. "Two years?"

"Yes. It's a standard clause in Hudson contracts. It keeps people from taking proprietary information with them when they go."

He stabbed his fingers through his short dark hair and moved a pile of papers on his desk as if he were looking for something and was irritated at not being able to find it. She fought the urge to spring forward and locate the missing item for him the way she always had in the past.

Helping him and taking care of him wasn't just her job, it had become something of an addiction—one she needed to kick.

"The timing of your tantrum sucks," he added without looking up.

She gasped and tried to put a lid on her anger. Hasty words and emotional outbursts never solved anything, and it wasn't like him to be rude. But then he wasn't often under this much pressure. The film had to be wrapped and ready before his grandmother Lillian Hudson died from the cancer consuming her body. They were getting close to completion since they'd already begun the postproduction phase, but the clock was ticking. Time was short and Lillian's remaining days were limited. Everyone involved was working around the clock and tense enough to crack.

Still, anger flushed any lingering reservations Dana might have had about hurting Max's feelings from her system. When she'd taken this job five years ago she'd intended only to get her foot in the door, gain a little experience and then move onward and upward in a year or two. She was overqualified to be the executive assistant to a producer and film editor—even one as acclaimed as Max Hudson. She had credentials—even if they were of the East Coast variety instead of the West Coast.

She'd always dreamed of producing her own films. But then Max had turned out to be an amazing boss. She'd found herself learning more from him than her years at university and her internships back home had taught her.

And then like a dummy, she'd fallen for him, which made leaving impossible. Until now. After watching him waltz off with yet another blonde last week, she'd realized that if the romantic setting of Chateau Montcalm in Provence, France, couldn't make Max see her as a woman instead of just an office accessory, then he never would.

She had put her life on hold to be near him for too long. She had to move on. Her brother often said that treading water did nothing but maintain the status quo, and she'd been treading and going nowhere. That had to end. Now.

She struggled to get control of her emotions so she wouldn't end up shrieking at him, and when she thought she had, she took a deep breath. "This is not a tantrum, Max. This is my career."

He looked up from his desk, his blue eyes glacial. "You'll have no career if you try to find work elsewhere in the film industry."

Shock slipped beneath her ribs like a sharp sword. Shock, hurt and betrayal. Max had a reputation for being ruthless in pursuit of his vision for a film, but he'd never been that way with her. "After all I've done for you, you'd blackball me?"

"In a heartbeat. Your leaving now would destroy our chance of finishing before—" He bit off the words and turned his head toward the storyboard hanging on the wall. But she didn't think he was focusing on the graphic depictions of each scene from the movie.

His jaw muscles bunched and his lips flattened. Watching him struggle with his feelings gripped her in a choke hold. She knew he was crazy about Lillian. They all adored the Hudson matriarch. And the knowledge that they would soon lose her was difficult to handle. But Dana knew Max was wrong about one thing. He could finish this film without her.

He visibly pulled himself together and his eyes found hers again. This time they were hard with determination and devoid of emotion. This was the face of the man she'd seen reduce misbehaving cast or crew members to Jell-O with a few terse lines. She locked her knees to prevent the same thing from happening to her.

"Dana, I won't let you make me fall behind schedule.

My grandmother wants to see the story of her romance with my grandfather on the screen. I will not disappoint her. And I will do whatever it takes to prevent you from sabotaging this project."

"Sabotaging!" She couldn't believe what she was hearing. She'd known he wasn't going to take this well, but to threaten her? When she'd started working for him five years ago he'd still been reeling from his wife's death. She'd done everything except breathe for him until he'd surfaced from his grief. And she'd continued to be his right hand ever since.

This was the thanks she got?

Fury simmered inside her. If she stayed in this suite one more minute she was going to say something she'd regret.

"I am going back to my room." It had taken everything she had to work up the nerve for this confrontation, and she'd crashed and burned because he was being an idiot. She needed to regroup, to replan. Because she couldn't go on. Not like this.

She pivoted on her boot heel and stomped out of his suite. A stream of Max's muttered curses followed in her wake. He called her back, but she didn't stop and she didn't go to her room. She couldn't. A sense of claustrophobia engulfed her. She bypassed the elevator, jogged down the emergency stairs and slammed out of the side exit of the hotel. Her long stride covered the parking lot as she headed…*somewhere*—she didn't know where, but anywhere away from the infuriating, selfish bastard in the hotel was preferable to here.

"Dana," Max called from behind her. She ignored him and lengthened her stride. "Dana. Wait."

She heard his footsteps quicken as if he'd broken into

a jog and then he caught her elbow as she reached a corner, pulled her to a standstill and swung her around to face him. "Give me a couple of months. Let me get *Honor* in the can. And then we'll talk."

"There's nothing left to talk about, Max. I've asked you for a bigger role and been refused so many times I've quit wasting my breath. I didn't spend all those years and all that money getting a degree in filmmaking to be an executive assistant."

"I'll give you a raise."

She tilted her head back and glared at him. He could be so obtuse sometimes she wanted to scream. "It's not about the money or even the project. I believe in this movie with all my heart, and I want to help you finish it. But the chance to produce the indie film won't wait for me. My friend's company needs me *now*. The only reason I have this opportunity is because their last producer died unexpectedly. I've already made her wait three weeks for a decision. If I turn them down or try to stall them any longer they'll find someone else. If anyone understands budget and time constraints as a producer, you should, Max. You know I have to move now."

She could practically see the wheels turning in his brain. His hand slid from her elbow to her bicep to her shoulder, his long, warm fingers infusing her flesh with heat that seeped through the fabric of her blouse and straight into her bones. It wasn't a sexual thing on his part. But it was on hers. She felt the noncaress deep inside.

She had a love-hate reaction to his touches. She loved how each caress made her feel all excited and jittery and breathless, but she hated how a simple brush of his fingers could weaken her knees—and her willpower—and turn her into putty in his hands.

And he didn't even notice.

Talk about adding insult to injury.

"Stay, Dana. I'll give you associate producer credits on *Honor*. That will give you better credentials whenever you decide to move on. Not that I intend to make it easy for you to leave. You're the best assistant I've ever had."

His praise filled her with a warm glow, and then reality hit her with a cold, sobering shower. He was talking about her work, not her personally. He'd never see her as anything more than a coworker. And she wanted more—so, so much more. But right now, with his fingertips gently massaging her shoulder, she was too addled to make a decision.

She shrugged off his hand. "I'll think about it and get back to you before we touch down in L.A."

"I won't be returning with you tomorrow. I need another week here, maybe two or three. I want your decision now."

Frustration and a sense of entrapment made it difficult for her to breathe. He knew if she agreed she wouldn't go back on her word. Unlike most of the inhabitants of Hollywood, her word was her bond. But if she stayed with him…how would she ever get over him and move on with her life? And if she couldn't do that, how would she ever have the family or the career she craved?

James, her older brother, her idol, would be so disappointed in her for waffling.

"We both know 'associate producer' is a pretty useless title, often no more than a boon given because someone did somebody a favor. I want more than credits, Max. I want hands-on skills. And I know you. There's enough control freak in you that you'd give me the title but none of the producer's responsibilities. I'd come away with a slightly better-looking résumé, but without any new abilities."

A nerve in his upper lip twitched, drawing her attention to the mouth that had monopolized so many of her dreams—a mouth she had yet to feel against hers in her waking hours. A September breeze cooled her skin and stirred his thick hair. She fisted her fingers against the need to smooth those dark glossy strands back into place.

"With the deadline we're facing, you'll be working around the clock if you take this position, and I promise you, this won't be a meaningless title. You'll get your new skills." *And you'll regret it,* his challenging tone implied.

She could feel herself slipping toward acquiescence and tried to pull back from the ledge to weigh the positives and negatives. As he'd said, any Hudson Pictures product carried clout and a guaranteed cinematic release. An indie film did not. The best she could hope for was acclaim at the Sundance or Toronto film festivals and possible success if that happened and the movie got picked up. But the market for independent films was exceptionally tight right now. Few were selling without big name stars. Her friend's flick had no box office draws in the cast.

Slim-to-none chances versus a sure thing. Some choice.

Focus on the outcome, her brother always said. In this case, the outcome was a chance to get named credit for working on a major feature film, one she truly believed in, and a credential for her résumé.

She sighed in defeat. She was only twenty-eight. Her dream of a family, of someone to come home to and a career she could be proud of, could stand a few months' delay.

Although she'd probably live to regret it, this was a chance she just had to take.

"I'll do it."

* * *

Friday evening Dana palmed the key to Max's Mulholland Drive house in her damp and unsteady hand, but she hesitated to slot the key into the frosted-glass-and-iron front door.

It was stupid to be nervous. She'd been to Max's house dozens of times since he bought the place four years ago, but never while he was here. He usually sent her to pick up or drop off something while he was tied up at his office, on a set or away on location. She'd been here several times since the day two and a half weeks ago when she'd left him in France. But tonight felt different.

Should she let herself in or ring the bell? He had to know she'd arrived. Not only had he summoned her the moment his plane landed and told her to drop everything and get over here, but she'd had to stop at the end of the driveway and punch in the security code to open the electronic gates. Whenever the gates were activated a chime sounded in the house. Had he slept through the summons? Or was he working? Either way, she didn't want to disturb him. She lifted the key.

The door opened before she could shove it in the slot and her heart tripped. Max, with a dark beard-stubbled jaw, a faded blue T-shirt and a pair of snug, worn jeans, stood barefoot in front of her. She'd never seen him dressed this casually before. He tended to dress for success at work, and he'd always demanded the same of his staff. Today's sleepy-eyed, just-out-of-bed look made her want to drag him right back to the rumpled and possibly still-warm sheets.

Don't go there.

She dragged her brain back from taboo terrain and studied his pale, drawn face and mussed hair. His body was probably still nine hours ahead on French time and thought it was the middle of the night. After several months in France it had taken her a few days to adjust. "Jet lag?"

"I'm fine. Come in. We have a lot to do."

Typical male. Refusing to admit weakness and stupidly ignoring the fact that he needed rest. "I take it you didn't sleep on the plane or nap when you got home?"

"No time. I could use a pot of coffee."

"You don't drink coffee, Max."

"I will tonight."

"I'll make it." She instantly wanted to kick herself. Taking care of him was her past role, not her current one. If she wanted him to give her new duties, then she had to stop doing the old ones.

"Thank you." He turned and headed back into the house, leaving a subtle trail of his cologne, Versace Eau Fraîche. She knew because she'd had to buy a bottle when he'd forgotten to pack his for a previous trip, and she loved the lemon, cedar and herb notes.

Her gaze traced the tired set of his broad shoulders. When she caught her eyes taking the old, familiar journey down his straight spine to his tight butt, which looked totally yummy in the jeans, she abruptly averted her eyes, tightened her grip on her briefcase handle and mentally shook herself.

Get over this obsession already. He's not yours. He never will be yours. Move on.

The two-story marble foyer echoed her footsteps as she followed him toward the elevator with her gaze firmly fastened on the back of his head. The doors enclosed them into the paneled space. She focused on the numbered panel until he leaned against the wall—another testament to his exhaustion. Max never leaned on anything. He was too dynamic for slouching.

"Max, you'd think more clearly if you slept a few hours."

"Later."

The doors opened onto the second floor. His multi-level house clung to the side of a hill. She knew the layout from her previous visits. The kitchen, living and dining rooms were on this level. His office, the screening room and his private den occupied the third. His massive bedroom and two others sprawled across the fourth floor.

She'd had a few brief stints in his bedroom, but sadly only to pack his suitcase or retrieve a file or a forgotten PDA. She'd never even dared to sit on his king-size bed, let alone crawl between the sheets the way she did in her dreams. And she knew from being asked to pack for him in the past that he didn't own any pajamas. Did he sleep nude or in his boxer briefs?

Not a journey her mind needed to take.

When she reached the sunlit kitchen she headed straight for the high end stainless-steel coffeepot sitting on the black-marble countertop. She'd overheard Max tell one of his brothers that he'd bought the appliance because most of the women who slept over couldn't wake up enough to leave without their caffeine. She didn't want to think about the parade of anorexic blondes through his life. Or his bed. They were a reminder that with her dark hair and eyes and olive skin she could never be what he desired.

"Where's the coffee?" she asked.

"Freezer." He sat in a chair at the glass-topped table with his back to the extraordinary view of the city, the distant ocean and the heated pool and spa below the window. Most of the rooms in his house overlooked the same spectacular vista. He dropped his head into his hands, exhaustion dragging his frame downward. The evening light streaming through the glass highlighted every tired crease in his handsome face.

She squashed the sympathy rising within her. He was the one who'd chosen not to sleep. But honestly, sometimes he reminded her of her two-year-old nephew who pushed himself harder when he started to tire rather than risk collapsing if he stopped moving. "The filters?"

He pointed to a dark wood cabinet above the machine and massaged the back of his neck. She yearned to step behind him and do that job for him, to tangle her fingers in his short dark hair and massage the warm skin of his neck. But she didn't dare. She'd done a lot of personal stuff for him as his assistant, but nothing *that* personal.

Instead, she retrieved the coffee and then opened the cabinet and located the paper filters. Within moments the energizing aroma of coffee filled the air. She heard the rumble of his stomach from across the room over the gurgling pot.

"Have you eaten, Max?"

"On the plane."

Apparently, even first-class food hadn't sated his hunger. "Can I fix you something?"

Old habits died hard. She'd have to work on breaking them after he recovered from his trip. Better yet, she'd hand those duties over to her replacement, if personnel ever found someone who could meet Max's exacting standards, and then she wouldn't have to worry about him anymore. That thought made her stomach twinge in an odd way. Who was she trying to fool? She'd always worry about Max.

"There should be some food in the fridge," his deep voice rumbled without its usual resonance.

"Max, we've been out of the country for months. I canceled your catering service, remember? And when I left you in France, you weren't sure when you'd be home. Since you didn't let me know you were returning until your plane touched down today, I haven't reinstated the caterers."

She checked the Sub-Zero refrigerator even though she knew she'd find none of the precooked meals she used to have delivered on a biweekly basis. As expected, the unit was empty except for condiments and a few bottles of beer. Nothing edible occupied the shelves or bins. The cleaning crew would have followed her instructions to remove any perishables the day after the film team left for France.

She'd have to take care of reinstating the caterers and the maid first thing in the morning. For money, which Max had in abundance, anything could be had—even on a weekend.

"Let me see what I can whip up." She raided his freezer and found only old chocolate ice cream, which she tossed in the trash, and a bag of meatballs. The meatballs held possibilities. Turning to the cabinets she searched and discovered a box of whole wheat pasta and a jar of marinara sauce. It wasn't the gourmet fare Max was used to, but it would have to do.

She located a pot for the pasta and another for the sauce and wondered who'd bought the items. One of his women? He didn't usually date the domesticated variety. He went for the leggy, actress wannabes who had banned carbohydrates from their vocabularies and their diets. Not that he practiced the old clichéd casting couch— she'd learned from observation that sleeping with him pretty much guaranteed a woman would never work with him. That didn't stop them from lining up.

She shoved the pot under the faucet and turned on the water. "Do you think you have everything you need to complete postproduction?"

"If I don't, then the second unit will deal with it once I make a list of my requirements."

The second unit filmed establishing shots that didn't require the principal actors. They'd make clips of the chateau or the landscape or distance pieces in which less expensive doubles could fill in for the actors.

With Max's editing talents and the magic of colored filters and computer software, those clips could be cut in between closeups and no one would ever know the scenes hadn't been filmed in sequence, in the same month or even on the same continent.

Dana had never been around for the second-unit shooting, since, like this time, she was usually sent home to clean up what had accumulated while they were away and to prepare for his return. She'd love to see how the second unit worked.

As producer, Max was usually the first on the scene and the last to leave. But with *Honor*, because he was also the film editor and the family wanted him to assure quality by doing the postproduction himself, he'd left the location before the second unit came in.

She loved the way Max gathered all the pieces of the movie puzzle together to make the final product seem like a seamless picture, and she'd learned a lot watching his process.

"Max, I know you like to be there till the last clip is filmed, but the rush job on the editing is forcing you to be here. I could go back to France to oversee the second unit filming for you."

"You're needed here. What's the status on the sound stages?"

From practice, she followed his jump in topic and poured the jar of sauce into the smaller pot. "They're ready for anything you might need. I checked and the sets look exactly like the photographs of the interior rooms of the chateau."

It always amazed her to see how the prop master and set dressers could identically re-create any place by using film, photographs and measurements. If she hadn't driven herself to the studio yesterday and fought the obscene Burbank traffic, she would have sworn she was still thousands of miles away in France when she'd toured the sound stages. But the real rooms of the chateau didn't have the soundproofed panels that the imitation sets on the movie lot had. Audio recorded here would be much clearer and have fewer outside interferences like airplanes flying overhead.

"Good. Have you eaten?"

His question surprised her. "No, Max. I jumped and came running the moment you called."

Like she always had. It was not as if she had a Friday night date to cancel or anything. Her feelings for Max had killed her dating life for the most part. She tried every now and then, but what was the point in dating a man who could never measure up to her boss? That was going to change. As soon as this movie was finished she would date again—lost cause or not.

"Make sure to fix enough food for two."

His consideration made her heart squeeze up into her throat. He was a nice guy, charismatic and confident…when he wasn't being a demanding perfectionist.

"You'll need your energy," he continued. "We'll probably be up all night. And keep the coffee coming."

Her hopes and optimism crashed. She turned away to hide her disappointment. She should have known Max's concern for her wasn't personal. All he cared about was work—the only mistress, other than his late wife, to whom he'd ever been faithful as far as she knew.

Would she never learn?

She couldn't bend over backward to please him at every turn the way she used to. That wasn't her job anymore. She had to find a way to remind him—to remind *both* of them—of the boundaries of her new role as associate producer.

And then once *Honor* was completed she would tender her resignation. Again. This time she wouldn't let him talk her out of it. She had more important things to accomplish in her life than being someone's invisible assistant, and wasting her time pining for her boss was not going to get those items checked off her list.

She squared her shoulders and stared at the man who'd played the starring role in her fantasies for the past few years. Beginning now, her actions were going to be all about her. Her life. Her dreams. Her success. She was going to go after the family and career she craved.

And no one was going to stand in her way. Not even Maximillian Hudson.

Two

Max fought the sensation of being trussed up in an invisible straitjacket Sunday morning. Having a woman move into his house even temporarily broke his twenty-four-hour rule, and he had that rule for a reason. Never again would he allow a woman to be more than a one-night stand.

But when Dana had fallen asleep sitting in the spare chair in his study just before sunrise yesterday he'd realized he couldn't ask her to work eighteen-hour days and then make the drive home. It wasn't safe. Instead of waking her and sending her on her way he'd let her sleep and left for the office so he wouldn't be around when she awoke. He'd barricaded himself in his office at Hudson Pictures all day Saturday.

He would not be responsible for another woman falling asleep at the wheel and ending up dead. His gut clenched as the memories rained down on him. His wife was gone, and he knew from experience that rehashing and regretting that night would not bring Karen back. Nothing would. He slammed the floodgates on the past the way he always did.

Reminding himself that his cohabitation with Dana was a temporary measure and nothing more than a way to squeeze more working hours out of each day, he brushed aside his disquiet. He wasn't doing this for Dana's benefit. It was a purely selfish action. If something happened to her, it would be close to impossible to finish editing *Honor* on time.

He shoved open the door to the first-floor guest suite, entered and dropped the small suitcase he carried beside the bed. "Leave your stuff in here."

Dana rolled her shoulders stiffly and yawned as she followed him into the room. She covered her mouth and the muscles in her arms shifted, revealing her excellent physical condition. He'd heard that she, like several of the employees, often made use of the personal trainers Hudson Pictures had on location for the lead actors. It showed.

Why had he never noticed that before?

He yanked his gaze back to her face. She looked tired. Not surprising since he'd called and woken her far earlier than most people got up on Sunday morning and demanded she pack a bag and get over here.

He should be exhausted, too, but he was charged by adrenaline, too much caffeine and too much to do. He'd snatched a couple hours sleep here and there, but he'd have to wait to catch up once he had the first cut of the film put together.

There were a lot of pieces to this project that would

normally be farmed out to others, but the family wanted tight control on the finished project. That meant he had more responsibilities than usual. But thanks to digital nonlinear filming he could do most of the work here on his computer instead of in the office where constant interruptions would slow him down.

He caught his gaze wandering over Dana again. Her usual work wardrobe was professional, conservative. Today's snug, ribbed orange tank top clung to her breasts, and she'd cinched her low-rider jeans with a wide leather belt, drawing attention to her rounded hips. She'd dressed too casually for the office, but they weren't going leave his house today, so he wouldn't waste time complaining or waiting for her to change.

She usually wore her long, dark hair up in a neat, no-frills style, but this time she'd clipped the strands up in one of those messy, I'm-getting-ready-to-shower styles that left her neck dusted with loose tendrils—the kind a cameraman loved when shooting a love scene or any other scene requiring a shot of a woman's vulnerable nape.

She hadn't bothered with makeup, but her smooth olive skin and thickly lashed dark eyes made cosmetics unnecessary. A makeup artist would love her, and if the male crew members saw her like this they'd be salivating over her. She looked approachable instead of her usual cool as ice.

Despite her skills in the office, Dana could easily be in front of the camera instead of behind it. Another thing he'd missed.

The fact that she had never used her womanly shape, big chocolate-brown eyes and lush red lips to wheedle her way out of hard work was a point in her favor. He'd experienced enough vain, demanding actresses to lose patience with high-maintenance attitudes long ago. The last thing he needed was more behind-the-scenes melo-drama. Movie sets were always full of drama of the un-scripted and unwanted variety. The *Honor* set had been no exception.

During the winter his younger brother Luc had become engaged, knocked up his fiancée and decided to leave Hudson Pictures for a horse ranch in Montana. In the spring his cousin Jack had discovered a son he didn't know he had and married the kid's mother. About the same time the family had learned of their grandmother's cancer after she'd had a frightening collapse. And then this summer his cousin Charlotte had become pregnant by the owner of the chateau where they'd been filming *Honor*.

If Max had his way, autumn would not yield any more real-life drama for the cast and crew and definitely not for him.

He shook off the past and focused on Dana. "I want you staying here until we finish the locked cut."

Her eyes widened and then her teeth pinched her bottom lip. "But the final cut could take months."

"We don't have months and you asked for this position. I warned you that you'd be working around the clock." He regretted letting her back him into a corner. But he hadn't had a choice. He needed an assistant to pull this off, and he didn't have time to train someone new on his methods. Dana knew how he worked. "If you can't handle it, speak up."

Her chin rose at his challenge and her cheeks flushed peach. "I can handle it. But when you said pack a bag I only packed enough clothing for a couple of days. I'll have to swing by my apartment and pick up more later."

"Fine. Let's get started." He headed for the stairs, hoping the climb would chase away his grogginess.

"Max, I need coffee first. It's not even six yet. And in case you don't know it, I stayed here until ten last night."

Thanks to his security system's ability to text his cell phone he knew how late she'd stayed. He'd deliberately avoided coming home until after she'd left, and then he'd rolled in around midnight. The pile of completed work she'd left on his desk proved she hadn't been sleeping on the job all day. But then Dana had never been one to shirk even the dirtiest assignments.

"You know where the coffeepot is."

"I left messages with the caterers and the housekeeper and asked them to resume services immediately," she said from close behind him. "They should return first thing Monday morning. Hudson's personnel director is trying to hire my replacement. In the meantime, unless you quit being so critical of every résumé you receive, you might have to work with a temp."

He stopped and turned on the stairs. From the tread above her he looked down at her upturned face, and against his will the swell of her cleavage drew his gaze. The sight hit him with an unexpected punch of arousal.

What the heck?

Dana worked for him. That made her off limits. He ripped his attention from her smooth skin. Only then did he notice she carried several canvas bags looped over her wrists in addition to her ever-present briefcase. "Is there a reason why you're telling me this?"

"Yes. I've run your office without a glitch for five years, Max. You need to know the effort that goes into that because you're going to notice some rough spots during the transition. I'll do my best to smooth them out, but you might just have to suck it up and deal with a few irritations."

The fire in her eyes and voice surprised him. Had Dana ever talked back to him before? He didn't think so. In fact, she'd almost been invisible in getting things done without drawing attention to herself. More than once he'd almost run into her because she was by his side before he even called for her.

"Nothing can slow us down."

"Max, I can't guarantee that, but I'll try to make sure nothing does. Let me unload the groceries and then we can get started. You may be able to work without breakfast, but I can't."

A subtle floral fragrance reached his nose. Dana's perfume? Why had it never registered before? And why was it intruding now? Not intruding, just distracting. She smelled good. He shook off the unnecessary awareness. He didn't have time for distractions.

"Give me those." He pulled the bags from her arms, carried them to the kitchen and set them on the counter. She immediately withdrew a covered rectangular dish from one and popped it into the microwave.

"What is that?"

"A breakfast casserole. I made it last night." She methodically unpacked the remainder of the bags while the microwave hummed, and she stored each item in the cupboards or fridge—fruits and vegetables, juice, milk, bread, eggs, a wedge of the cheese he preferred, two thick T-bone steaks, his favorite cut of meat.

The other night he'd had to escape to the balcony while Dana cooked the spaghetti. The domestic scene had brought back too many memories. Karen had loved to cook. During their brief marriage they'd spent many hours together in the kitchen of their old house laughing, loving and eventually eating whatever she'd whipped up.

That was back in the day when sharing a meal with his bride had been one of the highlights of his day, second only to making love with her.

Damn.

Karen had never set foot in this house, but he felt her presence everywhere he went these days. He blamed the disturbance on the script. Shooting the story of his grandparents falling in love reminded him of falling for his wife and the despair of losing her. He'd known he wanted to spend the rest of his life with his red-haired beauty within three days of meeting her, but he'd had only three years—years that had passed faster than a blink.

And now she was gone.

And it was his fault.

"When was the last time you ate?" Dana's voice plunged into the depths of his dark memories and yanked him to the surface.

He drew air into his tight lungs and searched his mind. "I don't know. Your spaghetti, I guess."

She scowled at him. "Max, that was thirty-six hours ago."

He shrugged. "I was working."

She rolled her eyes and made a disgusted sound. "And you always forget to eat when you're working."

Did he? Was that why she was always shoving food in front of him?

She filled a tall glass with ice and some of the pineapple juice she'd brought with her and set it on the counter in front of him. He sipped the sweet liquid while she bustled around. Moments later the scent of coffee brewing filled the kitchen.

"You don't need a new executive assistant. You need

a keeper," she muttered under her breath as she banged more items into cabinets.

The quiet anger in her tone raised his hackles. "What did you say?"

She turned, brown eyes flashing with temper, and parked her hands on her hips. "I said you need a keeper. I have your food and dry cleaning delivered and your house cleaned. I run your office, pay your bills and schedule your car maintenance and even your dentist and doctor appointments. You're a brilliant producer and film editor, Max. You can schedule a multibillion dollar project down to the dime and edit it down to the second, and heaven knows, you can work miracles with film and the cast and make sure everyone else's needs are met. But you can't manage your own life."

"What?" Karen had often said the same thing. That without her he'd be lost. She was right. That's why he had Dana.

Dana pushed her bangs off her forehead and sighed. "That's not your fault. You've never had to. You had your family and an army of servants and then your wife and now me to do all that for you. But you're going to have to learn. Your next executive assistant may not be willing to manage your personal life, and I won't be around forever."

"We've been over that. You can't quit."

Her gaze met his dead on, steady and determined, dark brown and serious. "I promised to see you through the end of *Honor*. And I am leaving Hudson Pictures once we're done. I negotiated the noncompete clause out of my new contract. You can't give me what I need, and I'm not going to let you hold me back anymore."

Her comment took him aback. Man, she was full of surprises today. None of them good. "I'm not holding you back."

"Yes, you are."

The sadness in her voice caught him at a loss. He didn't understand all this emotional crap, and he was too tired to try to figure it out. Was she PMSing or what? "What exactly is it you want, Dana? I gave you the promotion you demanded."

She glanced toward the doorway and shifted on her feet. "I need a life."

"You have a life and a job most people would kill for. You travel the globe and frequent five-star hotels and restaurants. You wear designer clothing to premieres and work with movie stars others only dream of meeting. The films we create make history, damn it."

"No, Max. You make history. I just watch from the sidelines." She dug in her briefcase, extracted her PDA, a pen and a pad of paper and then rapidly filled the page with her neat script. When she finished she pushed the sheet toward him.

"What is this?" Whatever it was, he knew from her expression that he wasn't going to like it.

"This is a list of people who make your world turn. Your caterer, dry cleaner, housekeeper, dentist, doctor, barber and the like. Until your new executive assistant is hired, you'll be dealing with these people yourself."

"Why won't you?"

"Because it's not my job anymore."

Speechless, he stared. Where was the efficient, quiet woman who'd worked for him for the past few years? "What in God's name happened to you in France?"

"I had a wake up call from my brother. He made me realize that my life was passing me by while I ran yours."

"You have a brother?" How could he not have known that? Come to think of it, did he know anything about

Dana's personal life? He searched his mind and came up with a blank slate. She didn't share; he didn't ask. He liked it that way.

But then he realized he didn't even know where she lived or where she was from originally. Going by the slight accent that slipped out now and then he'd guess she'd come from a southern state. He'd have to have personnel fax over a copy of her résumé.

"My brother, James, is two years older than me. He's a football coach at the university back home. Coaching was his dream, and he didn't let anything stop him from attaining it."

She pulled out a manila folder and slid it across the countertop. "Here's the schedule of your current appointments and a selection of the caterer's sample menus. Mark your choices, add anything else you want and then fax the sheets to the number on the top of the page. They'll coordinate the delivery times with Annette."

Confused, he frowned. "Who is Annette?"

She sighed as if she'd lost patience with him. "Your housekeeper. She's worked for you for four years."

He should have known that. But when was he ever home during the day? "What in the hell is going on, Dana?"

"I'm your associate producer now, Max. I won't be your caretaker anymore."

Caretaker.

He stiffened at the insult. "I'm thirty-three years old, not a child who needs a nanny. I can take care of my own damned needs."

A daring sparkle glinted her eyes and the edges of her mouth slowly curved in a mischievous smile. One dark eyebrow rose. "Really? Care to wager on that, Hudson?"

Something inside him did a queer little twist. He'd

never seen this side of Dana before, and he wasn't sure what to make of the change or if he liked it. "Oh, yes, I'll bet on it. Put your money where your mouth is, Fallon."

She shook her head. "Money means nothing to you."

Drumming his fingers on the folder, he ticked through the possible stakes. What did she have that he wanted? The answer was obvious. "If I handle all my personal junk without asking for your help, then you'll stay on as my assistant after we wrap *Honor*."

She bit her lip and shifted on her feet. "Your executive assistant, not an associate producer?"

"That's right. After this project you return to your old duties."

"And if I win?"

"I'll give you the best damned reference you've ever seen. I'll even make a few calls to help you get your next job."

Her lips parted and her chest rose as she took one deep breath and then another. Her bright orange top kept drawing his attention to her breasts. Her sedate, conservative clothing had never had that effect on him. He forced his gaze back to her face. Should he insist she go back to her professional clothing? No. That would be a sign of weakness.

"Be sure you want to wager this, Max. Because you won't win."

He was sure he didn't want to have to train someone new. Dana might have been around for a long time, but he remembered how many assistants he'd hired and fired before finding her. As she'd pointed out, she made his life run smoothly. She'd fit in from the first day she stepped into his office.

"I'm sure you won't win. Do we have a deal?"

He'd give her the responsibility she wanted with this picture, and if he played his cards right and showed her the harsh reality of an associate producer position, she'd see her job as his executive assistant involve a hell of a lot less work and stress. She'd beg to have her old job and her old hours back. Then his life would run smoothly once more.

She held up one finger. "If you win, I'll stay on for one year. That's the most I'll promise. Not that it's going to happen."

His competitive spirit kicked in. She ought to know better than to back him into a corner. He thrived on working under pressure. And he would do his best to change her mind about the one-year stipulation. "You have yourself a deal, Dana."

He held out his hand and she put hers in it. The contact of her warm, soft palm and long slender fingers against his sent a surge of electricity up his arm. He'd felt that jolt only once before.

The first time he'd kissed his wife.

He yanked his hand free.

Man, the *Honor* script was messing with his head.

He didn't have those kinds of feelings for Dana. Or anyone. And he never would again. Because the last time he'd let himself care about a woman she'd ended up dead.

Three

Max pulled away from Dana so abruptly he yanked her off-balance. "I'm going for a swim."

"What about work? You're the one who called me before sunrise and said we needed to get started. And what about breakfast?"

The microwave dinged as if to reinforce her point. Glad to have a distraction from the residual tingle in her palm, Dana wiped her hand on her jeans and then opened the door. The delicious smell of the ham, zucchini and mushroom strata filled the air.

"Later."

New job. New rules. No more passivity. She was part of his team now—not his support staff—not his gopher.

She grabbed his forearm before he could escape. His muscles knotted beneath her fingers. Heat seeped from his skin to hers. How would she ever get over him if she couldn't stop this instant awareness? She'd have to find a way. Somehow.

"Listen, Max, if you want to starve yourself and go without sleep when you're alone, that's fine. But hunger and tiredness make you cranky, and that makes dealing with you less than pleasant. When I'm around, you need to eat and sleep."

The stunned expression on his face made her want to take the words back. She'd jumped so far across the line of proper boss-employee conduct that she'd be lucky if he didn't fire her. But something her brother had said in his pep talk about putting up with the garbage you had to endure and eliminating the annoyances you could had struck a chord with her.

If she couldn't leave Max, then she had to make an effort to make her remaining time with him bearable. What did she have to lose? She'd already given up on winning his heart. "You can swim after breakfast."

He pulled his arm from her grip. "That's not safe. It causes cramps."

"Oh, please. That's an old wives' tale, and you know it. Stop making excuses. Sit down. I'll get you a plate."

She watched him mentally debate his reply and then, surprisingly, he nodded. "Let's eat outside."

A victory of sorts. She'd take it. She grabbed a tray and piled on the dishes, flatware, coffeepot and casserole. Max took the tray from her and headed outside to the wide patio.

After taking a moment to admire the flex of his thick biceps, she raced ahead to open the sliding-glass door and then closed it behind them. Today he looked more like the smartly dressed, composed boss she was used to seeing in his crisply pressed Pal Zileri trousers and a short-sleeved shirt. Thanks to dealing with his dry cleaning, she knew more about his favorite designers than she needed to.

A steady breeze blew her bangs into her eyes. She impatiently brushed them aside. Now that she was home she needed to make time for a trim. "You should probably find time to visit your grandmother today. She's asked about you."

He set the tray on the table and shot her a questioning look. "You've talked to her?"

The cool morning air smelled fresh instead of smoggy. She caught a whiff of his cologne and inhaled deeply before she could stop herself. "Of course. I've visited Lillian twice since we've been back. She's a bit frail, but her attitude is good, and she's as sharp and witty as ever."

He gave her a strange look. Dana shrugged and sat. "My family is on the other side of the continent and I miss them. So excuse me if I've adopted some of yours."

"Where?"

She blinked in surprise. "Where is what?"

"Your family."

How unusual. Max didn't ask personal questions. He kept the lines between business life and personal life very clearly drawn. "North Carolina. My father teaches filmmaking at the university in Wilmington and my brother coaches there."

"That's where you caught the movie bug."

"From my father? Yes. He always talked about coming to California and making movies, but family obligations kept him on the East Coast." Why was she blabbering this stuff? Max hated useless chitchat.

"So you're doing this for him."

"No, I'm doing it for me. He and I used to edit our old family movies together. It was a hobby we loved and shared. During high school and college I used to write screenplays, but—"

Shut up, Dana. You're blabbering again.

"But what?"

"Screenwriting's not exactly a secure occupation."

"Nothing in the entertainment industry is."

"No." That was why she'd been so thrilled to land a job with a heavyweight like Hudson Pictures.

She lifted the serving spoon to dish up the food, but hesitated when she realized she was about to fill Max's plate. It was a bad habit—one she had to break. How many times had she fixed his lunch when she prepared hers? In fact, if she knew he was going to be working at his desk instead of out schmoozing for lunch, then she usually spent the evening before preparing something special and then packed enough for two the next day. No more of that.

She served herself and set the spoon back in the casserole dish, letting him get his own.

He did so. "You'll have to send your family tickets to the *Honor* premiere."

Her fork stopped short of her lips. Who was this man? Usually exhaustion made Max grumpy. It never made him likeable and approachable. "They'd like that."

"I didn't know you and my grandmother kept in touch."

A chuckle escaped before she could stop it. Lillian had been a regular contact since the first day Dana set foot on Hudson property as Max's executive assistant. The eighty-nine-year-old might be subtle, but she was effective.

"Are you kidding me? I run your world and she checks to make sure I'm doing it correctly and to her standards.

She has a soft spot for you. Don't tell her I said so, but I think you might be her favorite grandson."

A tender smile curved Max's lips and the love in his eyes made Dana's breath hitch. If he ever looked at her like that, her new resolution to get over him would crumble.

No, it won't. You're past that. Remember?

Right. She'd promised to say yes to the next guy who asked her out. She might even sleep with him because it had been…forever since she'd had sex. Well, a couple of years anyway.

Step one in her twelve-step guide to getting over Max Hudson was to immerse herself in another man…or three.

Yeah, right. You never learned to juggle men.

Maybe it was time she tried. At least her heart would be safe that way.

Except for one fizzled relationship, she hadn't dated all that much since taking the Hudson position. Luckily she lived in an apartment building populated by attractive actors waiting for their big break. When she had to attend a Hudson Pictures function she asked one of her neighbors to accompany her. That way she always had a good-looking guy on her arm, and she did them the favor of giving them exposure and introducing them to a few powerful people in the biz. A win-win situation.

She pulled herself back to her present. "In all the years I've worked with you, you've never worked with an associate producer. What will my duties be?"

He seemed to ponder as he ate. "You'll liaison with the cast and crew."

"I've done that before."

"You'll be responsible for checking location details, making sure each of the cast has what he or she requires and you'll be troubleshooting."

Not what she had in mind. "This is beginning to sound like my old job."

"And until I have a new executive assistant it's my job. I'm delegating."

"Max—"

"Don't 'Max' me. You asked for this, Dana."

"If you'd look at the résumés piled on your desk, you might find a new E.A."

"I have looked and none of the applicants has your qualifications."

"That's because I was overqualified."

He frowned. "I don't have time to train anyone right now, and neither do you."

"But—"

"I'll also need you to check the log sheet."

She blinked at his change of subject and nearly groaned. Writing down each scene as it was filmed was mind-numbing. Checking it against the film was doubly so. She sighed. "What else?"

"Make an edit script."

Boring desk work. But, okay, she knew that was part of the process. She forced herself to keep eating although he was killing her appetite.

"Capture the footage and back it up. You do know how to work the editing software, don't you?"

"Yes."

She'd spent a lot of her nonwork hours learning the computer program that stored the dailies digitally on a hard disk. A good producer knew how to get his hands dirty in every phase of production. Putting the clips in order was busywork, but at least she'd get to see the raw footage and get a feel for how the film might come together. That part was exciting.

Max's vision for the story would determine the final product. His editing would set the pace, tone and emotional impact of the film and a million other things simply by the clips, shots and angles he chose to include or cut. Even the sound he chose would affect the final product. While editors might not get much of the credit, the editor could make or break a film.

And then something struck her. "Wait a minute. This is beginning to sound more like editing than producing. And why are you giving me the tedious jobs?"

Max didn't even blink at her accusation, nor did he deny it. "Because right now that's what I need you to do. The producer's primary job is to keep everyone happy, on schedule and under budget. Someone has to do the grunt work, and you need to learn from the bottom up."

She sat back, her appetite and her enthusiasm gone. "I have a degree in filmmaking, and I served several internships with Screen Gems at the Wilmington studios."

"You haven't used any of that knowledge since you graduated, and the technology has completely changed in what? Six, seven years?"

"About that. But I've done my best to keep up."

"Good. Then maybe you won't slow me down. We'll move faster if I don't have to stop and explain things every step of the way." Max took a few bites of his breakfast. "I'll also want you checking for continuity errors, specifically the clocks, candles, setting, cigarettes or anything else that might be an issue. Make sure they haven't changed from shot to shot. No short candles that suddenly get tall."

"That should have been done during filming."

"Right. And yet slipups make it into even megabudget films—even the ones that aren't rushed through post-production. But I won't have them in mine."

He finished his breakfast and rose. "Time for that swim."

She watched him climb the outdoor, circular iron staircase in the corner of the patio to the master suite and exhaled a pent-up breath when he disappeared inside.

He'd finally given her the job she wanted. But he wasn't going to make it easy. But if he thought he was going to force her back into her old job he was going to be sorely disappointed.

Because like her brother, she was no quitter. She might have gotten sidetracked from her goals for a while, but once she set her mind to something she stuck to it.

Like saving Max. Or saving herself.

Dana turned away from the sight of Max's tanned, muscular shoulders and arms cutting laps through the long pool below the window. No way could her brain function with that kind of distraction.

She was determined not to let Max or herself down, but when she stared at the overwhelming mountain of work on her desk and the long list she'd made of her assigned duties, she had to wonder if she was up to the task. Sure, she'd asked for the responsibilities, but Max had piled them on. His pointing out that she was a bit…rusty in her production skills hadn't helped her confidence any.

But she wasn't above cheating by calling on an expert for guidance if it meant keeping on top of her workload. She picked up the phone, dialed and pressed the receiver to her ear.

"Y'ello?" The deep southern drawl comforted her almost as well as one of her daddy's big bear hugs.

"Hi, Daddy."

"How's the new job, sweet cakes?"

She wished she could lie and say work was a breeze. "I'm feeling a little overwhelmed at the moment. I've e-mailed you a list of the duties Max has assigned me. Have a minute to take a look?"

"You betcha. Hold on a sec." She heard him tapping on the keyboard over the phone line and then the greeting from his e-mail provider.

Seconds later he whistled. "You're going to be earning that pay raise."

"It looks like I'll doing mostly grunt work and a lot of editing tasks."

"Yep. But you wanted to polish your skills, and he's going to make you."

"I have a question for you. What do I need to do next to keep ahead of things?"

She'd kept him posted via e-mail every step of the way because he was living vicariously through her. Today's list was just an update. She knew that if she failed in this position he'd be just as disappointed as she, maybe more so.

"You've been his right hand for years, so this isn't too different. Put every tool Hudson needs at his fingertips. With him juggling two jobs—producer and editor—his time is going to be tighter than ever. Help keep others on schedule for him whenever you can, and run interference with the troublemakers and squeaky wheels. Every project has them. Identify 'em as soon as you can and be proactive, otherwise their poison can spread."

"Got it."

"When you finish the capturing he'll start editing, and remember, an editor's job goes faster if he doesn't have to wait for the components."

She scribbled as fast as she could and hoped she could decipher her notes later. "After the basic editing the next editing components he'll need will be…" she searched her mind, "Sound, right?"

"If he's not calling in an independent sound designer, that's it. And you know where to find what you need, don't you?"

"I do." During college she'd been shocked to discover that most of the movie's soundtrack was added during the editing phase. Quite often the audio recorded on location wasn't up to par and dialogue or sound effects were added later.

There were audio libraries where film companies could buy or rent the sounds or background ambience they needed for a film. The roar of a passing subway train or the hum of a busy city street corner might be used in a dozen other films, but the typical moviegoer would never recognize it as one he'd heard before.

"I'll get right on it, Dad."

"That's my girl. Give him what for. Show him that a steel magnolia can whup a California girl any day. Have they hired the composer for the musical score yet?"

"Yes. It's not anyone I'm familiar with."

"Get familiar. You want to be on a first-name basis, so that glitches can be smoothed over quickly and painlessly."

"Got it." She wandered to the window and looked out to see if Max was still in the pool. He was pulling himself out, his muscles flexing under wet, tanned skin. Using both hands, he slicked back his hair. His wet trunks clung to him like a second skin, outlining his masculine attributes in excruciating detail. Her mouth dried and her pulsed skipped.

"Miss you, sweetheart." Her father's voice pulled her out of the lust zone. She turned away from the window.

"I miss you, too. Thanks for your help."

"Make sure home is your first stop after you put this one in the can. You're due a vacation, aren't you?"

She smiled. He father had never been anything but supportive of her career choice. Of course, that might be because they shared the same dream.

"Past due. I'll come home for a visit after this is all over. I'll see you then. Love you, Daddy."

"Love you back."

She disconnected and headed for the spare desk in Max's office. Thirty minutes and six phone calls later she had a list waiting when Max walked in. He looked refreshed from his swim. His dark hair was still slightly damp, and he'd donned her favorite DKNY outfit of gray pants and a white shirt with subtle gray stripes.

She rose and handed him the pages and a memory stick containing the audio files from the library. "I've contacted the sound library and found the items on your list. They're downloaded onto your flash drive. I also have the Foley artist on standby. I'll call when you're ready for him."

She loved watching Foley artists work. Once they opened their little briefcase of "toys" the sound specialists could re-create just about any noise to be perfectly synced to the audio tracks and inserted during the editing phase. Dubbing in voice audio wasn't nearly as interesting, but it still beat the monotony of logging and making edit scripts.

Max paused, his eyebrows raised in surprise. "Thanks. You've been busy."

She shrugged. "That's my job."

"Yes, it is." But there was a new respect in his eyes that hadn't been there before. His approval made her stomach turn somersaults and her entire body flush with pleasure.

Uh-oh. Getting over him wasn't going to be nearly as easy as she'd hoped. She'd just have to try harder.

"You have to trust me, Max. I won't let you down."

"We'll see about that."

And that's when it hit her. Max might be extremely charismatic, but he was also a loner. He didn't let anyone in, not even her. If he couldn't trust her after five years, would he ever?

"Give me ten minutes," Dana said over her shoulder Monday morning as Max followed her into her apartment.

He ripped his gaze from her butt, but not before registering her nice shape in a pencil-slim black skirt.

What was his problem? Finding her in his kitchen early this morning wearing skimpy shorts-and-camisole pajamas with her dark hair rumpled and streaming over her shoulders had clearly messed up his thinking. She'd been waiting for the coffee to brew or, more likely judging by her worshipful expression, praying to the coffeepot gods to send deliverance from her boss's brand of evil.

Maybe having her stay at his place wasn't such a good idea. He liked his space and his privacy. But they were getting more accomplished than they would have in the office.

He checked his watch. "We have a conference call in two hours."

"Max, I'll have my suitcase packed in no time." She dropped her purse and keys on an entry table made from glass and irregularly shaped but sturdy grayed branches. Driftwood? "Come in and make yourself comfortable."

He did a whip pan of the apartment, soaking up details

in a flash. He never would have taken his superefficient executive assistant for the relaxed beach-cottage type, but her rustic white-painted furniture with its bright blue cushions and citrus colored pillows combined with the box-framed seashells and artwork on her walls definitely looked as if he'd just walked in from the beach. Even the straw mats on the hardwood floor resembled the types he'd seen in coastal homes.

Not that he'd had time to see a vacation home recently.

He tried to sync the casual decor with the woman he knew and it didn't work. He was used to seeing Dana in conservative suits with her hair tightly pinned up—like she was now. He crushed the memory of her long, bare legs, flushed cheeks and heavy-lidded eyes. But damn, she'd looked sexy in his kitchen.

Forget it, Hudson.

Easier said than done. No matter how hard he tried to erase the memory, it kept popping up on his mental movie screen.

He ran a finger under his tight collar. "Did you rent this place furnished?"

She turned in her small living room, her brown eyes finding his. "No, it's all my stuff. Did you want something to drink while you wait?"

She spoke quickly, as if she were uncomfortable having him in her home. They'd decided to carpool today, since her apartment complex was on the way to the Hudson Pictures studios. It was too hot to wait in the car, so he'd followed her in.

"No thanks."

"Have a seat then. I'll be right back." She hustled down a short hall, and his gaze stayed focused on her hip-swinging gait until she turned a corner out of sight.

The golden, orange and red hues of a large beach scene hanging behind the sofa drew him closer. He could practically feel the warmth of the setting sun reflecting off the water and glistening on the ivory sand. He moved on to a second painting on an adjacent wall of a bright yellow hang glider sailing above the blue ocean. A third picture had caught the infectious grin of a child in a ruffled orange swimsuit playing on the beach with buckets and shovels beneath a colorful umbrella. The pictures, similar in style and technique, were well executed and looked so real he could almost hear the waves and smell the salt air.

He checked the artist's signature. All three were by a Renée Fallon. Fallon? A relative of Dana's? He'd have to ask.

A cluster of twenty or so framed photographs drew him to the opposite wall. He recognized a much younger Dana with an older man and woman and a preadolescent boy. She looked enough like the trio that he guessed they were her family. He turned back to the painting of the child, noting the similarities, the same big brown eyes, same smile and same coltish legs and long, dark hair. Dana without a doubt. So the artist did know her.

He scanned each photograph, and it was as if he were watching a much less serious Dana grow up in front of him. It wasn't until she hit what he would guess were her college years that her expression turned serious and her smile looked forced. What had caused the transition from carefree girl to serious woman?

In the next photo a group of young men in football jerseys surrounded a guy in his late twenties or early thirties. The guy grinned up at the camera, a trophy in his hands. He had Dana's coloring and a more masculine version of her features. She'd said her brother was a football coach. This had to be him. And then Max realized the boys crowding around him almost obscured a wheelchair. Her brother was disabled? She'd never said.

His gaze returned to the previous pictures where the guy had been a tall, muscle-bound athlete wearing a football uniform. What had happened?

You don't need to know. Your employees' personal lives are none of your business unless they impact their work.

But Dana had said a wake-up call from her brother sparked her decision to leave Hudson. That made the topic fair game.

A yawn surprised him. He blamed it on lack of sleep combined with Dana's decor. The space with its pale blue walls and beachy furniture made him think of kicking back barefooted with warm sand trickling between his toes and a cold tropical drink sweating in his palm. The room was surprisingly soothing.

Exhaustion hit him hard and fast. When had he had a vacation last? Maybe after *Honor* was finished…. No, after his grandmother… He snuffed the thought, rubbed a hand across his face and sat on the sofa. He didn't want to miss any of his grandmother's remaining days.

He glanced at his watch and leaned his head against the tall backrest. He'd give Dana two more minutes and then he'd yell for her to hurry up.

But visiting her apartment had stirred his curiosity. Who was the real Dana Fallon? The hyperefficient quiet assistant in business suits or the sexy, mouthy, tank-top-and-jean-wearing woman who'd arrived at his house on Sunday?

He suddenly had a strong desire to find out.

The urge to kiss Max awake was almost too strong for Dana to resist. Too bad *almost* didn't count.

"Max," she called quietly.

He didn't stir.

Two hours ago she'd come out of her bedroom and found him asleep. She couldn't remember ever having seen him so relaxed before. He'd practically dissolved into the cushions of her couch. But she shouldn't be surprised. She'd be shocked if he'd had more than two hours' sleep last night. He was pushing himself too hard— exactly the way he had after he'd lost his wife.

Why did men always think drowning themselves in work would cure a problem? It didn't. It only delayed dealing with the issue. And exhaustion made any problem much harder to handle.

While watching Max sleep, something inside her had melted, and she'd known she was in trouble. She'd wanted to cover him, tuck him in and kiss his smooth-for- the-first-time-in-forever forehead. Instead, she'd studied the shadows beneath his eyes that even his tan couldn't hide and decided not to wake him. She'd known he'd be irritated at himself for falling asleep and even more irri- tated with her for not waking him, but too bad. He'd needed the rest. Everyone at the studio would benefit if he had a nap, and he'd be sharper for the upcoming meeting.

She told herself she had nothing to feel guilty about, and it wasn't as if she'd been wasting time. While he'd slept she'd worked from her laptop at her kitchen table. But now his respite was over.

"Max," she tried again, a little louder this time. He still didn't stir. Dana dampened her lips and eased onto the cushion beside him. The warm proximity of his leg beside hers made her heart race. Touching him both appealed to her and repelled her. She flexed her fingers. She wanted

to stroke his smoothly shaven jaw—ached to actually—
but that would only make leaving him all that much
harder. And she was going to leave. Eventually.

She debated her options. Shake his leg? She checked
out the long, muscular thigh beside hers and discarded
the idea. Tap his arm? No, she'd always hated being
poked awake—her brother's favorite method when they
were schoolkids and had to catch the bus.

She cupped a hand over the shoulder closest to her and
gently shook him. "Max, wake up."

His eyelids slowly lifted and his unfocused gaze found
hers. His mouth curled in an easy, delicious, breath-
stealing smile. "Morning."

The groggy, rough timber of his voice made her
stomach muscles quiver. Wouldn't she love to wake up
to that every day?

"Good morning." Had he forgotten they'd already
played out this scene in his kitchen? She hadn't. How
could she forget his catching her looking like a ship-
wreck victim washed up on the beach? She'd been embarrassed to be caught in her pj's, but she'd thought he
was still sleeping when she'd staggered toward the coffeepot. He might survive on a couple of hours sleep, but
she couldn't—not without a few gallons of coffee to lubricate her mental wheels.

His hand painted a hot path up her spine. She gasped.
Then his fingers cupped her nape and he pulled her
forward. Too stunned to react, she let him move her like
a rag doll. Warm lips covered hers. Her heart stopped and
then lunged into a wild beat as his mouth opened over hers.

Shocked, but thrilled, she responded, meeting the slick,
hot glide of his tongue as he stroked her bottom lip for
just a second before reality smacked her upside the head.

Who does he think he's kissing? One of his blondes? His dead wife? She jerked free.

Max stiffened and blinked, the fog vanished from his eyes instantly and clarity returned. His hand fell away and his lips compressed. "I apologize. That shouldn't have happened."

She fisted her fingers and fought the urge to press them to her tingling mouth. "It's okay. You must have been dreaming."

His jaw shifted. "Must've been."

He lifted his arm, checked his watch and swore. "I've missed the conference call. You shouldn't have let me sleep."

Coming on the heels of her fantasy desire to kiss Max coming true, his accusatory tone rubbed her the wrong way.

"You needed the rest. I've called everyone involved and rescheduled the call until noon. It was no big deal, and no one was inconvenienced. If they had been I would have woken you. That's why I'm waking you now. We need to go."

She stood, removing herself from the temptation of kissing him again even if he did think she was someone else, and pressed her hands to her thighs to still their trembling. "I've left you a new toothbrush on the bathroom counter if you want to freshen up."

Not that he needed to. He'd tasted delicious.

Stop it, Dana.

He rose, standing so close his scent filled her lungs and his body heat reached out to encircle her. She told herself to move away, but her legs refused to listen. Instead, she found her head tipping back and wished he'd kiss her again, this time fully awake and cognizant of what he was doing and who he held.

As if he'd read her mind, his gaze dropped to her lips. Her pulse rate skyrocketed and her mouth dried. His eyes returned to hers, but while his pupils dilated, his lips settled into an almost invisible line of rejection. "Again, I apologize. It won't happen again."

Disappointment settled like a fishing weight in her stomach. "I—it's okay, Max. No harm done."

His gaze bounced to her wall of photos. "Is that your brother?"

Another abrupt subject change. But then he did specialize in them. It had taken her a while after she first started working with him to keep up. "Yes."

"What happened?"

"You mean what put him in the wheelchair?"

He nodded.

"James went swimming at a rock quarry with his college teammates. He dove in where he shouldn't have. We're lucky he's alive. He'd planned to play pro football after he graduated and then coach. He had to abandon the first part of his dream, but he never gave up on the coaching part, and he didn't let his disability stop him. He's the defensive coordinator and has plans to keep moving up."

"And the paintings? Who is Renée Fallon?"

He'd been busy while she'd been packing, and why did he have to ask personal questions now when her brain was still too stuck on that kiss to function? "My mother."

"She's very good."

"Yes, she is. We're all very proud of her."

Without another word, he swept past her and down the hall.

Dana quit fighting and pressed her fingers to her mouth. *Forget that kiss happened.*

He wasn't kissing you. Not in his head, anyway.

But that kiss, accidental or not, wasn't something she could ever erase from her memory.

In fact, she wanted another one.

And that blew her goal of escaping Max and getting a life of her own right out of the water.

Four

Hudson Pictures' studios in Burbank reminded Dana of home.

The property had a forties vibe that was both nostalgic and quaint. She loved everything about the place from the large, well-maintained buildings housing the sets and equipment to the small bungalows that made up the offices. It was the architecture of those bungalows that reminded her of her grandparents' waterfront community in Southport, North Carolina, which had been constructed in the same era.

She squashed a wave of homesickness and reminded herself she was living hers and her father's dreams. Not many people got a chance to do that.

As she hustled through the studio grounds beside Max she couldn't help getting mushy and emotional. When Dana had first started at Hudson Pictures, Lillian had personally guided her through the maze of buildings recounting the story of her life with Charles Hudson.

Oh, sure, Dana had recognized the subtle grilling the older lady had hidden behind the fairy-tale romance, but she'd been too enthralled by Lillian's exciting past to resent the inquisition. Lillian's blue eyes, eyes so like Max's, still came alive when she'd talked about those days.

Lillian had told Dana that it had been Charles's dream to make the story of their lifelong romance into a movie, but he'd died back in 1995 before seeing it to fruition. And now Lillian had adopted her husband's dream as her own—one last gift to him before she joined him, she'd told Dana over their last tea. She wanted the world to know what a wonderful man Charles had been.

Looking at the Hudson matriarch now, no one would guess the older woman had led a secret life as a spy masquerading as a cabaret singer in France during World War II. That's how she'd met Charles and their courtship had begun, and it was where they'd secretly married. When France was liberated, Charles had been ordered to fight in Germany, but he'd promised to return for his bride as soon as he could. He'd kept that promise, and then he'd brought Lillian here to the home and studios he'd built for her and made her a star. Lillian in turn had made Hudson Pictures a megasuccess, a privately owned filmmaking dynasty.

Dana sighed and pressed a hand to her chest. Every woman should have a larger-than-life romance like that. Her eyes grew misty just thinking about a lover who would cross the globe for her or stand by her through the difficult challenges of life. But so far, she hadn't been that lucky. She'd had boyfriends in high school and college, but nothing with forever written on it—not even close, but not for lack of looking. She found either friendship or passion, but she'd never managed to find a man who brought her both. And that was what she wanted more than anything.

She was determined to hold out for a true love like her parents', her brother's or Lillian and Charles's. With three excellent examples you'd think she'd have better luck.

"Dana."

She startled at Max's firm tone. "What?"

He stopped outside their office bungalow and stared down at her through narrowed eyes. "Did you hear a word I said?"

Her cheeks burned. "Um...no. I'm sorry. I was thinking about the *Honor* script and how lucky you were to convince Cece Cassidy to write it. She did a great job."

"Jack convinced her."

Upon Lillian's request, Max's cousin Jack had approached his former lover for the job. "He ended up with a great screenplay from her and found a son he didn't know he had—a double blessing."

Jack and Cece's romance was just one of several connected to *Honor*'s cast and crew. Was it too much to hope for one of her own before they wrapped? Apparently.

And then she noticed Max's scowl. "Lillian is thrilled to have a great-grandchild."

His frown deepened. "Is there anything else you'd like to share with me before we go into this meeting?"

She winced at the bite of his sarcasm, and then she wanted to smack her forehead. Duh. She'd forgotten that according to the Hudson rumor mill he and Karen had been trying to get pregnant when Karen died. Mentioning his younger cousin Jack's son had not been a good idea.

"No. I've made a list of bullet points that require attention and action right now, but I'm not exactly sure why your uncle David is calling this meeting, and he wouldn't say. I don't know if what I have is relevant."

She hurried through the door he opened for her and bolted toward her old desk, where she dropped her briefcase and withdrew a folder, which she passed to him. They had yet to sort out a new office for her, and since her replacement hadn't been found, there was no rush to vacate the space. Max had rejected each of the applicants' résumés personnel had sent over. He'd yet to call one single person in for an interview.

"Everything you need should be in here. Do I get to sit in on the meeting?"

"Yes. But I'll do the talking."

"Understood."

He'd barely spoken on the drive in. Was he still thinking about the kiss that, she suspected in his opinion, shouldn't have happened? She couldn't stop rehashing it. If only she hadn't jerked away...

What would he have done?

Nothing. He wasn't kissing you. He was kissing whomever he'd been dreaming about.

But what if she was wrong? What if he had known it was her?

Excitement made her shiver.

Get real.

All right, so chances were he hadn't been thinking of her. Should she tell him she'd enjoyed the kiss? Probably not. If she played her hand and he rejected her, it could get uncomfortable. Would she be able to handle the humiliation of running into Max at one Hollywood event after another? The Hudsons were powerful people. One word from any of them whispered in the right ear and she'd have a hard time ever finding a job anywhere in the movie biz.

That would be a disaster because the last thing she wanted to do was tuck her tail between her legs and run home, disappointing herself, her father and her brother.

But what if she could find a way to make Max notice her as a woman…?

She thought about her brother fighting the odds and winning, and about her father who'd found a way to achieve his dreams on the East Coast instead of the West, and her mother who made a living sharing her color-drenched view of the world with others. She'd faced rejection head-on daily until she'd finally found success.

Dana asked herself how she could be any less courageous.

She watched Max's stiff spine as he headed for his office.

Every member of her family took risks on a regular basis, with their hearts and their careers. She was the only one who always, *always*, played it safe. Coming to Hollywood was the only real risk she'd ever taken…and she'd done that only after she'd landed the job as Max's executive assistant.

It was time she found the courage to gamble on something that really mattered. And what really mattered was Max.

"We have a problem," David Hudson's voice said over the speaker.

Dana wasn't crazy about Max's uncle. He might be charming on the surface, but in her opinion he was a womanizer who never had time for his children. The only reason she didn't hate him was because he treated his mother, Lillian, well.

"What problem besides a shortage of time?" Markus Hudson, Max's father and the CEO of Hudson Pictures, countered.

Dana liked Markus, and she saw a lot of him because he was close to Max and often stopped by the office to chat. Markus was a wonderful husband, father and son.

While only Dana and Max occupied the office, Max's oldest brother Dev, the COO of Hudson Pictures, plus Luc, Max's younger brother who acted as PR director, had joined them on the conference call but had been silent thus far.

"What kind of trouble, David?" Max asked.

"Willow Films is making a World War II picture scheduled for release just prior to *Honor*."

Dana gasped and nearly dropped the pen she held for note taking. Willow was Hudson's biggest rival. There wasn't a lot of good feeling between the two film companies. In fact, the competition sometimes turned ugly.

"Worse," David continued, "rumor has it the story has some similarities to Lillian and Charles's. But I can't get anyone to tell me how similar the two films are."

"How accurate is your source?" Dev asked.

"I trust it," David replied.

Dana could feel Max's tension and see it in the lines on his face. His fingers fisted on his desktop. "Even if we could swing an earlier release at this late date, I don't think I can finish *Honor* any faster."

"We're not asking that of you, son." Markus's voice filled the room. "But we might need to put a PR spin on this to make our film sound bigger and better and different or Willow will kill our momentum."

"I'll get on it," Luc said. "But it would help to know more about their product."

"I'll see what I can get," David said, "but they're pretty damned tight-lipped."

Adrenaline rushed through Dana's system. One of her past boyfriends was an assistant director for Willow, and she and Doug had parted on good terms. In fact, he owed her a favor….

She sat up straighter as she turned an idea over in her mind. Could she get the information this group needed out of Doug?

She opened her mouth to volunteer, but sealed her lips without saying a word. Why make promises she wasn't sure she could keep? Best to test the waters first.

But the chance to do something to make Max notice her had fallen right in her lap. And she was determined not to blow it.

"Long time no see, babe," Doug said as he joined Dana at The Castaway in Burbank on Tuesday evening.

Dana had invited Doug to the restaurant in the hills overlooking the golf course because it had been his favorite back when they were dating. Once the sun set and the city lights twinkled below, the setting would be magical. Too bad it had never sparked romance between them.

"I'm glad you could make it on short notice." She rose from her seat and leaned forward to kiss his cheek. As usual, the doofus turned his head at the last second and she caught him square on the mouth. He was one of those people who kissed every female, young or old, on the lips, and because he was the total package—smart, ambitious, charming and attractive in a golden-boy kind of way— he could get away with it. Unfortunately, there had never been any chemistry between them, not even a tiny fizz. But they'd given it their best shot.

"Lucky you called when you did. The boss and I leave on recce at the crack of dawn tomorrow. I won't be back for at least two weeks, longer if it doesn't go well."

"*Ooh,* I'm jealous. I love scouting out potential locations. Where are you headed?"

"Can't say. Top secret. But it's somewhere warm and sunny with umbrella drinks." His blue eyes, shades paler than Max's, glimmered with amusement. He took his seat. "Congrats on the promotion."

"You heard?"

"Tinseltown is a small, gossipy community. Besides, you were once my girl, so I keep tabs on you. Liking the job so far?"

"Most of it. It has a steep learning curve, but I'm learning from the best." She wasn't going to tell him Max was working her fanny off, and she was lucky to get six hours of sleep each night or that she loved every minute of the torture.

"I'll bet it's a load of pressure with *Honor* nearing completion."

She smiled. He'd opened the subject, which made her job easier. As an assistant director, Doug assisted the director much the way she assisted Max. Doug didn't actually direct and he was okay with that. She'd have preferred the more creative position. But his job meant he knew a lot about ongoing projects.

"Yes, there is a lot of tension at the moment. I hear Willow has its own World War II film coming out soon."

"You heard correctly."

"Is it a romance?"

One corner of his mouth rose in a teasing smile. "Could be."

"Oh, c'mon, Doug."

He leaned forward and caught both of her hands in his on the table. It was a familiar gesture, one he'd done dozens of times before. "Why should I share with you? You work for the enemy, remember?"

"What do you have to lose? Everyone in Hollywood already knows the gist of Charles's and Lillian's story, and your picture is coming out first. Besides, I introduced you to the person who ended up hiring you for this job you adore, *remember?*"

Doug used to live in her building and had been her premiere date on more than one occasion before they'd tried and failed to be more than just occasional stand-in dates. She'd made the job connection for him at an after party.

"Good point." He released her, waved down the waiter and ordered a bottle of champagne. They had been together for about a year, and he hadn't forgotten her preference for Krug Brut Grande Cuvée. "Yes, it's a romance. I know how much you love sappy love stories."

"How similar is it to *Honor?*"

"It's similar."

She grimaced. That wasn't good. "That's going to make marketing on our end difficult."

"Not if you play up the differences."

That's exactly what Markus had said. "How are we going to know what those differences are?"

The waiter returned with the champagne. Dana impatiently waited for the whole tasting ritual thing to pass and then opened her mouth to repeat her question. Doug halted her with a raised finger.

"First we celebrate your promotion." He lifted his glass. She dutifully clinked her rim to his and sipped. The golden liquid bubbled down her throat leaving a nutty, toasted finish behind, but it failed to sooth her agitated nerves. She didn't need alcohol. She needed answers.

Doug covered her free hand with his. "Dana, relax. I didn't work on the film directly, so I don't know the details, but I might have a copy of the script at my place. You can follow me home and I'll check. If I don't, then I can probably get you a copy when I get back. After all, as you said, what could it hurt? It's too late in the game for any espionage stuff."

Surprise made her gasp. She couldn't possibly ask for any more. "Will that get you in trouble?"

"I don't think so. I'll test the waters first."

"I don't want to get you fired."

He winked. "I don't want that, either."

"I could kiss you, Doug."

"Please do."

That stilled her for a moment with a twinge of discomfort. "But you know—"

"Dana, just shut up and kiss me. I know it means nothing. But it raises my value to be seen with a hot chick."

Chuckling, she rose and leaned over the table without bothering to argue about his "hot chick" comment. She gave Doug a quick peck. It was like kissing her brother only Doug wore pricier cologne.

"Celebrating something?" Max's voice said behind her.

She froze an inch away from Doug's lips and then straightened and turned. The icy look in Max's blue eyes made her uneasy. "Uh…hi, Max."

Max wore his black Jack Victor suit with a white shirt and a black-and-white patterned tie. He looked delicious in a forbidding way.

Doug's chair scraped as he pushed it back and rose.

"We're celebrating Dana's promotion. I'm glad you were finally smart enough to recognize her worth."

She shot Doug a warning glance. Doug ignored her and offered Max his hand. "I'm Doug Lewis. We met a couple of years ago at the *Legions* premiere."

Max gave him a brief, hard shake. "I remember."

Max no doubt did. Dana didn't think he ever forgot a name or face. But at the time Doug hadn't been working for Willow. Should she tell him Doug had promised her a copy of the Willow script? No, better not. She didn't want to get Doug in trouble, and she didn't want to raise Max's hopes in case Doug couldn't deliver.

"Thanks for stopping by to say hello," Doug added in clear dismissal. "We won't keep you."

Aghast, Dana stared. Did the man have a career death wish?

Max's cold eyes found Dana's again. "My appointment is waiting. Don't stay out late tonight. We have a full schedule tomorrow. I'll meet you in the kitchen at six."

Having dropped that bombshell, he strolled across to the dining room. Her gaze followed him to a table where he joined his older brother.

Dana turned on Doug. "Are you crazy?"

"Whoa. He'll meet you in the kitchen?"

She sighed. "Until *Honor* is finished I'm staying at Max's house. It allows us more working hours if I don't have to commute."

"You've had it bad for him forever."

Her cheeks warmed. "He is my boss and I like and respect him."

"It's more than that and you know it. Opportunity is knocking, babe. Why not see if we can stir up a little heat?" He reached for her.

Groaning, she evaded him and sank back in her chair. "That's why you asked me to kiss you? You saw Max coming?"

He shrugged. "Maybe."

Doug had stirred up something all right. Max's anger. Max had looked furious to find her out partying when she should be at home working on *Honor*. She had a mountain of work on her desk and not enough hours in the day to get it done.

She prayed the copy of the Willow script came through. Only then could she fully explain to Max why she was consorting with the enemy.

"You look ready to breathe fire," Dev said as Max joined him at their table.

"My assistant is wining and dining when she should be at home working." That was the only reason seeing Dana kiss the guy had pissed him off. The urge to knock the kid back into his chair had nothing to do with the fact that she'd been kissing Max thirty-two hours ago.

For God's sake, she worked for him. The kiss had been a mistake—one he shouldn't, couldn't, *wouldn't* repeat. Had he learned nothing from his marriage? Business and pleasure were a volatile combination.

"You're out tonight, too."

"This is work. We're here to develop strategy to counteract the Willow competition. Damn, this time crunch is killing us."

"Rushing the film through production and postproduction has definitely added some pressure. But you can't expect her to work around the clock."

"Until this film is done we're all working around the clock. She knew what she was getting into before she signed on as associate producer, and she's being paid accordingly. If she'd wanted nine-to-five, she should have kept her old job."

Dev looked beyond Max's shoulder and his eyes narrowed. "How well do you know Dana?"

Obviously not as well as he'd thought given the discoveries he'd made in the past few days. Had he ever seen her smile the way she'd been smiling at her date? "Why?"

"Her dinner date is Doug Lewis."

"I've met him."

"He's Trey Jacob's assistant."

A knot jerked tight in Max's midsection. "Lewis works for Willow."

"That's right. And we have a possible leak. Think there's a connection?"

Instant denial sprung to Max's lips. He'd trusted Dana with everything for the past five years. But Dev had planted a seed of doubt and tendrils of mistrust took root. Would Dana betray him? Would she betray Hudson Pictures? If so, why? What possible motive could she have?

Money? He'd seen no signs of excess spending in her apartment, and she drove a four-year-old economy car. She wasn't into jewelry or designer shoes and handbags like so many of the actresses he dealt with.

A promotion? She'd have less of a chance of producing anything at Willow than she had with Hudson, and she was smart enough to know it.

Max scrolled through his memories. The *Legions* premiere hadn't been the only time he'd seen Dana with Lewis. "She's been dating him for at least two years."

"I'd say that needs looking into."

"I agree. I'll talk to her tonight."

"Tonight?"

He wished his brother hadn't picked up on that. "When I get home."

"You'll call her that late?"

"No. I'll see her. She's staying with me."

Dev's eyebrows shot up. "She's living with you?"

"No. *Staying* with me until *Honor* is completed."

"Same difference."

"Not at all. It's business. Working from my home office means fewer interruptions and a way to squeeze more hours out of the workday. She's downstairs in the guest suite. It's nothing personal."

That kiss had been pretty damned personal. His reaction to seeing her with bed head, no makeup and in her skimpy pajamas had felt personal. Why else would he have been dreaming about her when he crashed on her sofa? A seriously hot dream.

Planting one on her when he'd still been in that hazy half-awake state had not been one of his finer moments. He'd be lucky if she didn't cry sexual harassment. That would give the PR department a serious issue to work on.

"You're sharing a house. Trust me, women have expectations when that happens. Everything changes."

"Dana knows the score."

"I hope you're right." Dev got an *ah-ha* look on his face. "I get it. This is about Karen."

"No," Max denied quickly.

"Yes. You don't want Dana on the road late at night because of what happened to Karen. It's the same reason you always make your bimbos sleep over after sex instead of kicking them out like a smart man would. Better yet, you could go to their place, leave when you're done and avoid the messy mornings after."

"You're trying to connect unrelated incidents."

"Liar." But the insult was hurled in a brotherly tone. "The accident wasn't your fault, Max."

He didn't want to rehash this. Not now. Not while they had so much other garbage on the table. "I need a drink."

He scanned the area, searching for their waiter. It was because he'd had too much to drink that night while he was wheeling and dealing that he'd made Karen drive.

Is there a lesson here, buddy?

A familiar knot of tension balled between his shoulder blades. *Forget the drink.* "I shouldn't have let her drive."

"She was old enough to make that decision herself, Max."

"She was tired."

"Karen could have called for a driver. Wouldn't be the first time one of us has done that. Or she could have had a couple cups of coffee. God knows she had guts enough to speak up for what she wanted on the job. That night shouldn't have been any different."

Another reminder not to get involved with someone he worked with. He and Karen had had a great marriage most of the time, but when they had one of their rare arguments the bad mood had followed them into work and hung over the entire studio like a dark cloud. She'd been his executive assistant until he'd convinced her to quit, stay at home and try to get pregnant.

"Forget it. That's history. We have a current crisis to manage." He didn't need to be raking over old, cold coals tonight. If he did he'd end up drinking too much. Again. His pity parties didn't happen often, but when they did, they weren't pretty. That's why he usually carted himself out of town for the event. This year his tight schedule wouldn't allow it.

"You're right. Max, the similarity between Willow's film and ours might be coincidental. Congruity happens. And if it were any other film company I wouldn't think twice. But it's not another company, and if we have a leak then you have to consider Dana as the source."

He'd already come to that conclusion. "If I fire her, I'll never get the editing done on time."

"Then you won't fire her. Yet. You'll just watch her like a hawk. Can you handle that?"

She was already living under his roof. All he had to do was find a way to control the hours when she wasn't working or sleeping and since those would be few and far between until November, it shouldn't be too difficult.

"I have it covered. And I'll find out if she's leaked anything and if so, how much."

Five

Dana closed Max's front door and locked it behind herself as quietly as possible, then she turned and spotted a big shadow in the dark foyer. She startled and fumbled for the security panel, intent on setting off the alarm if she had to.

The light flicked on, identifying the shadow as Max. She pressed a hand over her racing heart. The gate chime would have alerted him to her arrival. "Max, you scared me."

"What did you tell Lewis about *Honor?*"

She smothered a wince. She'd been afraid he'd think the worst. "Nothing."

"He works for Willow."

She heard accusation in his tone, but until she had the script in hand and she was sure delivering it wouldn't get Doug fired, she couldn't give Max the whole story. Doug hadn't had a copy of the script in the pile at his condo. She'd have to wait until he could look around the office when he returned from recce.

"Yes. He works for Willow. He's been there a couple of years. And you might as well know now that I helped him get the job."

"So that you could exchange information?"

"No."

"Did you leak details of the *Honor* script to him?"

She pushed off the door and met his gaze straight on. "No, Max. Why would I do that?"

"You tell me."

That he didn't trust her ticked her off. "You think I sold information to our competitor?"

"Did you?"

The accusation stung. "I was trying to *get* information from Doug tonight, not give it to him. You wanted to know about Willow's upcoming film. I've known Doug a long time. I was hoping he'd tell me what we needed to know."

"Did he?"

"Not yet."

"You kissed him."

She shrugged. "Doug kisses everybody. It means nothing."

"Yesterday you kissed me."

Her mouth watered over the memory. She swallowed. "No. *You* kissed *me*. But I get that you didn't know who…you weren't awake or aware…that it wasn't me you were thinking of."

She was so uncomfortable with this conversation she could barely look him in the eyes.

"He's your lover."

She grimaced and curled her toes in her shoes. "He was. He isn't anymore. That ended years ago."

"Before or after he went to work at Willow?"

Why did he need to know this?

"About the same time. We didn't want to be accused of a conflict of interest, so we ended our relationship." By then they'd figured out they were better friends than lovers anyway. And yes, Doug had figured out she was looking for someone who could make her forget her boss. But Doug hadn't been that guy. No way was she going to tell Max that.

"Did you promise to meet him again?"

Heat crawled up her cheeks. Not in the way he meant, but she wasn't going to lie. "We didn't set a date."

"But you are going to see him again."

"I might. He's a friend." If he got the script, they'd definitely meet. He was supposed to call if/when that happened and set up a rendezvous. Waiting a week or three seemed like an eternity.

Max moved closer until he loomed over her and she had to tilt her head back to hold his gaze. "I could fire you for that conflict of interest you mentioned."

Her stomach sank. "You don't need to do that, Max. I swear I'm not sharing company secrets. I'm trying to help, not hurt Hudson Pictures."

"Will you sleep with him to get the information?"

She flinched and gasped. "No."

"Will you kiss him again?"

This was a weird conversation for a man who avoided personal exchanges like he would stepping on a fire-ant hill. "Probably. I told you Doug kisses everybody."

"Do you?"

She couldn't gauge his mood. She'd never seen him

like this…all edgy and male with a hint of aggression just below the surface. He wasn't drunk. His words and eyes were clear and she didn't smell liquor on his breath.

"No. I'm pretty selective who I kiss."

His eyes narrowed. "Are you?"

He closed the gap between them. Only an inch or two separated their torsos. Her breath stalled in her chest. "Max?"

"I knew who I was kissing yesterday. I always know who I'm kissing." He lifted her chin with his knuckle and covered her mouth with his.

Dana stood frozen with shock. Fast on the heels of that hair-raising circumstance came a potent cocktail of heat, arousal and adrenaline. His lips pressed hers open and his tongue sought and found hers in a slick, hot caress. A whimper of need slipped up her throat. Her nails bit into her palms as she struggled for sanity and fought the urge to wrap her arms around him.

She didn't have a clue what was going on or why he was kissing her. And she didn't care. She'd dreamed of this moment too often to question or fight it. His chest pressed her breasts and their thighs touched, and then his arm hooked around her and yanked her against him. Her heart raced and her skin flushed.

His heat scorched her, winded her, aroused her. The pressure of his mouth on hers intensified, bending her back over his arm, opening her mouth for deeper possession. She dropped her purse on the floor and gave in to the need to wind her arms around his middle for support as the room spun around her.

The warmth of his palm splayed over her hip and rose with torturous slowness to rest on her rib cage with his thumb just below her breast. Her nipple tightened in anticipation. She wanted him to touch her, ached for it. But he didn't.

His hold loosened and he stepped away. "Don't see Lewis again if you want to keep your job."

Dana struggled to catch her breath and unscramble her brain. "Wha-what if I can't promise that?"

"I'd think long and hard before I refused if I were you. Your job won't be the only one on the line."

And then he pivoted and climbed the stairs, leaving her alone in the foyer. Dana sagged against the front door with her heart pounding a deafening roar in her ears.

If she did as he ordered, she wouldn't get the answers Hudson needed. Surely once she had the script Max would understand and forgive her for ignoring his command?

It was a risk she had to take.

When he saw Dana smother a yawn, Max pushed away from his desk and stood. "Take a break."

Dana's brown eyes found his. "It's not even noon."

He couldn't think for the distraction of having her only yards away. He heard each shift of her body, every sigh and even the quiet rumble of her stomach, for pity's sake. Working in close proximity to her had never been an issue before. Why now when he didn't have time for this?

"We don't have time to correct mistakes that slip by because you're tired."

She snapped upright. "If I were that tired I'd take a break. I know my limitations. Do you, Max?"

"Of course." Had she changed perfumes? Her scent seemed stronger. Or maybe he was just more aware of it since that kiss last week.

Why had he kissed her?

Why had she kissed him back?

He plowed a hand through his hair and turned toward the window. He hadn't slept worth a damn since that night because he couldn't help wondering what she had been doing during those two hours after she'd left the restaurant with Doug Lewis. He'd worried about her driving on his twisty road after drinking champagne.

But mostly he'd wondered if she'd been in Lewis's bed.

And why did the idea of her naked and sweaty with Lewis make his gut burn? Must be because of the possible betrayal of Hudson secrets. If she'd shared the *Honor* script details, what else would she share?

The air inside the office suddenly seemed stuffy. He had to get out of this room. "I'm going for a swim."

Dana blinked, her long lashes briefly concealing the confusion in her eyes. "Okay, I'll cover the phones."

"No, you'll join me. We'll both be more alert after a break." And maybe the chlorine in the pool would kill her scent.

"But—"

"It's Saturday, Dana. No one important is going to call. Put on your suit. I'll meet you outside."

He left before she could argue and jogged upstairs to his room. Changing into swim trunks took only seconds and then he was outside on his private deck sucking up the fresh air and letting the sun bake his skin. Neither did anything to cure the restlessness riding him.

What was his problem?

He descended the circular stair to the flagstone patio. The blue pool water glistened, but a swim wasn't really what he needed. It was just a way to physically exhaust himself so that he could concentrate.

The door from the guest room to the patio opened, and Dana strolled out wearing a black bikini. He nearly choked on his tongue. She was toned where it counted, but soft where she needed to be. Honey-golden skin wrapped her curves in a mouth-watering package. Hunger hit him like a fist in the gut. How had he missed that she had a fantasy-worthy body?

He shook himself, trying to break the spell. This was Dana, the woman who'd been right under his nose, his right hand, for the past five years.

A woman who'd stood by him through some tough times.

A woman who might have betrayed him.

An idea infiltrated his brain like smoke slipping under a door. What better way to end the pillow talk between Dana and Lewis than by keeping her out of the other man's bed?

And the best way to do that was for Max to keep her so busy in his bed that she wouldn't have the time or energy to think about her ex-lover.

The idea sent a rush of heat through him, but his conscience countered with a warning prickle up the back of his neck. Sleeping with an employee was never a good idea. He'd learned that lesson the hard way. But he wasn't going to marry Dana. She'd already stated her intention of leaving Hudson as soon as possible—if she won the bet. The complication would be a problem only if she stayed on as his E.A.

Deliberately seducing her for personal gain wasn't the decent thing to do, but it would serve dual purposes. One, having her would satisfy his curiosity so that he could quit obsessing about her and get the damned film completed on time. She'd been interfering with his concentration since she'd moved into his house. Two, by getting closer to Dana he could find out exactly what she'd shared with Lewis and what Lewis had told her about Willow's upcoming flick.

He walked toward her and saw the exact moment she figured out something was amiss. She froze. Her lashes fluttered and her lips parted—her soft, delicious lips. He couldn't wait for another taste. God knows, the last two kisses had only whetted his appetite.

"Max?"

As he drew nearer he let his gaze devour the sleek curtain of her long, dark hair and the round curve of her breasts swelling above the black triangles of her top. Nice. Probably real. Real wasn't something you saw too often in Hollywood. Her chest rose and fell as if she were drawing quick, shallow breaths.

A glint of gold caught his eye, drawing his attention down her midline to just above her modest-by-Holly-wood-standards bikini bottom. A tiny piece of jewelry glimmered in her navel. Closer inspection revealed a heart dangling over the dimple of her belly button, its swing agitated by the fine tremor of her body.

Dana, his conservative assistant, had a navel ring?

He searched her face. Who was this woman who had completely hidden her true personality from him for so long? She stared back at him, eyes wide, pupils expanded, but not with fear or rejection. He saw hunger, a hunger almost as great as his own in her dark brown eyes.

If she'd given him one back-off signal, he'd respect it. The last thing he needed was an employee crying foul. But she gave no such signals. Instead she licked her lips and tilted her head to the side, sending a cascade of thick dark hair across her shoulder to semi-conceal one breast and shoulder. "I—I thought we were going to swim."

Her whisper swept over his skin like a caress, leaving goose bumps behind. Goose bumps? When had he last experienced those? And she hadn't even touched him yet. "Later."

He reached for her. She met him halfway, their bodies colliding with a gentle slap. The fusion of her smooth, hot, golden skin to his forced the air from his lungs. He paused to catch his breath, to wrestle for some measure of control, to remember why he was doing this.

She might have betrayed him.

She might be planning to betray him further.

But the knowledge didn't kill his appetite. He wanted her kiss so badly he deliberately denied himself the pleasure, grasped her upper arms and backed her toward the house. Anticipation made his mouth water.

Their bare legs brushed against each other, their bellies sliding with each step. Her breasts nudged his chest, her nipples tightened and prodded him, and her quickening exhalations puffed against his chin. Desire pooled in his groin and his muscles clenched. He could feel himself hardening against her. If she had any doubts where this was headed before, she couldn't possibly now.

He paused on the sun-warmed flagstones outside her room, giving rational thought one last chance to derail him from this irreversible course of action, giving her one more chance to object to crossing the boss-employee line.

"Dana, if we go through that door, I am going to be inside you."

She took a quick breath. Her hands cupped his shoulders and for a moment he thought she'd push him away.

But then she looked at him through her lashes with those passion-darkened eyes and coasted her palms down his biceps and back up to his neck. With agonizing slowness, she scraped her short nails lightly down his arms, over the insides of his wrists, across his palms, before the tips of her fingers hooked his. Sauntering backward with a hip rolling gait, she tugged him toward her room, making it clear she wanted this as much as he did.

Dana wanted him.

The knowledge rocked him, shocked him. When and how had that happened? Before she'd returned his kiss, he couldn't remember her ever giving him those kinds of signals. In fact, if anything, she'd mothered him, pampered him. Spoiled him, he admitted.

He reached past her to slide open the door. Cooled air rushed out of the house and over his skin, but did nothing to cool his desire. Once they'd crossed the threshold— literally, figuratively—there would be no going back. His feet sank into the carpet. He closed the door behind him, sealing them into the silent house.

The room smelled like her, looked like her. The *other* her. This woman he didn't know. She'd added candles and framed photographs of her family and potted plants to the room.

Who was this other woman? he asked himself not for the first time.

He caught her face in his hands and stroked her smooth skin and then threaded his fingers through her thick, silky hair. Her head tilted back, but he ignored the silent invitation. He caressed her neck, her shoulders, her arms, and then he transferred his hands to her hips and drew circles over her hipbones with his thumbs. She shivered and gasped. The sound hit him low and hard.

Easing his hands upward, he outlined her narrow waist and the bottom edge of her rib cage, savoring her warm, satiny skin. Her lids fluttered closed. He bent to kiss one, then the other. Her thick lashes tickled his chin, and her back arched, pressing her pelvis into his. Need stabbed him. He sucked a sharp breath through his gritted teeth.

Dipping his head, he sipped from the shadowy warmth beneath her ear. She angled her head to give him better access. This time he didn't refuse. The hot press of her hands at his waist jolted him. The unhurried caress of her soft hands up and down his sides urged him to rush, to push her onto her bed and bury himself inside her. He wanted her hard and fast. For that reason he kept a tight-fisted grip on his control.

Mindless passion was for college kids. Smart passion, delayed satisfaction brought greater rewards. And purpose. He reminded himself he was doing this for a reason, but that reason was a little hazy when she tasted so good on his lips and on his tongue.

Nuzzling the fragrant spot behind her earlobe made her shudder in his arms. Her nails raked his back and ripped an unexpected groan from deep in his chest. He drew back, putting space between him and fighting the temptation to say to hell with slow and easy.

He traced the V-neck of her top with one finger, his eyes focusing on the nipples beading beneath the thin fabric. He wanted those tight buds in his mouth, needed to roll them around on his tongue and taste her. Instead he circled the band of black around her ribcage and drew a line down the center of her belly. He repeated the circle around her navel and then the top of her bikini bottom.

She shifted impatiently, her smooth, warm thighs sliding against each other. "Max."

The half cry, half whimper got to him. He'd bet his Lamborghini she'd sound like that when he slid inside her the first time. And that couldn't happen soon enough. His patience evaporated. He reached for the knot at her nape and fumbled it free. The ties dropped and the fabric slid downward with excruciating slowness before finally baring her breasts. He swallowed hard at the sight of the dusky centers.

Dana reached one arm behind her back and loosened the other tie. The top floated to the floor. He flexed his fingers in anticipation and then cupped her warm, soft flesh in his palms and buffed her nipples with his thumbs. Her breath hitched. She bit her lip. He bent his head and took a puckered tip into his mouth.

Her taste was like nothing he'd experienced before. He savored her unique flavor and her scent filled his nostrils. Her fingers threaded through his hair, holding him close as she arched into him, her free breast branding his bicep. But he wasn't trying to escape. Not until he'd had his fill of her and cured this damned sudden and irrational obsession that had hit him like a bad case of the flu.

He shifted his mouth to the neglected soft globe and used the moisture he'd left behind to lubricate his massaging fingers on the first. Dana's fingers tightened, her nails scraping an arousing pattern on his scalp. He wanted more.

"Mmm. That feels good," she whispered brokenly.

Planting one knee on the floor, he hooked her bikini bottom with his thumbs and yanked it down her legs. She gripped his shoulders as she stepped out of her swimsuit, her touch hot and firm on his skin. He wanted her hands all over him, the sooner, the better.

Letting her nipple slide from his mouth, he looked up at her, at her red lips and heavy-lidded eyes, at the curve of her damp nipples, her small waist. But it was the tiny cluster of dark curls that beckoned him. He needed to taste her. Her golden skin, her sweet center, the essence of her arousal. But not yet. Not when his hunger was sharp enough to cut him.

He pressed a kiss to her breastbone, laved his way down her belly, toward the golden heart. He circled the jewelry with his tongue and she hiccupped a series of short fast breaths. As he strung kisses along her bikini line he used his hands to caress from her hips down the outside of her legs to her feet.

He curled his fingers around her ankles, grasped the delicate joints and urged her legs apart, widening her stance for balance because he intended to rock her world.

"Max?" she breathed.

He worked his hands upward on the insides of her legs this time, his palms coasting over warm, smooth soft skin. She was so damned touchable. The scent of her excitement grew stronger as he neared his target and his own desire pounded through his veins, urgent and unrelenting. He forced himself to take it slow when what he wanted to do was shoot to his feet and bury himself deep inside her with a single thrust.

He reached the back of her knees. She shivered at the scrape of his fingernails along the sensitive crease. He did it again with the same results. She clutched his hair and then released, clutched and released. Her short nails lightly outlined his ears, sending stimulating ripples cresting through him.

He finally reached her thighs and massaged their sleekly muscled length, working his way from her tensed quadriceps and hamstrings to her softer, warmer inner thighs. He traced her panty line with his thumbnails and her knees quaked. Encouraged, he leaned forward and traced the same path with his tongue, simultaneously finding her center with his fingers. She was hot, wet and ready for him. Her hands cupped his head holding him close.

Her fragrance filled his lungs and surged straight to his groin. The selfish urge to flip her on her back on the bed and ride her hard crossed his mind. Instead, he replaced his fingers with his tongue and laved the swollen flesh waiting for him, circling it, tasting it, exploring it until he found the spot that made her cry out and curl her toes into the carpet.

Her taste filled him with a desperate, ravenous hunger for more. More. More. His pulse hammered in his head, almost drowning out the sexy-as-hell sounds coming from Dana's mouth.

"It's too much. I can't." Her nails dug into his scalp. She tried to pull away.

He clamped his hands on her buttocks and intensified his oral caress. Her legs shook. She tasted so damned good, smelled so good, felt so good. He sucked her into his mouth and pumped his fingers deep inside her. Even without her moan to clue him in, he registered the exact second she quit fighting and went over the edge. Her cries filled the air and her internal muscles clenched his fingers.

He rode the wave with her, savoring each squeeze, each whimper, each spasm. And when her knees buckled, he held her upright. He kissed the pale skin between her curls and the twinkling heart and looked up at her. Her pleasure was a sight to behold. Dusky peach painted her cheeks and her lips were red and swollen from her biting them.

Her eyes slowly opened halfway and found his. The hand she had gripping his shoulder slid up the side of his neck, under his jaw and then she lifted his chin. "Thank you."

"My pleasure." And it had been. He rose and kissed her hard on the mouth.

Reality check. He'd been so eager to lose himself inside her he'd almost forgotten a critical component. "I've barely started. But we need a condom."

Her lashes fluttered and she lowered her chin. "I have some."

She bit her lip as if embarrassed by the confession, and then walked across the room. He enjoyed watching her move, and the tight curve of her bottom made him grit his teeth. Delicious.

Dana was a beautiful woman. How could he have been so blind?

She withdrew a plastic packet from her purse and turned. Despite the blush on her cheeks, there was a sexual sparkle in her eyes that grabbed him by the hormones and demanded his attention. But there was also a contradictory reticence lurking in the way her gaze bounced from his and the way she chewed her bottom lip. Her tight body language and a slight hesitation snagged his curiosity. He didn't know what to make of this from his confident executive assistant who handled conniption-fit-throwing actors and on-set disasters without breaking a sweat.

He took the package from her, pulled her close and covered her mouth with his. Her response started out tentative but quickly became so wild and uninhibited she pushed him close to the edge of control. He nipped her bottom lip. She bit him right back—not hard, just playful. Sexy. Enticing as hell. Hunger bolted through him like lightning.

He stroked her smooth back, her soft bottom, and she mimicked his every move, squeezing where he squeezed, scratching where he scratched. He tightened his arms around her, pulling her flush against his erection for one brief moment before bringing his hand between them to find her center. She whimpered into his mouth as he thumbed her still swollen flesh.

She yanked her mouth free. "Max, I want you."

"And you're going to have me as soon as you do one more thing for me."

"What?" Her body tensed in his arms and her nails dug into his shoulders. He quickened his caress. Orgasm overtook her.

"That's what I was waiting for," he whispered against her temple once she stopped shuddering.

Her lips and teeth found his shoulder, surprising him with a gentle love bite and punching him with another arousing jolt. She impatiently shoved his swim trunks down his legs and wrapped her fingers around his length. She stroked him long and slow from base to tip and back again.

His teeth clamped shut on a furnace blast of desire. It slammed him like a runaway trolley, winding him, making his head spin. He struggled to right himself and then kicked aside his trunks and tore the condom open with his teeth. She tried to take it from him, but he was so triggered he didn't dare let her. He grabbed her hand and redirected it to less dangerous territory—his waist. Only that ended up being more hazardous than he'd anticipated as her nails traced havoc-wreaking patterns on his skin with devastating results.

He rolled on the latex with an unsteady hand, ripped back the comforter and backed her onto the mattress.

She lay down and he caressed her long, luscious legs apart. He wanted to feast on her, to nibble from toes to earlobes, lingering and making her cry out again and again. He wanted that too much.

How could he want Dana this way when he'd never had a sexual thought about her before that kiss? He brushed aside the question and positioned himself. He intended to take it slow, to control his passion and keep his head the way he always did, but then she wrapped a hand around his nape, pulling him down for a kiss, and simultaneously hooked a leg behind his butt and pressed him forward. Slow and rational ceased to be an option.

He sank deep into her mouth and into the hot, slick glove of her body simultaneously. Hunger grabbed him by the groin and the throat, and a groan of pleasure barreled its way out of his chest. Instinct took over. He couldn't slow the thrust of his tongue or his hips. She met him stroke for stroke, engaging in a mental and physical tug of war for control. Reining himself in was no longer a sure thing. It was a damned risky proposition.

He fought through the animalistic drive riding him and tried to focus on her pleasure. This was about her, about keeping her from Lewis's bed. But damned if he gave a flip about his motives at the moment.

He swiveled his hips against her. She broke the kiss. "That f-feels g-good."

Her breathy, broken words drove him to repeat the maneuver again and again until her back bowed and her nails raked his back, his thighs, his chest. She nipped his shoulder—another gentle love bite—and that was all it took. He crossed the line, the point of no return. He pounded into her. Deeper, harder, faster. Again. Again. Her gasps and cries fueled him.

When he felt her tense, heard her breath catch, he did the same. Fighting his way back from the brink became a lost cause. Orgasm ripped through her, making her body squeeze his and forcing the air from her lungs in a sexy groan. And he lost it. His own release battered him over and over until he was spent. His lungs burned. His arm muscles quivered and then collapsed. He landed on her. It took seconds to regain his strength and lift himself from the warm, damp, soft cushion of her body. Not that he wanted to leave. And that worried him.

Her eyes remained closed, her lashes a dark fan on her flushed cheeks. But it was the smile curving her lips that nailed him right in the chest. He leaned down and brushed his mouth over hers.

What the…?

His arms snapped straight and then he rolled off her and landed on the bed. The bed that smelled like Dana. Like Dana and hot sex.

Why had he kissed her that way? He didn't do tender gestures. Not anymore. Sex was sex. Basic. Primal. Satisfaction of a need. And in this case, a way to protect his assets. No emotion required or desired.

But damn, he wanted to ask her about that smile. If it meant what he thought it did—that this was more than just physical release for her—then he needed to warn her. Temporary was his MO. His *only* MO. He would never marry again.

But if he warned her off and she got huffy, then his honesty could cause problems. One, she might quit. Two, she might pout and refuse to speak to him—the way Karen sometimes had. Three, anger might drive her back to Lewis. None of those options would help him get *Honor* completed on time.

So he'd have to suck it up and hope like hell she didn't get emotionally attached. Because happily ever after might make for a great film, but it had no place in his life.

Six

Dana couldn't stop smiling.

She lay flat on her back, eyes closed, fighting the urge to grin like a fool. Max lay beside her. She could hear his rapid breathing, feel his body heat and smell him. She inhaled deeply. Correction, she could smell *them* and the intoxicating aroma of their lovemaking. The urge to grin grew stronger.

Making love with him had exceeded her fantasies. And she couldn't ask for more. She was so happy they'd finally taken this step—even if she didn't know what had precipitated it.

The mattress shifted. She forced her heavy eyelids open in time to see Max leaving the bed. She soaked up the sight of his broad shoulders, tight butt, and long, muscled legs as he bent to scoop up his swim trunks from the floor. Yummy.

He disappeared into the adjoining bathroom without looking back. Something felt a little off. She chalked it up to the awkwardness of the first time with a new partner. Not that she had a whole lot of experience with that circumstance. And he did have the condom to deal with.

Rolling out of bed, she gathered her suit and shifted on her feet as she tried to figure out what to do next. Put the suit back on? Get dressed? Climb back in bed? She still hadn't made up her mind when Max returned dressed in his trunks.

His gaze rolled over her, lingering on her breasts, which tightened in response to his widening pupils and intense expression. His gaze coasted past her waist and hips to her legs and then slowly returned. His eyes stalled briefly on her navel ring before gliding up until they locked with hers once more. She saw suppressed passion but also caution in his eyes.

Her fingers tightened on the fabric of her swimsuit. A sudden and unexpected wave of insecurity made her want to cover up. He dated some of the most beautiful women in the world. How did she measure up? She certainly wasn't as skinny as his usual type. And she wasn't blonde.

"I'm going to take a quick swim and have lunch before getting back to work. Shall I cook enough for two?"

She blinked in surprise. He'd taken her to restaurants for working lunches, but he'd never prepared anything for her or even offered to fetch anything for her from the Hudson Pictures canteen. And while all he'd be doing was heating up something the caterer had left, that he'd offer to include her now made her feel all warm and fuzzy and cherished.

"I could make lunch." She'd rather stay here and cuddle with him. But they really didn't have time for that.

"I can handle it. You take a shower or…whatever it is women do after…sex."

Sex. She'd rather he called it making love. But he was a guy. A commitment-phobic guy. "Maybe I, um, could join you in the pool and then we could make the meal together."

"I'm going to swim laps." He turned on his heel and exited through her patio door.

Confused, Dana stared after him. Had that been a statement or a dismissal? Did Max regret what had just happened?

How could he regret what had been one of the best moments of her life?

And where did they go from here? Because for her, everything had changed. She no longer wanted to get away from Max, and she no longer wanted to win the bet. She wanted to win his heart.

Only the hum of the electronic equipment disturbed the silence of the room.

Dana sat at her desk in Max's home office and tried to focus on work, but her mind kept straying. She wasn't dumb enough to delude herself that Max was in love with her. Yet. His cool demeanor throughout lunch had proven that. There had been no tender, reminiscent smiles, no wicked glances promising more lovemaking to come later.

But he did desire her. She knew good acting when she saw it, and Max hadn't been faking his passion earlier.

So why the oppressive silence now?

Max's office chair squeaked as he twisted to face her. Her heart skipped in anticipation of what he'd say.

"How is the capturing coming?"

Work. She'd expected something…personal. She tried

to mask her disappointment. "It's going well. I should be finished in a couple of days."

He swiveled back and then stopped. "My family is having a dinner tonight. I'd like you to join me."

Happiness welled in her chest. He was including her—like a real date. That had to mean something. "I'd like that."

"We'll leave at seven."

She glanced at her watch. She had just over an hour to get ready. And then she realized she wasn't prepared—not to go to Hudson Manor as Max's date. "I didn't pack anything that would be appropriate for a night out. I'll need to go to my place to change."

"Back up your work and go. I'll pick you up in an hour." His neutral tone lacked enthusiasm and again, that niggling feeling that something wasn't quite right hit her.

She brushed it aside. They'd made love and he was taking her to his family dinner. As her brother had always claimed, as long as you're making forward progress, you're headed in the right direction.

And Max was picking her up at her house. It would be almost like a date. Their first date.

Dana's palms moistened and her pulse quickened as Max pulled his car to a halt in front of Hudson Manor. She'd been here several times before for functions related to work and to visit Lillian.

But tonight was different. Her role had changed.

Or had it?

It was hard to tell from Max's demeanor. He hadn't taken her in his arms and kissed her when he'd arrived at her place. In fact, he was acting as if they hadn't been lost in each other's bodies this afternoon.

She shook off her insecurities and looked up at the

Hudson's home through the car window. The French provincial mansion Charles had built for Lillian on Loma Vista Drive in Beverly Hills never failed to impress her. The gray stone facade with its wrought-iron decorative accents tripped every romantic switch she had.

Set on fifteen acres with two swimming pools, four tennis courts, stables plus a carriage house and a guest house, the estate had a fairy-tale quality that made it impossible for Dana to imagine living in such grandeur.

Charles and Lillian had filled the place with antiques they'd bought on their world travels, but the place didn't feel in the least like a museum. Every other time Dana had come for a visit she'd been very comfortable. Tonight, not so much.

Max came around to her side of the car and opened her door. He offered his hand to assist her out. She grasped him tightly, glad for the reassurance under the changed circumstances. What would his family think about him with *her?*

She climbed from the car, took a deep breath and squeezed Max's hand. She deliberately stepped into his body. "Thanks for including me tonight."

He held her pressed against his length for a moment, but then released her without a kiss, leaving her feeling a bit adrift. "You're welcome."

She kept pace beside him as they headed for the front door. Why hadn't he kissed her? Maybe he wasn't into public displays? "I can't imagine what it must have been like growing up here. It's quite different from my home."

"You get used to it."

She laughed at his dismissive tone. "I don't think so. According to Lillian when she gave me a tour, your house has fifty-five rooms. Mine had ten. There's a bit of a discrepancy."

He opened the front door and motioned for her to precede him. She entered the grand foyer with its marble floors, double-wide staircase and soaring ceiling. Until she'd visited Hudson Manor she'd had no idea there was such a thing as hand-painted wallpaper. Back home she and her mother had bought the stuff in rolls and redone the entire house themselves. It wasn't the same. Not even close.

"Who'll be here tonight?" She hoped he didn't notice the nervous quiver in her voice.

He shrugged. "Probably everybody except Luc, who's in Montana. He and Gwen are too close to the baby's due date to travel."

"Hudson Pictures will miss him as the PR director, but retiring to raise a family on a ranch does have its appeal."

His gaze sharpened. "You're interested in leaving L.A.?"

She shook her head. "Oh, no. I love the bustle and edginess of the city, but I was raised in a smallish town. I understand the appeal of a less hurried lifestyle."

The quick shuffle of feet drew Dana's attention. Hannah Aldridge, the sixty-something housekeeper who'd been with the family forever, hustled toward them. Her hazel-green eyes glowed with a warm welcome. "Good evening, Mr. Max, Ms. Dana. The family is in the front salon."

"The salon?" Max sounded surprised.

"Appears there's something to celebrate tonight."

Excitement stirred in Dana's belly. Was Max planning to surprise her by announcing their new coupledom to the family?

"What's the occasion?" he asked, dashing her hopes.

"That I don't know. You look lovely tonight, Miss."

Dana felt the heat climb her cheeks and smoothed a

hand over her black cocktail dress. She'd bought both the minidress and shoes at a studio wardrobe clearance sale. That was the only way she'd ever be able to afford designer apparel.

"Thank you, Hannah." A part of her wished Max had been the one to issue the compliment. Yes, his gaze had gobbled her up when she'd opened her door to him earlier, but he hadn't said a word about her appearance even though she'd taken extra care to look good tonight. "How is Lillian this evening?"

"She's well, and you're a peach for asking. Go on through. They're waiting for you."

On the short walk to the salon Dana tried to rally her courage. She told herself she knew these people and they knew her. She had nothing to fear. But the bats swooping and diving through her stomach didn't get the message.

The room fell silent the moment they crossed the threshold, tightening her nerves even more. How would Max explain their new situation? If he'd simply take her hand, everyone would get the message. But how would they react?

A chorus of welcomes greeted them. Dana forced herself to smile and wave at the nine people gathered in the room. Max broke away immediately to cross the room to his grandmother's side, leaving Dana by the door. Lillian looked as good as could be expected for her age and her condition. Her blue eyes twinkled and her expertly tinted auburn hair was perfectly styled. Her private nurse stood just behind her shoulder.

Dana felt a twinge of loss. Lillian's terminal illness was hitting them all hard, and while having time to prepare for her passing was a gift, that day was still going to be hard for everyone.

Max knelt, kissed Lillian's cheek and held her hands as he spoke to her so quietly Dana couldn't hear him. His gentleness and genuine affection for his grandmother tugged at her heartstrings.

At a loss, Dana tried to decide whether to join Max and interrupt his private moment with his grandmother or to impose herself on another group's conversation. Before she could decide Markus and Sabrina, Max's parents crossed the room toward her.

Sabrina, looking as elegant as ever in a designer evening pantsuit with her dark blond hair twisted in a French plait and her blue eyes sparkling, embraced Dana and kissed her cheek. "I'm happy you could join us, Dana."

"Thank you for including me."

Markus took her hand in both of his and gave it a squeeze. He looked to be in one of his jovial moods tonight. "It's the least we can do since our son is working you around the clock."

Her smile wobbled. Max must not have said anything about their being a couple now. But what could he say? He could hardly call his mother and say, "I slept with Dana today, so I'd like to bring her to dinner tonight as my date."

Okay, Dana admitted, maybe her expectations had been a little skewed. "I'm enjoying the challenge of my new position, and Max is teaching me a lot."

"May I fix you a drink?" Markus offered.

She did a quick scan of the room. Everyone seemed to be holding a glass. "A glass of white wine would be nice. Thank you."

"Sweet or dry?"

She wrinkled her nose. Living in California hadn't made a devoted wine fan out of her yet despite her vacation through Napa Valley on an educational winery tour. She'd learned a little about wine, but only enough to get by. "The sweeter, the better."

"I have something you might like."

Markus went one way. Sabrina took Dana's hand and led her in the opposite direction toward Max's brother Dev and the very slender brown-haired woman by his side.

"Dana, did you get a chance to meet Valerie Shelton, Dev's fiancée, in France?"

"I did, but only briefly. It's nice to see you again, Valerie." Dana shook her hand. Valerie was Dana's age, but seemed much more reserved. Dana had yet to figure out what about the cynical Dev appealed to the innocent and reserved Valerie other than looks and money. He was as rich and handsome as the rest of the Hudsons. But she'd always considered the COO of Hudson Pictures to be a bit aloof.

"It's nice to see you, too." Valerie gave her a shy smile. "I heard you've had a promotion since returning."

Sabrina nodded. "Dana is *Honor*'s associate producer now."

"That sounds exciting." Valerie glanced at Dev. The adoration shining in her violet eyes made Dana's breath catch. She hoped her feelings toward Max weren't as obvious to everyone around them. She'd have to be more careful.

Dev didn't seem to notice Valerie's tender regard. In fact, his cool blue eyes were watching Dana. Was he also concerned about her dinner with Doug? She prayed Doug would come through with the script so she could put both Dev's and Max's minds at ease.

Dana forced her attention back to Valerie. "It's a

dream job, but it's also hard work. No one wants to disappoint Lillian."

Markus returned to Dana's side and offered her a wineglass of pale gold liquid. "Try this, Dana. It's a German Riesling, 2006 vintage."

She accepted the glass and dutifully sniffed and sipped and rolled the wine around on her tongue as she'd been taught before swallowing. "It's very good. Nice and fruity. Thank you."

"Excellent. Let me know if you need a refill."

A tap on the shoulder made Dana turn. Bella, Max's baby sister, stood beside her. She had Max's blue eyes, and her grandmother's auburn hair. "Doesn't look like Max has you tearing out your hair yet."

"Not yet." Dana's gaze tracked him to the opposite side of the room where he now stood talking to his cousin Jack and David, Max's uncle and Jack's father, with his back to her. David was *Honor*'s director. She tried not to feel hurt by Max's neglect, but she had expected to be by his side tonight, not on opposite sides of the room.

Dana returned her attention to Bella. They'd known each other superficially for years because of Hudson Pictures, but not all that well until they'd gotten to know each other better while on location in France. Bella was not only beautiful, she was feisty and a lot of fun—when she wasn't wrapped up in her costar.

Dana scanned the room for Bella's man of the moment. Bella had played Lillian in *Honor*. Ridley Sinclair, a box-office star and Bella's current beau, had played Charles. Dana wasn't crazy about Ridley and thought Bella could do better than a guy so self-absorbed, but their off-screen romance had burned pretty hot.

"Is Ridley joining us tonight?"

"No. He's off doing…whatever." She waved a dismissive hand, but sounded a bit put out.

Markus patted his daughter on the shoulder. "I'll leave you ladies to catch up." He left to rejoin his wife.

Bella hooked her arm through Dana's. "Excuse us, Valerie and Dev. Dana, do you remember Cece, Cousin Jack's wife?"

"Yes, I do. Max worked quite a bit with Cece on fine-tuning the script." But Dana let herself be led to Jack, Cece and Max's side, hoping Bella hadn't seen the same lovestruck expression on her face that Valerie had displayed earlier. David stood on the fringe of the group.

Cece was a petite brunette, a brilliant scriptwriter and obviously in love with her husband. She grimaced as Dana and Bella approached. "They're talking shop again. Didn't Lillian forbid that tonight?"

"I did," Lillian called out. She winked at them and beckoned Dana.

"Excuse me," Dana said before going to Lillian's side. She kissed the papery cheek.

Lillian squeezed her hand. "You've made progress."

Dana drew back. "I'm sorry?"

"He was watching you while he was talking to me."

Dana's heart skipped a beat. She started to turn and look at Max, but Lillian caught her hand. "Don't look, dear. Never give all your secrets away. It gives a man too much power."

"Max was watching me?" she whispered.

Lillian nodded.

A blush scorched Dana's cheeks. "We're spending a lot of time together. Working," she added hastily, because there were some things you just didn't share with a man's grandmother.

On one of Dana's recent visits Lillian had confessed she'd known about Dana's crush for years and kept hoping her grandson would wise up. But she'd also warned Dana that Max's love for Karen had been all-consuming and her loss devastating. She wasn't sure Max would ever love that deeply again.

"Of course you are, dear. I'm glad he's giving you a chance to pursue your dream and that he brought you tonight. Keep up the good work. And remember, Dana, the best things in life are worth waiting for."

"Yes, ma'am. I'll try not to forget."

"Take care of him." The *after I'm gone* remained unspoken. But those silent words put a lump in Dana's throat.

"You know I'll do my best as long as I'm with him."

Lillian shoed her back to Max's side. Dana desperately wanted to take his hand, but didn't know if the gesture would be welcomed.

"No little man tonight?" she asked Cece.

Cece and Jack both smiled at the reference to their son—the son Jack hadn't known about until he'd tracked Cece down to ask her to write the script.

Cece shook her head. "We left Theo at home. This would be too late an evening for him."

"Good point." Dana had seen Theo only a few times, but he looked exactly like his black-haired, blue-eyed daddy, and he was completely precious. An old familiar ache squeezed her chest. Way back when, she'd believed she'd have several children of her own by the time she reached twenty-eight. "Let me know if you ever need a babysitter."

Cece grinned mischievously. "Don't make that offer lightly. I know your number."

Bella, her eyes brimming with excitement, shifted on her heels. "So is everything ready for the sixtieth anniversary bash and the movie preview?"

Jack nodded. "My staff has everything under control."

Bella looked at Dana. "I can't wait to see the first cut to see if I did Lillian proud. I mean, I saw the dailies, but…"

Dana touched her arm. "Bella, from what I've seen so far, you have nothing to be worried about. And once Max works his magic…"

Bella gave her a quick hug. "The three of us, you, me and Cece, are going to have to do some serious shopping. Oh, and we should probably include Valerie. I want a drop-dead gorgeous dress for this."

David rolled his eyes. "Shopping. That's one topic guaranteed to run any man away." He excused himself and went to his mother's side.

Max's gaze followed him and then he turned to Jack once David was out of earshot. "Is everyone behaving tonight?"

"Yes. Your father and mine are keeping it civil. For a change."

David Hudson did not get along well with his older brother or his brother's wife. There was a tension between them that Dana hadn't figured out yet despite the numerous interactions between David and Max. As director and producer they worked closely together.

Max scanned their little gathering. "Hannah said there was going to be a celebration. Anybody know what's going on?"

Jack shook his head. "No clue. Cece and I have no news. You?"

Dana tensed and waited, holding her breath, but Max shook his head. "Not me."

Her hopes sank like lead. She'd waited so long for it to happen that she really wanted to share the news that they were a couple. It was practically bubbling inside her.

Dev joined them with Valerie trailing behind. "I can answer your question." Dev turned to the room and used his key to tap on his glass. "May I have everyone's attention?"

He waited until the room fell silent. "Valerie and I eloped yesterday."

Gasps and surprised grunts filled the room. After a startled moment, Sabrina and Markus made their way across the room. Sabrina hugged her son and then her new daughter-in-law. Markus shook Dev's hand and then briefly embraced Valerie.

"Valerie, darling, welcome to the family," Sabrina said, and then turned her hurt eyes on Dev. "I wish you'd let me arrange your wedding. Your father and I would have enjoyed sharing such a special moment."

Dev shrugged. "We didn't want fanfare."

"A wedding on the estate grounds would have been nice," Lillian added.

"Oh, that's a lovely idea," Valerie gushed, but then seemed to regret her words. "But Dev and I couldn't wait."

Dana thought Valerie looked as if she would have liked some pageantry.

"Are you pregnant?" Bella asked bluntly, but not unkindly.

Valerie's cheeks turned crimson. She dipped her chin. "No. Oh, no. That's not what I meant."

An awkward silence descended. Dana moved forward to hug Valerie and break up the uncomfortable moment. "Congratulations. Perhaps I could arrange a belated bridal shower for you?"

Valerie's eyes filled with gratitude. "That would be nice, Dana. Although I'm sure we won't require any wedding presents. Dev tells me he'd like to live here in his suite of rooms."

"Every woman needs gifts. Sexy lingerie, for example," Bella said with a wicked smile that made Valerie blush more.

"I'll call next week and we'll work out the details." Dana stepped aside and let others offer their good wishes.

She glanced at Max and found his narrowed eyes focused on her. What was he thinking? From his forbidding expression she'd bet he wasn't remotely interested in following in his brother's footsteps to the altar.

All she had to do was find a way to change his mind, because there was nothing she'd like more than to marry Max on the grounds of Hudson Manor and begin her own fairy-tale romance.

Seven

"How did you know?" Max asked Dev after dinner when the men had retired to the patio for cigars and left the women inside to yap about the sixtieth anniversary gala.

"Know what?"

Max divided his attention between the women on the opposite side of the French doors and the far end of the patio where his father and uncle looked to be having another tense discussion. Jack was with them, running interference, Max would guess. "How did you know Valerie was the one?"

Dev puffed on his cigar. He exhaled long and slow as if the answer might be found in the smoke slowly dissipating in the air above their heads. "You're not expecting something sappy and romantic, are you?"

From his brother the cynic, who seemed to believe women were put on this earth only to procreate and provide entertainment? No.

"I just want an answer. Why Valerie? Why now?"

"I'm thirty-five. It's time to settle down. Valerie's well connected. Her father's a newspaper mogul and that could work in Hudson Pictures's favor when we need publicity in the future. She and I suit each other, and she won't give me a lot of backchat."

Like Karen had. His brother didn't say it, but he didn't need to. Max's wife had been quite opinionated. That she hadn't been a suck up or a pushover was one of the things Max had liked and respected about her. But she'd had a tendency to get in people's faces when crossed. Sometimes that had caused friction.

Dana was a hell of a lot more diplomatic.

He nixed the thought. There was no comparing the women and no reason to, especially now when the anniversary of Karen's death was just around the corner.

His gaze wandered to the woman in question on the other side of the closed glass doors. Her dress tonight had nearly knocked him to his knees. She'd gone from conservative, figure-concealing clothing to the kind that accentuated every curve of her luscious figure.

The wrap top of her black dress cupped her breasts and showed just enough soft skin to make him want to bury his face between the smooth globes and slip his hands beneath the short hem to see if she wore panties.

But he was stronger than that. No woman would make him weak with wanting again. He kept his head these days. No more getting swept away by passion. Reason ruled.

He forced his attention back to his brother and practical matters. "If you'd made a spectacle of the wedding instead of secretly sneaking off, it would have been great PR for *Honor*. Romance While Filming the Romance, or some similar headline. The press would have eaten it up. You know you wasted that opportunity."

Dev shrugged. "I know. But Valerie is an only child. You know what kind of production a traditional wedding would have turned into. Months of planning, too many trivial, irritating decisions… You know the drill. You did it."

Max knew. Karen had been an only child, too. Their wedding had taken a year to plan, and there had been times when the process had spiraled so crazily out of control he'd wanted to say to hell with it and elope. By the time they'd walked down the aisle he'd been relieved to have it over with and not to have to make any more decisions about stupid stuff like the color of the napkins and the like.

"Besides," Dev continued, "I didn't want to deal with the paparazzi, and we don't have time right now for all the cloak-and-dagger theatrics necessary to pull off a Hollywood wedding. Tents, helicopters, security."

"Amen to that."

"I preferred to close the deal as quickly as possible."

"That's it? Convenience? You weren't swept away by passion?"

Dev exhaled a smoky plume. "You do remember who you're talking to, don't you?"

Funny, he'd expected more from his big brother. But he shouldn't have. "Do you love her?"

"Like love worked so well for you." And then Dev winced. "I'm sorry. That was a low blow."

Love had worked for him. For a while. "Forget it. Did you at least get a prenup, so she won't take us to the cleaners?"

"What? You think I'm stupid?"

"No. I'm just looking out for our assets."

"While you're covering Hudson assets, what have you found out about Dana and Doug Lewis?"

"Nothing yet. I'm working on it."

"Any progress?"

He wasn't about to share his strategy. "Some."

"Let me know what you discover."

"As soon as I know it myself." And that meant he needed to turn up the heat and steam some information out of Dana.

And the desire to do so had nothing to do with how hot she looked tonight in that low-cut dress and those killer high heels.

Nothing whatsoever.

But damn, she looked amazing.

Good thing his hunger for her was temporary and could be turned off as soon as *Honor* hit the screen.

Otherwise, he'd be in trouble.

"The wedding announcement was a surprise," Dana said from beside Max in the darkened car on the way home from the dinner party.

Max kept his eyes on the winding road. "Yes."

"Did you know? Did Dev mention his plans at lunch?"

"No."

He heard her sigh and then the rustle of her dress as she shifted on the seat. Her scent and each sound she made seemed amplified in the quiet confines of the dark car. But the lack of light also kept him from checking out her legs the way he had on the way over to Hudson Manor. He was damned lucky he hadn't run them off the road.

How had he never noticed she had great legs before tonight?

"Does he realize what an amazing PR opportunity he missed? We could have had free airtime on every network and in a substantial number of magazines and web pages."

That's what he liked about Dana. Not only did she think like him, she reacted with logic rather than emotion. Karen had tended to go the opposite— He choked off that thought. He had to stop comparing the women. He'd promised Karen forever. The most he could offer Dana was for now, and then only because she might have the information he needed.

"He knew and he chose not to exercise that option."

"We could still use it to create a buzz. It could be our slant on making *Honor* stand out from Willow's film in case we can't find out what theirs is about."

She had a point—one too good to ignore. "I'll ask Dev to talk to PR. What do you know about Willow's film?"

He caught her sideways glance in the glare of an oncoming car's headlights. "You could have asked me that the other night instead of accusing me of sharing information."

She didn't miss a beat at his abrupt change of subject. She never did. It was as if she could follow the convoluted twists of his mind. No one else had ever done that. And she was right. He could have asked, but wondering if she'd betrayed him combined with seeing her kiss Lewis had crushed any tact Max might have had.

"I apologize. I should have asked."

"Doug said Willow's film is a romance. He didn't work on the project directly and hasn't read the script, but from what he's heard, there are quite a few similarities to *Honor*. I'm working on—" She stopped abruptly and turned to stare out the dark passenger window.

"You're working on what?"

"Nothing," she replied too hastily. "If I find out more, I'll let you know."

Dana was lying or holding something back. He wanted to know what and why. "When will you see Lewis again?"

Moments ticked past where the only sound was the car's tires on the road. "I'm not sure. He's on recce."

"But you plan to see him when he returns." He liked the idea even less now than he had before.

"Yes, Max. I'm going to see him. And you're going to have to trust that I won't share Hudson Pictures's secrets. If you can't trust me, then you need to fire me."

Trust her.

He'd trusted her for five years. Why was doing so now suddenly so difficult? Because Hudson Pictures very likely had a leak, and all indicators pointed to Dana as the most likely source. She had the info, the opportunity and the connections.

But did she have the motive?

If so, he hadn't yet figured out what it was. But until he knew for sure, he couldn't afford to give her anything that could be used against them.

The stroke of Max's hand down the length of her hair as they entered his darkened house just before midnight pleasantly surprised Dana.

But when he grasped a handful at her nape and pulled her to a halt he shocked her. Her breath caught. "Max?"

She heard the deadbolt click and then Max slowly reeled her backward, tugging just hard enough to make her nape prickle, but not enough to inflict pain. She never would have thought such caveman antics to be sexy, but the way her body instantly responded proved her wrong. Her skin tingled and her breath and pulse quickened.

He didn't stop until her back pressed against the length of his front. His chest and thighs were warm, hard and strong as she leaned into him. His breath steamed her cheek a second before his jaw, rough with evening beard, took its place. "Take off your clothes."

A lightning bolt of hunger made her gasp. "Here? Why?"

"We're going to take a moonlight swim."

Not a bad idea, but— "M-my suit is—"

"You won't need it." His free hand skimmed from her hip, over her waist to cup her breast. His thumb found her nipple and circled. Her flesh hardened beneath his caress. "Have you ever been skinny-dipping?"

She could barely think with the tangle of desire forming in her belly. "Um…no. What about your neighbors?"

"We won't turn on the lights." He released her hair and cupped her other breast with his hand. The dual massage melted her resistance, her arguments, and her ability to form sentences. He gave her a gentle shove into the center of the foyer. "Strip for me, Dana."

Moonlight streamed through the high windows, angling down on the floor, onto her, like a soundstage key light. Max remained in the shadows.

"Have you ever stripped for a man?" he asked when she hesitated.

Her heart pounded a path up her throat. "No. Not…um like this."

"Start with that sexy black dress. Take it off."

Adrenaline hit her with a dizzying rush. Her spinning head had nothing to do with the wine she'd drunk with dinner and everything to do with the words he'd just uttered. But nervousness dried her mouth. Her purse slipped from her fingers and landed at her feet.

She bent to pick it up.

"Leave it, and get naked for me."

But she just wasn't ready to do as he asked. "You first."

She heard him chuckle, low and sexy. She'd never heard that sound from him before and she liked it. She liked the way it rippled over her skin and made her quiver.

He stepped forward just enough to cast his body into the murky light, but kept his face in the dark. He shrugged out of his suit jacket and tossed it toward a settee. Next he worked the knot of his tie loose, and then yanked it free with a quick whip of sound.

"Shall I keep going?"

She'd had no idea Max had a naughty side, but that teasing tone was definitely the looking-for-trouble variety. She dampened her lips and nodded. "Please."

He unfastened his cufflinks and dropped them on the credenza. His watch followed. The clunk of metal hitting wood echoed in the high-ceiling space. He unbuttoned his shirt from the top down, revealing a widening wedge of his tanned chest with each passing second. He peeled off the shirt and tossed it on top of his jacket.

His hands settled on his leather belt, but stilled and then dropped to his sides. "Your turn."

She ripped her gaze away from the rippled definition of his muscles. Why would a man who looked like this work behind the camera instead of in front of it? She had no clue. The women of America would certainly appreciate the view she currently had.

"I—I—" She didn't know what to say. Feeling both excited and completely out of her element, she reached behind her back for the zipper. The tab slid down a few inches and then snagged. She tried to reverse it, but it wouldn't budge. "It's stuck."

"Turn around." He stepped into the light, giving her a glimpse of the hunger stamped on his face. His desire sent a thrill through her. Her legs trembled as she turned.

His hands cupped her shoulders, stroked down to her wrists and then back up. Her insides went all shivery— the way they always did when he touched her.

He brushed her hair forward over her shoulder. His warm breath on her nape was her only warning before his teeth lightly grazed her skin. A shudder quaked through her. His fingers manipulated the stuck zipper, his short nails scraping her spine as he worked. She had no idea how he could see with the lack of light. And then the tab rasped down. Cool air swept her back seconds before his palms, hot and strong, slipped beneath the fabric to grasp her waist. He held her in place while he strung a necklace of kisses along her shoulders and beneath her ear.

"Turn around and drop the dress," he ordered huskily in her ear.

Her entire body flushed with heat. On unsteady legs she pivoted only to discover Max had moved back into the shadows. But the glimpse of desire she'd seen earlier gave her the courage to be bolder than she'd normally be. She folded her arms at her waist and dipped her left shoulder. That side of the dress slid down to her elbow. She heard him inhale and repeated the action on the right side leaving her bare from the waist up except for her sheer black lace push-up bra. Only her crossed arms kept the dress up.

She straightened her shoulders and then slowly lowered her arms. The dress floated to the floor, leaving her in the bra, matching lace bikini panties and black heels.

His breath whistled out and he stepped forward into the light, but abruptly stopped. His nostrils flared and his hungry eyes burned over her, filling her with a sense of empowerment.

She lifted her hand and eased down one bra strap and then the other. Max watched through unblinking eyes. She opened the front clasp and peeled back the cups of her bra. His Adam's apple bobbed. She shrugged and her bra fell to the floor behind her.

Max's gaze devoured her breasts. The growing ridge beneath his zipper made her mouth dry. She dampened her lips, and then taking a deep breath, she stroked her hands from her rib cage to her waist and then her hips.

A quiet growl rumbled from him. She needed him to touch her, but he waited. Dana hooked her thumbs under her string bikini panties and pushed them over her hips. They slid down her legs and Max's eyes followed. She stepped out of them, but kept on her shoes.

When his gaze met hers again, her knees went weak at the barely controlled passion she saw in the hot blue depths. His hands returned to his belt buckle, made quick work of loosening the leather and unfastening his trousers. He kicked off his shoes and shoved his pants and boxer briefs to the floor. Next, he ripped off his socks and straightened.

The size of his erection shouted his desire more clearly than words. Max Hudson wanted her. That was something she'd prayed for for years and all that mattered at the moment. She'd work on making him love her.

He prowled toward her. "Do you have another condom in your purse?"

She barely heard his low growled question over her pounding pulse. She believed in miracles, in happily ever after and love at first sight, but mostly she believed in being prepared for all three. That was the reason she carried condoms. "Yes."

"Get it."

She crouched to reach the purse she'd dropped on the floor. Max surprised her by kneeling behind her. He curved his body around hers, wrapping her in a tight, hot hug. His arousal slid between her buttocks and came to rest against her wet center. She gasped. His palms caught her waist and his thighs flanked her hips as he stroked his length against her damp folds, moistening himself with her arousal. Then he leaned away, but only far enough to caress her shoulders and arms and length of her spine.

"You are beautiful, Dana," he murmured, "and very sexy."

Her heart squeezed with love. She'd waited what felt like forever to hear those words from him. She smiled at him over her shoulder and reached back to caress his bristly jaw, but she couldn't make out the emotion in his eyes in the darkness. "Thank you. So are you."

He cupped her bottom and lifted her upright as he stood. His sex remained pressed between her cheeks. His hands found her breasts and kneaded them.

"Get the condom. Now."

She was so turned on and her hands were shaking so badly she had trouble holding on to her purse, but she located the protection and dropped her bag again. The smack of it hitting the floor echoed off the walls.

He hooked an arm around her middle and yanked her backward. His chest blanketed her back with heat. He caught her jaw with his hand, turned her head toward him and took her mouth as if he couldn't wait another second.

The kiss was rough, hard and deep, with no warm-up

preliminaries, and the odd angle with him behind her made her feel a little powerless. But the vulnerability aroused her so much she could barely stand, because Max never lost control. That he was clearly on the verge of doing so now had to mean something.

Slightly off balance in her heels, she reached up and looped her arms around his neck, holding on as tightly as she could. His hands briskly raked her torso.

"To hell with the pool," he growled against her lips and walked her deeper into the darkness.

"Max, I can't see." Afraid she might run into a wall, she stretched her arms out in front of her.

"I know the way." With his hands on her waist he guided her forward only a few feet and then stopped. His short nails scraped the middle of her back. He grabbed her hands and lifted them. "Hold on."

Dana made out the shape of a door frame with her palms. Where was she? The doorway to her bedroom hall? "Max?"

His hands found her breasts. He kneaded her, tweaked her tight nipples and then buffed the stiff tips, causing an ache deep in her womb. A hot, open-mouth kiss scorched her neck, followed by another and another while his hands worked magic on her body. His touch was hurried, but sure and devastatingly effective.

He caressed her belly, circled her navel ring, and then finally, finally, slipped his fingertips into the curls between her legs. She was already slick for him.

He traced a devastating path over and around her sensitive flesh. She cried out as he found the right spot only to abandon it. At first she thought he just didn't realize what he was doing, but then he did it over and over, bringing her to the brink and then letting her fall back. Her breath came in pants and her legs trembled.

He strung a line of nips and kisses down her spine. His hot breath on her buttocks preceded an open-mouthed kiss that rocked her in her shoes. He rose and tugged the condom from the hand she had fisted against the door-frame.

"Hold on," he repeated, and then clutched her hips and drove into her from behind.

Dana gasped in surprise, in pleasure. This position took him so deep it stole her breath. He adjusted her stance and went deeper still, bending his knees and then rising to fill her again and again. She groaned out his name as desire stronger than any she'd ever experienced took hold of her.

Max had her off balance and confused, but he also had her unbearably aroused. How could she like this fast and furious coupling in the dark? It wasn't tender or romantic or any of the things she thought she needed from him. But she did like it. She liked the out-of-control passion, the unrestrained hunger. And she loved that Max was on the verge of losing control. She could tell by the ragged breaths steaming her nape, the tremor of his body against hers, his groans and the increasing pace of his thrusts.

He kissed and nibbled her neck. His hands caressed her breasts, her center. This position with him covering her like a stallion was so blatantly sexual, so primitive. He crossed her magic spot again, but this time he didn't tease her and move on.

He circled with devastating effectiveness and pressed his cheek to hers. "Let go for me, baby. Let go."

His roughly voiced command made her shiver, and then tension knotted into a ball. She imploded. Wave after wave of white hot heat shimmered through her. She

cried out and dug her nails into the wood. It took everything she had to remain standing, everything and Max's
support. His hands clamped on her hips and he plunged
faster. He muffled a groan against her neck as he shuddered against her back and again as the aftershocks
worked through him.

Dana fought to catch her breath and find her balance.
Once she did, she smiled.

Max had lost control. With passion like that, love was
sure to follow.

Max awoke suddenly. Something wasn't right. The
bed. The light filtering though his eyelids. He opened his
eyes and surveyed the room, trying to get his bearings.

Dana's room.

He turned his head. She lay curled beside him with a
hand tucked beneath her cheek and the other resting on
his chest. The corner of the sheet barely covered her
torso, and her dark hair streamed across the pillow.

A strong need to escape crawled over him. Why had
he stayed with her last night?

Because your legs were too weak to carry you upstairs.

His blood flow detoured at the memory of taking her
in the doorway and again when they'd finally staggered
to the pool sometime before dawn.

Why hadn't having her once satisfied his hunger the
way it did with other women? Even now he had to fight
the urge to tug the sheet away from her breasts and taste
her, slide into her, ride her into wakefulness. Why hadn't
sex in the dark been as anonymous as it should have
been?

But there had been nothing unidentifiable about her
scent in his nostrils, her taste filling his mouth or her body

gripping his intimately. Not even the chlorinated water had masked who he held in his arms. She'd still tasted and smelled like Dana.

What kind of hold did she have over him?

Whatever the hell it was, he intended to break it.

But not at the risk of delaying *Honor*.

Not wanting to wake her, he carefully lifted her hand from his chest and placed it on the mattress between them before easing toward the edge of the bed. His leg and butt muscles protested every shift. Oh, yeah. He'd known from the muscle fatigue last night, from the way she'd made him weak and quivery, that he'd pay for the acrobatics. He wasn't twenty anymore.

"Love you," she mumbled.

He went rigid. He didn't want her love. He didn't want any woman's love. But especially not one whom he suspected had betrayed him.

He twisted and looked at her over his shoulder. Her eyes were still closed and her skin still flushed from sleep. She must be dreaming.

What makes you think she's talking to you?

But if not him, then who? Doug Lewis?

The twinge in his gut was due to last night's gymnastics. That's all it was. Too much exercise.

Lewis was welcome to her—once *Honor* had been released.

And then if she was the leak, Max would fire her. It would be inconvenient to train her replacement, but he'd survive. He always survived. Even when he shouldn't.

But a niggle of doubt dug into Max's side. What if he were wrong? What if Dana was falling for him?

He couldn't let that happen.

But how could he stop it?

He'd have to tread carefully. Keep her close. But not too close. Push her away. But not too far.

He could stand anything for a couple more months. And then it would be over and his life could get back to normal.

And Dana would be gone.

Eight

Dana entered the kitchen not knowing exactly what to expect after last night's wild passion.

The smell of coffee greeted her, and her pulse tripped. Max had made coffee for her? That seemed like a good sign. But the kitchen was empty. She poured a mug of coffee.

It was barely six. Was Max already at work?

Movement outside drew her attention. Max sliced his way through the water cleanly, efficiently. Excitement coursed through her body at the memory of swimming with him just hours ago. Of course, swimming was an exaggeration. He'd pulled her from the bed, led her outside and towed her into the pool. Naked.

The lapping of the cool water against her bare breasts and bottom had been as sexy as a lover's caress. The fact that they'd been outside with pale moonlight and a gentle breeze on their damp skin had only heightened the intensity of the sensations.

Her nipples and her internal muscles tightened at the memory, and her gaze went to the rounded stairs at the end of the pool where he'd taken her. She'd had no idea she was such a hedonist, but she'd loved every minute of their sensual play. He'd loved her with his mouth, his slick, wet hands and his hard body.

Fanning her warm face, she blew out a breath and then opened the door and crossed the flagstone patio to the pool. She dampened her lips and wished she had the nerve to strip off and join him. She ached to make love to him in the bright sunlight where she could see his face and his eyes while he was inside her.

Instead, she kicked off her sandals, sat on the edge and lowered her feet into the water. She sipped her coffee while she watched Max swim. His daily laps and the home gym down the hall from her bedroom on the first floor explained his killer body.

He pulled up short and turned to her. "You're up early."

She shrugged. "So are you."

"Habit."

"Thanks for making the coffee." She loved the idea of sharing quiet mornings together and discussing the upcoming day.

"No problem." He waded toward her with water streaming down his torso. "Time to get to work."

The abrupt shift from personal to business threw her. "Before we do, I just wanted to say…Max, last night was…amazing."

His pupils expanded. He jerked a quick nod.

"But I—I don't know what to tell your family about us."

He stiffened. "Why tell them anything?"

She fought to conceal a flinch.

"Because of this." She pointed to the tiny love bite on her neck. That Max had been carried away enough to forget himself thrilled her. "Bella and Cece grilled me last night about who I was dating."

"What did you say?" His guarded tone set off tiny alarm bells in her subconscious.

"I managed to dodge the question because I didn't want to lie. What are we going to tell them?"

He hefted himself from the pool and reached for a towel. "It's none of their business."

"But…" She wanted them to know. She wanted *everyone* to know.

He inhaled, glanced away and then back to her. "Dana, revealing anything now is premature. Let's hold off and see where this thing goes. No need to get their hopes up if we don't work out."

If they didn't work out.

She was head over heels in love with him and he was just testing the waters, so to speak.

A sobering reminder that they still had a long way to go.

"Which is the real you?"

Max's question shattered Dana's concentration. She looked up from the breakdown sheet, which detailed the requirements for the few remaining scenes to be shot on the Hudson Pictures lot. "I'm sorry. What did you say?"

"Which is the real you?" he repeated. "The buttoned-up executive or this?" He nodded to indicate her denim skirt and lace-trimmed tank top attire. His gaze lingered on her flip flops and peach-painted toenails.

She'd deliberately dressed a little more casually while staying at his place. The goal had been to remind both of them that her role had changed. She wasn't his superefficient executive assistant anymore. When they went to work at Hudson Pictures she still wore her office attire because it looked more professional.

But she considered the fact that Max had been thinking about her a plus—especially since he was always front and center in her thoughts.

His gaze lingered on her breasts, and of course, the body parts in question tingled. How could they not? Max had that effect on her. Since they'd been making love, he'd turned her inside out with ecstasy more times than she could count. She knew Max desired her, but she was afraid sex was all he wanted from her.

"I'm both."

"Impossible. They're contradictory. And for five years I've seen no hint of the navel-ringed beachcomber." His gaze dropped to the jewelry concealed beneath her shirt.

"Why is it impossible, Max? You, as a producer, juggle a multitude of personalities. You have to be creative and smart enough to recognize a marketable script when it hits your desk. In preproduction you have to be a salesman and a PR man to a get financial backing for your project if it's not in-house.

"During production you're a clock watcher, babysitter and a peacekeeper on the set. As an editor in postproduction you have to be a visionary who sees the true message in the script and puts the complicated puzzle pieces of video, audio and special effects together to reveal that message." She shrugged. "If you can be that complex, why can't anyone else?"

"It's not the same."

"It is. We're all what we need to be for the people around us at any given time."

A line formed between his eyebrows. "Don't put me on a pedestal, Dana, and don't fall for me. What we have is great, as you said, but I'm incapable of giving you what you need. I can't love you back."

Alarm trickled down her spine like melting ice. Had he guessed her feelings? She'd tried to keep things light because she knew that's what he wanted. "Who says I'm falling for you?"

"You did."

"I've never said any such thing."

"You said it Saturday night."

Panic shot through her along with a stiff shot of humiliation. She vaguely recalled saying something like that in a dream the night they'd made love in the hall and again in the pool. *Please tell me that was a dream.*

The only thing she could do was brazen her way through this. "I must have been dreaming. I don't even remember who or what about."

He didn't look as if he bought her story. However, protesting more would only make her look guilty. She decided to go on the offensive.

"But, Max, your editing work proves you feel the emotions you claim you can't. You know exactly which shot to use to convey the most impact, when to use sound and when to let the characters speak.

"I once read that a great movie needs no dialogue— that the expressions of the characters show the story. You do that, Max. With your editing choices, you reveal the story through the emotions on the characters' faces, and it's amazing to behold."

"Being able to edit film is not the same as being able to experience emotions."

"I don't think that's true."

His scowl deepened. "You have too much faith in people."

"And you have too little. Maybe it's time you tried to trust again."

"And maybe it's time you stop trying to psychoanalyze your boss and get back to work."

She winced at the bite of his words and turned back to her desk. But that didn't mean she was giving up on Max Hudson. She'd only just begun her campaign to win him over.

Dana shut the front door and stopped. The house felt eerily silent. Max had been here when she left to go shopping and his cars were in the garage. He must be here.

Juggling the shopping bags, she headed for the stairs. She rarely used the elevator because she preferred the exercise after sitting at her desk for most of the day. She'd noticed Max did the same.

The second level seemed equally still. "Max?"

No answer.

She headed for the kitchen and unloaded her groceries and then carried the office supplies up to the third floor. Max wasn't there, either.

Maybe he was sleeping? She glanced at her watch. Barely nine. That would be an extremely early bedtime for him, but maybe weeks of burning the candle at both ends had caught up with him…unless he wasn't well? That could explain the odd, silent mood he'd been in all day.

She dumped her bag on her desk and once again headed for the stairs. His bedroom door stood open. She hesitated. They'd made love almost every night since that first time six weeks ago, but never in his room. She tapped on the door, but when he didn't answer she made her way inside the darkened room and flipped on the light. The bedroom and the adjoining bath were empty, as was the private deck outside his bedroom. "Max?"

Had she missed him on the patio or in the hot tub? She leaned over the rail and scanned the shadowy tiled area. Unless he'd hidden himself in a spot that the landscape lighting didn't illuminate, then he wasn't there. Where could he be?

She turned to go back inside and noticed a spiral staircase leading up to the roof tucked in the far outside corner. She'd never been up there before, had never even known of the rooftop access. The gate at the bottom was ajar. With her heart beating a little faster she made her way to the stairs and climbed. The flat roof made a great observation deck, but had only a low wall, no railing. Max sat in a folding chair with his back to her, facing the light-sprinkled valley below.

She struggled against a sense of vertigo. "Max?"

"Go back inside," he said in an unnaturally flat voice.

Then she noticed the whiskey bottle on the ground by his chair. "Are you okay?"

"Fine."

He didn't sound fine. She carefully made her way across the twenty feet or so that separated them. "I didn't know you had a deck up here."

"Dana, I don't want company."

But he sounded like he needed it. There was a hollowness to his voice that she'd never heard before. "Why?"

"Go back downstairs."

"And if I refuse, will you push me over?" The height was getting to her. There wasn't a second chair, so she eased down onto her knees on the pebbled surface beside him.

He glared at her, and the rising moonlight revealed the pain on his face. Her heart clenched in sympathy.

"What's wrong, Max? I'm not leaving you up here alone, so you might as well tell me."

"For God's sake, I'm not going to jump."

The words sent a jolt of panic through her. "I didn't think you were. But something drove you up here in the dark."

"It's none of your business."

"It became my business when you forced me to move in with you and even more so when you scared the daylights out of me by disappearing."

He swore. "She died three years ago today and it's my fault. Is that what you wanted to know?"

He turned his head away as if he wanted the words back. She'd known from old gossip that Karen had died in the fall, but she'd never heard the exact date. "Your wife?"

"Yes." He raked a hand over the back of his head and then reached down to recap the liquor bottle. There wasn't much missing. He must not have had much to drink, maybe a few sips.

"Why do you blame yourself? I heard she fell asleep at the wheel."

"We were at a party. She was tired and begged me to leave. But I was too busy wheeling and dealing to go home. So we stayed. I worked a few deals. Back then I was still busting my ass to prove I deserved my job."

He stared off into the distance. "When we did finally go, I'd had too much to drink, so I made her drive. I shouldn't have."

Dana covered his hand with hers. "If you'd been drinking, you did the right thing."

"She was pregnant. That's why she was so tired and why

she kept asking to leave early. She'd planned to tell me that night after the party. She wanted to celebrate. Privately."

Her heart ached for him. "I'm sorry, Max."

"She fell asleep at the wheel, ran off the road and hit a tree. She and our baby died and I walked away without a scratch."

She couldn't speak for the knot in her throat, so she squeezed his hand.

"When I got home from the hospital the next day I found the card and the pregnancy test, along with a non-alcoholic bottle of sparkling cider waiting in an ice bucket in the kitchen."

Tears stung Dana's eyes and put a burning lump in her chest. "That must have been like losing her a second time."

His gaze held hers in the semi-darkness. "Yeah. Exactly."

There was nothing she could say to lessen his pain, so Dana did the only thing she could think of. She climbed into his lap, hugged him and held him.

He stiffened at first, but eventually the tension drained from his muscles, and then his arms wound around her and he hugged her back. "No one else knows about the baby. Keep it to yourself."

That he'd shared such a painful secret with only her touched her and gave her hope.

"I will." She pressed her cheek to the warm raspiness of his beard-stubbled jaw. "You can't blame yourself, Max. You were doing your job by schmoozing and you were protecting her by not driving the car. It was an accident. A terrible, tragic accident. But it wasn't your fault."

His somber gaze held hers. "You'll never convince me of that. And that's why you can't love me. Because I will never allow myself to love you, or anyone else, back."

Her heart sank. At that moment she was very afraid that he might be right. And she was just as afraid she'd never get over him.

"Wake up." Max's voice jarred Dana from a sound sleep.

"What?" She blinked at the bright light in her eyes.

"Get up. You wanted to be a producer. Now you get to do one of the less desirable parts of the job."

"What's that?"

"Maintain the peace. We have to go haul Ridley's butt out of trouble."

She sat up in her bed and shoved her hair from her eyes. "Ridley's in trouble?"

"He's holed up in a nightclub getting drunk and obnoxious. We need to get him out before the paparazzi make paydirt out of him. *Honor* doesn't need the negative publicity. Throw on that black dress you wore to the family dinner and do it fast."

"I have to dress up to fetch Ridley?" And then she noticed Max was already dressed in black trousers and a white silk shirt left open at the neck to reveal a wedge of his great chest. He hadn't shaved, and the dark, beard-stubbled look was ravishingly sexy on him in a pirate kind of way. "You're going, too?"

"Yes."

"Because you don't trust me to handle it?"

"Ridley is unpredictable. You couldn't handle him alone."

"We have to go into the club to get him?"

"Yes, that means dressing the part or you don't get past the front door, which at this place is picky as hell. I stand a better chance of getting in with a beautiful woman on my arm."

The backhanded compliment made her all warm and fuzzy.

"You have five minutes."

She glanced at the clock. "It's three in the morning. Couldn't Ridley have partied at a reasonable hour? And is Bella with him?"

"No to both. Bella had the good sense to leave and call me when he turned ugly."

Dana threw back the covers and bailed out of bed. Max leaned against the dresser, arms folded, and watched her. Despite their intimacy, his scrutiny made her incredibly self-conscious. She hustled to her closet, snagged the dress in its plastic dry cleaning bag and debated locking herself in the bathroom.

But no. She wanted him to want her. That meant enticing him. It had been two weeks since the family dinner, two weeks in which he'd made love to her every night and then abruptly left her bed to sleep in his own.

She tossed the dress on the bed and dropped her chemise on the floor. Next she headed for her lingerie drawer and selected the black lace thong and matching push-up bra she'd bought in France on a whim but never worn. She stepped into the panties and then shrugged on the bra. Max's swiftly indrawn breath rewarded her bravado.

Digging deep for chutzpah, she paraded to the bathroom, but left the door open. When she checked the mirror, she found Max's gaze glued to her butt and bit her lip to hide a smile as she quickly washed her face, applied minimal makeup and ran a brush through her hair.

Returning to the bedroom, she dug out a pair of big, gold chandelier earrings and slipped on a gold heart-link necklace that fell between her breasts. Her nipples tightened under Max's scrutiny.

"You have one minute left." His voice sounded a tad huskier than usual and her pulse kicked in response.

She stabbed her feet into her highest black heels and felt a rush of adrenaline as Max's lids fell to half-mast and his nostrils flared. Fighting dirty was fun.

She removed the dress from the plastic bag and slipped it over her head, then twirled a slow circle. "Ready."

Max swallowed visibly, and Dana noticed the thickening ridge in his pants. Arousal slithered through her as he slowly pushed off the dresser and moved toward her. He didn't touch her but his eyes burned a path from her face to her toes and back.

"Grab your ID and let's go."

She would have liked a compliment on how she looked or acknowledgment that she'd dressed in under five minutes. But she'd settle for the obvious signs that he desired her.

Max strode from the room. Dana grabbed her purse, shoved the necessities into a tiny, beaded evening bag and hustled to catch up with him. In the attached garage he stood by the open car door—the silver Mercedes sedan this time instead of the black Lamborghini Roadster. She slid in and waited for him to round the car and climb into the driver's seat.

"Does this happen often?" she asked.

He shrugged and reversed out of the garage. "Depends on the actor. Some are more of a headache than others."

"And why don't their managers or agents babysit them?"

"Sometimes they go by the 'any publicity is good publicity' fallacy. At the moment we—Hudson Pictures—have more to lose if this turns ugly. And Bella called me."

The last line snagged her. Max adored his baby sister although he, like his father, tended not to be obvious about his feelings. That was one of the things it had taken her a good chunk of her five years with Hudson to learn. The Hudson men didn't show their feelings openly. She was used to her father and brother, whose bear hugs and obvious affection left you in no doubt of their feelings.

He exited the electronic gate, hit the road and accelerated. "The plan is to get in and get him out with as little fanfare as possible. The paparazzi will be lurking like vultures and may even get right in your face, so watch every move you make and every word you speak. If anyone asks, we're going to check out a new club we've heard about."

"I've heard about Leslie Shay. Does she have a personal vendetta against the Hudsons or something?"

"Or something. She's one of the worst paparazzi vultures. If we're lucky, she followed Bella, and we won't have to deal with her."

"If we're not?"

"Then the fact that you and I were seen together might be tabloid fodder tomorrow."

She couldn't exactly dread that. She wanted everyone to know they were an item.

"Thanks for including me tonight, Max. I want to learn every aspect of the business—the good, the bad *and* the ugly sides of it. I guess I just never heard you talk about this part."

"That's because I don't. This part of the job doesn't need to be discussed. It just needs to be handled and discreetly. Trust me, Dana, you do not want the babysitting part of the job. Actors are worse than children and they get in more trouble with bigger stakes. One stupid star can kill a movie's box office potential. Producing isn't a glamorous job."

"I never thought it was. I'm the one who handled the petty squabbles you were too busy to deal with. Remember the actor who complained that his trailer wasn't the biggest on the lot, the one who demanded only bat guano coffee and the actress who wanted five pounds of green M&M's delivered every Monday? You delegated those to me."

He grimaced. "This is bigger. This isn't going to be a back-lot headache. This has the potential to blow up in our faces."

"I understand, and you can count on me." She wanted to cover his hand on the gearshift, but didn't think the gesture would be welcome. To heck with it. She did it anyway.

His fingers, his entire arm, stiffened and then relaxed. "Thanks for coming without complaining."

She squeezed his hand and then put hers back in her lap. She didn't want to push him too far too fast. "I'm happy to help. Besides, I'll get to see the inside of one of the 'in' clubs."

A few moments later they arrived at a club Dana had only read about in the tabloids. Max pulled up at the front door, tossed the keys to the valet and circled to her side of the car.

"Don't make eye contact with the crowd," he cautioned as he assisted her from the car. "And remember, don't answer any questions."

Excitement hummed in the air from the minute she stepped on the sidewalk. People milled around the club entrance to catch a glimpse of the stars going and coming. Some looked like fans. Others were clearly paparazzi. Max swore under his breath, leaned close and pressed his mouth to her ear. The feel of his flesh on hers made her shiver.

"Shay is here. Tall, skinny brunette to your left. Keep moving. Keep your mouth shut."

Dana took a quick look from under her lashes to identify the woman. Flashbulbs went off, but she kept hustling to keep up with Max.

"Max," called a voice from the reporter's direction, "who's your new girl? Going to follow in your brother's footsteps with wedding bells?"

Max didn't comment. He stopped at the front door and spoke to the big, black-suited goon guarding the entrance. Dana couldn't hear the conversation, but the stiffening of Max's body didn't bode well. She leaned around him to see refusal stamped on the bouncer's face and knew she had to think fast.

"Please, it's my first time. Bella promised me I'd love it here." She batted her lashes for added effect. When that didn't seem to work on Stone Face, she winked. "She also bet me five hundred bucks I couldn't get her brother to bring me."

The guy looked her over from top to bottom, returning to ogle the cleavage her new bra had created. "Yeah, sure, go on in."

He shoved open the door and the sound of raucous music hit Dana like an explosion. The bass drum vibrated the fabric of her dress. She squeezed between Max and the bouncer and darted inside. The door closed behind them. She hesitated while her eyes adjusted to the darkness and the strobe lights. The smell of cigarettes and cigars permeated the air.

Max wrapped an arm around her waist and pulled her close. "You're good."

She grinned up at him. "Now let's go find our man."

"Bella said he was in the back room when she left." Max cut a path through the loitering clientele.

Dana tried not to gape at the famous faces they passed, but she couldn't help it. This was the A-list crowd, something she'd never be a part of, and while she was used to dealing with movie stars on the set, clubs like this were out of her realm.

She scanned the faces of the famous and the hangers-on and then bounced back to one. That looked like Ridley in the corner, but it was dark and hard to be sure, and the guy wasn't alone. Bella wouldn't like that if it was Ridley.

"Isn't that him? Kind of hard to tell with three women piled on top of him."

"That's him. Now let's convince him to walk out with us."

Ridley was dark haired, of medium height and handsome if you liked the type of guy who knew he was attractive and always had an agenda—Dana didn't—and he was totally oblivious to their presence until Max lightly kicked the toe of his shoe.

"How's it going, Ridley? I heard you needed a ride home."

Judging by his drunken glare Ridley wasn't happy to see them.

"Excuse us, ladies. Ridley has a prior engagement." Max peeled a pair of hundred dollar bills off his money clip and handed it to one of the women. "Next drink's on me."

The trio vanished. "You had no right to bus' up my party," Ridley slurred.

Max leaned down, said something in Ridley's ear Dana couldn't hear, grabbed his hand in what looked like a handshake—but judging by the bulge of Max's biceps was much more—and yanked the drunk actor to his feet.

Looking ticked off, the star of *Honor* gave Dana a lecherous look. "I'll go if I can sit in the back with her."

"Don't even think it," Max growled at him. His jealous tone sent a thrill through Dana. If he was jealous, he had to feel something, didn't he?

"Let's get the hell out of here without causing a scene."

The three of them left the club and piled in Max's car, Ridley alone in the back and Dana in the passenger seat. Max turned to glare at him. "If you want to work for Hudson Pictures again, you'll clean up your act."

Ridley sat in sullen silence for the next thirty minutes. Max dumped him at his home and headed back for Mulholland Drive.

"That went relatively well," Dana ventured.

"Just remember that if you read something in the paper tomorrow it doesn't make it true."

He meant the wedding plans the reporter had mentioned. "I wouldn't dream of trusting any information that didn't come directly from the source."

"Good. Let's go to bed. You're going to pay for tormenting me with that little performance you gave while getting dressed." The fire in his eyes lit a corresponding flame in her.

But making Max want her was the easy part. Making him trust her and want to keep her forever was going to be the real challenge.

Nine

Dana jerked to a stop on the patio Monday morning when she realized Max was on his cell phone.

He had his back to her and her gaze automatically took the familiar tour from his broad shoulders to his tight butt.

"Handicapped access to all premiere events." His words penetrated her lust. "Dana's brother is in a wheelchair, and I don't want him to have any difficulties while he's here. Make sure all obstacles are removed."

Emotion gripped her in a stranglehold. Max had mentioned making arrangements for her family to attend the premiere. She'd expected to have to handle the details herself, but she had been so slammed with her new duties that she had yet to get around to following through.

"I've already booked the airfare and hotel for all five of them."

Five? He had to mean her parents, her brother, her sister-in-law and their son, Dana's precious nephew. She couldn't wait to see them, but the premiere was months away. First they had to get through next month's first-cut showing at Hudson Pictures's private sixtieth anniversary party.

She clutched the phone in her hand to her chest. This was the man she'd fallen for, the one who cared enough to make sure the important people in his life—and hers, apparently—were taken care of.

"Thanks." He turned and spotted her. "Did you need something?"

She swallowed to ease the lump in her throat and held out the receiver. "It's Luc."

Max took the cordless phone. "Luc, what's the news?"

He listened for a moment and then a sad smile curved his lips. "Congratulations. How are Gwen and the baby?"

Dana walked to the edge of the patio to give him privacy. She scanned the cityscape below and the distant ocean. Today a haze hung over it all, diluting the sun. As much as she enjoyed living in California, she missed the cleaner air back home and the changing seasons. In Wilmington, October meant brilliant fall leaves and pumpkins for sale on every corner. Here, fall was just a word on the calendar. The temperature fluctuated only about thirty degrees all year.

Max joined her. "Gwen had the baby last night. A boy. They named him Charles after our grandfather, but they plan to call him Chaz. Luc will e-mail pictures when he gets home from the hospital."

Given what Max had told her about Karen's pregnancy, she wondered how he felt about the news. It was impossible to tell from his poker face and neutral tone. "Is everybody okay?"

"Yes. I need to send something."

"You mean *you* need to shop for a baby gift?"

He opened his mouth and closed it again as her emphasis on "you" sank in. "Yes."

In the past, as his executive assistant, buying gifts would have been her job. She waited for him to ask for help. If he did, she'd have to point out that he was losing that silly bet they'd made when she moved in three weeks ago.

"Would you like a list of appropriate shops?"

"And have you claim victory? No. I'll go online and see what I can find."

She should have known he wouldn't cave. The man was too stubborn to concede defeat. Thus far he'd handled each of his personal items without her assistance. Of course, there had been few of them, and he did have the cheat sheet she'd made for him that first day to help. But then again, Max budgeted money, schedules, cast and crew for his pictures. Juggling a few personal appointments shouldn't be too difficult.

And now that things had changed between them, did she really want him to lose the bet and give her a glowing referral to another movie studio? No.

She decided to switch to a safer subject. "You're making the travel arrangements for my family?"

He nodded.

Travel arrangements had been her job as his E.A. If she hadn't already been in love with him, she would have fallen head over heels at that moment. "Thank you, Max. I could have done it."

He brushed off her thanks with a dismissive wave. "They weren't the only ones I had to make. We have too much to do to waste time yakking. The first cut isn't the final cut, but I want it to be as perfect as possible for the anniversary party and we have only a few weeks left. Let's get to work."

And then he turned on his heel and walked away, leaving Dana feeling both elated and alone. At times like this when she needed to share her excitement and he turned his back, she wondered if she'd ever break through that tough shell he'd built around his heart, or if she should throw in the towel and admit defeat.

Click, click, click went the pen in Dev's hand. *Click. Click.*

The repetitive sound was beginning to get on Max's nerves. He rocked back in his home office chair and looked at his brother, who'd parked his butt on the corner of Dana's desk.

Dev stared back, tension drawing his features tight and making Max wonder if his big brother's honeymoon was over, and if he was regretting his month-old marriage.

Click. Click.

"Spit it out, Dev. What has your neck in a knot on a Saturday afternoon?"

"We're down to the wire for November's sixtieth anniversary party and the first viewing. You have only a few more weeks. Are you going to be ready?"

"The first cut will be ready." Thanks to Dana's help and more hours of overtime than he'd ever put in before. But for his grandmother he'd do anything.

"What about Dana? You have scripts and treatments for potential new projects rolling in daily. We need to know if we can trust her before we start making decisions on what to shoot next."

"I've kept her too busy to screen new projects. If she

knows anything about where Willow got their information, she's not talking. How's married life?"

"Don't change the subject. You've had weeks to find out if she's our snitch. If you haven't, then you're not trying."

"I am trying, damn it. The script similarities could be coincidental."

"We both know that's unlikely."

Yeah, they both knew it. If it had been any other film company, they'd have blamed the situation on coincidence. But not with Willow. There was too much bad blood between Hudson Pictures and their number-one rival, and the contributing incidents had escalated in the past few years—years since Hudson had employed Dana, a woman who had admitted she was overqualified for the position. So why had she taken the job?

Max shoved himself to his feet and walked to the window. Was Dana the leak? Given his suspicions, he couldn't believe he'd spilled his guts to her about Karen and the baby. He'd deliberately kept that shameful piece of information to himself. No one else knew. Not even Dev.

What was it about her that made everything so damned easy? Too easy. They shared work, meals, conversation and sex. Incredible sex. Like this morning in her tub. What had started as his offering to wash her back had turned into—

Damn. Had the air-conditioner quit working? He stepped into the hall to turn the thermostat down a few degrees and then returned to his seat.

Why couldn't he quench his thirst for her despite being with her almost twenty hours a day? He didn't want to want her. He sure as hell didn't want to like or respect her. But he'd given her his dirtiest producer duties, and she'd done them without question or complaint. Her willingness to do the undesirable jobs and her perspective on the editing impressed the hell out of him. She'd offered several damned good suggestions.

The more she gave, the more he demanded from her, and she delivered over and over, no matter how hard he tried to make her regret backing him into a corner.

If she'd betrayed him with Lewis, would she work this hard? Or was she busting her butt just to get him to let down his guard and uncover more she could use against him?

If so, for what gain? Was she on someone else's payroll?

He didn't want to believe it.

"Max, we need to know if she's the source. What are you doing to find out?"

His brother's surly tone, combined with Max's own frustration over the situation, hit him the wrong way. He scowled at Dev. "I'm sleeping with her to keep her out of Lewis's bed and to find out if she sold us out. What more do you want me to do?"

A gasp jerked his attention to the doorway. Dana stood frozen in the opening, her fist an inch from the wood as if she'd lifted it to knock. She looked at him through pain-flooded brown eyes as the color drained from her face.

"You—I—how could you?"

Regret clutched Max's chest and coldness seeped over him. He'd heard the front door close minutes ago, but he hadn't heard the gate chime, which meant she hadn't left and returned. Because she hadn't gotten around to it? Or because she'd stayed behind to eavesdrop on a private conversation?

He stood and started toward her. "Dana—"

She held up a hand to stop him. "Was I just part of the job to you? Just another mess Hudson's producer had to clean up?"

The hurt in her voice ripped him right down the middle. "No."

"You didn't want me to keep my job because you needed my help with *Honor*. You wouldn't let me quit because you didn't want me to take what I knew elsewhere. God, you even told me that in the beginning, and I was still dumb enough to fall in love with you."

Fall in love with him. The words crushed him like a fallen set wall, immobilizing him and making it impossible to fill his lungs.

She couldn't love him. He didn't want her to love him.

He didn't want to have this conversation in front of his brother. "Get out, Dev."

"What?"

"Leave."

Dana's chin rose. "Why don't I make it easy for both of you? I'll leave. I can be packed and gone in five minutes. Out of your life and off Hudson Pictures's payroll."

He couldn't let her go. Not yet. She knew too much. "If you walk out that door you'll never work in Hollywood again."

She gasped and paled even further. "You bastard."

"Max—" Dev started.

"Get out, Dev," Max repeated, and when his brother didn't move he added, "Now."

"Don't screw this up," Dev said low enough that Dana wouldn't hear him before he stormed out.

Max silently held Dana's gaze until he heard the roar of an engine racing out of the driveway. "You were going shopping. Why didn't you?"

She flinched as the accusation in his voice sank in, and then marched over to her desk, snatched up a piece of paper and waved it in front of his face.

"Because I forgot my shopping list. I was going to cook a special dinner for you because it's Halloween. It's a tradition my mother started when James and I outgrew trick-or-treating so we wouldn't feel as if we were missing out on all the fun. But forget it. Get your own dinner."

She crumpled the paper, threw it at the trash can and missed. Dana never missed. She folded her arms. "I can't work with someone who doesn't trust me."

"You have no choice. You signed a contract."

"The contract doesn't say I have to have sex with my boss or live in his house. From now on, I'm doing neither."

Her words hit him like a whip. "We'll have more interruptions at the office."

"Too bad."

Memories of fighting with Karen followed by days of her pouting silences forced their way forward. If Dana acted the same way, then completing *Honor* on time was in jeopardy. He'd have to cut corners and he never cut corners.

But he couldn't compel her to stay here or to work here. He didn't need the legal department to tell him that could be construed as kidnapping. "I'll help you pack up your work."

"I can handle it."

But he couldn't trust her to do so. "I'll help you and then I'll deliver the boxes to the office."

Comprehension dawned on her face. "You don't trust me not to drive straight to Doug or whoever it is you think is buying your secrets."

He couldn't deny it.

Her body went rigid. "I'll tell you what, Max. You pack up the office. I'm going to deal with my clothes. I'll see you at the office Monday morning."

"What about tomorrow?"

"Tomorrow is Sunday. I'm taking a day off." She turned on her heel and strode out of the room. Her footsteps clattered down the stairs.

He was going to lose her.

And considering he didn't know whether she was guilty or innocent, that realization bothered him far more than it should.

Dana sank down on her bed and then sprang right back up again to pace her bedroom. Anger, hurt and betrayal swirled inside her like a noxious cocktail.

She should have known her relationship with Max was too good to be true. She'd thought they'd been growing closer, especially after he'd confided in her about Karen and the baby.

But Max hadn't suddenly discovered he desired her after five years. He'd been using her. She didn't know how he could have made love to her—correction, had *sex* with her—so tenderly and so passionately, if he'd felt nothing.

But apparently, he had no problem faking it.

Or was she just too stupid to know the difference between real and pretend passion? She'd believed she knew what good acting was. But he'd been so good he'd fooled her.

She had to get out of his house—the sooner, the better. Her heart was broken, her career in jeopardy and her dream of having a career and family she could be proud of...*dead*.

All she wanted was to get through the next four weeks. When *Honor* was finished she'd… Darn that bet. Unless Max blew his end of it soon, she'd be trapped. Assuming he didn't fire her. And why wouldn't he if he didn't trust her? Getting fired for selling company secrets—even if she hadn't—would make it impossible to get another job in the industry.

She yanked open the closet, pulled out her suitcases and slung both onto the bed. She popped them open and stared at the gaping insides. When she'd unpacked them she'd been full of hope, full of love and dreaming of possibilities.

"Fool," she muttered, and grabbed an armload of clothes. She cramped them in the first case without worrying about wrinkles or removing the hangers. After mashing the mound flat, she added more and more until both the closet and dresser were empty and each piece of luggage overflowed.

How could you love a man who would treat you this way?

She marched into the bathroom and gathered her makeup and toiletries. The extra large box of condoms she'd bought after she and Max became intimate mocked her.

So much for being prepared for love.

After shoving her loot into luggage, she sat on one lid to squash it closed. Her hands trembled so badly she could barely get the latch to catch. She had the same problem with the second.

Next she dropped to her knees. The temptation to stay there on the carpet and sob grabbed her by the throat, but she forced herself to keep moving. She was not going to cry over this. She'd loved Max and decided to leave him once before. The world had not ended then and it wouldn't now. She would survive.

Although it might not feel like it.

Why hadn't she listened when her conscience and his grandmother warned her that Max might not ever get over his wife? Even Max had told her. But she hadn't believed him.

The collapsible crate she'd flattened and hidden under the bed was hard to reach, but after she pulled it out and wrestled it back into shape she loaded it with her pictures, candles and plants. She continued her frantic denuding of the room until no trace of her presence existed.

How would she face Max at work day after day knowing what he'd done? Knowing that he'd coldly and calculatingly penetrated her body, her mind and her soul and he hadn't cared?

Taking a deep breath, she rubbed her dry burning eyes. Only ten yards separated her from her car and escape. She didn't want to run into Max. She eased open her door and checked the hall. Empty.

Grabbing her keys and the crate, she hustled down the hall, through the foyer and out the door. She wedged the crate into the passenger seat of her car and straightened. She did not want to go back into that house. But what choice did she have? She would not give him the satisfaction of making her call and ask him to have her belongings delivered.

Bracing herself for a possible encounter, she put one foot in front of another until she reached her room. When she did so without incident, she closed the door, sagged against it and exhaled a pent-up breath. The bed drew her gaze like a magnet. For the past five weeks she'd been making love and opening her heart to Max in that bed. And he'd been taking her for a ride.

How ironic. He thought she'd betrayed him, but he was the Judas.

A knot expanded in her chest, making it difficult to inhale. She wanted to go home—not to her apartment—to North Carolina. Back to the loving arms of her family. But she couldn't disappoint them. And she wouldn't disappoint herself. And there was the bet. Part of her wanted to say to hell with it. But the other part of her had too much pride to welsh.

She swallowed to ease the lump climbing up her throat, grabbed both suitcases by their handles and turned her back on the memories. She would forget, and she would get over him. Eventually.

She checked the hall again and again found it empty. How stupid of her to think he might care enough to have anything else to say.

Dragging her luggage, she made one last pass down the hall and across the foyer. She paused at the front door. She'd never set foot in this house again and, despite everything, that realization left her feeling a little empty. She loved this house on the hill with the beautiful vistas from every room.

She loved its owner more.

Get over it, and get on with it.

She yanked open the door and jerked to a halt. Max stood beside her car, looking heart-stoppingly handsome in his Ravazzolo trousers and Canali shirt. A wolf in designer clothing.

Drawing a deep breath for courage, she strode forward.

He stepped between her and her car's trunk. "Dana, you don't have to go."

How could he say that? "Yes, I do. You used me, Max, and you don't trust me. That pretty much says it all."

She used her remote to open the trunk. "Excuse me."

After a tense, silent moment Max took the suitcases from her. His hands brushed hers on the handles, and she couldn't believe after what he'd done that her body dared to tingle from the brief contact.

After loading the cases he shut the trunk and just looked at her, searching her face with those dazzling blue eyes.

Lying eyes, remember?

She refused to let him see how much he'd hurt her. Turning her back on him so he couldn't see her unsteady hands, she removed his house key from her key ring and then pivoted and held it out. "This is yours. I no longer need it."

When he didn't take it, she reached out, took his hand and slapped the key into his palm. She felt the contact with his warm flesh deep inside, and that only angered her more.

Why him? Why love a man who would deliberately hurt her?

She wasn't capable of saying another word. Her voice box had burned up. She turned and climbed into her car. And then she peeled out of the driveway, barely missing the wrought-iron gates because they opened too slowly.

She didn't look back because she didn't want to remember what a gullible, lovestruck fool she'd been for Max Hudson.

But one thing was certain, she would never, ever let herself care for anyone like that again.

Falling in love had been eradicated from her goals list.

Max wasn't sure what he'd find when he reached his office Monday morning, but it wasn't the old Dana.

At second glance, he realized that was not the old

Dana sitting behind her desk. The previous version would have greeted him with a glass of orange juice and a smile that started his day on the right note.

This Dana had donned one of her conservative suits and scraped back her hair like before, but her pale face wore no welcome. Her eyes lacked their usual luster, and her movements were stiff and tight. There was no glass of juice.

Would she pout and make working conditions difficult the way Karen had when she was ticked at him? Either way, Dana had shown up and he had to be grateful for that. After the way she'd left him Saturday evening, he'd half-expected to never see her again.

Dana rose as he entered and offered him a large manila envelope. "Dev brought this by earlier. He needs you to look at it ASAP and get back to him."

Her tone was cool, but professional. No snit fit in evidence. "What is it?"

"I don't know. The envelope is sealed. I'm no longer your assistant. I didn't open it."

He wanted his assistant back. "Thank you. Any messages?"

"They're on your desk. And your two o'clock appointment has confirmed." He started to turn away. "Max, there's one more thing." She lifted a script from her desktop and handed it to him. "This is a shooting script of Willow's World War II film."

Surprised, he searched her expressionless face. "How did you get a copy?"

He knew the answer: Doug Lewis. And the burn in his gut was anger. Nothing more. She'd seen the guy again when he'd specifically asked her not to.

"It doesn't matter how. But next time, before you

accuse someone of selling company secrets, you should do your research first. The screenwriter is a former Hudson employee. He's using a pen name, but that was easy enough to penetrate with the online copyright registration site. I checked with human resources and he was fired seven years ago 'for cause.' I've written his real name right there." She pointed to the top of the cover page. Max recognized the name immediately. The guy had been a troublemaker.

"After you've read the script you might want to forward it to the PR department so they can put their spin on the promo."

He'd wronged Dana. Hurt her. Used her. Betrayed her. "I'm sorry, Dana."

"It's a little late for sorry. Now if you'll excuse me, your associate producer has to solve a minor crisis on the back lot. I've asked human resources to get you an executive assistant temp. She should be here by nine."

Dana walked away without a backward glance, and it felt as if the energy in the room and his enthusiasm for the project followed her out.

But completing *Honor* wasn't about him. It was about his grandmother and granting her last wish. He gritted his teeth and peeled his gaze off the curve of Dana's departing butt. The answers he and PR needed might be inside the script he held, but the pages wouldn't give him what he wanted.

He wanted his former relationship with Dana back— the one they'd had before France. He wanted her trust. And he wouldn't mind more of the mind-melting sex.

But he had a feeling he'd lost both forever.

Ten

"Dana tells me she might be leaving us," his grandmother said when Max joined her on the settee in the sunroom. "Something about pursuing her career goals elsewhere."

Dana had been to see his grandmother again. Why didn't that news surprise him? "Yes, ma'am."

"I thought she had a career with Hudson Pictures—especially since you finally recognized her talent."

He wanted to get up and pace, but his grandmother's shrewd blue eyes pinned him in place.

"She might move on once *Honor* is completed." Unless he held her to that bet. It had been a struggle, but not once had he asked for her assistance on the day-to-day garbage of his life. He'd had no idea how much Dana did to make his life run smoothly both on the job and away from it. Her word was her bond. If she made a promise, she'd stand by it. He could make her stay.

But did he want her to, knowing how she felt about him? Was it fair to ask that of her when he couldn't give her what she needed?

"Do you have anything to do with that decision?"

He didn't want to talk about Dana. Didn't want to think about how empty his house had been these past sixteen days without her. Didn't want to think about the candle the maid had found in the guest suite bathroom or the fact that he kept it on his nightstand so he could smell the beachy scent as he tried to fall asleep.

And he wasn't interested in spilling his guts or getting a lecture about being stupid. "I might."

A small, reminiscent smile touched her lips. "Everyone believes your grandfather and I were a match made in heaven, but we didn't always get along. Like you and Karen, we fought, we made up. Love is like that—fire and ice. But you and Karen never had those warm, balmy days when it felt good to just float along together side by side. It was always one extreme or the other. Love that's going to last needs those restful days, too."

Not liking the direction of her conversation, he shifted on the cushion. "I came to talk to you about the film."

"I don't need to talk about the film. I know how the story goes. I'm trying to tell you the part I left out when I talked to Cece." She laid a pale blue-veined hand over his. "I won't be here much longer, Maximillian. I want to see you happy before I go."

Her words made everything in him clench in denial and then in loss. Soon she would be gone and there would be no more quiet conversations like this one.

"I am happy," he insisted automatically.

"No. You *were* happy. For the most part. And then Karen died. I know that hurt. I know you wished you could have taken her place and that you didn't want to go on without her. I know, because I felt the same when your grandfather left me.

"But it wasn't my time, and it wasn't yours. We still have work to do here. I had my sons and my grandchildren, and Charles's story to tell. That kept me going. You might want to think about what or who kept you going."

"My job."

"Oh, it was much more than work that made you get up each day."

"What are you talking about?"

"That's for you to figure out, Maximillian. But remember, those who loved us, Karen and my Charles, would want us to be happy—even if it's not with them."

She waved for the nurse who stood behind her shoulder at all times.

"Grandmother—"

"I'm tired, dear. Go back to work. I know you have a lot to do and only a week to do it in. And while you're there, consider convincing Dana to stay."

"Dana, would you come in here, please?" Max's voice said via the intercom.

The summons was the last thing Dana wanted to hear. Seeing Max every day and working with him despite the canyon between had been painful and difficult. She'd clung to her professional demeanor by a fraying thread, but she missed the old warmth between them.

"Yes, sir." She pushed herself to her feet.

In the three weeks since she'd moved out of his house she'd gone through the motions. She worked herself to the point of exhaustion only to wander around aimlessly at home too tired to sleep. On the positive side, she'd lost that ten pounds that had stubbornly clung to her hips despite diet and exercise, but she couldn't seem to work up any excitement about it. Other than making dress shopping for the anniversary party easier, the weight loss was irrelevant.

She tapped on Max's door. In the past she would have automatically gone in after knocking, but not anymore.

"Come in."

She took a bracing breath and opened the door.

He rose as she entered. Before, he wouldn't have. His gaze took in her scraped-back hair and tailored cinnamon-colored pantsuit. "Sit down."

She sat. He did the same. She hated the new stiff and formal atmosphere between them.

"I've finished the first cut. I want you to take a look at it."

He'd been putting in a lot of hours. She wasn't surprised he'd finished early. "To check for continuity errors?"

"To prepare yourself to introduce the film at the anniversary bash."

Surprise stole her breath. She searched his face, but then suspicion took over. "Why me?"

"You've gone above and beyond the call of duty since this project began, and your dedication deserves a reward."

"That's not necessary, Max. I was only doing my job."

His blue eyes showed remorse. But it was too little too late. "Dana, I owe you."

The only thing she wanted from him was something he couldn't give. "You don't owe me anything except a good reference."

His eyes narrowed. "I haven't lost the bet."

Dread filled the pit of her stomach. "You wouldn't hold me to that."

He rocked back in his chair and laced his fingers over his flat abdomen. "Why wouldn't I?"

Her heart raced and her palms dampened. She *had* to get away from Hudson Pictures when *Honor* was done. She couldn't stay. "Because you don't trust me."

He shrugged. "I made a mistake."

She licked her dry lips. "I don't want to stay here, Max. Release me from the bet."

"No. You're mine for a year."

Max was late.

Dana couldn't remember the last time he'd been late for anything. She scanned the people milling about the room again, wondering if she'd somehow overlooked him in the gathering of *Honor*'s cast and crew and special guests waiting for the unveiling of the film's first cut. But she didn't see Max among the expensively garbed guests.

The rest of the Hudson family was already here. Even Luc and Gwen had flown in from Montana with the baby, but they'd left the baby at Hudson Manor with a sitter tonight. Dev, Luc and Jack were with David. Sabrina and Markus were sharing a glass of champagne by the piano where a musician played music from the movie score. The other Hudson women, Cece, Valerie, Gwen and Bella, had clustered around Lillian, who'd been determined to come tonight despite her declining health.

Dana supposed she could join them, but she was too agitated. She'd heard the phrase "alone in a crowded room" before, but until tonight she hadn't understood it. Now she did. In this group of perhaps a hundred guests she felt like an outsider, but that was probably because her conscience was bothering her and she'd isolated herself. She'd never broken a promise in her life, but she was seriously considering welshing on her bet with Max.

Could she live with herself if she tucked her tail and ran home after the *Honor* premiere next month?

Probably not.

But she might have to learn to.

She needed her parents, needed her father's bear hugs and her mother's gentle wisdom. Talking over the phone just wasn't the same as a face-to-face discussion, which was why she hadn't told them what was going on in her personal life. At the very least, she would take a long vacation and go see them. She'd earned it.

But first, she had to get through the next few weeks.

She exhaled what she hoped would be a calming breath and brushed a hand down her silk gown. She'd wanted basic black for the evening, but Cece and Bella had convinced her to buy a burnt orange halter dress with beading around the straps and the gathered bodice. The gown was attention-getting and form-fitting and not at all her usual style.

An air of excited anticipation hummed in the air, but nothing could get started without Max. Where was he? She considered digging her cell phone out of her evening bag and calling him. Before she could, Max strolled through the entrance. Her heart and lungs simultaneously contracted. He looked devastatingly gorgeous in his Armani tux. Of the three tuxes he owned, this one was her favorite.

He turned and spoke to someone behind him. Dana forced her gaze from his tall, lean form to see who'd accompanied him. She wasn't sure she could get through her presentation tonight if he'd brought one of his vapid blonde dates. Seeing her replacement in the flesh would be hard to take.

But her parents stood behind him. Surprise made her gasp and press a fist to her chest. What were they doing here? They weren't supposed to come until the premiere. There was no one she wanted to see more right now.

She hurried across the room, dodging hors d'oeuvres and champagne-carrying waitstaff and other guests. Max spotted her as she approached and smiled. That tender, indulgent twist of his lips made her stomach flip-flop. She forced herself to look away, brushed right past him and threw her arms around her mother first and then her father.

Her eyes burned and her throat clogged up. As if her father sensed her inner turmoil—he always had in the past—he squeezed tighter.

"What's going on, baby girl?" His gruff whisper made her chest tighten. With colossal effort, she pulled herself together, gave him one last hug, pasted on a smile and drew back. Bawling now would not be a good thing.

"What are you doing here?" She hoped they wouldn't notice or comment on the shakiness of her voice. But the tightening of their expressions said they'd taken note.

Her mother took her hand in both of hers, offering silent support. "Max thought we might enjoy sharing your big night."

Max. Dana's eyes found his. How could she ever stop loving him when he did wonderful things like this?

"Thank you, Max." She was proud she managed to keep her tone level.

"You're welcome. I'm only sorry your brother and his family couldn't make it. They'll be here for the premiere." His gaze traveled over her. "You look beautiful tonight, Dana, and as vibrant as one of your mother's paintings."

Her breath caught. That was exactly the reason she'd

allowed herself to be talked into this dress. It reminded her of home, of peaceful long walks on the beach at sunset gathering shells with her mother. The color was exactly the same shade as the sun's reflection off the water just before it slipped into the ocean.

Stop being so nice. She wanted to scream the words at the top of her lungs, but she bit her tongue. She wanted to hate him, to walk away without feeling guilty and then forget him.

Tall order.

"Thank you," she mouthed, but the words just wouldn't come out.

He checked his watch. "It's almost showtime. Are you ready?"

She cleared her throat. "Of course."

"Good. Let's introduce your parents to my grand-mother and my parents then I'll show them to their table."

Before they could do as he suggested, raised voices yanked their attention to the far side of the room. David and Markus stood toe-to-toe, at it again. The brothers' arguments were legendary, but Dana had expected them to be on their best behavior tonight.

David took a swing at Markus and missed. Shocked, Dana watched as Dev and Jack, who stood nearby, jumped into the fray.

"Excuse me." Max took off across the room.

Dev grabbed his father. Jack did the same with his, but David struggled, and shouted, "Tell him, Sabrina. Tell him you slept with me. Tell him we were lovers."

Gasps rent the air and then the crowd went quiet as if holding their collective breaths and waiting for more. Markus cursed his brother and struggled, but Max and Luc joined the effort to keep the men apart.

"Tell him his precious baby girl is mine," David shouted. "Tell him Bella is mine."

A shocked silence descended. A woman's pained cry broke it. Dana looked toward the sound. Bella paled and pressed a hand to her mouth. She staggered forward to her mother. "Is that true? Is David my father?"

Tears streamed down Sabrina's cheeks. She cast an apologetic glance at her husband and then her daughter. "I—I—yes."

Well, that explained the tension between David and Markus.

Even from yards away Dana could see the pain on Bella's crumpling face. Bella turned on her heel and raced from the room. Dana's heart ached for her. She turned to her mother.

"I need—"

"It's okay, baby, go to her."

Dana didn't ask twice. She took off after Bella, raced outside and caught the sight of her blue gown going behind one of the office bungalows. Dana followed and found Bella leaning against the building gulping air and obviously fighting tears.

"Bella?"

Bella waved a hand as if to say either go away or she was okay. Dana knew she wasn't okay. She recognized when someone was hanging on to their composure by a thread. She'd been doing the same just moments ago. But as painful as her broken heart might be, it seemed trivial compared to Bella's shattered world.

Without a word, she put her arm around Bella's shaking shoulders, offering support.

"I can't believe…I mean…*David*." Bella shuddered. "How could she? He's a jerk."

Dana shook her head. She'd been thinking the same thing. What could Sabrina have possibly seen in her brother-in-law? "You'll have to ask your mother that. But you know David can be quite charming when he wants something."

Bella gulped several breaths. "My father—I mean, *Markus*—is he going to hate me?"

"Markus is still your father in every way that counts. I'm sure he's shaken up by this, too. He looked shocked, and you'll probably have some stuff to work through. But Bella, he's loved you for twenty-five years. He's not going to stop just because of David's big mouth. Daddies don't do that. Daddies love their baby girls no matter what."

It was as if a lightbulb went off in her head when she heard herself say the words. Her father would always love and support her—even if she disappointed him by letting go of their dream of making it big in Hollywood.

She couldn't work for Max anymore. And if that meant she couldn't work in Hollywood, then she would find work elsewhere. There were production studios all across the country. She'd build her credentials elsewhere and then when she was strong enough emotionally and professionally, she could return to Hollywood—if she still wanted to.

"This is just not my day." The ironic humor in Bella's voice caught Dana's attention. "First Ridley. And now this."

"What about Ridley?"

"He dumped me. Can you believe that? The jerk actually dumped *me*."

Good riddance. She kept the words to herself, but she understood Bella's pain. "Isn't he here tonight?"

"He will be. But he's coming with someone else."

Dana gave Bella an empathetic hug. "Men can be idiots."

"No kidding. I don't want to go back in there, Dana."

"I'm sure everyone will understand if you don't."

"But I can't hide out here. *Honor* means everything to Grandmother. I can't let her down. And I can't let those morons know they hurt me. But as soon as this is over I swear I'm heading somewhere until the gossip dies down. I'll go back to Europe and find a quaint little Italian village to hide out in…or something."

"That's the fighting spirit. And who knows, I might go with you."

Bella's big blue eyes searched Dana's. "He hurt you, didn't he? My dolt of a brother—*half* brother."

"Heartbreak isn't fatal. I'll survive. You and I both will." And she knew it was true—even though it didn't feel like it at the moment. "My office is just around the corner. I have makeup in my desk if you want to drop in and do a repair job."

"Ugh. I need it, huh?"

Dana wrinkled her nose. "A little touchup wouldn't hurt. I'll go with you."

"I'm keeping you from introducing the film."

Dana smothered a wince. "If they can't wait, then Max can introduce it. It's his masterpiece, after all."

"Is it a masterpiece?"

"Bella, you did an amazing job. Lillian will be proud. So let's go back in there and, as my daddy would say, let's show 'em what we're made of."

The crowd was getting antsy. Max glanced at his watch.

His father and David had been sent to opposite sides of the room like spoiled children. His mother sat pale and drawn by his father's side. Bella and Dana had disappeared during the fracas. He hoped Bella was okay with the bombshell. But checking on her would have to wait.

Canceling the showing of the first cut wasn't an option. They needed feedback from tonight's viewing for the final edit. The film was already scheduled for the premiere and the theatrical release. Those dates were set in stone.

Surely Dana would come back since her parents were here. He'd promised her the opportunity to introduce the film, but he could see his grandmother's energy flagging. He couldn't wait much longer before he'd have to begin without Dana.

Dev gave him a "get on with it" signal. Max realized time was up. He was on the verge of taking the stage when the doors opened and Dana and Bella strode in with their backs straight, their heads high and their hands linked. They made a striking picture in their jewel-colored gowns. Bella wore cobalt blue and Dana carnelian.

He'd seen Dana in premiere finery before, but he'd never seen her look more beautiful, more confident or more determined than she did right now. Her dark hair draped her shoulders like a dark satin curtain, the ends teasing the cleavage revealed by her low-cut dress. His fists clenched in memory of the silky strands threading through his fingers, dragging over his skin and wrapping around his—

He cut off the thought as a bolt of desire shot through him, and he looked away from the tempting sight of her womanly shape.

His grandmother beckoned and Dana and Bella immediately went to her side. The rest of the Hudson women closed ranks around them.

His grandmother grasped Dana's hand and pulled her close. He couldn't make out what she said, but suddenly, one thing became very clear. Dana hadn't just adopted his family, they had adopted her. She was a part of them, one of them. She belonged.

Why in the hell was he the only one afraid to let her in?

Who was he kidding? He'd already let Dana into his life. As she'd pointed out, she'd been running his life for him for years. And lately he woke up thinking about her each morning and lay in bed at night thinking of her while he waited for sleep to give him a few hours of oblivion.

Her smile was like his personal ray of sunshine.

Sap.

Sad, but true. When had she become so important to him? He didn't have a clue. She'd become an integral part of his life. There was only life before Dana and life since.

He didn't want there to be a life after Dana. The idea of her leaving opened a crater of emptiness in his chest.

But she was right. He was holding her back. She was too smart and too talented to waste her skills in an executive assistant position. She'd proven she knew how to look at the big picture, see all the components and juggle them the way a producer has to. Her hard work had made it possible for him to finish the first cut with days to spare.

Hell, who was he kidding? Dana had made it possible for him to get through every day since—

Then it dawned on him. That was what his grandmother had meant when she'd asked him who kept him going each day. Dana did. How could he have missed it? She'd prodded, challenged, and even fed him to keep him from crawling into a hole after Karen's death.

Dana had resurrected him.

And even if it was the right thing to do, he didn't want to let her go. She'd claimed she'd fallen for him. If he hadn't killed her feelings with his distrust, could he appeal to her romantic heart and convince her to stay and give them a shot at the kind of love his grandparents had shared?

Dana straightened, nodded at his grandmother and then strode across the room. Like a woman on a mission she climbed the stairs to the stage and stepped behind the microphone.

"Good evening, everyone. I hope you've enjoyed our entertainment thus far."

A scattering of laughter broke the tension in the room. This was the Dana he'd come to love.

Love.

He shook his head at the realization. He'd been so busy avoiding the intense instant attraction he'd had with Karen that he'd missed the simmering volcano of his relationship with Dana slowly building up pressure until it finally erupted in white-hot passion.

How long had she loved him? How long had she waited for him to wake up?

He zoomed in on her beautiful face and hoped he wasn't too late.

She smiled at the crowd. "I promise the night will only get better from this point, and the only drama you'll see will be on the screen. Tonight Hudson Pictures brings you an amazing tale of bravery, heroism and true love—the kind of love that we all aspire to have one day. A love that withstood the test of time and every challenge the world threw at it.

"Ladies and gentlemen, may I present *Honor,* the one

and only true, authorized story of Charles and Lillian Hudson's lifelong adventure."

"Wait," he shouted before the lights went dim and raced for the stage.

Dana's shocked gaze found his as he jogged up the stairs. The crowd rumbled as he crossed the platform toward her and stopped behind the microphone. When she tried to leave, he caught her hand and held her by his side.

He turned to the crowd. "Every movie has a message, and the message you'll find in *Honor* tonight is that true love is worth waiting for. It holds strong through adversity and stands the test of time.

"A love like my grandparents' is a rare and special thing. It's easy to find someone who'll stand by you during the highs, but not nearly as easy to find someone who has the fortitude to stand by you during the lows or keep speaking to you when the road gets a little rocky.

"The credits will tell you Dana Fallon was the associate producer on this film. What they won't tell you is that she's become part of my family, part of my life. And I can't imagine a day without her by my side. She has been my true partner for the past five years."

He heard Dana gasp, but kept going. "My grandmother asked me recently who or what made it possible for me to get up every day. What kept me going? The answer is Dana kept me going."

He turned to face her and saw tears brimming in her beautiful brown eyes. She tried to tug away, but he wouldn't let go. He didn't ever want to let her go.

"A very wise woman told me that a great love not only has fire and ice, but warm, balmy days where you drift along happy and content just to be with the one beside you. Dana, you are the only woman who has ever brought me all three.

"What we share is that same unbreakable bond my grandparents had. And I hope I haven't been so slow on the uptake that you've given up on me."

She hiccupped in several breaths and a few tears spilled over—tears that couldn't hide the love shining out at him like a warm beacon.

"You were right. You have too much talent to waste as my executive assistant. You've proven you deserve to be a producer, and you'll be a damned good one. But I'm selfish enough to hope you'll make room for me in your life as you shoot to the top."

He dropped to one knee. She pressed her fingers to her trembling lips. "I've been a blind, stupid fool. But please allow me to share not only the good times with you, but also those days when you're challenged."

He carried her knuckles to his lips. "I love you, Dana. You've made me a better, stronger person. And I want to spend the rest of my life with you. Marry me and let me give you that romance of a lifetime that you dream about."

She cupped his chin, stroked his jaw and then traced an unsteady finger over his lips. "I love you, too, Max. And nothing would make me happier than sharing my life with you. Yes, I'll marry you."

He shot to his feet, pulled her into his arms and swung her around. He kissed her and tasted tears and happiness, but mostly he tasted love. It felt good not to hold back, not to be cautious or afraid.

Applause rocked the room, and then a shrill whistle rent the air. He reluctantly pulled back, lowered Dana to her feet and turned toward the direction he'd heard the sound.

His brothers were laughing and pointing at their grandmother. She beckoned them over to her table.

Holding tightly to Dana's hand, he led her off the stage to his grandmother's side. "Did that whistle come from you, Grandmother?"

"Of course it did. I may be old, but I haven't forgotten all my tricks yet. It's about time you came to your senses, Maximillian Hudson."

She tugged off her diamond engagement ring and offered it to Max. "You could not have said it better. Dana is family, and I would like for my future granddaughter-in-law to have this, the ring from the man I love."

A shocked squeak of noise bubbled from Dana. "Lillian, I couldn't."

"Unless you hate it, you can and you will."

"Of course I don't hate it. It's beautiful."

"Then let the boy put it on your finger."

Max took the ring, kissed his grandmother on the cheek and knelt before the two women he loved. "Dana, may I?"

She offered her trembling left hand.

"With this ring, I promise to always try to be the man you need me to be."

Dana's smile lit up the room like sunshine. "You already are, Max. You have been for a very long time."

Max wanted to be alone with Dana. He wanted to drag her back to his place and make love to her without the emotional barriers between them. But there were two-hundred-plus people, including his grandmother, waiting for their first viewing of *Honor*.

"Roll the tape," he shouted, and seconds later the lights dimmed.

He dragged Dana to their table as the opening score swelled. Reluctant to release her for even a moment, he shifted their chairs so that they sat shoulder-to-shoulder and thigh-to-thigh. Her warmth, scent and love seeped into him.

He knew each frame crossing the screen backward and forward, but this time he viewed his grandparents' love story from a new perspective.

He realized love didn't make a man weak. It empowered him, made him braver, stronger and better as part of a whole than he had been alone.

The film that he and Dana had created together was easily the best work of his life because he had shared the burdens as well as the triumphs with her. They made a damned good team.

And as the credits rolled at the end and the house lights came up he saw the happy tears streaking down his grandmother's face, and knew he'd done her and himself proud because in telling her story he'd found the courage to live and love again.

* * * * *

*Wondering if Valerie's marriage to the
infamous Devlin Hudson is what she dreamed?
Then don't miss this exclusive short story
by* USA TODAY *bestselling author Maureen Child.*

Vegas weddings had always brought to mind tacky little chapels, Elvis impersonators as the justice of the peace, and plastic bouquets.

But when Valerie married Devlin, he somehow managed to make it both quick and beautiful. They'd been married in the chapel attached to the brand-new luxury resort, Treasures. Surrounded by stained glass, a glorious garden and the soft sigh of classical music, they'd exchanged vows with the last rays of a beautiful sunset spearing into the flower scented chapel.

It had all seemed so perfect a few hours ago, Valerie mused, sitting in the dark of Treasure's penthouse suite. She stared out the wide bank of windows and the brightly lit sprawl of Las Vegas, some thirty stories beneath her. Life pulsed down there, frantic, eager, desperate. But here, alone in the luxury of a darkened suite, she felt none of it.

"God, I was an idiot," she muttered quietly.

She should have told Devlin she was a virgin. Should have let him know that he was her first. That she was nervous as well as excited. Maybe if she had, things would have turned out better. For both of them.

Pushing up from the low slung couch, she walked barefoot to the wall of glass, put her hands on the cool panes and stared directly down at the street below. Neon shone back at her like fallen stars from an alien sky. She stared so hard, the lights began to blur and she closed her eyes, instantly opening a mental doorway to her memories.

The wedding had been so lovely. Devlin so handsome. So tall and strong and quite simply, mesmerizing. Valerie had been swept along on a thick tide of romance. Running off to Vegas instead of doing what society would have expected and throwing a huge, elegant wedding had seemed…romantic. And it had been. For a while.

Valerie's forehead rested against the glass and she squeezed her eyes shut even more tightly. Memories crowded her mind and made her squirm with discomfort.

She'd wanted Devlin. Her body had been achy for weeks as if in expectation of her wedding night. But nervousness it seemed, was much stronger than excitement. At the dinner they'd shared in one of the hotel's private dining rooms, she'd tried to drown the flocks of butterflies in her stomach with champagne. But the nervous flutters had only grown, expanding with the alcohol to make her clumsy, tense and more edgy than ever.

Devlin had been smooth and kind and gentle. As if he'd sensed her uneasiness, he'd kept conversation light, almost impersonal. Then, on the elevator ride to their suite, he'd kissed her, stealing her breath and briefly stilling the frantic worries racing through her mind.

But once in their suite, alone together in the palatial bedroom with its massive bed and flickering candlelight throwing dancing shadows on the walls, Valerie's body had betrayed her completely. She'd locked up so tight, it was a wonder she hadn't given off sparks.

She wanted him, but fear and nerves and anxiety had just been too much to conquer. Plus, the champagne had made her head fuzzy and her stomach unsteady. When he came to her, unbuttoning her dress, sliding it off her shoulders, taking her mouth with his even as his fingers tweaked at her hardened nipples, Valerie had started shaking. Shaking so badly she could hardly stand up and she'd batted at his hands like a crazy person. She'd just needed air. Some time to think. To get used to everything he was making her feel.

But he kissed her deeper, longer and want began to win the battle over anxiousness.

In seconds they were on the bed and Devlin was leaning over her, positioning himself between her legs and Valerie had opened for him, sure that once he was inside her, everything would be fine.

It hadn't been.

"Are you all right?" Devlin's voice came out of the dark, from somewhere behind her.

Oh, no. She couldn't face him. Couldn't look into his eyes and see regret over marrying her. But it wasn't as if she could avoid facing him forever. Valerie shut off the flood of painful memories, swallowed hard and whispered a lie. "Yes. I'm fine."

"Then why are you in the dark?"

Because she didn't want the light. She wanted to lick her wounds and that was better done in the shadows. Alone. How was she supposed to face him? How could she look him in the eye knowing that he was remembering everything she was? That the image of their botched lovemaking was no doubt overshadowed by the fact that he'd had to hold her hair back for her while she threw up every drop of champagne she'd consumed?

Could there ever have been a more disastrous wedding night?

"Dev, can we not talk about this?"

"Why? Are you still sick?"

"God, no." Her head pounded and her mouth felt like the Sahara, but the nausea was gone. "I just don't want to have to discuss it, okay?"

"That's the problem, isn't it? You not wanting to talk about it. Damn it, Val, you should have told me you were a virgin."

She laughed softly. "Well, I'm not now, am I?"

"If I'd known, it could have been different. It didn't have to be like that."

Slowly, Val turned her head to look at him. Standing across the room from him, he was mostly hidden in darkness, the dim reflection of the city lights not bright enough to reach him. Even now, even remembering the pain and embarrassment of their first time together, Valerie's body hummed with need.

She hadn't found that magic she'd heard so much about. But that was her fault and she knew it. If she hadn't had so much champagne. If she hadn't kept her virginity a secret. If she hadn't been so damn nervous—worried about doing something wrong—everything might have been better.

But it was too late now to get a second chance at a first time. That moment was lost forever.

Wrapping her arms around her middle, she held on

tightly and tried to sound matter-of-fact. "It's okay, Devlin. I'm fine. You're fine. I'm sure it'll be better the next time."

It *had* to be, she thought. After all, there was nowhere to go but up. Besides, she loved him. Wanted him. Wanted this marriage.

Devlin took a step toward her and stopped when he saw her back up almost instinctively. He felt like some raving caveman. Damn it, he hadn't had a virgin in his bed since he was fifteen and had coaxed Debbie Colucci into the back of his father's limo.

How the hell could he have possibly guessed that Val would be a virgin? He hadn't even known there were any virgins left. *Until* he'd entered her small, tight body and felt her stiffen in reaction to the pain he knew he'd caused her.

Shoving one hand through his hair, he sighed heavily and shook his head. He'd let his own need take control, that was the problem. If he'd been paying more attention, he'd have noticed the way she was drinking their champagne. The subtle signs of nerves she'd displayed as soon as they entered the bedroom.

But he hadn't been thinking at all. He'd been feeling. The roar of lust, the rush of desire. He'd seen her, wanted her and taken her. Not realizing until it was too late that she was an innocent.

Well, he couldn't give her back that innocence, but he for damn sure could give her some space now.

"Look, I'm going downstairs. Hit the blackjack tables for a while. You…" He shook his head again and turned for the door. "There's a Jacuzzi in the bathroom. Go have a soak. It'll help."

"You're leaving?" She sounded surprised.

But hadn't she been the one to leave their bed and

come to the living room alone? Hell, he told himself, she didn't know what she wanted. Why would she? So he'd make the decision for her.

"Yeah," he said. "I'll be downstairs an hour or two. Give you some time to yourself."

"Devlin—" Now she took a step toward him, and he was the one to retreat.

Dev didn't want to talk about their disastrous lovemaking session. He didn't want to explore what he was feeling, didn't want to look into her wounded eyes any longer. What he wanted was copious amounts of scotch and the impersonal feeling of getting lost in a crowd.

"Just try to relax," he told her. "Get some sleep. We can talk in the morning."

"I can't believe you're leaving. On our wedding night."

In the dim light, her eyes looked shattered and confused and Devlin almost changed his mind about leaving her. And that wasn't a good idea.

He didn't want to hurt her, but he also didn't want to be dragged into an emotional debate he had no interest in. They were married, yes, but he'd never pretended that this was a love match. He'd never promised that soul-deep connection. And now, he knew that the best thing he could do for her was to back off, whether she knew it or not.

"Valerie," he said softly, "the wedding night's over. Why don't we just leave it at that and move on? All right?"

When he left, he closed the door quietly behind him, but not before he heard her begin to cry.

* * * * *

PROPOSITIONED INTO
A FOREIGN AFFAIR

BY
CATHERINE MANN

RITA® Award winner **Catherine Mann** resides on a sunny Florida beach with her military flyboy husband and their four children. Although after nine moves in twenty years, she hasn't given away her winter gear! With over a million books in print in fifteen countries, she has also celebrated five RITA® Award finals, three Maggie Award of Excellence finals and a Bookseller's Best Award win. A former theater school director and university teacher, she graduated with a master's degree in theater from UNC-Greensboro and a bachelor's degree in fine arts from the College of Charleston. Catherine enjoys hearing from readers and chatting on her message board—thanks to the wonders of the wireless internet that allows her to cyber-network with her laptop by the water! To learn more about her work, visit her website at www.CatherineMann.com or reach her by snail mail at PO Box 6065, Navarre, FL 32566, USA.

To my delightful and talented editor,
Diana Ventimiglia.

One

His hands roved her bare body, melting her with the warm heat of his strong caress.

Bella Hudson bit her lip to hold back an embarrassing groan. Barely. She called upon all her training as a Hollywood actress to stay silent while Henri worked his magic on her oiled-up body.

Muscles melting, she buried her forehead deeper in the massage table's face cradle. The scent of aromatherapy candles soothed her nose while Christmas carols sung in French mixed with ocean sounds to caress her ears.

Pure bittersweet pleasure. Very bittersweet.

Sixty-two-year-old masseur, Henri, was likely to be the only man touching her for quite some time since her jerk of an actor boyfriend stomped her heart just last week. And wow, that thought sure kinked up her neck again, encroaching on her peaceful retreat.

She and her precious dog, Muffin, had escaped to France for some much-needed soul soothing at the seaside Garrison Grande Marseille. Garrison hotels always provided the best in pampering, peace and privacy.

And crossing the Atlantic guaranteed she wouldn't risk accidentally running into Ridley or, worse yet, *Uncle David.*

Men. They were all rats. Well, except for Henri, who was too old for her and married, but oh my, he worked wonders with heated river stones along her lower back.

"Henri, are you and your wife happy?" She stared through the face cradle at Henri's gym shoes as he swapped out the stones beside her treasured little Muffin, snoozing away in her pink doggie carrier.

"*Oui*, Mademoiselle Hudson. Monique and I are very 'appy. Four-tee years, three children and ten grandchildren later. My Monique is still beautiful."

He continued to laud his wife and family, his adoration so thick it threatened to smother her.

Or make her gag.

She'd really thought Ridley loved her, only to have him say he'd been too caught up in the romance of their starring roles in the movie about her grandparents' WWII romance. She'd really thought her parents loved each other, too.

Wrong. And wrong again.

Her mother had cheated. She'd slept with her own brother-in-law and now Bella's uncle David was actually her daddy David. Her two cousins were actually her half-siblings. Good God, her family was ripe to be featured on an episode of *Jerry Springer*.

Even river stones couldn't ease that ache.

A low-sounding beep echoed through the room. A series of clicks eched. Had the whale sounds traded up to dolphin calls?

Henri yanked the sheet up to her shoulders. "M'selle Hudson, quick, get up!"

"What?" she asked, not quite tracking yet.

Her eyes snapped open. She blinked to adjust in the dim light and found Henri blocking someone trying to push through the door.

Someone with a camera.

Crap. Crap. Totally tracking now, Bella bolted off the table and to the floor. Her feet tangled in the sheet and she pitched forward.

"Paparazzi. Run!" Henri barked as Bella struggled to regain her footing. "Run. M'sieur Garrison prides himself on protecting the privacy of his clients. He will fire me. Then my wife, she will *keel* me. She is crazy mean when she gets angry."

So much for Henri and Monique's happy marriage.

"Where the hell am I supposed to run to?" Bella spun away from the door—and the camera—making sure to anchor the sheet over her backside. She dashed to Muffin's quilted pink carrier and grasped the handle.

She couldn't wedge past Henri and the photographer struggling to raise his camera over Henri's head.

"The screen," Henri gasped. "Move the screen. There's another door behind. I will hold off this piece of garbage, M'selle Bella."

Henri might have strong hands, but he appeared to be fighting a losing battle. It was only a matter of time before the paparazzi passed him.

Clutching the Egyptian cotton in one hand and the rhinestone-studded carrier in her other, Bella raced to the antique screen painted with Monet-style murals. Sure enough, she found a narrow exit decorated with a large red bow. She butt-bumped the bar, creaked the door open and peeked out.

She looked left and right down an empty corridor, less ornate than the rest of the hotel. Labeled office doors were bedecked with simple holiday wreaths. There might be some after-hours workers around, but running into them beat the hell out of sprinting through the wide-open, high-ceilinged lobby with crystal chandeliers spotlighting her mad dash toward the elevator.

"Okay, Muffin, cross your paws, 'cause here we go."

Her sweet little fur baby yawned.

Bella tucked into the dimly lit hall, empty but for ornately carved antiques. Her bare feet pounded along the thick Persian carpet on her way past a lush green tree, tiny lights winking encouragement. She paused at the first office.

Locked. Damn.

She ran her hand along door after door on her way down. All locked. Double damn.

An echo sounded behind her. The sound of someone running. She glanced over her shoulder and…

Click. Click. Click.

She recognized the sound of a camera in action too well. The short but bulky photographer had over-powered Henri.

Bella ran faster, Muffin's cloth cage bumping against her leg. She wasn't a novice in ditching the press. She'd been aware of the media attention on her family since she was born twenty-five years ago.

Gilded, framed photos of employees stared at her in a weird pseudo voyeurism. She rounded the corner and yes, yes, yes, found a mahogany door slightly ajar. No lights on. Likely empty. She would lock herself inside and call for help.

Panting, she raced the last few steps, slid through the part in the door.

And slammed into a hard male chest.

One without a camera slung over his shoulder, thank heaven, but still a warm-bodied—big-bodied—*man*. She looked up into his cool gray eyes. She didn't need to check the formal photo by the door to confirm the identity of this dark haired, billionaire bachelor. At only thirty-four, he'd already been featured on plenty of "most eligible" lists. This ex-patriate bad boy had broken hearts from the Mediterranean to South Beach.

She'd fallen into the arms of hotel magnate Sam Garrison.

* * *

Sam stared down into the panicked blue eyes of film star Isabella Hudson.

Where the hell were her clothes?

He was used to dealing with eccentric behavior from his star-studded guest list. But a woman running around in nothing more than a sheet? That was a first.

He kept his eyes firmly locked on her panicked face and mussed red hair while waiting for her to clue him in. No need to check out the luscious cleavage on display. He could feel every voluptuous curve of the near-naked beauty pressed enticingly against his chest.

"Media," she gasped, pressing her breasts more firmly against him. "Paparazzi!"

Damn. His libido took a backseat to business. God, he hated the press.

He prided himself on his hotel's privacy, an essential element in attracting high-profile clientele. A breach like this could cost him. Big time. *Nothing* was more important to him than his hotels.

Not even a potentially distracting pair of amazing breasts.

Where was the man she'd been trysting with? Must be a wimp if he'd left her to face the media on her own while clad in nothing more than a sheet, her body slicked up enticingly.

Was the guy married? Or a high-profile politician? His mind raced with possible publicity landmines. This temperamental actress could spell big trouble.

Sam gripped her by the shoulders, her silly, pink dog carrier thumping him in the knee. "Stay in my office. I'll take care of this."

"Thank you. But hurry, please." She backed into the office, her foot peeking out from beneath the sheet to show a gold toe ring. "He's right around the corner—"

Footsteps pounded down the hall.

Sam had spent the past ten years of his life delivering on the promise of privacy and luxury at his branches of the family's exclusive Garrison Grande Resorts. Even a resort magnate had to roll up his sleeves and play bouncer on occasion.

Today, apparently, was one of those occasions.

He stepped back into the empty reception area leading to his office. Waiting. Waiting. Waiting to pounce.

Behind him, he could hear Bella scooping her dog out of the carrier and soothing the restless pet until the bell around the dog's neck quieted.

The footsteps grew louder. Closer.

He stuck an arm out and clotheslined the media hound. Sam lunged out just in time to press a Berluti loafer flat against the guy's chest as he tried to arch up. Bella's dog yipped from inside the office.

Applying more weight, he made sure the burly man became one with the floor. Yeah, he recognized this peon. The guy freelanced for a national gossip magazine.

Or rather he *had* worked. Because by morning, the guy would be fired.

The dog barked louder as if in agreement.

"Security will be escorting you out," Sam growled lowly. "You are no longer welcome here. Your magazine will no longer be given access to any press conferences held here if they keep you on staff."

A big-time loss to the magazine that would guarantee the guy's walking papers.

"I'm just doing my job," the photographer gasped.

"And I am doing mine." Sam pressed his foot down more forcefully.

The guy with the camera cowered. Yeah, he'd gotten the no-trespassing message loud and clear.

Sam eased pressure. "If you manage to land another job, perhaps you will remember to be more *polite* to my guests in the future."

The dog growled, launching through the door and into the hall.

Dog? More like a… Hell, he didn't know what to call the bristly little beast that looked more like a slightly mangy steel wool pad of indeterminable breed.

"Muffin!" Bella squeaked, peeking out the door.

The photographer lurched, grappling for his camera. Like hell.

Sam yanked the camera from the relentless guy's white-knuckled grip. Muffin leaped with surprising lift for a dog so small. The photographer started to arch upward again. Sam scowled. Muffin landed on the guy's face.

The photographer sagged.

Muffin growled with an underbite and a protruding lower tooth that gave the mutt something close to a Billy Idol snarl. Sam flipped the camera over and popped free the storage disk. He rubbed the tiny bit of plastic between his fingers, his brow furrowed. Then he smiled.

"Muffin," he looked down at the dog, "fetch."

He flicked the card full of six-figure photos to the ugliest little mutt he'd ever seen.

The pooch snapped the "treat" out of midair. *Crunch. Crunch.*

The photographer slumped back with a whimper.

Bella laughed from the doorway. Husky. Uninhibited.

Sam jerked to look over his shoulder at her.

She fisted the sheet tight between her breasts, flame-red hair tumbling down to her shoulders with a post-sex look that called to his libido. No question about it. The American starlet was drop-dead gorgeous. He'd noticed her before when their paths crossed at the occasional high powered party, but her up close appeal now packed an extra punch.

A security guard jogged down the hall, snapping the thread of awareness. "Do you need help, M'sieur Garrison?" Henri the masseur called.

Ah, she'd been getting a massage. He should have guessed, but something about this woman just screamed sex and he'd jumped to conclusions. Regardless, he needed to deal with the crisis at hand.

"Haul this piece of trash out of my hotel and make sure he's never allowed back in." He'd grown up experiencing firsthand what hell these sorts of muckrakers brought to people's lives.

Sam watched the guard drag the dejected photographer into a stairwell, then turned his attention back to the sexy diva.

She knelt beside her dog, sheet cupping the sweet curves of her bottom. "Muffin, give it up." She pinched at the memory card clenched in the pup's snaggletoothed mouth. "I appreciate your help, sweetie pie, but I don't want you to choke."

Sam snapped his fingers.

The dog whipped her furry head around, spitting out the plastic card as she hastened to pay attention.

Bella's eyes went wide with surprise. She gathered up her pet, just managing to keep the white sheet from slithering to her feet.

Desire spiked through him, stronger this time, followed by something else. Determination.

Bella Hudson would not be sashaying out of his life anytime soon tonight.

Two

Bella faced her rescuer. Her very hot rescuer.

Muscular Sam Garrison dominated the corridor outside his office with the same authority he reputedly brought to the boardroom. She tried to distance herself by looking at him with a more analytical eye.

His chestnut-brown hair was trimmed military short, his gray gaze more like piercing steel. He appeared strong enough to take on anyone, anywhere, but even with the sleeves of his crisp, white shirt rolled up, he didn't look the sort to dirty his hands with this type of work often. Everything from his perfect haircut to his high-end loafers shouted privilege.

"Thanks bunches for your help with that reporter."

She fisted her hand on the sheet, securing the scant covering, and thrust her other hand out to shake. "I'm Bella Hudson."

Sure he probably already knew who she was. Most people recognized her on sight, thanks to all the pre-publicity for *Honor*. Posters with her face were plastered all over the U.S., U.K. and France. But it seemed rude to assume someone already knew who she was. Besides, she liked life to be as normal as possible.

Well, as normal as it could be for a girl sprinting around in nothing more than a sheet as she escaped a rabid reporter.

"I know who you are." He extended his hand. "Sam Garrison."

"I know who *you* are," she echoed, her hand sliding into his callused grip, enfolded in heat, hidden from sight by the size of his hold.

Oh, boy.

Any hopes of staying aloof scampered away like leaves in the fall wind. Not that she felt cold. *Nooo.* Heat tingled up her fingers, infusing warmth through her veins from tip to toe. Too much. She'd come here to escape these sorts of feelings, damn it.

Bella snatched her hand back. "Uh, so," she shifted from bare foot to foot, "where did a rich dude like you learn street-fighting moves like that?"

The hotel mogul Garrisons were reputed to be worth more than even her family, who'd made their money from Hudson Studio's box-office hits. From European boarding schools to holidays in Fiji, she hadn't exactly grown up without means, but the Garrisons had wealth that ran deeper with houses around the world. They had a Rolls Royce lifestyle all the way.

"Wealthy people don't know how to fight?" He urged her through his office door into the empty reception area, out of the hallway and away from possible onlookers who might straggle through even after regular work hours.

"That's what bodyguards are for." She just hadn't expected to need one inside a Garrison Grande spa, for crying out loud.

"I fight my own battles—always have." His steely eyes went harder for a flash before he smiled.

Suddenly she felt very, very alone with him since everyone else must have clocked out for the night. That left her alone with Sam Garrison in the lush reception area leading to his office just beyond the open door. Alone with a very sexy male at a time when by all rights she should be swearing off *any* guy, much less this one, a known ladies' man.

She'd met him briefly a few times in the past since the Hudsons and Garrisons frequented many of the same fund-raisers, parties and galas. It was a part of the whole networking game for their high-powered families to be seen in all the right places.

Sure she'd registered he was handsome in the past, but given he was nearly ten years older than her, he'd been out of her range before. What made him so much more compelling tonight? All he'd done was clothesline a reporter.

A shiver of excitement tripped up her spine.

She kept her expression bland—thank goodness for those acting skills of hers. The rogue attraction must be a by-product of raw and vulnerable emotions after her breakup. Not to mention the shock of learning about her uncle and her mother's long-ago affair.

All the more reason to retreat to her room for a bubble bath. Far, far away from any man until she had her equilibrium back. "Thanks again for coming to my rescue. Now how can I get back to my room without flashing the entire lobby?"

"My apologies for this mess." He knelt to scoop up Muffin then crossed to tuck the dog back into the carrier. Had he even heard her question? "We pride ourselves on privacy for our clientele. Rest assured the breach in security will be investigated and addressed."

"It's all right." Stepping on the edge of the sheet, she kicked her foot free and shuffled across to take Muffin's carrier from Sam. "I certainly don't enjoy being hounded by the press, but I understand it's the price I pay for having been born into this family and doing the job I love. Most of the time it's okay." She paused to clear the hitch in her throat. "I'm just having an especially tough month."

He kept his hand on top of the dog carrier, preventing her from picking it up. "Then please give me a chance to make your month take a turn for the better."

Whoa, hold on there, buster. She backed a step from the gleam in his eyes, her heel sinking deep into the lush carpet. "Getting me some clothes to wear would certainly help. I don't even want to risk going out into the hall."

"I have an elevator right through there in my office that will take us straight up to my suite." He stepped closer. "My staff can deliver your clothes there, and dinner, too."

"Dinner?" she squeaked.

He didn't push nearer this time. He simply smiled, his steely, gray eyes glinting with appreciation. "Our chef is internationally known. I will instruct him to make anything you request."

What about a hamburger to go? Because she should run, run, run. Run back to her penthouse for more spinsterish plans—watching a chick flick with Muffin, her third in as many days. Where again she would probably cry her eyes out. Where—yet again—she would see the beautiful French sunrise all by her lonesome.

How flipping pathetic. She needed something to jar her out of that sad routine. She needed to prove she wasn't falling apart.

She eased her grip on the dog carrier and reassessed Sam Garrison. Perhaps he could provide just the distraction she really needed tonight. And it wasn't like there was a chance in hell she would fall for any smooth talker's charms again. Anything that happened between the two of them would be *her* choice with her eyes wide open.

Bella secured her sheet and straightened her shoulders. "Does your cook make doggie treats?"

* * *

He'd lured her to his suite.

With a gourmet meal, a little persuasion and a bit of luck, he would lure her into his bed as well.

Sam sampled the remains of his chardonnay while Bella sat across from him at the intimately small table in the alcove overlooking the moonlit water. Candle-light flickered, casting an ivory glow over her face.

She'd swapped her sheet for a voluminous white robe bearing the hotel's crest on the pocket. Clothes would show up soon—but not too soon. He hadn't seen the need to rush and risk her leaving before he had a chance to persuade her to stay.

The leftovers of their meal remained on the table and antique serving cart. He'd sent away their server after the hotel employee had unveiled the duck in a black currant sauce.

Bella hadn't even blinked. She'd been too busy eating. He liked a woman who enjoyed her food. He'd wondered if the world-class cuisine would be wasted on an anorexic Hollywood type who dined only on watercress and wine.

He had the wine part right.

She alternated sips of his cellar's best with tastes from the wooden board filled with samples of cheeses and fruit. Her face bore the smile of a content woman.

Even her dog was happily snoozing on a pile of gold tasseled pillows on the sofa after snacking on the baked puppy treats his chef had whipped up.

Bella dabbed the corner of her mouth with a linen

napkin. "This was all amazing. Far more relaxing than even a massage." She reached for her wineglass beside the single rose in a vase. The neck of her robe parted slightly to reveal the creamy curves of her breasts. "It's just what I needed after a real bitch of a month."

She had mentioned that in the hall earlier as well. He knew the look of a woman burning to vent and the more she talked, the longer she would stay. Conveniently, that would give him more time to win her over.

He set aside his drink, focusing his total attention on her so she could tell her celebrity tale of woe. An unflattering photo? A former friend spilling lies for a payoff? "Why has your month been so terrible?"

She hesitated for a moment before shrugging. "You must be the only person on the planet who hasn't read a newspaper."

"Gossip magazines you mean?" He spit out the words. "I stay away from them."

"Smart man. I wish my job allowed me that luxury." She downed half the remaining fine wine as if it were nothing more than water. A bracing breath later, she continued, "My grandmother has breast cancer, my boyfriend dumped me and my uncle's really my dad."

He whistled low and long. Not what he'd expected at all. "That *is* one helluva month."

She glanced up from her drink. "Thank you."

"For what?"

"For not offering platitudes that really don't fix anything." She set her crystal stemware back on the table. "I prefer a no B.S. attitude."

He simply nodded, refilling her glass. He hadn't realized the family matriarch—Lillian Hudson—was battling for her life. Lillian was somewhat of a legend around France, her homeland until she met and married a young American soldier during WWII. "This is your grandmother you made the movie about?"

"Yes. Since my grandfather died thirteen years ago, Grandmere—I'm the only one to call her Grandmere, actually, but that's besides the point." Bella paused to sip her wine. "She's made it her mission to bring their wartime love story to the big screen. We were afraid she couldn't live long enough, but with the film making its debut in a week on Christmas day, it looks like she'll have her wish. She's weak, but hanging on. This project has come together in time to celebrate the sixtieth anniversary of Hudson Studios. It's perfect timing."

"It must have been tough playing your grandmother in the movie, especially now." He didn't keep up with Hollywood bios, but he seemed to recall that while Bella Hudson had made great strides in independent films she'd yet to achieve a breakout role.

She toyed with her napkin, twisting it tight. "People think my casting was some kind of family gift, but I had to fight to get that part. And I'm so glad I got the chance. Making a movie about my grandparents' World War II romance was an honor—all the more fitting since the movie itself is called *Honor*. Are you familiar with their story?"

"Only what I've read in news releases about the

movie." He lied a bit, but hearing her sexy voice stoked his senses. And talking about her grandparents softened the strained edges around her eyes.

He suspected the telling would relax her far more than any wine and he most definitely wanted to make Bella feel at home.

She eased back into her chair, toying with the stem on her wineglass. "My grandfather was a U.S. soldier when he met my grandmother here in France. She was a struggling cabaret performer. They secretly married. After the war, he brought her back to the States. My grandfather Charles founded a movie studio so Grandmere Lillian could bring her talents to the big screen. He made her a legend and she made his fledgling studio a huge success. It's a fairy-tale story." Her eyes sparkled more than the crystal in the candlelight.

"Sounds like you have romance in your genes."

Her smile faded fast. She rose from her chair, taking her drink with her as she turned her back to him and crossed to the window, boats bobbing in the busy French port outside.

"My belief in romance took a serious hit recently." Her voice trembled. "My mother had an affair with her husband's brother. My parents have split up as a result. I always thought they had such a great marriage and now everything has come crumbling down."

He shoved back his chair and walked over to her, stopping an inch shy of touching her. "I'm sorry to hear that."

She glanced over her shoulder at him, fiery spirit

replacing any tears in her eyes. "I'm not sure why I'm spilling my guts to you this way."

"Maybe you just needed to tell someone rather than having the press tell it all for you."

She tossed her head, her hair a flame-red contrast against the white robe. "Perhaps."

The exotic perfume of her shampoo mingled with the scent of the massage oil slicking her skin. His body stirred in response, but he could control himself.

The payoff would be worthwhile for both of them if she decided to stay—and it needed to be her decision. "I'm afraid I don't have any reassuring words to offer you, Bella. My Garrison cousins are all jumping on the marriage bandwagon, but I'm still a cynical soul when it comes to tying the knot."

She laughed low, her eyes lingering on his face a second longer than casual interest. "Did your parents have a crummy marriage, too?"

He slid around to stand beside her, leaning one shoulder on the picture window overlooking the Mediterranean Sea. He normally didn't roll out his life story for strangers, not that his private life was any secret after the way the press raked his mother over the coals. Anything he said, Bella could find out on her own.

So why not use those same facts to wrangle his way a little closer to her? It wasn't like any of the information upset him anymore.

He stuffed his hands in his pockets to keep from reaching for her too soon and risk spooking her. "My parents never had a marriage at all. My father was a scam artist looking to hook up with a wealthy Garrison. Mom fell for him at first, got pregnant, but wised up before actually tying her life to the jerk."

Her hand fluttered to rest on his arm. "I'm sorry, for your mother and for you."

"No loss on my part. He's an ass. He tried to get custody of me once, but everyone knew he was only interested in the trust fund that came with me. The courts threw out his case once three women showed up with marriage licenses bearing my dad's name."

"He'd been married before?"

"But never divorced."

"Ouch," she gasped. "Your father was a bigamist?"

"*Big* time." This wasn't something he talked about, but if sharing it would gain him traction in winning over Bella, then why not? He'd long ago hardened himself to the facts that made up his parentage. "Mom was forty-one, single, pregnant and hounded by the press."

Her eyes went wide. "Your mother was forty-one when she had you? From the way you told the story I thought she was younger."

His mother had once told him that she hated being a cliché most of all—the old maid taken in by a younger Lothario. Sam hated most of all that the press had hammered home that image to his mother. They'd made her life miserable to the point she'd become a recluse, living in a barrier island bungalow off the coast of Southern Florida.

He stared back at young and vibrant but too vulnerable Bella. Would the media wear her down? Or would she develop Teflon defenses over time?

And speaking of relationships and breakups… "You mentioned an ex-boyfriend."

She looked down and away, out the window again. "My costar in *Honor*. Ridley the Rat."

He stroked a strand of her hair back over her shoulder, leaving his hand there, caressing the inside curve of her neck. "Ridley the Rat, huh? I'm glad he's out of the picture."

Bella studied him through narrowed eyes, but she didn't pull away. "Your empathy factor is sadly lacking."

He slid his fingers into her hair, cupping her head. "But my attraction factor is not. Ridley the Rat is an idiot."

"Oh." Her pupils widened and she swayed closer toward him in unmistakable attraction.

Enough dancing around the subject. Time to let her know how much she affected him and see if she felt the same. He dipped his head and skimmed his mouth over hers. Her breathy sigh, and the downward glide of her eyelashes encouraged him.

He traced the seam of her lips until she parted for him and finally her hands slipped up his arms to rest on his shoulders. A jolt of desire shot through him, instantaneous. Undeniable. He deepened the kiss, stroked, searched, learned the taste and feel of her.

She edged closer to him, returning his kiss with

an enthusiasm that made him hard with desire. Her soft curves grazed his chest, her fluffy robe warm from her heat. He could keep pushing the point and he was fairly certain she would follow him all the way into his bedroom a simple door away. Her response indicated as much. But he needed to *hear* her total, unreserved surrender.

Sam eased his mouth from hers, his hands sliding down her back to loop loosely around her waist. He watched her, waiting for her to open her eyes again.

Finally, her lashes fluttered open again, her blue gaze passion glazed. "Wow."

Yeah, "wow" pretty much summed it up. He wasn't sure what it was about her kiss that sent him so high so fast, but this woman packed a hell of a punch to his libido. He didn't want to think overlong how much a simple kiss rocked him. He gathered up his shaky control and focused on winning her over for what he wanted most.

More.

More of her.

Tonight.

"Wow," she said again, her voice steadier this time.

He glided his knuckles along her jaw, the silky feel of her skin making him ache all the way to his teeth. He wanted to discover if she felt this good all over. "My eyes followed you more than once at parties we both attended over the years. But you don't need me to tell you what a gorgeous woman you are when there are magazine covers devoted to stroking your ego."

"I hardly know you." Yet her face dipped toward his touch. "You're polite and this dinner was lovely, but I'm not even sure I like you."

"Ah, but do you *want* me?"

Three

Bella gripped the edge of the winter-cool window-sill to keep from falling straight into Sam's muscular arms. Even the romantic Marseille skyline twinkling beyond the pane seemed to be special-ordered for seduction. With the power of his kiss still zinging through her veins, she couldn't deny the obvious to him, much less to herself.

She wasn't sure why he affected her so much, so quickly. She didn't like to think of herself as shallow, falling into bed with a man because of his looks. But then hadn't she done just that with Ridley?

God, even thinking of how easily he'd tossed her aside still hurt. Ridley had said he loved her. He'd even discussed getting married. All lies, lies she hadn't seen through because she'd been too caught in the romantic air of filming her grandparents' story. She'd been ripe for the picking when Ridley showered her with his flowery charm.

Apparently he was an even better actor than she'd given him credit for.

She scrubbed memories of him from her brain. Thoughts of him now, while she was with Sam, felt disloyal somehow. For tonight, in this moment, she would be totally with this man, a man who issued bold, blunt statements of fact rather than fake, empty, flattery.

Yes, she wanted Sam. Yes, she needed something to ease the pain inside her and it seemed being with him might help her forget for at least a night. But no way could she let him think she was a total pushover.

She tipped her chin, the heat of his touch still tingling. "You're certainly not lacking in the ego department."

He trailed a finger along the lapel of her bathrobe. "I'm only stating facts here. You're a gorgeous woman. I would have to be dead not to notice."

His words soothed her wounded ego. People complimented her often enough, but so many of them were sycophants and suck-ups, she discounted much of what they said. She couldn't miss the straightforward sincerity in Sam's eyes.

Still, a wounded part of her needed to push. "A person's worth is about more than looks."

"Of course." He stepped closer, the tangy scent of

his aftershave tempting her to breathe deeper. "But initial, animal attraction shouldn't be discounted."

"Is that what's happening here?" she asked, even when she already knew the answer to that one.

She was completely out of her depth, wavering on weak-kneed hunger for him, and it was a feeling unlike any she'd ever experienced. Animal attraction sounded just about right for her instinctual need to touch him.

"What do you think?" He rested his hands lightly on her shoulders, broad palms gently massaging away her tension.

And self-control.

"I'm thinking that maybe you believe sleeping with me might make for good publicity, or that you want the novelty of sleeping with an actress." Had she actually said that? She hadn't even known the fear existed until the words fell out of her mouth.

"Damn, lady, that's a hefty load of insecurities." He gave her shoulders a final squeeze before pulling his hands back. "Let's unpack that one issue at a time." He held up one finger. "First, I don't need you or the damn press in order to be successful. I'm managing quite fine on my own. In fact, I could buy your family business twice over." He ticked off a second finger. "Second, if I wanted novelty, there are other women I could turn to who wouldn't accuse me of chasing them for their money."

Her eyebrows shot upward. "You really aren't lacking in ego."

"Women chase me for my money. That's nothing to be proud of."

A hesitant smile tipped her mouth. "I really don't have anything you need."

"Now, there you're wrong." He stepped closer, his body totally flush against hers, his hard muscles a sweet temptation against her.

"I am?" she gasped, the musky scent of him swirling through her with that one breath.

"Since the second I saw you running down that hall, I have wanted to get closer to you. So much so that I'm damn near about to explode if I don't get my mouth on some part of you soon."

The intensity of his rumbling voice stroked her senses as artfully as his touch, his kiss, everything about this moment drugging her, dragging her away from any good intentions.

She knew he had a reputation with women, and in a strange way that made this encounter somehow safe. She didn't have to worry about risking a relationship. Her heart wouldn't be in jeopardy.

Casual affairs had never been her style, but then her life had never been this upside down. Why not take what she needed? What he so clearly wanted, too.

Maybe she'd been hoping for a little adventure when she'd taken the elevator up to his private suite tonight. But then, perhaps being wrapped in Sam Garrison's arms was the balm her wounded spirit needed. And who better to seek this moment of mindless pleasure with than a man who knew all about the joys of hot, one-time encounters?

"Birth control?" she asked, that issue the last hurdle between her and jumping into his bed.

"In the other room." His hand slid behind her back, anchoring her against him. "Is that a yes?"

She touched his face, her fingers testing his raspy five-o'clock shadow. "Yes, definitely yes."

A low growl of appreciation his only response, he scooped her off her feet and carried her across the sitting area to the door ajar, leading into his bedroom. Dim lighting from the crystal chandelier showcased the king-size bed with a large painted panel of the French countryside over the bed.

The burgundy-and-gold brocade comforter was turned back invitingly. Champagne waited in a bucket by the bed along with chocolate-covered strawberries.

She thumped him on the shoulder lightly. "You were planning this all along when you placed the order for supper?"

"What can I say? I was hopeful as hell from the second you slammed into my chest wearing nothing more than a sheet."

So he'd been hopeful. Yet he'd still given her plenty of chances to say no. He might be a player, but he was a player with honor.

Time to stop thinking.

Time to feel and forget.

Raising her face for his kiss, she smoothed her hands over his hair, finally allowing herself the indulgence of feeling its texture. Soft along the top, a bit bristly as his hair tapered off at his neck. She savored the pleasure of being kissed by a man who knew how to do it so beautifully well.

Beside the sprawling king-size bed, he lowered her to her feet, her toes nearly disappearing in the carpet. Her hands roved his back, the fine fabric of his shirt soft against her fingers, a thin barrier over the hard muscled expanse. A thin barrier she quickly unbuttoned and stroked away to reveal the cut of muscles, more defined than she'd imagined. And her imagination had been darn impressed.

What other pleasant surprises waited for her? He had far more clothes on than she did and she did not intend to be the only one naked in this room.

Desperation gripped her with a frantic need to soak up everything she could from her time with him. This was her amnesia drug of choice. A way to forget everything. A way to relieve the tension Henri had said riddled her muscles. She couldn't imagine herself in a relationship anytime soon and she couldn't see herself indulging in a string of meaningless encounters. This, *Sam,* could be her last chance for the sweet pleasure of a man's bold stroke for quite a while to come.

He kissed his way down the sensitive curve of her neck, nudging aside her robe with his chin, only an inch. She'd expected him to whip away the belt quickly. Instead he took his time, lavishing attention in the curve of her shoulder.

"Faster," she said, unbuckling his pants frantically as he toed off his shoes and socks.

"Slower," he commanded, lowering her to the bed, sinking her into the downy fullness. Her robe parted. He froze for an instant before he exhaled hard. "I knew you were beautiful, and it's obvious you have a great body, but damn. Just damn."

Maybe he was only dishing out flattery to win her over... Hey wait, he didn't have to win her over anymore. She was already naked and ready in his bed.

Unwilling to wait any longer, she arched up and hooked her thumbs in his waistband. "How about we get rid of those pants so I can enjoy you, too?"

His hands covered hers as she swept away his trousers and boxers, the bristly hair on his muscular thighs sending a shower of awareness stinging through her. She let her eyes rove him in a "wow" moment all her own. His broad shoulders spoke of strength beyond the boardroom, a strength she'd experienced firsthand when he'd so effortlessly carried her. She glanced back up to his angular face—handsome in a stark way—softened by an intriguing dimple in his chin.

In a flash of insight, she realized she'd chosen Ridley's opposite. Other than dark hair, Sam shared little in common with her more wiry, smoothly good-looking ex-lover. She shoved away thoughts of another man.

No one and nothing else would intrude on this.

Sam tapped her on the shoulder lightly, encouraging her to fall back on the mattress. He snagged a bottle of champagne from an ice bucket beside the bed. Deftly, he popped the magnum, angling it over her body so the frothy overflow splashed along her stomach.

"Sam!" she squealed at the cold kiss of bubbles against her overheated flesh.

He dribbled champagne along her stomach. Cool droplets gleamed on her skin, sending a shiver through her. He dipped his head to taste and tease her with his tongue. Lower, lower and lower still he slowly dribbled a thin trail of amber liquid between her legs.

Wicked determination lit his eyes as he tasted her. Carefully, again and again, just enough to tease her higher without sending her over the edge.

He glanced up at her with heavy lidded eyes. "You make me drunk."

"We didn't have *that* much wine with dinner." She wouldn't be able to delude herself later that this had been an alcohol-induced mistake.

He gripped her hips, his naked body sliding up and over hers. "You misunderstand. I said '*you* make me drunk.'"

"*You* flatter me."

"I am known for being brutally honest."

His undisguised admiration numbed her bruised ego more effectively than any bottle of champagne. Bella flipped Sam to his back, leaned toward the silver tray by the ice bucket and plucked up a chocolate-covered strawberry between her teeth. She brought her mouth to his and shared.

He nipped at the fruit, closer and closer until their lips met. His kiss tasted of strawberries and champagne, and she couldn't deny the power of his touch along her skin. His touch brought the perfect forgetfulness.

Sam held her kiss while reaching to the bedside table for protection. He sheathed himself before she even had time to totally register what he was doing, but grateful all the same that he'd possessed a whisper of restraint enough to do so.

He gripped her hips and positioned her over him, nudging against her as he stared up into her eyes. Slowly, she lowered herself onto him, taking him, letting him take her with bold strokes that scattered any remaining rational thought.

Heat rose and she threw herself into that swirl of sensation. Total oblivion. Complete forgetfulness of all the things that had driven her here in the first place. Into his bed.

She writhed more urgently against him, ready for release, almost there already…. He flipped her to her back and took control and kept that sweet finale from her, coaxing her to the edge again and again until her fingernails scored his back.

Still, he tormented her by slowing the pace, damn him. She'd had enough of men ruling her life and her emotions. She would take what she wanted, *when* she wanted it.

Bella locked her legs around his hips, sensation rolling through her as fast as their wet bodies slid against each other. Almost… Almost…

There.

Her muscles tensed as pleasure pulsed through her so hard and fast a cry burst free. Dimly she registered his hoarse growl of completion as she rode the wave into total satisfaction.

Replete, she sagged beneath him into the fluffy comforter. The scent of champagne, strawberries and lovemaking filled the air, but she knew it would all fade soon enough.

Her escape from reality would end at sunrise.

Sun peeking on the horizon, Sam tucked the sheet more securely around Bella as he carefully slid from the bed. Her hair splayed over the pillow, her bare arm gripping the coverlet as if securing it for another great escape.

Muffin stared at him quietly from the foot of the bed, wide eyes unblinking, Billy Idol snarl in place. He'd never been much of a dog person, but at least the mutt wasn't an annoying yippy barker.

He shifted his attention back to Bella. No question that Ridley guy had done a number on her ego. The rat's timing sure sucked, with her grandmother's illness and her true parentage coming out.

She'd mentioned the press had already started printing stories about the mess. Media hounds would eat up her misfortune faster than wolves devoured a fresh carcass. The very reason he preferred to stay as far away from them as possible.

By all rights he should say goodbye to Bella once she woke. He'd certainly intended to when planning out this seduction.

He'd expected great sex. But he hadn't expected to want more.

She'd made it clear this was a one-night-only deal for her, too. Now he had to convince her otherwise.

He wasn't sure how long it would take for them to work each other out of their system. He wasn't even sure how long he could put up with the media circus that would undoubtedly follow her wherever they went together.

The one thing he did know? He would have to tread warily with her, given her recent experience with men. Of course, he wasn't an inept jackass like that Ridley moron.

A soft knock sounded from beyond the sitting area, out in the hall.

Right on time.

Sam shrugged into his robe and strode past the remains of their meal to answer the door. Bella's mutt pattered across the floor to join him. Sam blocked the pup with his foot.

His personal assistant, a middle-aged Englishman, stood in the hall, his eyes going wide for a flash at the sight of the dog. "Here are the clothes you ordered for Miss Hudson, along with a new room key."

"Thank you, Parrington." Sam stayed in the entry,

not wanting to expose Bella to the other man's eyes. "And the security breach?"

"One of the ladies at the registration desk started dating the photographer a couple of weeks ago." Parrington reached for the PDA clipped to his belt. "I have the name here."

"No need to tell me now. Just send the information to my e-mail. The guy probably seduced the woman for her connections here." A self-serving ass just like his own father. "Thank you for looking into this. I appreciate that no more stress will be visited on Bella Hudson while she is with us."

"Rest assured." His assistant nodded crisply.

"Good. Good. Well done." Sam closed the door again and stared back into the bedroom at Bella. She still slept soundly.

His body stirred at just the sight of her. He wasn't sure what made her different, but he still wanted her even after their night filled with lovemaking and what he wanted, he got.

He knew she'd only slept with him as a balm to her bruised ego. No doubt she planned to hotfoot her way out of here when she woke. Most times, that would have been a relief. But he wasn't ready to say goodbye to her yet. He had other plans.

Plans to delay her leaving France.

Plans to get her back in his bed.

Mind set, he picked up the phone and dialed.

* * *

Bella picked through the layers of sleepy fog until she could pry her eyes open. She blinked twice and...

Oh, my God. She'd really slept with Sam Garrison because sure enough, she could hear him in the shower. What the hell had she been thinking?

She scrubbed her tousled hair off her forehead and stretched, her body tender from a night of uninhibited lovemaking. She eyed the empty champagne bottle and a fast flush heated her face. She eyed the clock and groaned again at how late she'd slept.

What seemed like such a good idea last night now seemed totally reckless. How could she have thought she could sleep with a man without giving something of herself?

The shower turned off.

No, no, no, she wasn't ready to face him yet, wasn't sure if she would ever be. All of her reasons for jumping into bed with him—her breakup, her parents' marital train wreck—now had her eying the door for a fast escape before she risked even a corner of her already bruised heart.

She inched quietly out of the bed, farther and farther until one leg slipped off the mattress. She toed the floor and eased herself the rest of the way out from under the covers. Careful not to make a sound. Determined to get away before he finished his shave and she had to make morning-after talk with a man she barely knew but had slept with anyway.

She prided herself on being so much better than many of the promiscuous Hollywood party types.

Hell, she'd even managed to keep her clothes on in her movies so far. She was a *serious* actress, a deep person who rescued pound puppies rather than spending a gazillion dollars on a vanity pet.

And yet at the first sign of heartache, she'd thrown away her clothes and inhibitions.

Speaking of clothes, she needed something to wear. She would settle for the robe, if need be—

Her gaze fell on a stack of clothes resting on the gold-striped sofa, Muffin resting her head on top of the pile. Bella raced across the room for the jeans and frilly top—hers. Sam must have sent someone into her room.

She scruffed Muffin's head before gently moving the dog aside. "Sh... Stay quiet, sweetie."

Under the dog's head, a room card rested on top of the clothes. Thank goodness. With a little luck and a lot of stealth, she could make it out of here undetected with her pet.

She scooped up the clothes. Sam's thoughtfulness tugged at her.

Or was Sam just eager to see her leave by making sure her clothes were ready? Insecurity nipped her heels harder than Muffin bounding after her, bell around her neck chiming.

"Shhh, shhh, shhh, Muffin."

Bella took off the collar so the bell wouldn't chime and alert him to her escape. She would put it on again once she returned to her room.

No way in hell did she plan to be featured in any

photos—or relationship—with one of the world's most eligible bachelors.

She slipped on the clothes and her gold Escada sandals quickly, tucked Muffin back in her carrier and made a beeline for the door. Half in, half out, she stared back at the bathroom door. Wistfulness whispered through her. What if they'd showered together?

God, she was a sucker. "What if" nothing. They'd enjoyed amazing sex, two adults who wanted no ties.

It was over.

She closed the door behind her and took the elevator to the penthouse floor. Almost home free. She should walk Muffin, but she wasn't ready to be seen in public yet. She turned to the elevator operator....

He nodded. "Do you need help with your little pet, mademoiselle?"

She loved it when people read her mind. "Yes, thank you. She just needs a quick walk. Her leash is looped on the side of her cage here," she rattled off instructions at light speed as if that would bring about her escape all the faster. She passed over Muffin's carrier, blowing a kiss to her little sweetie.

The elevator dinged, the doors opened and she raced the last few feet to her door, ready for a shower, fresh clothes—and a new hotel. She whipped her key card in and out, shoved open the door.

And she came face-to-face with the last person she expected to see.

Four

Bella gripped the door to her hotel suite, resisting the urge to bolt back into the hall. It wasn't like she had to face a pack of wolves. Seated on the floral loveseat was her cousin Charlotte, thumbing through a newspaper, one of her favored Jamin Puech beaded purses beside her.

A cousin who was actually her half sister since they shared the same father.

What a convoluted family tree. Bella had three brothers she'd grown up with, and now her two cousins were actually half siblings.

Charlotte Hudson Montcalm lived with her French aristocrat husband at the Chateau Montcalm, a palatial estate outside Provence, a fair ways from this port city. What in the world was she doing in Marseille?

And more particularly why was she in Bella's hotel suite, sitting there as serenely perfect as the white calla lilies on the coffee table in front of her?

She loved Charlotte, but wasn't ready to deal with their changed relationship. Sorting through the tumultuous emotions would take time. She wasn't ready to see *anyone* associated with her tangled family tree.

Then why had she decided to hide out in the very country where her cousin/half sister lived with her husband Alec?

Bella sighed, wishing that annoying voice of reason niggling at the back of her mind would take a nap. Freudian slips were a real pain in the butt.

She closed the door behind her and stepped deeper into the sitting area. Light streamed through the window, whispery gold curtains pulled wide to reveal the harbor with sailboats and ringed with quaint whitewashed buildings.

Pulling a smile, Bella opened her arms for a hug, determined to act as normal as possible. "Hello, Charlotte. What a pleasant surprise to find you here waiting for me."

Her cousin's signature perfume reminded her of summer vacations together, staying up late and trying out makeup together.

"And hello to you, too." Charlotte stood, her stomach large with her advanced pregnancy. Still the blond-haired, blue-eyed beauty carried herself with her usual sophistication. They were the same age and during their teenage years, Bella had felt freckled and chubby next to her willowy cousin.

Bella hugged her taller cousin—sister. Damn, it was tough to rewire a lifetime of programming.

Easing back, she reminded herself none of this was Charlotte's fault. "What are you doing here so far from home?"

Bracing a hand behind her on the arm of the sofa, Charlotte lowered herself back to sit again. "Alec and I flew over this morning to shop for the baby and learned you were here, too."

An odd coincidence, but Charlotte's serene smile showed no sign of subterfuge. Alec had planes at his disposal ready to be used at a moment's notice.

Charlotte pulled back, her brow puckered with worry. "Why didn't you tell me you were in Marseille?"

Bella sat in the tapestry wingback chair. A light breakfast had already been laid out on the antique tea cart—small baguettes, jams and fresh fruit beside a carafe of coffee, starched linen napkin lying beside the silver tray.

The thought of food churned her already nervous stomach. "Would you like something to eat?"

"Does a bird sing? Of course I would like something to eat." She grinned. "I'm pregnant."

Bella watched as Charlotte tore off a piece of bread. "How did you find out I'm staying at the Garrison Grande?"

Charlotte smoothed her hands over her baby belly. "Alec heard it from one of his business contacts."

The truth exploded in her mind. "From Sam Garrison."

Charlotte's silence and neutral smile answered clearly. She swirled the silver knife through the glistening preserves and smoothed a dollop of raspberry jam on top of her bread.

But when would Sam have had time to do this? They'd only met up the night before and they'd spent every waking moment together....

Charlotte speared a melon ball. "Okay, yes, he called early this morning."

While she'd been sleeping, before his shower. The only question was had Charlotte truly already been here shopping or had she dropped everything to fly over just because Sam sent up an SOS. Regardless, her half sister had gone to a lot of trouble for her. Bella poured a cup of black coffee and took a sip to wash down the lump in her throat.

"I appreciate your stopping by, but why would Sam call you?"

She barely knew the man and already he was tampering with her life. She'd come here to feel closer to her grandmother. If she'd wanted to see her sister, she would have called her. Now she was stuck in an awkward situation where she appeared rude.

Charlotte waved the silver jelly knife lightly. "Who knows what men think most of the time? I do know that you shouldn't be staying at a hotel. You should be at the estate with Alec and me."

Damn, damn, damn Sam for interfering. "I didn't want to risk bringing the media down on you. Stress is the last thing a pregnant woman needs."

"I'm completely healthy—and ravenous." She popped the last pinch of bread into her mouth. She chewed slowly before saying, "Are you staying away from me because of our father?"

Bella snapped back in her seat. She hadn't expected ever-poised Charlotte to be so blunt. Hearing the truth of her parentage still cut straight through to her heart.

"Why would I do that? Mother and Uncle—" she winced "—David are the ones at fault, not you. They're the ones who cheated on their spouses."

"Looking at me could make you remember we're half sisters rather than cousins." Her blue eyes darkened with pain.

For the first time, Bella considered how all of this must have hurt Charlotte. David Hudson hadn't been much of a father, always too busy to spend any time with Charlotte or her brother, but he was still their father. The way he'd torn apart the fabric of their family with his betrayal was terrible.

Bella mentally kicked herself for being so self-centered in her grief. Charlotte deserved reassurance. She reached past the wooden tea cart to squeeze her hand.

"I loved you before; I love you now." As she said the words, she realized they were true.

Her issue was with their father, David. How strange to think she wouldn't be here without him, yet at the same time it felt as if he'd stolen her real father from her—Markus, the man who'd brought her up, the man who'd declared her Daddy's pampered girl, the man who'd been kept in the dark for years just as she had.

Until the whole ugly secret had come to light.

Blinking back tears, she snatched the rolled linen napkin from the silver tray and dabbed her eyes. She was tired of crying over this. She needed to quit feeling sorry for herself and move on. "I'm sorry. You're right that I was avoiding you. I have to confess, I wasn't sure if I could even speak to anyone about this without crying."

Yet somehow she'd managed to tell Sam the whole sad and sordid tale. Memories of strawberries and champagne bubbled in her brain, stirring a phantom taste on her tongue.

Charlotte clasped Bella's hand. "It's just going to take a while to settle into this new family tree."

Was it wrong to want the old one back? Was it wrong to be damned indignant on Markus's behalf? So much anger could sour her insides quickly. She could sure use some of Charlotte's serenity right about now.

"Wise words." Bella nodded, ready to talk about anything but this. "How do you feel? Is everything going well with the pregnancy?"

"Totally perfect. I'm huge, but happy." Her joy sparkled as brightly as her diamond ring catching the sun when she straightened her pearls. "Alec is spoiling me shamelessly. He even says pregnancy is sexy." She rolled her eyes. "I laugh, but I'm secretly soaking it up. It's no secret I had a hard time trusting him after the way our father treated my mother."

Bella tried not to flinch every time Charlotte used the word *father*. How could she ever grow accustomed to thinking of him that way? She'd always thought she had her mother's blue eyes. Now looking into Charlotte's flashing blue gaze, she saw the real source of her eye color.

David Hudson.

She struggled not to cry and risk another outpouring of sympathy from Charlotte that would only make the urge to feel sorry for herself all the stronger. Blast Sam for pressing this on her before she was ready. "Thank you for coming to check on me. That was truly a sweet thing to do. No matter what, we're family."

"I'm glad to hear you say that." Tears filled Charlotte's eyes this time. "I was afraid things would be uncomfortable between us."

"We'll be fine." She wished she could be so certain about how things would work out with the rest of her relatives.

"So will you stay with Alec and me?"

And watch her sister wallow in all that newlywed love and happiness as the two of them waited for their first child?

Not a chance.

Charlotte may have found peace and happiness in

spite of their family's crummy track record with marriage. But Bella just wasn't feeling it for herself.

She patted Charlotte's hand. "Thank you for the generous offer, but I'm afraid I've already hidden out from the press as long as I can. I need to get back to the States for the premiere of *Honor.*"

Charlotte pressed a palm to her back. "Only a few more days until the Christmas debut. I wish I could be there, but a flight that long really wouldn't be wise for me this late."

"Everyone understands. You have to put the baby's health first."

Charlotte's smile wavered. "I just hope our grandmother can hold on long enough to see this baby."

Facing Lillian's impending death was difficult for the whole Hudson clan. Bella felt as if her whole family was falling apart.

Charlotte sniffed. "Enough tears. I'm meeting Alec in an hour. Please, keep in touch."

"Of course, I will." Bella hugged her cousin-turned-sister a final time before walking with her to the door with a farewell wave.

She stayed in the open doorway, watching Charlotte step into the elevator—

Just as Sam stepped out.

Bella gasped and started to back into her room but, oh, my God, she was too late. And hey, wait, she had a bone to pick with him anyway over the heavy-handed way he'd interfered in her life. She stiffened her resolve and waited to face him, toe-to-toe. She had a lot of mixed emotions roiling around inside her these days and he would make a perfect target for a good, old-fashioned shout down to release the pressure.

Sam closed the last few feet between them and walked her backward toward the suite again.

Stopping in the open doorway, she put her hands on her hips and wished she had on heels for height. "Why are you here?"

"Well, good morning to you, too, Bella." He held up his hands, a filmy gold scarf dangling from one, large-framed sunglasses from the other. "I'm here to kidnap you."

From the look on Bella's face, this wasn't going to be as easy as he'd planned.

"Come on," Sam urged, "at least talk to me inside, so we don't risk some reporter seeing us."

Not a chance in hell would that happen here, but she didn't need to know that.

Huffing, she spun on her heel and headed back into her suite. He closed the door behind them.

He'd hoped a visit with her cousin/sister would soften her up, help her deal with some of her frustration. He'd also hoped reminding her of her family connection to this area would entice her to stick around awhile longer. His instincts were never wrong when reading people in the business world. Why should handling Bella be any different?

He would be analytical about this. Emotions were messy and led to mistakes, a truth he'd learned from his failed engagement to Tiffany Jones. He'd certainly missed the boat on reading that woman. She was the daughter of a respected business acquaintance, and Sam had considered settling down after attending yet another wedding for one of his Garrison cousins.

A momentary weakness.

Tiffany wasn't worth his trust. She'd slept with a yachting friend of his, then had the gall to try and blame it on Sam for not paying enough attention to her. He might not be the most attentive man on the planet, but he'd been straight-up honest with her from the start about the demands of his career. She'd responded by accusing him of loving his job more than her.

He'd realized she was right and called it quits between them.

Sam shoved aside doubts. He'd taken care of the Tiffany situation before it spiraled out of control into a lifetime mistake. Thank God they hadn't gotten around to setting a date or sending out invitations. He hadn't totally screwed things up.

And Bella wasn't looking for forever. In fact, he was going to have to work his ass off to wrangle a few weeks with her. She was as committed to her career as he was. That boded well for them.

Although her scowling silence wasn't exactly promising.

Sam looped the gold scarf around Bella's neck playfully. "Come on." He tugged lightly, drawing her deeper into her suite. "Smile."

"Like hell." She whipped the scarf out of his hand and off her neck. "I'm mad at you."

The best defense was a good offense. "If anyone has cause to be angry, it's me. You ran out without saying goodbye. If I'd done that to you, I would be scum. Why is it any different when you skulk off?"

She pitched the wadded scarf at his chest. "You've got to be kidding."

"What?" He snagged the whispery fabric before it slid to the floor. "Only women get to be indignant over someone running out after sex?"

She opened her mouth, then hesitated. Her brow furrowed with confusion. Ah, he had her off-balance. Good. Let her wonder if maybe he wanted some postcoital cuddling.

Bella shoved her tangled hair back from her face. "I'm sorry for not saying goodbye." Her frown shifted into a scowl. "Now you can apologize to me."

"For what?"

She crossed her arms over her luscious chest. "You know what you did."

"I saved you from the press yesterday. Damn, I'm a real bastard."

She jabbed him in the chest with one finger. "You called Charlotte."

"Says who?" he hedged.

"Are you denying it?"

Apparently she knew already, so he confessed, "I'm not denying anything."

He walked past her, deeper into her room, making it tougher for her to usher him out. He ran a cool hotelier's eye over the polished sheen of the antiques, the designs unapologetically European. There might be a forty-six-inch flat screen with surround sound at any given U.S. Garrison Grande, but the curtains here were raw silk and the floors polished bamboo.

Here, he'd cultivated a rich, old-world feel all the way down to the paneled murals on the walls. "I called Alec this morning. I was worried about you."

Her plump lips went tight. "You have to realize from what I told you that my cousin is really my half sister." She dropped into a tapestry wingback chair. "I'll deal with that when I'm good and ready."

He looked around but saw no sign of the padded pink dog crate. "Where's Muffin?"

"One of your helpful staff is walking her."

"Good." He nodded.

"Maybe you can go find her for me," she said, her hint to leave none too subtle.

"About Charlotte…I thought you might need someone to talk to." He plucked a couple of grapes from the breakfast tray and popped them into his mouth.

"That's my decision to make."

"Hey—" he thumped his chest "—I'm trying to be nice here."

"No hidden agendas?"

"Who me?" He pinched up another purple grape.

"Said the spider to the fly."

"Forgive me?" He brought the plump fruit to her

mouth, caressing it along her lips, reminiscent of how they'd fed each other strawberries and champagne.

She bit the grape, nipping his fingers none too gently in the process. "Not yet."

Yet? That meant he had a chance to get in her good graces again, a prospect that became all the more important as even her playful bite sent a bolt of heat straight to his groin.

Bella swallowed the grape, her tongue flicking over her lips.

"What did you mean about kidnapping me?" she asked, her voice throaty and confidential.

Victory shot a second jolt through him almost as strong as desire. "I thought you might like to spend time in France somewhere other than cooped up in a hotel."

Her nose scrunched. "And run through the gauntlet of reporters? I don't think so."

He looped the scarf over her head and dropped the sunglasses in her lap. "Put those acting skills of yours to work and change up your walk a bit, take on an accent. Leave the rest to me. I'm willing to bet you could plow through your entire Christmas shopping list before a single photo is snapped…unless you would rather go home."

She winced.

Good. Score one for his master plan.

"Come on, Bella. I have Christmas shopping of my own to take care of and I could really use your help in choosing something for my mother. So?" he pressed. "Are you in?"

"Well, I haven't had time to shop for gifts." Finally, her face cleared and she sighed. "All right. Find my dog and you can take me shopping."

He held back his smile of victory.

"I need to shower first."

His body stirred at even the thought of her naked under the spray of water. Too bad he couldn't convince her to skip shopping altogether and spend the day in bed together.

She jabbed a finger into his chest. "You are not invited to join me."

"Muffin and I will be waiting."

Five

If only every day could end with coffee and a handsome man, the Eiffel Tower silhouetted in the distance.

Bella tightened the gold scarf draped over her head, but she'd ditched the large sunglasses since the sun was setting. Besides, they were indoors, tucked away in a corner of a small Parisian café. The scent of espresso wound through the restaurant, the soft chatter of native speakers soothed her with its melodious cadences.

So far Sam had done a brilliant job at evading the press, arranging a limo and extra security at one side entrance while spiriting her away to a private car out another. The plan had gone off without a hitch, but then he was full of surprises today.

Sam had told her he intended to take her shopping. He hadn't mentioned they would be flying to Paris in his personal jet.

They'd left her dog at the hotel. Sam had reassured her that his assistant—Parrington—would take care of Muffin's walks, food and water. Muffin would be happier playing, after all, rather than being carted around in her carrier all day.

He was right. Besides, juggling the little crate and her packages could be tough. She'd bought so much, they'd already left a load in their chauffeured car. She hadn't had time to do any Christmas shopping with the hectic prerelease publicity schedule for *Honor.* She'd certainly fixed that problem now.

Somewhere around the fourth store, her anger at Sam for interfering had diminished to mere irritation. She didn't totally trust him. After all, what man actually wanted to go shopping? Yet he hadn't made even one move on her since they'd left the hotel. She would simply keep a wary eye on him.

A guitarist in the corner crooned "The First Noel" in French while Bella sipped her black coffee contentedly, eyeing the rest of her dessert and wondering if she dared pack on more calories. The answer? Definitely. The *poire au chocolat*—a Bosc pear, cooked in wine, dipped in chocolate, served with whipped cream—was irresistible.

She speared another bite, as the couple at the next table left, speaking in French at the speed of light.

"I'm never going to fit into my dress for the movie premiere if I let you keep feeding me like this."

He cocked a brow. "You look fabulous and you know it. Quit fishing for compliments."

"Ouch." Her irritation sparked higher. "That wasn't very nice."

Of course, most people had no way of knowing how hard an actress had to fight to stay competitive in an absurdly weight-conscious business. Bella had never been one of those stars accused of being anorexic, after all, she liked her food. But to remain in an industry where she was photographed constantly, she had to be extremely disciplined. One day, when she'd had enough of Hollywood, she planned to celebrate with a ten-day doughnut spree. All doughnuts. All the time.

He toasted her with his coffee, the bone china absurdly delicate in his large hand. "I'm a no B.S. kind of guy."

"I guess there's honor in that." She forced down miffed feelings and savored another bite, her eyes closing in ecstasy. "I love food, but it's true what they say about the camera adding pounds. I work out a lot. I decided early on I would not spend my life living on rice cakes and cocaine."

"Admirable." He seemed surprised, darn him. "Did your personal trainer come along?"

She snorted and quickly dabbed her lips with her napkin. "Don't have one. Sure I consult with trainers on how to target problem areas, but honestly, I have such a large entourage following me around with a camera documenting everything I do, I prefer to exercise alone. Well, except for Muffin of course. Muffin needs lots of exercise too or she misbehaves. So when I walk on the treadmill, she runs circles around me. I enjoy bike rides and she trots alongside. If she gives out, I have a carrier attached to the back of the seat...."

She paused mid-ramble and stared across the table at Sam who was watching her intensely. The sunset through the window cast shadows on his leanly handsome face. Had he truly been listening or was he a B.S. artist after all? Because she truly didn't have a clue why he'd signed on for a shopping trip today. Most men would have avoided this like the plague.

Bella ducked closer to him, careful to keep her voice low so the waiter angling past wouldn't overhear. "Why are we doing this? What do you hope to gain?"

"I enjoyed last night," he said simply. "I don't see why it has to be a one-time deal."

She'd been wondering, half expecting this all day, but hadn't wanted to face the inevitable discussion. Spending time with him had been more fun—laid back and easy—than she'd expected.

Now that was coming to an end. "Weren't you listening to me when I poured my heart out to you over supper? My life is a mess. I'm not in any shape for a relationship."

She wasn't in any shape to withstand more hurt.

"I never said I wanted a relationship." He set his

coffee back on the small café table and leaned on his elbow, closer, intent. "No offense meant, but I am most definitely not looking to marry you."

She leaned back, her cheeks puffing out a sigh that played with the flickering candle in the middle of their table. "Wow, no need to soft soap it."

"You're the one who asked for reassurance."

She was mad at herself even more than at him. She resented the pull of attraction even as she seemed unable to back away. "I didn't ask for anything except a change of clothes to get back to my room. You don't seem to understand." She struggled for the right words. "I am hurting, really hurting. Despite how it seemed last night, I'm not the casual-sex sort. What we did was…an anomaly."

"Stupid me." He grinned. "I thought we ate strawberries off each others' bodies."

She slapped her napkin on the table. "Quit trying to make me laugh."

"Why? You just said again how much you're hurting. Is it so wrong of me to want to make you smile?"

"As long as I still have my clothes on." Was that possible around him? Even with her defenses on full-scale alert, she couldn't help but notice the ripple of muscle under his shirt as he'd carried her packages.

Or how the appealing scruff of his five-o'clock shadow along his jaw gave him an edgier, sexy appeal. She itched to test the texture beneath her fingertips.

Against her better judgment, her fingers began crawling across the table. The very small table.

Another couple of inches and she would throw caution to the wind—

Snap, snap.

The unmistakable click of cameras sounded behind her. Damn it. Her stomach clenched in frustration—and disappointment.

Sam's face hardened. "Head down."

So far the photographer had yet to get in front of her. Sam pitched cash on the table and looped his arm around Bella's shoulders. She ducked into the strength of his protective embrace. Luckily, they'd already stored all their shopping bags in the car, so they were unencumbered to make a break for it.

He raced straight toward the restaurant's kitchen door, hurrying her alongside while shielding her face. They pushed through the double swinging doors, steam blasting through carrying the scent of frying meats. Pots clanged loudly as voices shouted instructions back and forth. A humidity-limp plaid Christmas bow hung over the clock marking six o'clock.

Sam pointed across the crowded kitchen, past the cooking island down the middle. "The back exit is that way."

"Our coats?" The winter temperatures felt all the colder to her after a lifetime in sunny California.

"Already taken care of." He rushed her past a chef in a tall white hat, the industrial stove sizzling with sliced vegetables.

An attendant stood by the back door, their coats draped over his arms. Sam had obviously made contingency plans for evading the press. She had to admire his thoroughness.

"Merci." Sam shrugged into his black coat while their accomplice helped Bella with her longer one of white wool.

He shuttled her out into the empty back lot, the crisp air echoing with cathedral bells chiming "Silent Night." The lot was very empty other than their waiting transportation, thank goodness.

Sam's arm around her shoulders, he sprinted toward the Mercedes parked nearby, exhaust chugging into the early evening. "Hurry up, Cinderella, before this sucker changes into a pumpkin."

The chauffer swept open the door. Bella slid in as Sam launched into the other side. Her heart pounded from the exertion as much as the threat. She knew too well how quickly a frenzy of reporters could cause an accident by jumping all over a car. Once their car pulled out onto the main road, two motorcycles roared away from the curb.

The press had found them.

Their driver raced through the streets of Paris at a breakneck speed, motorcycles speeding closer behind. Her pulse thudding in her ears, Bella double-checked her seat belt. Sam pulled out his cell phone, issuing instructions for the crew on his plane to be ready for takeoff. Otherwise, silence hovered heavily in the vehicle as she checked anxiously over her shoulder.

Mere minutes later, they pulled into the small

private airport, through a security gate. Sam's silver private jet waited, the crew prepped and ready outside.

She leaped from the vehicle. A few yards away, the paparazzi on motorcycles screeched to a halt behind the fence. They wouldn't get any farther, but their cameras had mighty powerful lenses.

"Hurry!" He ushered her up the airplane steps. "That security guard isn't going to hold up much longer."

Two men wearing vests with reflective tape unloaded her packages from the trunk at lightning speed while she raced up the metal stairs.

Inside, she unlooped her scarf and sunk into the leather seat. Gasping for air, she couldn't recall feeling this breathless in a long time. She should have been frustrated, angry even.

Yet for some reason it had felt more like an adventure with Sam at her side.

Because she'd never doubted he would take care of the situation? "I can't believe you managed to elude them all day."

Sam sidestepped the media center dominating most of the space. He secured his seat belt near the wine refrigerator at an old-fashioned bar. Sparkling cut-crystal glasses hung upside down above a black, granite prep area. "It helps that you speak fluent French when shopping or ordering meals."

"As do you."

His fluency in the language shouldn't have surprised her since he worked here, but it did make her wonder what other surprises he had in store.

"People see what they expect to see. We appeared to be two locals finishing up last-minute Christmas shopping."

Still, Sam had a knack for ditching the press beyond anything she'd seen before. And given the high-profile Hollywood sorts who made up her regular circle, she'd seen some mighty adept press dodgers.

The airplane engines roared louder, the craft easing forward, faster, until the nose lifted off. With a smooth swoop they were airborne. The neat pile of her shopping bags barely moved from where they rested in a corner.

And it was quite a hefty pile.

She'd checked off everyone on her growing list of family members. Buying for her grandmother had been particularly difficult—and sad. What did you get for a person who wasn't expected to live much longer?

She hoped she'd chosen well.

God, what was she even thinking wasting her grandmother's final precious days apart? Or worse yet, what if her grandmother died before Bella could say goodbye?

The holiday cheer she'd found with Sam seeped away. Even the twinkling lights of the Eiffel Tower were fading in the distance. Her escape was truly over. Time to face reality—and Beverly Hills—again.

She needed to tell Sam that while their day shopping together had been special, come morning, she would be leaving for California.

* * *

Sam could see Bella mentally pulling away from him as clearly as if she'd risen from her seat and hopped out of the plane.

He wasn't sure what had changed, but most certainly he'd lost some ground. He needed to get her talking again so he could find the right opening. No great hardship, actually. Spending time with her today—even out of bed—had been surprisingly entertaining.

She hadn't shopped like a diva with the world at her feet. There hadn't been any special requests for private showings or traipsing up the aisles with complimentary champagne in hand. Bella spent most of her time admiring the different style crèches, delighting in everything from delicate crystal figurines to rustic wood carvings. She'd slid a huge donation into a charitable collection plate when she thought he wasn't looking, then turned around and purchased a miniature *père Noël* bell on a ribbon to drape around her neck—his own personal Christmas elf.

The tinkling of that small bell had charmed and seduced him all day long.

She was a total turn-on even totally clothed.

Bella shifted in her seat, her green silk blouse inching open to flash him a hint of creamy skin. "Thanks for helping me with my shopping," she said, jump-starting the conversation for him. "This worked out perfectly since I really do have to get back home tomorrow."

Damn. Time was shorter than he'd anticipated, but lucky for him, he already had business dealings lined up in California, the most recent in Los Angeles. He could combine work and pleasure quite easily.

He just needed the right opening to suggest a visit to her side of the Atlantic. "And where exactly is home for you?"

"At the family estate on Loma Vista Drive in Beverly Hills. I stay in the guesthouse." Her brow puckered. "Where do you actually live?"

A promising move that she asked more about him. Sam stretched his legs in front of him as the plane droned through the dark sky. "Most of the family is located in southern Florida, but Garrison hotels have been expanding of late. I've taken on more traveling responsibilities as many of my family members are marrying and settling down. I oversee most new projects in the works."

"But where do you *live*?" she asked again as she propped her chin on her hand.

"In my hotels." Everything was provided for him. Why bother keeping a condo or home that would leave him losing valuable work hours commuting?

"The epitome of a rootless bachelor."

"That would be me. A no-commitment guy. No worries about me leading you on." The truth should put her at ease.

Studying him, Bella twisted a lock of hair then stopped abruptly as if realizing how damn sexy she looked with that simple gesture. "I don't want you to get the wrong idea."

"What idea would that be?"

"The sex was amazing, no question." She chewed her bottom lip for a blood surging second that threatened to send him reaching for her again. "But I'm not interested in any kind of relationship, even a no-strings fling."

"Who said I am?"

"Then what are we doing here?" She gestured between them.

"I'm making restitution for the inconvenience caused by my hotel's security lapse. My business is everything to me." Now to start easing into his plan for more time to win her over. "In fact, I have a new hotel opening in the U.S. I would have been heading back to the States soon to check on the progress anyway."

"You take your commitment to your guests above and beyond." She eyed him suspiciously. "Where is the new hotel?"

"Los Angeles, actually." True enough. The hotel was almost ready to open as the latest in Garrison Grande Incorporated's successful expansion plan.

Her brows pinched together. "Yeah, right. You just happen to have a hotel in the town where I live," she said suspiciously. "Where in Los Angeles?"

He recited the address, a piece of prime property he'd busted his ass negotiating for.

Her eyes went wide. "You really do have a hotel there?"

"Bella, it's not like I could or would lie about this. It's easy enough to check out."

"Of course. I'm sorry." The defensiveness eased from her shoulders and she relaxed back in the white leather seat. "I'm just not sure what to think of you yet. You've been so nice, but then you went behind my back to call Charlotte, albeit with seemingly good intentions."

She shoved her hand through her wind-tumbled red hair. "I just don't know what to think these days. I'm probably being prickly and a little paranoid. I'm nervous about going back and facing everyone again at the premiere of *Honor*. It's difficult enough dealing with Grandmere's cancer. I'll also have to face my parents and pretend I'm okay with everything." She exhaled long, her cheeks puffing. "Then of course Ridley will be there."

Ridley the Rat? Jealousy kicked around inside his gut. Sam stroked his jaw. "I imagine seeing him at the premiere will be tough."

She pressed her hands to her forehead. "I don't even want to think about it. Which makes me mad at him all over again. The premiere of *Honor* on Christmas day should be one of the best days of my life and he's wrecking it. He'll show up with his new bimbo girlfriend and I'll be there with my dog."

He leaned toward her. "Use me."

Her hands fell to her lap. "What?"

The more he thought about it, the more it made sense. He'd been looking for an opening and she'd just handed him the ideal opportunity. "Take me as your date to the premiere. Use me to show that loser ex-boyfriend of yours that you aren't shedding any tears over him. At the risk of sounding as if I have an overinflated ego, magazines seem to think I'm a fairly eligible bachelor."

"So I've seen." She toyed with the thin velvet ribbon around her neck, nudging the small bell just above the top button on her blouse. A hell of a distraction for his eyes. "But *use* you? Wouldn't that be shallow of me?"

"Not if we're both in agreement."

"What do you gain from this?"

Bella back in his bed?

But a smart man would lead with another argument and no one had ever called him a fool. "For starters, I get to take a breather from appearing on all those damn 'most eligible bachelor' lists. Every time they publish one, a fresh flock of matchmaking mamas shows up at one of my hotels. It's insulting to me and to their daughters. Not to mention a real pain in the ass."

"Okay, I can understand that." She nodded slowly. "I have to leave tomorrow."

"Not a problem." He only slept for a few hours anyway. He could wrap up business and be ready by sunup. He'd been planning a trip later next week after Christmas anyhow. "Any other questions?"

"Yeah," she said empathically, "a big one. Why me?"

"Because I can be honest with you about this and know you're not going to run to the press."

She smiled grudgingly. "You have me there."

"You agree?" That easily. Hot damn. Peeling her clothes off her after that premiere would make for a night to remember. He would pleasure her so thoroughly he would wipe Ridley Sinclair from her memory forever.

"We're not sleeping together again."

"Seems like you're cutting your nose off to spite your face with that one." He held up a hand to stop her protest. He knew to quit when he was ahead, and he'd definitely taken a huge step ahead in getting her to agree to let him hang out with her over the holidays. "But, hell, who am I to judge? No sex. We'll leave first thing tomorrow morning. Agreed?"

She hesitated only a moment, frowning briefly before her face cleared. "I have the feeling I'm going to regret this…but…yes. We'll go to the Christmas-day premiere together."

Six

As Bella sat on Sam's plane the next morning on her way back to the States, she couldn't believe she'd actually said yes to his outrageous proposition.

Petting Muffin in her lap, Bella stared out the window at the Atlantic Ocean peeking below while the plane zipped in and out of clouds. Footsteps echoed as Sam walked to the front of the plane, toward the kitchenette for a snack, his long legs eating up the space in only a few strides.

She knew one thing for sure. Sam was a damn good businessman. He'd presented the case well for sticking together awhile longer, knowing right where she was most vulnerable. Her pride stung at the thought of facing Ridley alone.

Yet Sam *had* agreed to her no sex stipulation.

Her gaze dipped to his fine tush showcased in casual blue pants. In a weak moment she wondered what he would look like filling out a pair of well-washed jeans?

She shook off the too-enticing fantasy. She'd meant what she'd said about no sex, especially not now when she was so confused and, well, weak when it came to his appeal. She wasn't one for flings, in fact didn't have much of a dating past other than Ridley because of her drive to break out in her career.

Had Sam been lying about keeping his distance, or was he really genuine about seeing benefits in helping her out? Maybe he was just one of those gallant guys who couldn't resist a woman in distress.

After the way his mother had been treated, Bella could understand how he would have developed that tendency. Maybe he didn't really have a hidden agenda. Perhaps he genuinely had business to accomplish and figured he would be a good guy along the way.

Her initial idea for facing Ridley at the premiere had been to borrow one of her brothers for the evening. But how lame was that? Sam would make for a powerful piece of eye candy to distract gossip-hungry people from wondering why she and Ridley were no longer an item.

She could ruminate about this all morning, but regardless, her escape to France was officially over. She couldn't hide from her family's drama anymore. Thanks to Sam, she wouldn't be facing everyone alone.

Bella sagged back in her seat, sliding the shade closed over the small oval airplane window. She scrubbed her fists along her gritty eyes. She hadn't slept well, tossing and turning all night as she worried if she'd made the right choice in coming back to the States with Sam. A yawn stretched her face.

The bed behind the privacy door was inviting, but she feared sending the wrong message. Hell, she feared her own willpower weakening if she crawled onto a mattress with Sam anywhere near. She was better off making use of the additional sleeper chairs out here.

Was she cutting off her nose to spite her face, as he'd said?

No, damn it. She wasn't in any position for a new relationship. It wouldn't be fair to him or to her.

Caffeine, yeah, that was the ticket. She just needed more caffeine to jolt her awake and get her brain working again.

She unbuckled her lap belt, placed sleeping Muffin on the seat and strode forward to the small kitchen area where Sam had headed a few minutes earlier. "Anything with caffeine up here?"

Sam's back tensed at her words, his shoulders rising ever so slightly. He shoved his hands in his pants pockets and turned toward her. "Coffee, tea, soda, your choice. Let me know and I'll pour it for you. The steward is up with the pilot right now."

"I can serve myself." She sidled by him in the

narrow galley kitchen. Very narrow. The heat of his body permeated through her thin blouse, his chest grazing her breasts. "What are you having?"

"Just bottled water." He angled past and out of her way, even as his silvery-gray gaze stayed locked in tight on her.

Bella opened the stainless-steel mini-refrigerator and pulled out a Diet Coke from the rows of neatly arranged beverages, fresh fruits and cheeses inside. She considered fishing through the dark mahogany cabinets for a cup and ice, but her hands had started shaking right about the time his body had rubbed ever so enticingly against hers. She wrapped a napkin around the can and popped the top.

A bracing gulp later, she worked to establish some emotional distance again. "I appreciate your help with the Ridley issue, but I want to make sure you understand. No more interfering with my family like you did by calling Charlotte's husband."

"Wouldn't dream of it."

"You're lying."

He leaned against the bulkhead, his feet crossed in front of him. The sun glinted through the oval window highlighting hints of russet in his deep brown hair. "You sure are a charmer today, Bella." He smiled wide and wicked. "Why would you accuse me of something so devious?"

She wadded her napkin and tossed it at his chest. "Because you have a reputation for being ruthless when you want your way."

Beyond his success in the work world, she'd heard rumors he changed women with the season.

"I make no secret of being a driven, determined person." He cocked an eyebrow. "Of course that could mean you're reckless in climbing onto my airplane."

"Ha-ha. Not amused." She passed him his bottled water. "If we're going to give this 'friends' thing an honest go, then you need to be truthful with me."

Sam stiffened, only a hint and only for a second, but enough to make her wonder what he was covering up.

He reached for his drink, taking it with his left hand, rather than his right, which he kept stuffed in his pocket.

Like he was hiding something.

She thought back to when she'd come to the galley. He'd only been drinking water. What else could he have…

An awful, awful possibility—probability—flooded her mind. She'd seen the look and stance often enough when walking in on people at inopportune times at parties or raves.

Oh, my God. Sam was hiding more than she'd thought, something she never would have considered. "What were you doing here before I walked up?"

"Getting a drink of water, like I said." His face went totally blank.

His complete lack of expression spoke louder than anything else. He should have been at ease.

She planted her hands on her hips. "Like hell. I've

been around Hollywood types all my life. I've seen more than my share of alcohol and drug abuse." Disillusionment threatened to swamp her even as her anger topped the charts. "You're popping pills."

His jaw dropped open for a flash, then snapped shut. But he didn't deny it.

She stood her ground. She might be hurt, but she was also mad as hell and she wasn't backing down. "I may have to put up with that kind of behavior from those I work with, but I absolutely will not tolerate it in my private life."

His frozen face cleared and…he laughed. Not just a chuckle, but head-back, full-out laughter that muffled even the drone of the airplane engines. Was that what his drugs did for him? Separate him from reality so thoroughly he found this amusing?

Steam built inside her, fuming, filling her with anger and cynicism. That made her all the madder. She shouldn't care what kind of man he was. He should mean nothing to her.

But this disappointment on top of everything else was just too much. "Don't you *dare* mock me. I'm serious. Get out. Get out now."

He scratched his forehead. "I'm afraid I can't accommodate you there. We're in the air, in *my* plane."

She stomped her foot. "Damn it, you make me so mad sometimes."

His laughter faded, but his grin remained. "Good God, you're even hotter when you're fired up."

His eyes sparked with awareness, his gaze locking

on her face so long she suddenly felt self-conscious. "I'll just go back to my seat."

She started to turn and he caught her arm. The heat of his familiar touch seared through her lightweight sweater. He stared down at her with somber gray eyes. "I'm not popping illegal drugs."

He pulled his other hand out of his pocket, a pill bottle in palm.

She shoved his wrist away. "Prescription drugs, then. Abuse and addiction all the same. Go get high somewhere else."

He thrust his hand forward insistently. "Look at the label."

She frowned. "The label?"

"I'm taking allergy medicine."

Oh crap. She'd let her temper take control and screwed up. She owed him a whopper of an apology. "You have allergies?"

"I am a human being, last time I checked anyway." He held up the bottle and rattled the pills. "Humans get sick."

"What are you allergic to?" Unease prickled up her spine with an impending sense of doom as she crossed her fingers, hoping he wouldn't say what she feared.

He dropped the bottle of allergy meds back in his pocket and faced her straight on. "I'm allergic to dogs."

Ah hell.
His secret was out.

He'd done a decent job at hiding his allergy to her dog before, popping pills and trying to put distance between himself and the mutt. Their shopping jaunt in Paris—with Muffin staying back at the hotel—had given his sinuses a break. But the recycled air in the plane was really wreaking havoc with his allergies.

He hated weakness, any lack of control over his mind or his body. Ever since his mother had brought home a chocolate Lab puppy for his seventh birthday he'd known extended exposure to dogs made his sinuses go haywire.

Bella's hand floated to her chest, over her heart. "You took allergy pills so you could be with me?"

Her blue eyes glinted with a wonder that made him itchy. "Vanity dogs are a must for a large number of my clientele. So the hotel allows small pets."

True enough, but the passing contact wasn't enough to cause a problem. Still, she didn't know he'd put the call in to his doctor for the meds just so he could be near Bella—and Muffin.

Her look of wonder faded to irritation, her chest heaving with indignation. "Vanity pets? *Vanity* pets! Muffin is *not* a vanity pet."

"Well of course not," he said, unable to peel his eyes off the flush spreading along her milky skin. "That is not one of those purebred, froufrou animals."

Bella relaxed and started swiping a few stray dog hairs off her black jeans.

He couldn't resist needling her. "She's too damn ugly to be a vanity pet."

"Ugly?" she gasped, her hands fisting. "I cannot believe you just called my precious Muffin ugly."

The door leading to the cockpit creaked open.... Then closed again as the folks up front must have realized no one was in danger.

Damn, Bella was hot when she got all fired up, which led him to keep right on stoking the flames. "Good God, have you checked out your dog's Billy Idol snarl lately?"

"Shush!" She glanced back at the sleeping dog as if somehow the animal might understand his words. "She's a sweetie pie."

"I never said she wasn't—"

"Last time I checked—" she staked closer, jabbing a finger in his chest "—it's the inside that counts, not appearance. If I turned ugly tomorrow, would you stop being my friend?"

"We're friends?" That was a start.

"We *were*."

Were? Past tense? Not so fast, Bella. He advanced a step, pushing his chest against her poking pointer finger. "So you consider yourself beautiful."

She snatched her hand back and crossed her arms. "I don't consider myself vain. Understanding strengths and weaknesses is a part of the business."

Something niggled at him about her reasoning. "Am I to assume you believe you're only chosen for roles because of your looks?"

"I want to be taken seriously as an actress. That's why I fought so hard to get the lead in this film." Her fists unfurled and she studied her nails. "My brothers were always the brains in the family."

He thought of a thousand ways she'd shown her innate intelligence in the short time he'd known her—her knowledge of French architecture while they'd been shopping. Her quick wit. He could think of a number of other examples, but he suspected she would just brush those aside in embarrassment.

What a strange dichotomy she presented. One of America's hottest women was a mass of insecurities.

Since he couldn't tell her what he really wanted to—that she was so damn hot and smart he wanted to take her behind that curtain and tangle up with her on the bed until they landed in the States—he opted for, "I'm sorry for saying your dog is ugly."

Muffin perked up in the leather chair, her ears twitched. Damned if that mutt actually could understand humans.

The dog jumped to the ground and scampered to her owner. Bella scooped her up and snuggled her scruffy pet under her chin. "Muffin forgives you. But it may take *me* a little while longer."

"For what it's worth, I think Billy Idol is a badass." He winked, stroking a finger along Muffin's chin, then Bella's.

She froze.

Her chest rose and fell faster, her lips parting with each gusty breath. Memories of their night together flared to life in his mind until he could taste her, feel her even without touching. He was right to link up with her this way. They both deserved more of what they'd shared in his suite. He wouldn't let her be so foolish as to throw away a chance at enjoying the chemistry between them until it ran its course.

He stroked her cheek with his knuckles. When she didn't twitch away, he leaned toward her, already anticipating the explosion of sensation that would come just from sealing his mouth to hers—

The PA crackled to life. "Mr. Garrison," the pilot's voice called over the speaker, "we're heading into some turbulence. You will both need to buckle into your seats, please."

Bella blinked fast, clutched her dog closer and angled past him double-time without a word. Her silence and evasive eyes were all the more telling than any words of dismissal.

All talk of friendship and no sex be damned, she wanted him, too. Now he just needed to show some restraint until that desire grew so taut *she* came to *him*.

Bella stood on her front stoop with Sam as the sun hovered low on the horizon. While it was only suppertime in California, she was suffering from a serious case of jet lag. A car's motor sounded in the distance but continued around the drive toward Hudson Manor's twelve-car parking garage.

Sam pressed a hand to the door frame, stopping her from passing. "So this is your place."

She leaned against the railing, not as eager to leave as she would have expected. The whole allergy

pills incident still whirled around in her head. He
may not have taken the meds just for her, but he was
continuing to do so because of Muffin and that
tugged at her heart.

Beyond that, she was relieved to see his unmistakable disapproval of drugs. She'd witnessed firsthand
the ruin too much money could bring to people who
snorted their wealth up their noses. "I moved here to
the guesthouse a few years ago to live on my own.
Of course it's obvious I didn't move too far away
from my relatives."

She'd made her big independent stand by moving
across the lawn and redecorating the two-bedroom,
one-story cottage in a shabby chic, Bohemian style
totally at odds with the French Provincial formality
of Hudson Manor.

She'd needed to step out of her very large family's
shadow, find her own style and voice. Right after
moving in, she'd painted each room according to different moods. Blue ceilings to evoke the sky. Green-
painted hardwood floors with sea-grass mats to
ground her in the natural world. Her bedroom ceiling
was dotted with stars. She'd even used a constella-
tion map for accuracy but regretted that the night
sky was permanently set to October. She made a
home for herself rather than letting some decorator
stamp his own personality onto her life.

Security lights flickered on as the sun drifted
deeper into the horizon. Her childhood house loomed
in the distance, a fifty-five-room white stone and

wrought-iron mansion. Fifteen acres of sculpted landscape afforded plenty of privacy here.

Privacy with her whole big family all around. She eyed the lengthy garage in the distance and all the doors were closed. She tucked deeper onto the porch so a sprawling tree would block them from any curious eyes in the main house.

She stared up into Sam's mesmerizing gray eyes, allowing herself a moment to just sink into their appeal. "Thank you."

"For what?"

"For bringing me home, for the shopping trip in Paris, for clotheslining the reporter, for offering to come with me to the premiere, for taking allergy pills." She stared down, scuffing her red heels along the stone step. "For respecting my stance on no more sex."

"I respect your opinion, but make no mistake, that doesn't mean I agree."

She pressed a hand to his chest, his really hard and hot chest. "Hey, I mean it when I say I'm not going to invite you inside, not even for coffee."

"I'm a man who stands by his word." He picked up her hand and linked their fingers. "As much as I detest media attention, maybe if I feed the hungry press hounds for a few days they might get off my back."

Since she intended to be an actress for as long as the industry would hire her, her life would be full of media frenzy indefinitely. Sam had made his feelings about the press known. Sure she wanted privacy at times, but she also appreciated the hand they played in helping her promote her work.

That put her lifestyle in direct conflict to his. She didn't have to worry about him pressing for more. His short-term offer must be as genuine as it sounded.

Great news.

Right?

So why did it leave her wanting to squeeze his hand, yank him closer and steal up all the kisses she possibly could?

Her mouth dried and she forced herself not to moisten her lips. "Good luck with your new hotel."

A hotel nearby in Los Angeles. A hotel that could bring him back again in the future.... She stopped those thoughts short.

"Luck? Hard work makes luck more inevitable."

"I like that." She was actually finding she liked *him* and that was a dangerous thought to have while standing on her front stoop. Too easily this man could entice her to toss aside her intentions to keep him— any man—at arm's length until her life settled back down again. "I spend a lot of time with diva sorts, male and female, who barely carry their own bottled water, much less a suitcase."

Damn him for being so muscular and charming and enticing. What would it have been like to meet him before she'd made the mistake of falling for Ridley? Back during a time when she'd believed her parents had the perfect marriage and happily ever after was for real.

She would have invited Sam into her home, into her bed.

He leaned toward her as he'd done on the airplane. She'd wanted him then, wanted him even more now, a need made all the more painful because she knew just how good they could be together. Her body flamed in response, memories of champagne kisses still fresh in her mind. He angled closer—to open her door.

Sam placed her suitcase in the entryway and set Muffin's carrier alongside.

"Goodnight, Bella." He backed a step, waving once before turning toward the limousine. "I'll be in touch."

Touch. She shivered with want. It was going to be a long night.

Seven

Sam sprawled on the backstage studio sofa watching the television screen in the green room while Bella finished an interview on the *Tonight Show*. Muffin perched on her lap, wearing a plaid Christmas sweater. The mutt actually quietly behaved for the cameras as Bella encouraged viewers to rescue a pet from the pound for the holidays.

God, she looked hot in a frothy green dress, silver sequins belting it just below her breasts. Her hair flowed over her shoulders in a deliberate disarray that spoke of steamy, out-of-control sex.

He'd seen just that hair style on her—for real.

Sam shifted uncomfortably. He'd kept his distance up to now, restricting contact to phone calls. She didn't even know he was here at the Christmas Eve taping, but he figured this would be a great time to start rumors flying about the two of them before they showed up together at tomorrow's premiere.

A network intern refilled the water glass beside him. He nodded his thanks to the young woman, but kept his eyes firmly planted on the television screen.

Bella had spent the past two days doing interviews while he'd attended to business at his hotel. He'd given her space, easy enough to manage with their movie premiere date just around the corner. He'd seen the want in her eyes on her front stoop the night they'd arrived in the States. A couple of days to ponder that and let it grow could be a good thing.

Except that it had backfired by ramping up his desire for her as well.

Sam knocked back half his tonic water and studied the interview in progress. Framed by the TV screen, Bella smiled flirtatiously at the talk-show host, her hand fluttering to rest on his arm.

The talk-show host loosened his tie in a moment that made the audience laugh. Sam wasn't chuckling. The NFL quarterback sitting on her other side—having finished his interview—hadn't taken his damn eyes off her plunging neckline since he'd risen to hug her too tightly when she'd walked across the stage.

Sam bit back a curse. He understood the PR game. Bella wasn't Tiffany. And even if Bella's inviting smile and batting eyelashes were genuine she'd made it clear Sam had no claim to her.

The host leaned closer across his desk, L.A. skyline superimposed behind them. "What's the deal with you and your costar Ridley Sinclair? You two were a couple and now I hear there's another guy in the green room waiting for you."

Bella stroked her dog with undue attention as if stalling to gather her thoughts. "You've been checking out the green room?"

The camera shot shifted to a split screen image of her—and of him. Damn. He'd meant to surprise her, but not this way.

Making it all the more awkward, the camera angle had included a vase full of red roses interspersed with holly sprigs. The flowers were all over the back-stage area as part of the holiday decorations, but the audience didn't know that. It looked as if he'd brought the bouquet for Bella.

Not a bad idea, if he'd thought of it, but he had gift plans of his own for tomorrow. He shot a laid-back smile and wave to the camera, stifling an itch at the media attention.

To her credit, Bella recovered quickly. "Hi, Sam." She blew him a flirty little kiss. "Thanks for the flowers."

Muffin raised her head and yipped.

The host grinned and—thank God—the screen returned to the regular image of the stage. "Tell us more about this new man in your life, Sam Garrison. I understand he is the owner of a string of Garrison Grande hotels."

Bella stroked Muffin in a gesture Sam had come to recognize as self-soothing. "Sam owns the Garrison Grande Marseille near where we filmed parts of the movie and he has a new hotel here in L.A. We'd planned to spring the news at the premiere tomorrow—" her mouth tightened slightly "—but you've found us out."

"What about you and Ridley Sinclair?" the host pressed.

"Ridley and I—" she waved a dismissive hand and laughed lightly "—went out a few times while making the movie, nothing more. I'm afraid the PR people may have gone a little overboard with all those joint publicity shots and, so, that's how rumors start. What can I say? It played well for the film."

"Ah, could you have been leading us on all the time with the Ridley rumors in order to hide your other relationship in the works?"

She batted her eyelashes. "Now would I mislead the press like that?"

The audience rumbled with laughter.

Damn, she was good at maneuvering people into believing her time with Ridley was nothing more than a couple of shared hamburgers. Yet, she'd never once lied in any of her answers to the talk-show host.

The interview was wrapping up and soon enough he would see Bella, another brief brush to remind her of the chemistry they shared simply by standing in the same room. She probably had Christmas Eve plans anyway and he wasn't much for holidays. His mother had ventured out to spend a week with her

South Beach relatives, and he had work to clear away if he intended to devote all of tomorrow to Bella's premiere and post gala.

The green room door opened and Sam rose to his feet, a surge of excitement just over seeing Bella knocking him a little off guard.

Except it wasn't Bella. Rather, an older man walked in, slickly dressed, wearing an ostentatious ascot. The guy looked vaguely familiar, but Sam couldn't quite place him.

Medium height, dark hair, probably around fifty, and he had a Hollywood smile. This fella was definitely a part of the industry.

The man made a beeline for the intern with a clipboard. "Hello, lovely lady, I hope you can help me."

The assistant giggled, sidling closer. "Yes, sir? What can I do for you?"

"I'm here to check up on the star of my film— Bella Hudson."

"Your film?" Her eyes went star-struck wide.

"I'm the director of *Honor*." He thrust out his hand. "I'm David Hudson."

Anger pumped through Sam at the man who'd betrayed and dishonored his family. A man who'd knocked a spirited woman like Bella off-kilter. Something Sam intended to make sure it didn't happen again tonight.

Bella secured her hold on Muffin's short leash and rushed down the busy hall toward the green room.

She tucked sideways past a line of pet trainers waiting their turn for an interview. Muffin growled at the snake handler with his mammoth reptile curled in a cage.

Ewww.

Skin crawling, she focused her eyes forward, past signed and framed photos of prior guests with the host, toward the door at the end of the hall. Where Sam waited for *her*. How sweet that he'd showed up in support. They'd spoken on the phone since returning to the States, but hadn't planned to see each other until the Christmas premiere.

Her stomach fluttered, catching her unaware. Viewing him on that studio screen shouldn't affect her this much. Yet still she doubled-timed down the corridor.

Pausing outside the door, she fluffed her hair with her nails, checked the string straps of her seafoam dress, and smoothed the flirty hem down to where it stopped just above her knees. Muffin danced around her legs in protest over having the leash tugged.

Bella glanced down. "Sorry, precious."

Damn. How many times had she asserted to Sam that looks didn't matter? She forced her arms back to her sides, shaking out her hands to release nerves.

Deep breath. She strode slowly through the door as if in no hurry at all, Muffin trotting alongside. A girl with a clipboard stood by the refreshments cart, jotting notes beside the empty sofa where Sam had been sitting. Bella twirled, looked around, but the room was otherwise vacant.

She walked over to the young intern taking stock of the coffee supply. "Excuse me?"

The intern spun to face her, pageboy haircut swishing in her enthusiasm. "Yes, Ms. Hudson. Can I help you with something?"

Bella waved toward the sofa where the video screen had showed Sam earlier. "What happened to the man who was waiting back here?"

"Which one?" She clutched the clipboard to her chest. "The younger hunk or the older charmer?"

"The young hunk, without question," she answered, surprised at the hint of territorialism that crept into her voice.

"He left with the older gentleman."

"Oh." Disappointment stabbed. Had he met up with a friend? Or brought along a business acquaintance, merely stopping in for her PR on his way to something else? He'd made it clear more than once that his work came first. She couldn't resist asking, "Any idea who was with him?"

The star-struck intern's eyes gleamed with excitement. "I sure do. Mr. Garrison was with the director of your movie."

Ah crap. She grabbed the edge of the sofa to bolster her suddenly wobbly knees.

Uncle David. Not her uncle. Her real father. Had come here. No. No. No.

Her heart thudded hard in her chest, darn near thumping to her stomach. She accepted she would have to face him at the premiere, but that should be hectic enough for her to be able to stay away from him. She wasn't ready for a face-to-face, especially a surprise meeting. Not yet. Maybe never.

What if she'd seen him, now, unprepared? Her throat tightened. Had he come simply because of the movie? Of course he had. He didn't care about her any more than he cared about his other two children. The bastard.

And Sam had left with him.

Why?

Her mind churned. Sam knew how she felt about her biological father. He could only have lured David away to spare her the stress of an unexpected visit. It was thoughtful, and yes, even helpful, but... She couldn't help but think how he'd interfered again, much as he'd done with Charlotte.

God, he confused her, thoughtful but pushy.

And he took allergy pills to be near Muffin.

Bella flopped on the sofa beside the vase of roses speckled with holly. Disappointment over not seeing Sam pinched harder than her silver Ferragamo heels.

Harder than she would have expected given she'd known the man less than a week.

She was a total mess, in no way ready to deal with complicated relationships. And she doubted her mind would be any more settled by the time she saw Sam at the Christmas premiere.

Bella couldn't imagine a Christmas more exciting—and tumultuous—than this one.

Sitting in her unabashedly frilly bedroom retreat with a hairdresser working behind her and a friend beside her gabbing away, Bella glanced at the clock. Forty-five minutes until she would leave for the opening of *Honor*.

Forty-five minutes until she would see Sam.

She hadn't even been able to speak with him after her Christmas Eve interview when he'd left with David. As much as she feared her out-of-control emotions around Sam, curiosity was eating her alive.

Along with irritation.

Bella fidgeted on the pink-paisley vanity chair as the hairstylist pinned loops of hair in place. She'd expected Sam to be more ardent in pursuing her. Maybe he'd really meant what he said about this merely being a convenient arrangement.

Damn it, she hated sitting still because it gave her too much time to think. She preferred to be moving, busy, active.

Tough to do when having her hair yanked. At least she didn't have to hang out alone. Her brother Max's fiancée Dana kept her company while Muffin snoozed in her puppy bed—a small white wrought-iron model that matched Bella's larger version across the room. The stylist worked his magic while Dana rambled on about family gossip. Dana was the one to comfort her when the news about David and her mother Sabrina's affair came out.

Dana was there for her now, already dressed for the big event in a sleek bronze dress with yellow diamond accent jewelry that complimented her olive skin and luminous dark brown eyes. Uber-efficient Dana wouldn't be a mental mess over some guy. Dana glided around the room straightening covers, tossing a discarded nightie in the hamper, straightening a stack of scripts for future projects her agent had messengered over for Bella's consideration.

The male hairstylist from Hudson Studios tapped Bella's shoulders. "Sit up straight, please."

Perched on a vanity chair in only a camisole and tap pants, she forced herself not to slump while her red hair was twisted into at least a gazillion swirls.

She cut her eyes toward Dana since she wasn't allowed to move her cramping muscles. "Thanks for hanging out with me. I would have died of boredom without you. I'm sure there are things you would rather do with your Christmas than babysit me."

Dana dropped into a floral, ruffle skirted armchair. "You're family. And besides—" she grazed her fingers over the yellow teardrop diamond resting in the V of her low-cut gown "—what woman doesn't like to be draped in a mint's worth of jewels? It's not every day I have the excuse to wear this kind of bling."

"You're a gem yourself. My brother's a lucky man." She resisted the urge to chew off her peachy lipstick. "It's kinda sad that it takes a movie premiere to bring the rest of our family together for the holidays. If nothing else, everyone should be here for Grandmere."

Even if that meant she had to put up with the

debacle between her parents and David. Would there be some kind of blowup with the three of them in one place? It sucked to think the best she could hope for was painfully thick tension. She couldn't ignore her gratitude that Sam had saved her that tension the night before.

Dana grimaced. "Umm, I guess you haven't heard via the Hudson grapevine, but while you were in France, Dev and Valerie separated."

"What?" Her oldest brother had split up with his wife? "Already? I had my doubts about them, but still, they only eloped a few months ago."

"I realize he's your brother, but you have to know he never treated Valerie very well. Maybe this will make him wake up before he loses her altogether," Dana said logically, pointing out a missed thread of hair to the stylist.

How could she keep a cool head about things like this?

Bella held still in spite of the yanking tugs on her hair. At least they didn't have to worry about the stylist spouting gossip, not if he wanted to keep his high-profile job with the studio.

Of course so far it wasn't as if she and Dana were revealing state secrets. "I'm not holding my breath on Dev scrounging up an empathy gene."

Dana crossed her legs, gold strappy high heel dangling off her toe. "What's the scoop with you and this hotel mogul?"

"It's nothing serious." Which was exactly what

she'd asked for, yet she couldn't help feeling miffed at his no-show lack of attention.

"He came all the way from France to Beverly Hills just to 'hang out' with you."

"He has business here." And he'd protected her from David. Yet hadn't so much as met her for coffee. Although that hadn't stopped her from having her driver detour by Sam's new hotel to scope out the project he had in the works—a mighty high-end impressive project.

"Business? Uh-huh. Whatever."

She wasn't sure if she wanted Dana to be right or not. "I appreciate your optimism, but I'm fairly certain long-term romance just isn't in the cards for me anytime soon." *If ever.* "Think about it. Dev broke up with his brand-new wife. My parents aren't speaking to each other. We don't even need to go into how crummy Uncle David's marriage was before Aunt Ava died. I don't mean to be a wet blanket, but how are you not shaking in your shoes over becoming a Hudson?"

Dana leaned forward. "Max and I are happy. So are Luc and Gwen." Bella's brothers, Markus's biological sons along with Dev. "And what about Charlotte and Alec? Even Jack and CeCe beat the odds and got back together again."

Jack and Charlotte—Bella's new half siblings. Good Lord, her family tree had more branches than a national savings and loan—and about as much stability.

The hairstylist held up an industrial-size bottle of hairspray. "Close your eyes, Ms. Hudson."

Bella squeezed her eyes closed as the mist of organic hair product swirled around her. "Face it, Dana. There's still plenty of time left to screw it up."

Dana sneezed. "Thanks. Keep that up and next time I'm going to sneeze on your dress."

Half a bottle later, the hairstylist put away his spritzer bottle and started packing his supplies. Bella peeked through one eye and stood. Turning her head from side to side in front of the mirror, she checked out the Grecian-inspired updo.

Dana slipped the specially crafted gown from the hanger and held it for Bella. "Okay, sweetie, time's a-wasting."

Bella turned from the mirror and stepped into the dress. She pulled the cool fabric up her body, then shimmied out of her camisole, flicking it free.

Dana zipped the dress up the back slowly. "Spin around and let us see."

The ivory velvet strapless with a beaded top—a Marchesa creation just for her—draped her curves to pool at her feet in a style somewhat reminiscent of her dash with a sheet down a hotel corridor back in France.

Except this time she had a full face of makeup and upswept hair. She wore her grandmother's diamond necklace in spite of the offers from major jewelers to display their wares. Bella placed her hand over the necklace, her rapid heartbeat thudding under her touch.

Nerves tap-danced in her stomach over how *Honor* would be received. Over her combustible family gathered in one place. Over seeing Sam when he kept her constantly off-balance. The evening could shatter into a debacle so easily.

Dana clapped her hands. "Well, sweetie, it's time to go."

Sam couldn't take his eyes off Bella.

In fact, hadn't been able to look away since he first saw her when he'd picked her up and still couldn't now that the limo was pulling up outside the theater. Her grandmother's 1940s Bentley, just ahead of them, inched to a stop by the red-carpet walkway.

Not that he'd been able to talk to Bella or, more important, touch her since her brother Max and his fiancée Dana rode with them, relegating everything to small talk. Of course their presence also helped him stay the course in keeping enough distance from her so Bella would come to him on her own.

The limo inched toward the red carpet spread from the edge of the curb all the way into the sprawling steps leading into the historic theater. He kept his arm along the back of the seat only allowing his fingers to lightly brush her neck, about all the temptation his libido could stand. Bella presented a mix of pristine untouchable beauty in that ivory creation, yet the strapless top of the dress tempted him with the creamy curves of her shoulders and generous breasts.

He could envision her wearing that diamond necklace and nothing else.

Patience.

Camera flashes clicked at strobelike speed outside

the limo's tinted windows. Security guards had the street blocked to outside traffic, cordoning off the area for the slow parade of vehicles toward the theater. People dressed to see and be seen strode up the red carpet, posing for photos, stopping for the occasional impromptu interview with entertainment reporters.

Fans packed either side behind the gold ropes lining the path. Bodyguards in tuxedos did more to keep the fans in check than any decorative cord.

Just ahead, the Bentley's chauffeur opened a door. Family matriarch Lillian Hudson stepped from the limousine, aided by both her sons. Markus and David wore traditional tuxedos and composed faces. No one would guess they were at each other's throats because David's long ago affair with Markus's wife Sabrina had been explosively revealed.

The brothers were putting on a good show at civility for their mother. This was almost certainly her last Hudson Studios movie premiere.

Lillian Hudson walked up the red carpet, her steps even if slow, a son remaining on either side. Sam could see subtle signs they were supporting her. But from what little he'd heard about the woman, he was certain she wouldn't even consider using a walker or wheelchair at this particular event.

A strong lady, no question. With her auburn hair, Sam could see flashes of Bella in this woman. However, apparently even Lillian's strength couldn't beat the breast cancer.

Was the hair a wig due to her treatments? If so, it

was a damn good one. She hid her illness well. Somehow, she made the sedate pace seem regal rather than frail in her deep blue gown and sapphires.

A true timeless beauty and star.

Bella's head was turned toward the window, her eyes sparkling, as were her future sister-in-law's. Even her brother seated across from them cleared his throat.

Sam squeezed Bella's shoulder. "Come on. No crying. You beautiful ladies will wreck your makeup."

Bella pulled a wobbly smile, leaning into his touch. "You're right. It's just emotional seeing her tonight."

She needed him. A surge of protectiveness shot through him.

He started to answer her but the opening door cut him short. "Your fans await."

She held his gaze for a second, confusion whispering through her eyes. Her hand fell to his thigh. "Thank you."

Without another word, she turned away, stepped out and waved. His leg damn near on fire from her simple quick caress, Sam followed, palming the small of her back. The flashbulbs clicked as fast as ticker tape, blinding him. As much as he enjoyed touching Bella, he hated dog-and-pony shows, but he would put on a good face for her. She deserved her moment.

Then the reporters' questions started in a flurry of shouts.

"Miss Hudson, tell us more about this new man with you."

"How did you meet?"

"What happened to Ridley Sinclair?"

"Did you break Ridley's heart?"

A host from a major network talk show—someone who could stand on the red carpet side of those golden ropes—rushed forward with her microphone. Bella squeezed Sam's arm in a signal to stop.

The reporter screeched to a halt, her plastic surgery all too evident up close, with eyebrows millimeters away from her hairline. "Look who we have here, the leading actress of *Honor*, Bella Hudson. Good evening, Bella. You look marvelous darling. Tell us about your dress and jewelry."

Bella posed for the camera, showing off a side angle of her gown while a camera swooped an extra spotlight on her. "I'm wearing a Marchesa original." Her hand swept up to her neck and her ears. "But the diamonds are totally Hudson, gifts from my lovely grandmother who this film honors tonight."

The reporter leaned closer, winking at her camera lens before turning to Bella. "Our viewers are dying to know if it's true that you and Ridley Sinclair are no longer an item."

Bella tucked nearer to his side. "Sam Garrison is an important part of my life."

"Garrison? Oh! One of American's most eligible billionaire bachelors." The reporter's eyebrows disappeared into her brunette coif. "Who called it quits between you and your leading man in *Honor*?"

Sam angled toward the mic. "I have to confess to

being the bad guy here. My apologies to Mr. Sinclair, but once I saw Bella, I knew I had to have her."

Bella smiled up at him in gratitude that the reporter must have mistaken for adoration since she sighed and dramatically fanned her face. "Oh, my, the steam factor is hot here tonight, ladies and gentlemen."

Sam cupped Bella's shoulder. "We should move on. We wouldn't want to hold up the show."

He ushered her through two more interviews, and couldn't help but admire her ease with the whole chaotic mess. He wanted to get his show on the road and park themselves in the theater.

A group of females screamed to his left. He jolted, ready to body block any threat from out of control fans…. Only to see the female attention was directed firmly behind them.

Ridley—the rat and moron who'd let Bella slip away—stepped out of the limousine with a *Sports Illustrated* swimsuit model on his arm. A moody lock of hair stayed perfectly styled over one eye.

Bella stiffened, her smile brittle.

Sam brushed his mouth over her ear. "I hear that anorexic airhead's vanity dog has a boring smile."

Bella relaxed against him, tipped her head back and laughed. The reporters turned their frenzy back onto her. Cameras clicked away, the flashes firmly on the two of them while Ridley helped his date untangle her heel from the hem of her skimpy Band-Aid dress.

The sound of Bella's happiness beat the hell out of all the bells he'd ever heard from the French churches. She sang through his veins more and more. Patience was paying off, but he wasn't done playing his hand. Time to make his big move toward getting the press talking and winning Bella's favor.

He escorted her past the last of the outdoor media into the crush of servers and early arrivers inside the lobby, decorated evergreen trees towering up into the cathedral ceiling. Twinkling lights and gilded angels graced the fragrant boughs. Red roses and poinsettias filled massive urns. Garland looped the gold rails leading into the historic theater.

And a fresh batch of reporters waited. Sam might hate the profession on principle, but he wasn't against using them to his advantage for Bella.

He paused at the top of the lengthy staircase, skimmed the corner of her mouth. "Merry Christmas, Bella."

He slid a black-velvet jewelry box into her hand, the sort that contained bracelets. A photographer elbowed a supporting actor out of the way to thrust her telephoto lens closer. Little did any of them know what was *really* inside.

Sam ducked his head closer to hers again. "You may not want the press to see what's actually in here."

Her eyes went wide, her pupils dilating with excitement. Tucking the box close to her chest, Bella untied the bow, creaked open the box and found...

He'd given her a small designer dog collar. Pink. With an engraved tag that read Muffin.

Smiling, she tipped her face up to thank him and

Sam sealed his mouth to hers. Nothing long or drawn out, but unmistakably romantic for the cameras.

Enough to make the press spread the news—and knock him on his ass.

Bella blinked up at him wide-eyed, a little confused. The single kiss had rocked him more than he'd expected. His hands-off policy the past few days had messed with his restraint. He'd scripted the kiss but sure as hell hadn't planned on how much it would floor him.

Sam slid his hand to the small of her back, gently urging her back into the moment. "Let's go see a movie."

He'd come here for her. Now he had to figure out how to stay around after the premiere so he could see what surprises their next kiss might have in store.

Eight

Bella settled into her seat in the historic theater, balconies overhead packed in the sellout premiere. She should be taking note of everything around her, cementing this breakout moment in her memory. Yet she could only think of Sam beside her, his thoughtful gift in her beaded ivory handbag.

His kiss still lingered on her lips.

While Sam asserted that looks didn't matter, his strong presence certainly appealed to her on an elemental level—tall and striking in his traditional tuxedo and clean-shaven face. Surprisingly, he'd been patient with the reporters even though she knew that sort of media fanfare must be driving him nuts. Yet, he'd put up with it smoothly for her.

The biggest surprise of all, though? Seeing Ridley. She'd been so nervous about crossing paths with him, of the stab of pain and betrayal she expected his presence to bring and...*nothing*. Ridley actually looked small and rather foolish in his bolo tie up next to Sam who didn't need props to carry a room with his charisma.

She leaned toward Sam and whispered, "Thank you for my lovely gift."

"You're welcome." His aftershave teased her senses. "Merry Christmas."

"I have something for you, too." The day they'd gone shopping in Paris she'd bought him a little brass antique bell to remember her by.

"Is it what I really want?" he asked, his intent clear from the wicked glint in his eyes.

Her breasts tightened with awareness, anticipation. *Undiluted want.* "I don't believe what you're referring to would fit under a tree."

"I work out. I'm very limber."

She laughed, drawing eyes toward them. She lowered her voice again so it wouldn't be heard over the WWII tunes piped in from the sound system. "Why didn't you wait for me after the *Tonight Show* interview?"

She'd been dying to ask him ever since they'd met at her place to rendezvous with the limo, but Dana and Max had been there, prohibiting her from delving into any conversation about David.

"I ran into a business acquaintance and we had to

leave." He tugged a lone lock of hair along the back of her neck. "You look incredible tonight."

"Don't try and sidetrack me." She knew full well how easily he could distract her mindless through just a touch. "I know you ran into David. Why did you make him leave?"

He stroked the back of her neck, along her vertebra sending delicious shivers down her spine. "I hope you're not going to bite my head off here like you did over the Charlotte incident. It won't go well with the image we're working to portray."

Trust was tough, but she couldn't miss how he'd had her feelings in mind, how he'd cared enough to try and shield her. "Actually, I want to say thank you. I really would rather not talk to him at all anytime soon." *If ever.*

"You're welcome."

His somber gray gaze held her still. He simply stared at her as if no one else in this overflowing theater existed. Memories of his sensually intuitive touch in France flooded her senses, tempting her to throw caution out the window and dive headfirst into an affair with Sam. The heat of his gaze shut out the rest of the world, her attention dipping to his mouth as she wondered how his kiss would taste.

Why not indulge? At the moment, she couldn't seem to come up with a single argument against giving in to the demands of her desire.

The lights dimmed, forcing her to divert her attention forward to the movie screen. She'd seen the rough cut of the film and of course knew every scene by heart. Still there was something magical about watching a movie—one including her—play out officially.

Sam's hand slid over hers. For appearances or support? She linked her fingers with his, the rough texture of his callused grip sending a fresh wash of tingles over her.

Sam's thumb stroking the sensitive inside of her wrist, Bella watched her grandparents' love story unfold, starting with how her grandfather had worked in Marseille. A U.S. soldier, he'd been part of a spy cell for the Allied Forces. The screen scanned a panoramic view of the small sea port—the very one near Sam's hotel. In fact she'd enjoyed that view during supper the night they'd made love.

The present and past merged in her mind as a young Charles Hudson met and was captivated by Lillian Colbert, a spirited young cabaret singer in a nightclub. Their romance traveled a rocky path as Charles suspected the sad-eyed beauty could be a collaborator with the occupying German army.

Bella gripped Sam's hand, the turmoil of her grandmother's life surging through her much as the musical score swelled throughout the theater. Bella had said those words that Lillian had lived, linking them even beyond the appearance and blood they shared.

She could feel the agony of her grandmother's grief when Charles was injured and on the run. Lillian rescued him and hid him, first in her tiny apartment above the club, then forced to take refuge at a friend's country estate. Bella's heart pounded with exhaustion, fear, exhilaration as she relived the chase scene when Lillian and Charles made their getaway.

Her fingers went numb and she realized she'd been squeezing Sam's hand so hard she'd cut off circulation. She pressed her palm to her fluttering stomach, even knowing what came next, cheering inside when Charles discovered that Lillian was actually working for the French Resistance. The risks and bravery of her grandparents blew Bella away all over again. Under constant threat of discovery, Charles and Lillian teamed up to further the Resistance's cause, secretly marrying.

The scene blended to their wedding night— passionate, explosive and apparently a part of the movie Sam was not enjoying. His jaw visibly clenched as Ridley/Charles kissed down her neck, tugging the simple string at the top of her peasant blouse. The scene wasn't overly graphic, shot mostly in close-ups of their faces or a far away silhouette with their bodies under the covers. The window behind them gusted loose curtains around them, the wind increasing with the rise of their passion, ending with close-ups of their hands clenched together over her head, tighter, then slowly unfurling.

Had Sam actually growled?

She couldn't deny a hint of excitement even as she wanted to roll her eyes. She leaned toward him, her mouth to his ear. "I wore a body stocking under the covers for that scene."

"I didn't ask," he said tight and low.

"I wanted you to know."

He grunted.

"Ridley wore tighty whities."

A smile ticked the corner of Sam's mouth before she settled back into her seat and returned her attention to the movie alive with the liberation of France.

Charles had to leave his new bride behind and return to the fight in Germany, but during their tearful farewell he promised to return at the end of the war. Battle weary, he kept his promise and reclaimed his waiting wife. Bella watched the camera pull out on a panorama of her grandparents passionately kissing, profiled against the Marseille shore.

And to Bella, those two people on the screen *were* her grandparents.

The audience exploded with applause and cheers, a standing ovation rippling to life. As words scrolled across detailing Charles and Lillian's life together in the United States, Bella's mind swirled with memories of sitting on her grandfather's knee while he humbly told the stories behind his many medals. She missed him, could almost smell his cigar smoke. They all could have used his calm logic right now to set their family back on track.

Although she knew she couldn't possibly miss him nearly as much as her grandmother did. Their love had been special. Rare.

With the triumph of a beautiful romance surging inside her heart, would Bella now know when it came to her life? She couldn't settle for an affair. She was an all-or-nothing person.

Sam downed his club soda during the after party bash hosted at the Hudson family estate on Loma Vista Drive in Beverly Hills. It was mind boggling how many people chose to spend their Christmas night at the Hudson home, but then Hollywood was all about being seen in the right places.

He'd had enough of their schmoozing for an entire decade.

In particular he'd had enough of watching slimy wheeler-dealers in the industry put their paws all over Bella. Not that she seemed to do anything to stop them. She smiled and flirted and damn near drove him over the brink as live band music grated in his ears.

Uniformed waiters wove through the crowded living room with canapés and champagne. Having overseen the decor for five Garrison hotels, he studied Bella's childhood mansion as he stood in the formal living room. The interior was very French Provincial, but not overtly stuffy, with antiques he would wage money had come from around the world. Marble floors stretched throughout a grand foyer with a mammoth evergreen nestled between double-wide staircases, pastel lights glittering along the branches. Hand painted wallpapers and fifteen-foot ceilings all made for a classically grand mansion.

"Sit down."

His head whipped around to find Lillian Hudson tucked in a wingback chair by the garland-strewn fireplace. "Pardon?"

She rested a thin hand on his arm, her veins showing through near translucent skin. "Sit down, young man, before you start a brawl."

Sam eased into the wingback beside her, releasing the button on his tuxedo jacket. "My mother raised me better than that, ma'am."

"I'm glad to hear it, but even my Charles lost some of his silver-spoon ways after seeing one of my smoky on-screen kisses." She waved her hand, only a slight shake betraying her health crisis. "All of this is just for show. Bella's a good girl."

He really didn't want to talk about Bella's sex life with her grandmother. "Yes, ma'am. I understand that."

His eyes lingered on Bella still in her off-white dress from the premiere. Men pressed drinks into her hand that he noticed she stashed on the mantel behind her.

Seeing her on the big screen had impressed the hell out of him. He'd heard of her growing reputation in indy films so he'd expected a decent performance. He hadn't been prepared for her to blow him away. He admired her talent, although he would be hard-pressed to get that love scene out of his head.

Without question, *Honor* would catapult her to the next level in her career.

"She's having a difficult time right now." Lillian leaned on the arm of the chair, angling closer, her blue eyes still bright and alert. "Her mother and father are just pretending to be polite tonight for my sake, but I know they're still separated."

"She has told me about what happened with her parents." He gently skirted the issue of the affair that produced Bella.

"Really? That's surprising." Her gaze darted to her wayward younger son David who smartly kept a full room's distance between himself and the rest of his family. "I'm ashamed of what David did. I'm afraid I spoiled him with my pampering. I should have treated him as I did my oldest."

The insight was interesting, but he'd watched his mother blame herself for another man's actions for too long to let Lillian go to her grave with that weighing on her heart. "Ma'am, if you'll pardon me for a moment, I believe adults are responsible for their own actions. No blaming others for their own mistakes."

A slow smile spread over her face with a charming allure that broadcast well what a heartbreaker she must have been in her day. "I like you, young man."

He patted her hand gently. "The feeling is mutual, ma'am."

A light scowl puckered her forehead. "Be good to Bella or I will haunt you from the grave."

Crap. What did a guy say to something like that? He wasn't used to being caught off guard. In fact, never was. "Umm, ma'am—"

"Loosen up, young man." She patted his face. "I'm making a joke." Her hand fell away limply, her spark giving way to exhaustion in a flash. She reached to her other side to an older woman in a simple black dress. "Hannah? I am ready to retire."

Sam helped Lillian to her feet and offered his arm until she was safely away from the jostling crowd.

He pivoted back around, searching the crush for Bella. All he had to do was look for the largest pack of men, since they seemed drawn to her like magnets to metal. He retrieved his drink and watched, reminding himself that he would be the one finishing out the night with her.

And he intended to make damn sure her dreams included *him*.

Her hand tucked in the crook of Sam's arm, Bella strolled leisurely across the Hudson Manor lawn toward her home in the guesthouse. Her filmy gold wrap trailed behind her in the gentle evening breeze on a standard sixty-degree December evening. Champagne and success left her slightly tipsy, even if she had fed plenty of bubbly to unsuspecting potted ferns.

A looming angel fountain spewed water backlit with Christmas red. White lights swayed along branches of trees lining her path past the tennis courts back to her place.

She couldn't have dreamed up a more perfect setting—or a more intriguing man.

Bella tipped her face up to Sam, her heels sinking in the soft earth. "Thank you for sharing your Christmas with me."

"I'm here to serve."

She looked away, staring at the ground to keep from tripping over roots. "I appreciate how you handled the publicity about Ridley. Even my family bought our act." She glanced up again. "Maybe you should be nominated for an Academy Award."

He palmed her back, steering her around a wrought-iron bench. "I'm not acting when I say how much I want you."

"I thought we agreed no sex talk." Her beaded bag dangled from her arm, her gift for Sam inside.

"No—" he smiled "—you said there wouldn't be sex. You never specified anything about talk of sex."

She didn't want to wade into those waters, not tonight when surely it would lead them into an argument—or lure her into a temptation she wasn't sure she could resist. Hadn't she realized tonight that she couldn't tread into this awkward terrain with him? In spite of her behavior earlier this week, she wasn't a fling sort of girl.

Bella sprinted forward and turned to face him, walking backward. "Tell me about your family."

"That was a fairly transparent attempt to change the subject." He stayed step to step with her in a near dance move.

"As long as you get the message." She tugged his bow tie. "Isn't your family missing you over the holidays?"

"I'm an adult. As for immediate family, there's only my mother. She never had another child, so I don't have any siblings, just lots of cousins. Mom ventures out of her island hideaway to spend most holidays with them in South Beach. They all have kids and she enjoys being with children at Christmas."

"She must be expecting some grandchildren from you." Had she really blurted that? She stumbled to a stop at the base of the three steps leading up to her cottage.

"That's none of my business. Forget I said it." Flustered at her blunder, she rested her hands on his chest without thinking. "Thank you again for coming with me tonight."

His eyes went from guarded to predatory in a spine-tingling flash as sure as the stars overhead.

"My pleasure." He leaned toward her, his mouth hovering just over hers, the heat of his breath teasing her with a phantom touch. "If I had my way, I would pleasure you even more tonight. If we *were* still having sex, I would take you back to the limousine. I would tell the chauffeur to drive until I say otherwise. Then I would close the privacy window."

Her very vivid artistic imagination flourished to life with possibilities for playing out a sexy fantasy she'd never tried before. She started to tell him to stop, but what harm could come from words?

"All night long I've been thinking about taking your hair down." He tugged the lone loose curl, his knuckles grazing between her shoulder blades. "Of how it would feel tumbling down into my hands."

She struggled to keep her eyes from fluttering

closed. "All the hairspray could wreak havoc on your allergies."

He laughed low. "I'm willing to risk it." His hands skimmed her arms to cup her waist. "The zipper along your back has driven me crazy all evening long. If I tugged it down, would you be wearing a bra or are you totally bare for me?"

Her breath hitched somewhere around her ribcage. She should make up a tale of boring underwear and save herself the extra ache when she sent him away tonight. But the truth fell out on a breathless, "The bra is built into the dress."

He growled. "Since we're not having sex, I have to guess you are only wearing panties."

She nodded weakly. "Tap pants, actually."

"Satin?"

She nodded again.

"Creamy colored like the dress. Like your skin. I still remember the silky feel of it under my mouth, sheened with champagne. I couldn't even drink the stuff tonight for fear it would send me out of control from wanting you." His lips grazed hers, just barely, but more than enough to ignite her flames through her veins. "God, you look amazing. Every man in the room was thinking what a lucky guy I am."

His words swirled through her already champagne-woozy mind and lowered defenses. She clenched his lapels, stretching up, craving a full-out kiss.

He slid away at the very last second, his hot breath caressing her neck. "If we were having sex, I would skim away your tap pants so we could celebrate in the best way. Don't you agree?"

She swayed toward him, entranced. Aching. He kept his mouth poised just below her ear, so near her eyes drifted closed as her body already anticipated a nip along her earlobe, warm kisses down the sensitive curve of her neck down to her shoulder. Her head fell back limply at merely the possibility.

Damn it.

She straightened upright again. What was she doing? Only a few hours ago she'd sat in the theater determined to follow an all-or-nothing approach to any future relationships. Yet here she already stood wanting more than anything to say to hell with it all and spend the night naked with Sam, celebrating the premiere the old-fashioned way.

He tapped her lips. "No need to answer. Because according to you we're not sleeping together, something that won't change unless you tell me otherwise."

She wanted to say yes, her body positively on fire for his touch, but the hope from the end of *Honor* still prodded her to want more, reminding her that trust and forever were rare gifts in a world full of lies and broken relationships.

She couldn't miss the competitive gleam in his eyes, an emotion that would muddy the waters of any possible relationship because she wouldn't be sure of his motives.

Did he want her?

Or merely want to win?

Her indecision must have shown because he eased away, scrubbing a hand over his jaw. "All right then." Sam backed down the steps. "Merry Christmas, Bella."

He pivoted back toward the line of limos along the driveway. She gripped the railing to keep from bolting after him. Her purse thudded to the porch, jingling a reminder that she had forgotten to give him the Christmas bell.

As she watched Sam climb into the limousine, she wasn't sure if she'd just made a stand—or thrown away a once-in-a-lifetime chance.

Nine

Four weeks later, Bella flopped backward on her wrought-iron bed, the train on her burgundy Vera Wang gown swooshing around her. She should be turning cartwheels tonight after winning the Screen Actors Guild's Best Actress Award. *Honor* also picked up Best Picture and Best Director, a real coup for a breakout surprise hit.

Accepting that trophy had been amazing, and the after party advantageous as she schmoozed with Hollywood bigwigs until the wee hours with Sam standing by her. During the party—in fact over the past month—he had been the perfect escort and a total gentleman, honoring her request for no sex.

Damn.

That man was driving her absolutely batty.

Bella rolled to her side, staring out the window as the first morning rays shot golden streaks across the sky. Besides escorting her to both the Golden Globe and Screen Actors Guild Awards, he'd taken her out to elaborate dinners and society functions to feed publicity as *Honor* continued to dominate the theaters and the news.

He'd also surprised her with a lighthearted day of fun at Disneyland, followed by a stop at a local animal shelter to drop off a monster-big donation check. Most touching, he'd patiently joined her for quiet dinners with Lillian in her grandmother's chambers as the end stages of her cancer confined her.

Afterward, Sam would walk her across the lawn and drop her off at her door with a peck on top of her head like she was a flipping kid. Just as he'd done again tonight.

She dropped a pillow over her face to muffle her shout of frustration.

Yet how could she complain? He'd followed her request for helping dispel any rumors she might be carrying a torch for Ridley.

After Sam had escorted her to the Golden Globe Awards earlier in the month, magazines and television media had reported everything from supposed matching love tattoos to a secret wedding in Las Vegas. Gossip rags even digitally altered an image of her with a small baby bump that circulated the news prominently enough for Dana to rush across the lawn and demand Bella hike up her shirt to prove she wasn't expecting.

She pitched aside the pillow and scooped up Muffin from the foot of the bed. "What should I do about this guy?"

Muffin cocked her head to the side, her snaggle-tooth look bringing reminders of Sam's teasing label of a Billy Idol snarl. Bella ruffled a hand along her dog's bristly fur. "I guess you're not able to help out too much on this one, huh?"

If ever she'd needed someone to talk to, someone she could trust not to spill her secrets... She straight-ened. That very person was just across the lawn. Her grandmother. Lillian had always been an early riser and was now even more so since she slept in short spurts throughout the day and night.

Bella rolled from her bed to her feet, rushed to her closet and yanked out the first thing her hands fell on. She slid the side zipper down on the form-hugging gown, kicking the train out of the way and peeling the dress down. She shimmied into jeans, tugged a V-necked tight T-shirt over her strapless bra and left the rubies on. Hopping into her heels on the way out the door, she snagged the trophy she'd won and called for Muffin to follow her.

Breathlessly, she raced across the lawn, her loose French twist shaking free with each reckless wobbly step as she sprinted past the angel fountain. Muffin trotted closely at her heels, up the steps and into the foyer. The little dog dashed toward the kitchen where the cook always kept special puppy treats.

Bella's heels clicked over the marble floor on her way to Grandmere's first-floor quarters. A live-in nurse had moved into the bedroom next door to be close after Lillian had been released from the hospital.

Gathering her tattered composure, Bella tapped lightly on the door.

The door creaked open an inch, the housekeeper Hannah on the other side. "Oh, Ms. Bella, come on in. Mrs. Hudson is awake and she always perks up when she sees you."

"Thank you, Hannah." Bella squeezed her arm and stepped inside. "Good morning, Grandmere. I brought you something."

She placed her Screen Actors Guild Best Actress Award on the bedside table. Already, she breathed easier now that the familiar air of the soothing room surrounded her. Tall vases of flowers—live and silk—filled the airy room along with Lillian's personal photo collection. She'd met dignitaries from around the world in her career, starting with her work in the French cabarets to the years she spent as the toast of Tinseltown.

There were also pictures of her with other stars, but there were many, many more of her surrounded by her family. Bella appeared in a handful of the images framed in matching ivory mats with gilt frames, the spill of Hudsons around her. And on Lillian's beside table rested her most treasured photo of all, one taken the day she and her husband eloped. So much love emanated from Lillian's family gallery.

Not until recently had Bella started to look for hints of unhappiness in the scenes from her childhood.

Her grandmother moved her arm from over her eyes, the pinch of pain at the corners of her mouth easing into a smile. "Thank you, sweet Bella. You've all made me so happy with the movie. First Golden Globe Awards and now this. Come tell me about tonight's ceremony."

Wearing a deeply pleated linen nightgown with a matching wrapper, Lillian still clothed herself with the simple grace that had marked her unpretentious style all her life. A blue ribbon held a cameo locket about her neck, the keepsake memento Bella had played with as a child. She knew if she pressed the tiny latch on one side, she would find a black-and-white picture of her grandfather in uniform beside the image of a tiny cottage along a winding French river.

"That's why I'm here." She winged a prayer for forgiveness for that little lie.

The housekeeper gathered up a breakfast tray with most of the food untouched.

The nurse checked the IV drip, before backing toward the door. "I'm going to step out for a few minutes and let you two have some privacy. Just ring if you need anything," she said before following Hannah out the door.

Her grandmother weakly adjusted the pillows piled behind her, her head swathed in a rose satin scarf rather than her wig. She'd resisted having a hospital bed brought into her room, insisting she would spend her final days in the bed she'd shared with her beloved husband.

"Sit here, Bella dear." Lillian patted the spot beside her.

The hint of a French lilt in her voice washed over Bella with warm familiarity. She had spent so many hours as a child, curled in her grandmother's lap listening to stories and singing together.

"I'm not so little anymore." She settled carefully onto the edge, her heart squeezing with pain over how fast time flew, how soon her grandmother would be gone. She fought back tears Lillian had long ago told her she didn't want to see.

"Come closer and quit worrying you will break me. I have wonderful painkillers." She waggled her arm with an IV taped in place. "Remember when you used to run in here early in the morning so we could talk before the rest of the house came to life?"

Beautiful memories flooded her with a joy and peace she desperately needed right now. "Grandpere always went to work early and I knew I could have you to myself." Bella swung her legs up, crossing them to sit by her grandmother, the underlying antiseptic air of a sick room mingling with Lillian's scent, an old Chanel formula she had worn her entire life. "I wish you could have gone with us to the awards ceremony last night."

"Hannah and I watched every moment on my television." A plasma-screen television had been mounted over the fireplace mantel once Lillian became bed-bound. "The awards are nice, but beyond that, I am so proud of you and pleased with how you portrayed me in the movie. You did yourself and the family very proud."

Lillian's compliment meant…everything. Stifling a blush, Bella traced the intricate pattern on the gold brocade spread. "All I did was bring your wonderful spirit to the screen. You're amazing, Grandmere."

As much as she had longed for the lead actress role in *Honor*, she'd also been terrified of falling short. Her grandmother was a remarkable woman with an unmistakably dynamic presence, a presence that had made her a big screen star in her own right.

A twinkle lit Lillian's blue eyes. "Your young man looked quite handsome, too, although a mite irritated about those men fawning over you." She peered above her bifocals with a wicked rather than censuring twinkle. "That dress of yours was rather risqué, don't you think?"

Sam had actually noticed the men speaking to her? Could have fooled her. "I've looked at your photo albums, Grandmere," Bella teased, "and you've worn a risqué dress or two yourself."

Lillian laughed lightly. "That I have, that I have." Her laughter faded. "I'm glad nothing came of your relationship with that Ridley."

"I thought it would make you nostalgic to see the two of us together since we made the movie, revived those days when you fell in love. He even looks like Grandpere." Had that perhaps been a reason she let herself be drawn in by Ridley's playboy charm? In some hope of living out her grandmother's grand romance for real? A disquieting thought, to say the least.

"He may have looked like your grandfather and he may be a fine actor on screen, but off screen? *Non, non.* The man was nothing like my Charles. Besides, it rarely works for two actors to marry each other. You've chosen well with your new man. He has his own power and success in a different arena from yours."

"I'm glad you approve." Bella looked away quickly, afraid her grandmother would read the truth in her eyes. Whatever the truth was right now.

"Tell me more about him. He is so quietly polite during the dinners we've had. He always leaves you and me to do the gabbing." Fresh air toyed with the curtains at the window.

"Well, in spite of what the media reports, I am definitely not pregnant." Bella hitched her shirt up to just below her breasts.

Grandmere clapped a hand over her mouth and laughed, a raspy sound but unmistakable mirth. Too soon, the laughs turned to coughs.

Bella passed her grandmother a cup of ice water with a bent straw. Lillian sipped with labored draws until her throat cleared again.

"Thank you, dear. Of course I know you are not expecting. We have always talked about everything.

That is why I am surprised I haven't heard more from you about Sam."

It wasn't for lack of having him in her thoughts that Bella hadn't shared more. She was so confused about how she felt, about what was happening between them, she didn't know what to think, let alone what to say. "We're still in the early stage, waiting to see what happens."

Lillian's mouth pursed thoughtfully. "Trust is difficult. The Garrisons have had their problems like any family, but they persevere. I respect that. Your grandfather always said they were ruthless but honest in the business world. You'll need someone that strong to keep you grounded in this profession. I found that kind of man in your grandfather."

Grandmere thought Sam was like Grandpere? Now that had never crossed her mind and she wasn't quite sure what to do with the notion yet.

"Bella?" Lillian pulled her back into the moment. "I know you've suffered some hurtful surprises of late, but be kind to your father."

Startled, Bella wanted to cry out *which one*? Markus, the man who made her his pampered princess for twenty-five years? Or David, the man who'd wrecked her parents' marriage with the affair, the man who'd been nothing more than sperm donor in making her?

She held her tongue, however. Lillian was entitled to blurt random dictates like this since—with a heart-lurching ache—Bella knew grandmother wouldn't be around much longer to direct the stage around her the way she'd done with a firm but gracious hand her whole life.

Except Grandmere had a reputation for petting David, her one flaw. Had David been a bad seed, which led Grandmere to favor him because she knew he was weaker than his brother? Or had she made him weak spoiling him?

They would never know for sure, however one thing was certain. David Hudson led a self-centered life, wreaking havoc all around him.

She couldn't burden her grandmother with her own heartache, not now. The comfort of Lillian's presence would have to be enough. "Of course, I'll be nice to him, Grandmere."

"Good, good. I knew you would do the right thing. You've always been the tender-hearted one. You may have inherited my temper, but you never could hold a grudge." Her grandmother sighed, sagging back into her satin-covered pillows. "I am tired. Please get Hannah to come sit with me while I take a nap."

Bella squelched the twinge of disappointment that she hadn't really broached the topic she most needed to discuss. Guilt seared her throat that she'd spent precious moments dancing around the matters that were most important to her.

Bella pressed the call button and within seconds the housekeeper rushed through the door. Stout but spry, with graying hair and kind hazel-green eyes, Hannah had been with the family for thirty years, always making sure the large and boisterous family ran smoothly. "I'm here, ma'am. You just rest."

Bella eyed her grandmother, panic welling. How many "naps" did Lillian have left? The doctors had said it could be any day now. They'd been hopeful for more time, however, since Lillian had already outlived medical expectations. "I'll stay. I don't mind, really. I want to."

"No, no, you go," Lillian insisted. "I need to take my medicines and change into a fresh gown first. Please, it will make me happy to think of you with your Sam."

She looked deeper into her grandmother's weary eyes and saw beyond the words to her need for privacy with her pain. Bella leaned to hug her gently, carefully avoiding the IV. "I love you, Grandmere."

"I love you, too." She cupped Bella's face. "Be happy."

Bella slid from the bed, backing toward the door so she could smile at her grandmother until the very…last…second.

Once in the hall, she sagged back against the wall and let the tears flow. Heartache and helplessness flooded through her, pushing more tears streaming down her face, more than she thought one person could shed. This hurt far more than she'd felt that night in Marseille when she'd ended up in Sam's bed for a few hours of forgetfulness.

Grief threatened to drive her to her knees. There was so little time left. Thinking about how quickly life could change forever made her reevaluate her all or nothing mindset when it came to Sam. Life was fleeting. Right now was what truly mattered, this moment, because there might not be another.

She stiffened her spine, straightening away from the wall and swiping the back of her wrist over her eyes. She was a fighter like her grandmother. What she wanted, she went after.

And right now, she wanted Sam.

Sam sat behind the desk in his executive office at the new L.A. Garrison Grande Hotel due to open within another two months. Construction noise echoed a floor above as workers reinstalled crown molding. He should go up there and inspect the progress, stretch his legs, air his mind out about the headache item that headlined today's gossip columns. He pitched aside two newspapers folded open to the offending item—a thorn from his past coming back to jab him on a day he was running on fumes from the late night with Bella at the awards ceremony and party.

Although in retrospect, he should have seen this coming. He creaked back in the oversize leather chair, the only addition he'd made to the sparse temporary office space. A permanent manager would be hired once the place opened. That had been his plan from the beginning since this wasn't his type of town with its see-and-be-seen attitude.

He should be used to this kind of crap in the newspaper by now. At least Bella appeared immune to all the gossip, in fact seeming to welcome anything that advanced her acting career. So much so, there were times at those functions where it was all he could do not to deck the latest industry letch looking down her dress.

His phone buzzed just as his doorknob turned. The intercom echoed with his interim secretary's high pitched voice, "Mr. Garrison, you have a—"

Visitor.

Bella stood framed in the doorway, her hair a damn sexy mess. She struck a wide legged pose in red heels, jeans and a curve hugging T-shirt with a ruby and diamond necklace that cost more than most cars. Given her wild-eyed look, he assumed she must have seen the latest bombshell in the newspapers.

His secretary, a pencil jammed in her hair bun, peeked over Bella's shoulder. "Uh, Mr. Garrison…"

"It's okay. Close the door and hold my calls, please." Once the lock clicked, he gathered his words to explain. "Bella, about—"

She held up a finger, tossing her head, flicking her fiery hair over her shoulder. "Don't say anything. Me first, because I don't want to waste even a single second here."

Ohhh-kay. That would give him more time to gauge her mood.

She flung aside her oversize gold purse.

Thud.

She peeled her T-shirt up and off.

Whoosh.

What the hell? He damn near choked on his tongue. Bella sent the wisp of cotton sailing in a fluttery white flight across the room to land on his computer.

Apparently she wasn't here about the latest in the news. He'd been biding his time when it came to her no-sex request, waiting—painfully at times—for her to come to him. He just hadn't expected her turn around to be quite so dramatic.

One hip jutting, she stood across from him in a red strapless bra and the glittering ruby necklace, her low-rise jeans displaying her diamond belly-button ring and a mouth-drying expanse of creamy skin. "So Sam Garrison, has anyone ever told you you're a tease?"

He scrubbed a hand over his jaw to keep his shock from showing. "Run that by me again?"

She strutted forward, her wild hair and curves and do-me heels spiking his heart rate through the roof. She slid a hand into her pocket, pulled it back out and slapped it on his desk, leaving behind…

A condom packet.

"Okay, big guy, it's time to put up or shut up."

Ten

Bella bolstered her nerve, determined to see this through with Sam, to live in the moment. She'd certainly succeeded in shocking him silent.

She planted her heels deeper in the lush carpet, the rest of the office, however, was sparse. He'd obviously set this up as a temporary operating post with a large mahogany desk, a media center in the corner and one long leather couch—presumably for naps.

A lone banker's lamp rested on the corner of his desk beside newspapers. He'd replaced the on/off chain with the small bell she'd finally given him one evening after supper with Lillian.

His sentimental gesture filled her with reassurance

she was doing the right thing by coming here. By seducing *him*.

His steely eyes narrowed sensually. "I take that to mean the no-sex rule is now null and void."

"You would be right." She tapped him on the chest right over his red silk tie, nudging him backward until he reached his large, leather office chair. Empowerment surged through her. There was something to be said for living in the moment. "But I'm the one in charge today."

With a gentle two-handed shove on his shoulders, she urged him to sit. He could have stopped this at any time. No question who held the physical strength edge here. Yet for some reason he seemed to be through with his tease-and-tempt games.

Was it really as simple as he'd been waiting for her to make the first move all this time? Her pulse quickened at the thought he truly wanted her that much. That perhaps going out together wasn't just about scaring off matchmaking mamas in search of a wealthy son-in-law.

Sam had a lot more going for him than his bank balance. Not the least of which was the searing look he gave her that made her knees weak and her breath catch. Pulse fluttering wildly, Bella toyed with the clasp between her breasts and freed her bra. Cool air whispered over her, her nipples tightening in response, tingling in oversensitive need for a firmer caress.

He whistled low and long. "Woman, you are driving—"

"Shh." She leaned forward, pressing a finger to his lips and bringing her breasts closer to him. Sam's tangy aftershave mixed with the scent of freshly painted walls.

His hands crept up and she clamped his wrists, denying herself for the moment. But for a moment only.

"This is my show, Sam Garrison. Unless you have an objection."

He shook his head slowly, his gaze locked steadfastly on her. "None that come to mind."

"I'm glad to hear that, because I believe we've both had enough of this waiting game. You have to know how frustrating it's been denying myself these past weeks when you were doing your damnedest to charm me...then walk away. No more walking. No more waiting."

She lowered his hands back to the armrests on his oversize office chair. His eyes stroked her instead, his knuckles turning white with restraint. Good. She'd planned every moment of this on her drive over to his office, hoping she'd see the same fierce hunger in his expression that she'd been feeling for weeks.

Now, she shimmied out of her jeans, thumbing her panties down as well, the fabric teasing her skin already hungry for contact. She kicked the clothing free until she stood before him in only red spike heels and a ruby necklace.

Desire burned in his eyes, encouraging her to

continue. One slow, sultry step at a time she closed
the distance between them. Bella straddled his lap,
her knees on either side of his legs, and cupped his
face in her hands.

Sealing her mouth to his, she kissed, nipped,
tasted while brushing her breasts against his crisp
white shirt. The starched fabric rubbed arousing
friction against her needy nipples, the silky tie caressing sensually between her breasts, until she rocked
her hips against him in desperation to ease the deeper
ache. She unbuckled his belt, opened his pants and
freed him to her soft and stroking touch.

His grip on the wooden armrests tightened until his
biceps bulged. "Things are moving mighty fast here."

"That's only a problem if you're a one-shot kinda
guy, and I happen to know from past experience with
you that's not the case. So what do you say we make
it fast this time to take off the edge then take things
slower the next time on your desk…" She kissed the
side of his mouth, breathing in his breath, locking
gazes. "And on your sofa."

He pressed warm kisses down her neck that fired
a trail of sweet sensation through her restless body.
The chair rocked as their kisses grew more frenzied,
wheeling backward until it lodged against the wall.

Drawing slightly away, she reached behind her for
the condom she'd brought along, praying he had
more stashed away somewhere because she actually
hadn't thought further than this one time. She tore
open the packet with frantic, shaking fingers until

finally, after weeks of waiting, she could sheathe him with slow deliberation.

Rising up on her knees, she then eased herself onto him, taking him into her body deeper and deeper until she settled on his lap, her knees tight against his hips. Delicious shivers of pleasure prickled along her nerves.

"Enough," he growled, standing, holding her in place.

She locked her legs around his waist and looped her arms around his neck. Her desire spiked at his bold move and she dug her nails deeper into back.

Sam swept an arm over his desk in a clearing swoop to the side before lowering her onto the slick mahogany. Standing between her legs, he moved, thrust, drove them both higher with pleasure.

His hands freed and her ability to speak scattered with her thoughts, he played his fingers over her body, her breasts as she held on to furniture this time, anchoring herself in the moment, the muscle-melting sensations rising at such a rapid rate already she...

Flew apart.

Pleasure pulsed through her as she thrashed her head from side to side, biting her lip to keep from crying out. Still, he thrust, belying her words of a quick finish until he'd taken her to completion a second time. This time she couldn't control the moans of ecstasy from slipping past her lips as she arched upward and he quickly sealed his mouth to hers. He clasped her to his chest until he finished pulsing inside her, his face tight against her cheek, his growl strained between his clenched teeth.

His arms slackened and Bella collapsed back onto his desk with a gusty sigh.

"Wow, Sam, that was…Wow." She focused on the shimmering after-tingles, her heart not even close to slowing down its frantic pace.

"I agree." Bracing one hand on the desk, he smoothed her hair back from her face as he drew in ragged gasps.

She centered herself in this moment for as long as she could, drawing it out to avoid a return to rational, painful reality. Or maybe things would be all right after all. She and Sam could move into a new stage of their bizarre courtship/friendship. They could start a full-out affair that might truly lead to something more.

She turned her head to the side to kiss his wrist, then frowned. She eased up onto an elbow and reached for the discarded newspaper featuring a photo of Sam…embracing a woman she'd never seen before.

The headline blared: Garrison Cheats on Hudson, with Fiancée?

Sam buttoned his pants, pronto. Given the horror in Bella's eyes as she stared at the newspaper headline, he needed to enact damage control without delay. "I was just going to talk to you about that before we got sidetracked."

Bella scrambled off the mahogany desk and gathered her clothes at lightning speed. She yanked on her panties and jeans. "I can't believe I didn't see this coming." She whipped her strapless bra off the floor and back in place, her voice dripping with disillusionment. "I am such an idiot." She tugged her shirt over her head. "Thanks for your help this month but I'm outta here."

The burn at her quick acceptance of the worst and speedy rejection blindsided him.

"Hold on." He grabbed her wrist before she could bolt out the door. "Simmer down and let's discuss this rationally."

"Simmer down? Simmer down!" Bella jerked her arm free and stalked over to his desk. She stabbed the nearest newspaper with her finger. "What the hell is this?"

He lifted the paper and read the headline proclaiming he was cheating on Bella Hudson by seeing fiancée Tiffany Jones. The spread included a photo of him with Tiffany at a New Year's party a year ago, making it seem they'd spent *this* December thirty-first together.

The article even included a photo of a tearful, "wronged" Tiffany spilling her tale of woe, likely looking for her fifteen minutes of fame along with a hefty payoff for the article. "This is total bull. You know as well as I do how gossip rags can make things up out of thin air."

Didn't she?

Her indignation visibly ramped until her fiery hair damn near crackled with electricity. She paced restlessly, snatching her purse off the floor, her path leading her closer and closer to the door. "So you're saying this picture of the two of you super-glued together on New Year's Eve was altered?"

He scratched the kink in his neck, remembering why he hated the press so damned much. "Not exactly."

She stroked the doorknob as if already plotting her sprint away. "This picture is real?"

He hesitated.

"You *do* know her." Her hand closed around the knob. "Please don't insult me by saying she just catered the party."

He knew Bella had a temper, but he still couldn't believe she was so pissed off so fast. All her trust issues be damned, this was just an article. Irritation at her piled on top of his anger over Tiffany's stunt. Bella should know full well what the media was like. She'd grown up under the microscope herself.

He worked to keep his voice low and level. "This photo was taken a year ago when Tiffany Jones and I were seeing each other."

"Why didn't I ever hear about it?"

Her suspicious tone kicked at his already thin rein on his own temper. How had things spun out of control so damn fast? Only minutes ago they'd been locked together in a mind-numbing release.

He mentally kicked himself for not taking up this topic with her before he accepted the tempting offer she'd made when she walked in. "Not everything I do gets reported. In case you haven't noticed, I prefer to stay away from the camera's lens."

Something that had frustrated Tiffany. In hindsight, he could see she had dated him for the attention she'd thought his wealth would bring her way.

Bella released the doorknob, a sign of promising progress. "Why is she speaking out now?"

Like he was a mind reader? If that were the case he would know how the hell to reason with Bella. "For attention. For money. For revenge because I ended our engagement."

"Fiancée?" Any sign of softening disappeared in a snap, her blue eyes darting shards of ice his way. "She really was your fiancée like the paper says? When?"

"I broke it off at Thanksgiving." A very messy breakup where he'd nearly had his head taken off by a Ming Dynasty vase Tiffany had hurtled his way. Yet he hadn't even thought about her in weeks, a further affirmation he'd made the right decision in ending things with her.

"Mere weeks before you met me?" Her voice rose with each word. "We've been together for over a month now and you never thought to mention you'd been engaged?"

"We weren't planning anything serious and then I honestly didn't think of her."

She wrapped her arms around her waist defensively. "I don't believe you."

"What?" His sense of honor roared. He wouldn't deny he was ruthless, but by God, he did not cheat.

"I don't believe you." Her chin tipped, her eyes full of hurt as well as anger. "Why should I? Everyone knows your reputation with women and I chose to ignore it. Well, not anymore."

"I'm not going to stand here while you call me a liar." He turned his back, walking to his desk to put distance between them. He was not the sort of man to stare down a woman in an attempt to physically intimidate her, but he also wouldn't put up with these irrational accusations.

Sam pivoted behind his desk to face her again. "I've spent the past weeks with you in front of the press, supporting you, helping you save face while you flirted with every damn man in sight."

Her head snapped back. "What are you talking about?"

"At the parties." A month's worth of exasperation boiled to the surface. "It gets old sitting around with my thumb up my—" he cleared his throat if not his anger "—sitting around while you let other men paw you."

Her eyes went wide with shock, then she shook her head in amazement. "I could almost laugh at your jealousy, almost." Her face went emotionless and she hitched her purse higher on her shoulder as if readying to walk the hell out of his life. "It seems neither of us trusts the other and without trust we have nothing."

Bella grabbed the doorknob again, her spine regally stiff with Lillian-like poise. "Thank you for your help with the promo issues these past weeks. It's obvious our time together is over."

She opened the door and left.

Bella hitched her bag even more securely onto her shoulder and marched past Sam's secretary, head held high on her way into the hallway. She wouldn't give anyone the satisfaction of seeing her cry, especially not someone who worked for Sam and probably knew that Tiffany person.

Likely Sam had been telling the truth about breaking up with Tiffany before he and Bella met. But this made her realize just how little of himself he'd ever shared with her. All those romantic gestures through the month had simply been about getting her back in bed. She'd been such a gullible sucker. She been right to run out of his office before her still-humming body lured her back into his arms.

Construction work thundering overhead echoed the pounding in her ears. She should have known better. She'd heard about Sam's reputation as a player. She'd seen firsthand how easily relationships fell apart in her family. Yet she'd naively thought she and Sam could be different just because he'd spent four weeks wooing her.

He was simply a damn good multitasker.

Her hurt feelings over Ridley felt like nothing in comparison to the heartache jack-hammering through her now. Somehow during this past month, Sam had eased the ache of Ridley's callousness, her parents' betrayal, and the imminent loss of her grand-mother, she'd felt a certain comfort in knowing she could lean on Sam through it all.

She'd been right to expect all or nothing, and wrong to come over here so impulsively. Except it hurt so damn bad to be on the nothing end of that deal.

A custodian rolled a cart down the hall, casting a quick curious glance at her. Bella scrounged a feeble smile and swiped away the tears she'd been so desperate to hold in. Her hand came back smudged with mascara and makeup.

Damn it. She needed to get out of here.

Rushing toward the elevator, she fished in her purse for a tissue and mirror, shuffling aside her wallet, brush, her cell phone, a bag of doggie treats for Muffin...

Wait.

She thumbed the elevator button and backtracked to the pink phone flashing "missed call." She stepped into the empty elevator as she retrieved her messages.

Her brother Max's voice came over the phone. "Bella, call me as soon as you get this message. It's important."

Her stomach clenched. It couldn't be.... Not now. Not yet. Not when so much of her life was falling apart. Her fingers shook so hard she could barely operate her cell phone as the elevator whooshed down five floors. Finally, she connected to her brother's number just as the door chimed on the main floor.

"Please, please, pick up," she chanted while the phone rang.

The ringing stopped. "Bella." Max's somber voice erased all hopes of escaping the worst news. "I'm sorry, kiddo. It's Grandmother. She passed away a half hour ago."

Eleven

Eleven

Three days later, Sam sat in his Marseille office, wondering why the hell he was still staring out the window at the harbor rather than getting back to work. Bella had walked out on *him*, for crying out loud. She'd even ignored the brief message he'd left on her voice mail once he'd calmed down enough to offer a neutral territory discussion.

His phone buzzed—the line used by his personal assistant. Sam jabbed the speakerphone button.

"Yes," he answered, his voice clipped and rude, he knew, but he'd asked not to be interrupted.

"There's someone on line one—a Charlotte Montcalm," Parrington announced. "She insists on speaking with you. She says it's about Ms. Bella Hudson."

Was Charlotte Hudson Montcalm calling on Bella's behalf as some kind of olive branch? He wasn't sure how he felt about third-party negotiations on something that should be between him and Bella, but he also realized he couldn't ignore the call. "Thank you, Parrington."

Sam tapped line one. "Hello, Mrs. Montcalm."

"Please, call me Charlotte."

"Charlotte, what can I do for you?"

"I'm sorry to bother you at work, but since you reached out to Alec and me about Bella last month I have to think you must care about her in some way."

"No offense meant—" he creaked back in his office chair, staring out at the harbor Bella so loved "—but this is something between Bella and me."

"I agree. But when she's hurting so much right now, more than ever after such a difficult year, I just can't keep my peace. I've learned the hard way that it doesn't help to keep my feelings to myself."

"Bella's upset?" Over their breakup?

"Our grandmother passed away three days ago. I'm unable to attend the funeral because of my pregnancy, and Bella could really use some support."

Sam creaked his chair upright. Lillian Hudson had died? How had he missed that in the news?

Perhaps because he had been avoiding newspapers—even television—like the plague since storming out of his L.A. hotel and flying back to

France. He'd been so sickened by Tiffany's drama and the heartache it caused with Bella that he damn well didn't care to see a follow-up story.

"Well," Charlotte continued, "I've said my piece. I hope you'll set aside whatever it is that's keeping you in France and be there for her right now."

Still too stunned by the news of Lillian's passing, he didn't begin to know how to respond to Charlotte's request.

"I'm very sorry for your loss," he said finally. Then ended the conversation with, "Thank you for calling."

After a cool goodbye from Charlotte, the dial tone droned over his speakerphone for…he wasn't sure how long before he stabbed the button.

Lillian Hudson had died. Even knowing this day was coming, it must be crippling to Bella. He'd viewed the special bond between the two women often enough over the past month.

Charlotte was right that Bella would need support, but she had her friend and future sister-in-law Dana. She had her brothers. She'd already made it clear she didn't want him around first in his office and then by ignoring his call….

A call that must have come right after her grandmother died.

Hell.

He shoved aside his own angry feelings long enough to think about this from Bella's perspective. She'd made it clear on the very day they'd met that she had trust issues, and with good reason. He should have realized that and pushed more assertively to be heard.

Why wasn't he fighting as hard for Bella as he would for a company? Normally, he would never back down from a little controversy. Obstacles in his path had always been new challenges to conquer. Could he have taken a page out of his mother's book, ducking out on life? His mom may have chosen a mostly solitary existence in her little beach retreat, but he'd buried himself in his work with just as effective results.

He'd cut himself off to the point he didn't hear Bella. Because if he heard her, he would have to acknowledge how damn much it would hurt to lose her. He would have to face the truth that had been nudging at the back of his brain for more than a month.

He'd fallen in love with Bella Hudson.

The last of the guests had left Hudson Manor. So many had come by to visit after Lillian's funeral, Bella had wondered if she would have to hold on to her "brave face" well into the night.

Even her best acting skills couldn't carry her through this loss much longer. Her grandmother's death had hit her even harder than she'd expected, compounded by her breakup with Sam until her heart swelled with so much hurt she wondered how much longer before it burst.

Now that the house had cleared, some of the remaining family members had decided to retire to the manor's private screening room—Charles and

Lillian's favorite feature—and watch old home movies. At least in the darkened theater she wouldn't have to hide her emotions any longer.

Thank goodness David had bowed out after the last guest left. Bella decided she really couldn't think of him as anything other than her uncle. She'd never been close to him and a simple, sad quirk of genetics wasn't going to change that. David had known he was her father all her life and chose to stay silent. She could even write that off as a man attempting to keep peace in his family, but he had also ignored her as thoroughly as he disregarded his two children with his wife.

The man truly had no feelings for his offspring. He didn't deserve anything from her. She would forgive him like her grandmother had asked, but that didn't mean she had to open her heart to a man who'd never cared for her.

First into the home studio, Bella slid down a row of luxury theater seating in the middle, pushing down her seat for the best view. She kicked off her black heels, tugged her dress over her knees and scooched down low in the deep leather chair. The whole cavernous room was decorated in black and white except for large color movie posters of the most successful Hudson Picture's films.

Her brothers filed in—Dev, Max and Luc—each hugging her on his way past. Her cousin/half brother Jack joined them, all the wives and fiancées filling seats until wow, what a legacy Lillian had left.

Suddenly everyone quieted.

Sabrina and Markus walked down the aisle, united in their grief if nothing else. They weren't touching or even looking at each other, but they were here together for their children and in honor of Lillian.

Sabrina, a strikingly handsome woman with dark blond hair and blue eyes, slid on the end beside Luc, her body stiff and defensive as if she feared being asked to leave.

Markus, distinguished but with perhaps a few extra strands of gray in his dark hair, circled round to the other side to sit beside…

Bella.

Her eyes watered and she blinked back tears before she wrecked what little makeup she had left. He patted her hand as selections from home videos of Lillian started rolling, through her early years with her husband and small children, to her years as the grandmother of a rapidly expanding family.

An image of Max in a cowboy outfit appeared, complete with chaps and a hat. Except he hadn't known to wear his jeans, and only had on little boy underwear. Much needed laughter rolled through the theater, Dana leaning closer to her fiancé, clasping his arm and smiling.

Max shook his head. "Where's the video of the summer Gran organized us all into an acting troupe? We could use some footage of Luc and Jack in tights during Gran's Shakespearean week."

More laughter echoed up to bounce around in the high ceiling. Bella couldn't help but wonder what boyhood memories Sam carried with him as an only child. He'd mentioned numerous cousins. Had they included him?

Next on the screen came a clip Bella remembered well, her seventh birthday. Grandmere had organized a Pierrot and Harlequin theme, complete with stylized clown costumes true to the era. The day stayed etched in her mind, the taste of strawberry cake, the sound of carnival music.

On the screen, a younger Markus stepped into the camera's sites, past the jugglers, carrying a scruffy little puppy with a pink Pierrot ruffle around its neck.

Seven-year-old Bella sprinted across the lawn with a high-pitched squeal, her pointy clown hat toppling to the side in her haste to hug her father and the dog—Muffin number one who had passed away just three years ago.

Without thinking, Bella clasped her father's hand as she absorbed the image of such pure love on the screen in front of her. Markus squeezed her fingers gently, turning to smile at her.

He dipped his head and said softly, "I've missed you, princess."

He'd always called her that, his princess. She hadn't realized until now how much she'd missed hearing it. Bella swallowed down the lump in her throat thicker than that long-ago cake as she thought of her grandmother's request to be kind to her father. In Bella's mind, that was Markus.

"I should have called or come straight to you," she whispered, everyone else caught up in the ongoing family video clips. "I'm sorry. I was so busy feeling sorry for myself and resenting Mom, I didn't think enough about you."

"I made my own mistakes in the marriage. It's rare that any marital trouble is only one person's fault. I just hate how this has affected you." He cleared his throat. "I miss the sparkle in my little girl's eyes."

She couldn't hold back the words and blurted quietly, "But I'm not your little girl."

"That's where you're wrong," Markus said firmly. "David may have cost me my wife, but he can never take you away. You are my daughter."

She'd felt that in her heart—known that she could never think of David as her father. But, oh God, it felt so good to hear that Markus—her daddy—felt the same way.

He opened his arms and she fell straight into his familiar embrace.

"Love you, Dad."

"Love you, too, princess." He patted her shoulders and it felt right, familiar.

Easing back into her seat, she sensed a pair of eyes watching her and her father. She searched down the row and locked gazes with her mother. Heartbreak had stamped fresh lines in her mother's face. New strands of gray streaked Sabrina's blond hair. Without question, her mother was suffering for her mistake.

Her mother wasn't perfect, but who was? They undoubtedly had a way to go in repairing their relationship after so many years of lies, but now wasn't a time for holding grudges. How strange to finally figure out at twenty-five that her parents were human, but there it was. And she loved them both.

Bella smiled across the row at her mother. A shaky smile spread across Sabrina's face in return. The tears hovering in her blue eyes glinted even from a distance in the darkened family theater.

In that moment, Bella realized it didn't matter what David had done, what her mother had done twenty-six years ago. This was her family.

A light slashed across the theater from the back, someone opening the door. Frowning, Bella looked over her shoulder and gasped.

Sam stood silhouetted in the open doorway.

Her heart swelled with something other than pain. Relief, happiness, and yes, love flooded through her as she watched him walk down the aisle, coming for her. Strong and supportive Sam who'd actually never given her any real reason to doubt him, yet she'd run at the first sign of trouble.

In a flash of inspiration she acknowledged life wasn't a matter of all or nothing, black and white issues. It was about people trying their best to love and be loved.

As she loved Sam.

* * *

Sam watched Bella rise from her seat in the dim media room. She scooted sideways past Markus toward the aisle—and she was smiling. Thank God.

He'd crossed the Atlantic, plotting his strategy the whole way for how to win her back. As he'd considered all the possible scenarios, he'd never imagined she would actually be glad to see him.

She strode barefoot toward him, her conservative black dress swishing around her knees, her high heels dangling from her fingers.

Bella stopped in front of him, her family craning to look over their shoulders. "Sam, you're here."

He kept his hands in his pockets for now. "I just heard the news about your grandmother."

"The funeral was this afternoon." She slid one shoe, then the other back on. Keeping her voice low, she spoke into his ear so as not to disturb the backdrop of children's laughter in the family video highlights splashed on the big screen.

He leaned closer to keep her openly gawking relatives from hearing. "Do you think we could go somewhere more private to talk?"

"Absolutely." She slipped her hand into the crook of his arm, turning him toward the open door.

A low buzz of whispers sounded behind them as her family huddled together. His family soon, if he had his way in winning Bella over. But even as a damn good negotiator in the business world, he knew he needed to take this one step at a time. "Where's Muffin?"

Bella glanced up. "She's in my house. I left food out and the doggie door open. I didn't think a funeral would be an appropriate place for her."

He kept his silence—as did Bella—while crossing the yard to her cottage. On impulse he stopped beside the angel fountain.

What the hell was up with that because he was never impulsive? Until now. Until Bella.

Sam turned to clasp one of her hands in his. "I truly am sorry about your grandmother."

She leaned to drag her fingers through the water, the wind blowing through the trees adding a crispness to the fifty-degree evening. "There's never a good time to say goodbye."

He shrugged out of his suit jacket and draped it over her shoulders. "I wish I could have been there for you this afternoon."

She glanced up quickly, her hand leaving the fountain to secure his jacket. "Even after how we left things?"

Was it his imagination that she'd turned her face toward his lapel and breathed deeply? Inhaling his scent?

He drank in the site of her after four days apart, cataloguing the small facets he loved about her. The restless hands that talked for her when she spoke. The red hair as vibrant as the woman herself. God, he could stand here staring at her all night, but that wouldn't get things moving.

"Do you still believe I'm hiding an engagement

to Tiffany?" No need hedging, he went straight for what mattered most. "Because there's no way I can prove when she and I broke up. You're going to have to take my word on it."

"I need you to understand I'm in a job where affairs and broken relationships are a dime a dozen. And then there's my family..."

His gut clenched as he faced the possibility she could still boot him out on his ass. "Is that a no to believing me?"

Her eyes went wide. "No. Uh, I mean no! I do believe you. I understand firsthand how bad gossip magazines can be about fabricating a whole story out of one small thread." She hugged his jacket closer. "Your actions speak louder than words. I should have believed you and I'm sorry."

"Thank you. I'm sorry too about being a jealous jackass. I may be a driven person, but I pride myself on being honest about what I want. And right from the beginning I have wanted you, Bella. It may have started out about sex, but you've got to know there's more going on between us."

He slid his hands up to cup her face, for emphasis, for her undivided attention, for the unsurpassable pleasure of simply touching her. "Bella, I've fallen in love with you."

She gasped, her eyes filling with tears.

Ah hell. He'd botched it already. "This probably wasn't the best day to spring that on you—"

She clapped a hand over his mouth. "Stop. This

is exactly what I needed to hear. Even more so, what I wanted to hear, because Sam, I was so wrong to walk out on you. I was so, so wrong to let the actions of others influence me into denying what has been growing between us these past weeks."

Bella slid her arms up and around his neck, his jacket slipping off her shoulders to the ground. "Because I have fallen in love with you, too."

Relief surged through him, driving him to lift her up for a kiss, deep, intense, echoing with a need to cement this moment and his love for her.

Bella stroked her hands over his head, down his neck, cupping his shoulders. "Sam, I do trust you, but I need to hear that you trust me, too. The whole media and schmoozing are a part of my job. Future movies will involve a love scene, so I'll be slipping into that body sock again."

He had to admit he didn't feel like cheering over that notion, but without question there would be parts of his job and life she would have to adjust to as well. They both needed to adapt. "What if I come to the studio when you're filming those scenes?"

"Hmm…" The worried pucker between her eyebrows smoothed. "I seem to recall my grandmother telling me that's what she and my grandfather did whenever she had a kissing scene in a film. I can't think of a better role model for romance than the two of them."

Her eyes filled with nostalgia and a hint of tears.

Again he regretted he hadn't been there for her earlier. But he intended to be there for her now.

And for the rest of their lives.

He thought of all she would have to get used to as well. "My main base is in Marseille and your work is based in Hollywood." He reminded himself of his vow to work as hard for her as he did for his work, harder even. "I can shift my headquarters here to the new hotel in L.A."

"Hold on." She halted him with a hand to his chest. "Does it have to be all or nothing? Could you split time between the two places? Hollywood is fun, but it would be nice to run off to France for the privacy we both crave. I even have a sister there."

"That sounds doable to me," he assured.

She would make a damn fine negotiator in the business world. They'd made a solid first step at blending their different lifestyles, giving them the time they deserved to build on the love they'd found together.

He hooked his jacket off the ground, shook it out and draped it over her shoulders again. "I stocked up on my allergy pills. What do you say we find Muffin and end this day together?"

She tucked against his side, sliding her arm around his waist. "I think that's the best proposition I've heard all year."

Epilogue

One week later

Champagne, chocolate-covered strawberries and Sam—the best way to celebrate amazing news.

Bella leaned over Sam's naked body to snag another strawberry between her teeth. She shared the plump fruit with him until they'd both nibbled their way into a sultry kiss. Given how things were still low key for the Hudsons following Lillian's funeral, Bella had opted to commemorate her exciting career milestone in a private celebration with Sam.

Sam kissed a smear of chocolate from the corner of her mouth. "Congratulations on your nomination for an Academy Award."

In addition to Bella's Best Actress nod, *Honor* had also been nominated for Best Director and Best Picture. Grandmere was no doubt cheering them on from heaven. "I'm lucky to have had such an inspiring story to enact."

Muffin yipped from her puppy bed, her new pal in a larger doggie bed beside her. Bella had surprised Sam for his birthday yesterday. She'd done some investigating about breeds of dogs that worked best for allergy sufferers. Through a pet rescue network she learned of an elderly man heading into a nursing home who couldn't keep his three-year-old Portuguese water dog. Muffin was still most definitely a fixture in their home, but now she had a more allergy friendly pal in Bear.

They had actually made quite a few changes and plans in a few short days. Bella had accepted two movie offers, a drama and comedy, both offers coming in with paychecks that put her on par with top grossing actors in Hollywood—and sent her to remote filming locales. Sam had reassured her he could use the opportunity to scout potential sites for new Garrison Grande hotels.

Plans had also been made to visit his mother's barrier island home in Southern Florida. Their lives were intertwining with seamless ease more and more each day.

Sam tugged the pink floral comforter more securely in place as he sat up. "This is supposed to be your celebration, but I sure do like my gift." He snapped his fingers. "Bear, come."

A fifty-pound mass of curly black hair, Bear resembled an oversized poodle. He bounded across the room, Muffin trotting at his heels. Both animals leaped onto the bed, turning circles until settling into a nest of covers.

Sam leaned back on the headboard. "Did you notice Bear's new collar?"

"It's buried in all that fur. I must have missed it."

"Check it out."

Sam really was getting into being a pet owner, something that warmed her heart. But then, Sam had a way of doing that on a regular basis.

She inched closer to the big ol' cutie and furrowed her fingers into his hypo-allergenic fur. A bright red collar peeked through, leather, but rather plain in her opinion. Still she didn't want to hurt Sam's feelings. "Very nice, and, uh, manly."

"Did you check the buckle?"

He seemed so enthused, she hung in there, twisting the collar around and found an odd lump at the buckle. "What's this?"

She looked closer. Oh, my God. A ring box.

The small black-velvet jeweler's case had blended into the color of Bear's fur. Bella's stomach tap-danced with nerves and excitement and then trepidation because what if this wasn't what it looked like? What if Sam had bought something else for Muffin as he'd done with the collar at the premiere of *Honor*?

It must be a new bell for Muffin's collar, she decided. Her emotions firmly reined in, Bella untied the gift cradled in her palm, determined to put on a happy face since Sam seemed so jazzed. They hadn't been dating long, after all, so there was plenty of time for an engagement, something she wanted more than she ever would have imagined possible a couple of months ago.

Sam slid his arm around her. "Aren't you going to open it?"

"Yes, of course." She smiled quickly and brushed a quick kiss over his lips before creaking the lid wide to reveal…

A whomping big princess-cut diamond solitaire in a gold setting.

Bella squealed and threw her arms around Sam's neck.

He laughed. "I take it that's a yes."

"Yes!" She punctuated her affirmation with a kiss, once, twice, repeating "yes" and kisses again and again. The dogs barked together, nudging her and Sam to join in the fun.

Happiness swelled inside her as Bella scooted back and held up the ring box. "Put it on my finger, please."

"My pleasure." His gray eyes twinkled as brightly as the jewel. He slid the ring slowly, reverently on her finger until it settled in place, a perfect fit. "I love you, Bella Hudson."

She smiled. "How convenient since I love you, too, Sam Garrison." She squeezed her fingers into a fist, making darn sure that ring stayed put. "I want us to do this right. Forever."

He slid an arm around her shoulder, pulling her

closer. "Obviously that's what I want, too, or I wouldn't be proposing."

She stared down at her ring, chewing her bottom lip. "Hollywood marriages have notoriously low odds."

He tipped her chin up. "I'm a whiz when it comes to the odds."

She believed him, trusted him, had faith in Sam's determination to make things happen for the best between them. Thanks to him, she also had regained her faith in forever.

Sam reached into the bedside table and pulled out two dog biscuits. He pitched one into a neat landing on Muffin's bed, followed by the second, which landed on Bear's bed.

"Well, my future wife, what do you say we finish up this celebration in style?"

Sweet anticipation curled inside her at the thought of all the celebrations ahead of them. "Again, my husband-to-be, I say yes, yes, yes." She sighed at his bold stroke up her side. *"Yes…"*

* * * * *

Can Valerie and Devlin make their marriage work?
Find out in this exclusive *short story by*
USA TODAY *bestselling author Maureen Child.*

Scene Four

"You're leaving?" Devlin looked from the open suitcase on their bed to his wife's calm, detached expression. *"Now?"*

Val's eyes shuttered and her features were remote, deliberately blank. She only glanced at him before turning to walk to the elegant, cherrywood dresser against the far wall.

"Yes, now. There's really no point in staying any longer, is there?" Her voice was quiet, tinged with sadness, but her movements were sure, steady.

Devlin's pulse pounded until he heard the echo of his own heartbeat thundering in his ears. He hadn't expected this. Hadn't seen it coming. Though, he told himself now, he really should have.

Things hadn't been good between them from the beginning. Their marriage had gotten off to a bad start with that disastrous wedding night and had never really recovered. He spent most of his time at the studio, avoiding coming home, and Valerie was unhappy living at the family mansion. She'd wanted them to get their own place, but Devlin hadn't wanted to take the time. With all the postproduction work on *Honor*, he already had more than enough to contend with.

He hadn't loved her, but he had wanted her. Now though, sex was uncomfortable, for both of them. Since that first night, he'd never again let his own passions reign free. He'd maintained a strict control over his desires, so much so that making love to his wife was almost a formal event. A chore to be ticked off a to-do list.

She was embarrassed and uneasy, as if she knew he was holding back and so she wouldn't allow herself to fully engage in what was happening between them, either. They were two strangers who occasionally shared a bed.

Not the marriage he's envisioned, so it was hardly a shock that she wanted to leave. Though his ego was taking a beating and, damn it, she'd picked a hell of a time to acquire a backbone.

"The movie premiere is tomorrow night," he reminded her. As if she could have forgotten. It was all anyone in the family had been talking about for weeks.

"I know, and I'm sorry to miss it," she said, carefully stacking her lingerie into a corner of the suitcase. "I'm sure it'll be wonderful."

"Damn it, Val, what am I supposed to tell the family?"

She looked up at him and her eyes were filled with pain, regret and shadows of things he couldn't read or understand. "I don't care, Dev. Tell them whatever you want to tell them. This isn't about your family. This is about us. And it's just not working."

"And leaving will fix it?" He sounded unreasonable even to himself, but he didn't care.

Once the media got hold of this, he thought in disgust, the premiere of *Honor* would be lost in the sensationalism of yet another Hudson marriage disintegrating. Instantly, his mind filled with images of his parents' long-standing marriage and the indisputable fact of his mother's treachery. His own mother had cheated on Dev's father. Why in *hell* should he be surprised that his own wife was now walking out?

"I'm not trying to fix anything, Dev," Valerie said, moving now to the walk-in closet. "I don't think there's anything *to* fix."

"What's that supposed to mean?" He shoved both hands into the pockets of his slacks and glanced with irritation around the bedroom.

After his marriage, Devlin had moved Valerie into his rooms at the Hudson family mansion. The entire right wing was theirs, and with several bedrooms and sitting rooms, there was enough privacy afforded them that they might as well have been in their own home. Which, he conceded had been a bone of contention between them from the start.

But it was convenient and easy to get to work and why the hell would he want to move?

Now, he stared at the interior of his own bedroom as if it were a strange new place. Until that moment, he hadn't even noticed that Valerie—at least he assumed it had been she—had brought in Christmas decorations, hanging tiny white light around the framed paintings, red candles set in holly wreaths positioned on top of the dressers and tables and there was a cinnamony scent in the air, too. How had he not been aware of that before?

His wife stepped out of the closet with several items of clothing draped over one arm. She paused briefly, looked at him and gave him a sad smile. "Devlin, I thought you'd be happy I was leaving. You never wanted a marriage."

"Excuse me?" Fresh irritation erupted inside him. "I am the one who proposed. The one who swept you off to Vegas. The one who moved you in here— into my bed."

"Exactly," she said, shaking her head now as she walked to the bed and the open suitcase. While she packed, she told him, "We moved here. Into *your* place. Not ours. Into *your* bed. Not ours. You wanted a wife who would be some sort of decoration, I guess." She lifted one shoulder into a half-hearted shrug. "You expected me to slide into your life and not create a ripple, and I tried. Really."

"Yeah, you gave it a real try. A couple months and then you split on Christmas Eve. Do you want applause?"

Valerie sighed, closed the suitcase, zipped it shut, then pulled it off the bed to stand beside her. This was so much harder than she thought it would be. She didn't want to leave him, but staying was destroying her by inches.

Lifting her gaze to his, she took one long, last look at him. His cool-blue eyes, the shadow of dark whiskers on his cheeks, his broad shoulders and the stiff, unrelenting posture of his stance.

Her heart broke at the thought of never seeing him again. Even knowing that their marriage was a sham, that he felt nothing more for her than he would for a slightly annoying guest in his house, Valerie wanted to cry over the loss of him.

But she wouldn't.

She'd done enough crying in the last few weeks to last her a lifetime. She was finished being quiet and accommodating. She was through trying to be the wife he wanted instead of the woman she was. It was time to admit that loving him wasn't enough to build a marriage. She needed his respect. She needed him to love her back. And that was never going to happen.

"I'm sorry, Dev. Sorry to be leaving before Christmas. Before the premiere. But it's better this way and eventually you'll see that."

"Right. I'm sure. While I'm answering reporters'

questions about the breakup of my marriage instead of talking about the movie we've all sweated blood over for months, I'll remember you saying this is best."

Valerie blew out a breath and picked up her pale-pink sweater from the end of the bed. Shrugging into it, she then lifted her hair free and let it fall around her shoulders. "You're angry."

"That's a fair read of the situation."

"I understand.

"Great, thanks. Wouldn't want to be misunderstood."

His voice was sharp, sarcastic and the glitter in his eyes told her fury was crouched inside him, tightly leashed. Well, why wouldn't it be? He never allowed himself to completely relax with her. His passions— be they anger or desire—were always carefully banked. As if he couldn't be bothered to show her the *real* Devlin Hudson. As if she weren't important enough to engage him fully.

Sighing again, she said, "This is really as much my fault as yours. I never should have married you knowing you didn't love me."

He stiffened. "Love? That's what you want? Not a very trustworthy emotion to bet a life on. Look at my father. He loved my mom. She betrayed him."

That wound was still fresh and deep, Valerie saw. "There are two sides to a marriage, Devlin. Maybe you ought to talk to your father before you condemn your mom so easily."

"She broke her vows," he said, his tone stating emphatically that there was no excuse for that. "I didn't. I've been faithful to you, Valerie."

"I know that," she said. "This isn't about our sex life—this is about our *lives*. And I want more for mine."

"More than what?" He stalked around the edge of the wide bed where they'd spent so many awkward hours together. Just the memories of those encounters filled Valerie with grief for what might have been.

Every time he came to her, he was so stiff, so controlled, so damn careful, that Valerie knew he was remembering that first time. That night would *always* be between them. She hadn't been able to break through the walls Devlin had built around himself and she'd finally gotten tired of trying.

Gripping her shoulders he yanked her close, and she tipped her head back to stare into the eyes that had fascinated her right from the beginning.

"I've given you everything anyone could want, Valerie. You live in a damn mansion. You've got servants, money and the time to spend it anyway you choose. What the hell else is there?"

Valerie's heart broke a little as his demand seemed to echo around her. Keeping her gaze locked with his, she gave him a sad smile. "Oh, Devlin, don't you see? The fact that you can even ask that question is enough to prove that we have nothing."

"You're not making any sense." He let her go so suddenly, she staggered back a step or two.

"Yes I am. I only wish you could see it."

"Fine." He pushed one hand through his thick,

black hair, then waved that hand at the bedroom door. "You want to go? Then go."

Shaken, sad and holding her broken dreams close to her shattered heart, Valerie pulled up the handle on the suitcase and rolled it behind her to the door. But before she left, she turned for one last look at the man she still loved so very much.

"Devlin, I never wanted your money. Or your mansion. All I wanted was your love. Since I can't have that, there's really nothing to stay for, is there?"

Then she left and Devlin was alone.

* * * * *

SEDUCED INTO
A PAPER MARRIAGE

BY
MAUREEN CHILD

Maureen Child is a California native who loves to travel. Every chance they get, she and her husband are taking off on another research trip. An author of more than sixty books, Maureen loves a happy ending and still swears that she has the best job in the world. She lives in Southern California with her husband, two children and a golden retriever with delusions of grandeur. Visit her website at www.maureenchild.com.

To my niece, Maegan Carberry,
for always having the strength of spirit
to go her own way and fight for what she believes in.
I love you.

One

Another high-pitched squeal from the outer office went through Devlin Hudson's brain like an ice pick.

That made the fourth secretary this morning to receive either a vase full of flowers, a stuffed animal of some kind or a huge box of candy.

"Valentine's Day should be abolished," he muttered.

"That's the spirit, Boss."

He shot a quick look at his assistant, Megan Carey. The fifty-something blonde shook her head at him as if he were a personal disappointment.

"No comments from you, thanks." He knew from long experience that it was best to cut Megan off at the pass rather than let her start in on whatever was bugging her.

"I'm not saying a thing."

"That'd be a first," he said, just under his breath.

Dev was under no misapprehension. He might be the oldest sibling in the Hudson family. Might hold a position of power in the Hudson Pictures dynasty. Might even have a glare that could freeze agents and actors in their tracks. But Megan Carey ran his office—and therefore his world—and assumed the right to speak her mind no matter what he thought of the idea.

"But," she said, just to prove his thoughts right on target, "Valentine's Day is tomorrow."

"Good God." He nearly groaned. "We've got another full day of deliveries to live through."

"Man," Megan murmured, "the Romance Fairy never paid you a single visit, did she?"

"Don't you have work to do?" he countered, fixing her with a cold stare he usually reserved for over-budget directors.

"Trust me," she said with a dramatic sigh, "talking to you about this *is* work."

He almost smiled. Almost. "Fine. Say it so I can get on with my day."

"Okay, I will."

As if anything could have stopped her.

She laid a stack of phone messages on his desk, then planted both hands on her substantial hips. "Like I was saying. Valentine's Day is tomorrow. A wise man would see this as an opportunity to send his wife some flowers. Or candy. Or both."

Dev snatched up the while-you-were-gone messages and fixed his gaze on them as if she weren't there. As if ignoring her would make her go away. It didn't work.

"I'm thinking," she continued, "that any wife

would be happy to hear from her husband on such a special day—"

"Valerie and I are separated, Megan," he reminded her tightly. Dev didn't want to talk about his marriage, his wife or the fact that she'd walked out on him. On *him.*

But now that Megan had brought it up, his brain picked up the torch and ran with it.

Dev still could hardly believe that his wife had left him. For God's sake, *why?* They'd gotten along all right. She'd had an open account at every store on Rodeo Drive and the free time to do all the shopping she wanted. They had lived in his suite at the family mansion, so she hadn't even had to concern herself with dealing with house-keepers. All she'd had to do was live with him.

Which, apparently, hadn't been enough of a draw to keep her there.

So now, he was a husband whose wife lived in an upscale condo in Beverly Hills, who was often photo-graphed shopping or doing lunch at some trendy restaurant in town and who might, for all Dev knew, be *dating.*

His fist tightened around the stack of messages until the papers folded in on themselves like a broken accordion. Dating—his *wife*—unacceptable, he told himself even as he realized there wasn't a damn thing he could do about it.

"That's right boss," Megan said, approval ringing in her tone. "You're *separated,* not divorced."

"Megan," he ground out, "if you value your job, you'll drop this. Now."

She snorted. "Oh, please. You couldn't run this place without me, and we both know it."

A deep voice spoke up from the doorway. "If he fires you, Megan, I'll hire you at twice the salary."

Dev looked at his brother Max. "Hell, I'll pay you to take her."

Megan frowned at both of them. "I should quit. Just to prove to you how indispensable I am around here. But I won't, because I'm just too good a person to watch this place fold without me."

She left with her nose in the air and a final scowl for both of them as she turned to close the door behind her.

Dev leaned back in his black-leather chair. "Why don't I fire her?"

Max strolled across the huge office and took the chair opposite his brother. "Because," he said as he sat down and got comfortable, "she's been here thirty years, has known us both since we were kids and would probably kill us both if we *tried* to get rid of her."

"Good point." Dev shook his head and let his gaze slide around the room. He barely noticed the framed movie posters hanging on his walls, the conference table, the wet bar, the functional yet comfortable furniture or even the view of the back lot of Hudson Pictures' studios that lay outside the wide windows.

This was his world. This was where he did the work that made him happy.

So why the *hell* wasn't he happy?

"What was she on you about now?"

Dev shot Max a quick look. "She thinks I should send Val flowers for Valentine's Day."

"Not a bad idea," his brother mused, steepling his fingers together. "I just sent Dana sterling roses and a giant box of Godiva. Why shouldn't you send something to Val?"

"Are you insane?" Dev shot to his feet and stalked the perimeter of the room. "You want to buy into this Valentine thing for your fiancée, fine. But Val walked out on me, remember?"

"Not really surprising, was it?"

"What's that supposed to mean?"

"Well, come on, Dev. She was nuts about you and you hardly noticed she was there."

He stopped dead, swiveled his head to glare at his younger brother and said, "My marriage is none of your business."

Max only shrugged. "I'm only saying that if you put as much effort into keeping your wife happy as you did with placating whiny directors, you wouldn't be alone right now."

"Thanks very much, Mr. Newly In Love and Newly Annoying."

Max smiled. "I admit it. I'm grateful to have found Dana. After I lost Karen…"

Dev winced. He hadn't meant to bring up his brother's late wife or the misery he'd lived through for so long. "Look, I'm glad you're happy. But that doesn't mean everybody else is looking for what you have."

"You should."

"Damn it, Max, did you come here to lecture me on my love life? What are you, some love guru now?"

"Hardly!" Max laughed shortly. "But since Megan was already on your ass, thought I'd join in."

"Thanks so much. But no thanks. Love is for morons."

For the last year, the entire Hudson family had been

tumbling into love and marriage and happily ever afters. And they were damned irritating on the subject—all of them.

Well, Dev wasn't convinced. They were in the movie business. Hudson Pictures *sold* happy endings to the public. That didn't mean that Dev believed in them.

"Says every man who doesn't have a woman around on Valentine's Day." Max shook his head and grinned.

Dev shot Max a hard look that didn't do a thing toward dimming his brother's self-satisfied smile. "I can't believe even you're buying into this. Valentine's Day? You're serious? Every male in the world knows that the holiday was invented by card manufacturers and candymakers. It's a woman's holiday, little brother. Not a man's."

"A little candy, a few flowers and some wine and there's a great evening for both of you. Of course," Max mused, "you wouldn't know anything about that, would you? Oh, no. You're the guy who let his wife leave him on Christmas Eve. Mr. Romance."

"You know something? You're far less amusing now that you're in love."

"Funny," Max mused. "Your marriage didn't change your personality at all."

No, it hadn't. But then, Dev told himself, he hadn't gone into his marriage claiming to be "in love," either. He'd married Valerie because he'd needed a wife and she had fit the requirements perfectly. She had good connections —press, media, corporate—and she looked lovely on his arm.

At least she *had,* until she left him. Not that he missed her or anything. He was fine with Val being gone. Completely fine.

"Exactly my point," he said firmly. "I'm the same man I was when I got married."

"And that's a damn shame," Max told him.

Frowning, Dev walked to the wide bank of windows and stared out the glass. There were acres of land out there, all belonging to Hudson Pictures. There was the back lot, where dozens of different sets stood, just waiting for camera crews to arrive and bring them to life again. There were actors and extras, stagehands and electricians. The studio back lot was a small city and he was its mayor.

But instead of seeing his domain, nestled deep in the heart of Burbank, Dev's mind furnished a mental view of Beverly Hills. Where Valerie now lived in a condo that he'd never seen the inside of.

Glancing back at his brother, Dev kept his voice low and demanded, "What's that supposed to mean?"

"It means, Dev, that you could use a little lightening up."

Max turned his chair so that he was facing Dev. "Val was your shot at actually having a real life and you let her waltz right out the door."

Gritting his teeth, he shifted his gaze back to the city view. He didn't want to talk about his marriage. Not with Max. Not with anyone.

The irritation that had spiked inside him the night Val left—Christmas Eve, no less—was still with him. He was Devlin Hudson. Nobody walked out on him. At least no one ever *had* until Val. And dealing with the very public aftermath of his marriage's collapse had left Dev with a bitter taste in his mouth and his hackles continually on the rise.

Every newspaper and gossip rag in the city had speculated as to the reason for Val leaving him. There'd been paparazzi after the two of them for weeks and though he hated to admit it, even to himself, Dev had sunk so low as to checking out the tabloids just to catch any news of what his wife was up to.

He turned abruptly, walked back to his desk and sat down again. Only when he had the breadth of the desk between him and his brother did he say, "Did it ever occur to you that I was the one who wanted the separation?"

"Nope." Max shook his head, leaned back in his chair and stretched out his legs, crossing his feet at the ankle. He looked as relaxed as a man could get in an eight-hundred-dollar suit. "See, Dev, that's not your style. Once you make a deal, you stick to it. So, no, you wouldn't have asked her to go. The only thing I can't figure out is why you *allowed* her to leave."

"Allow?" Now Dev laughed and folded his hands together atop his abdomen. "You do a lot of 'allowing' in your relationship, do you? I think Dana would disagree."

For the first time, Max frowned, clearly trying to imagine using the word "allow" and Dana in the same sentence, then looked slightly less relaxed. "Touché. Okay, maybe *allow* was the wrong word. But what the hell were you thinking letting her leave you? It was clear to everybody in the family that Val was nuts about you."

She had been, Dev remembered as Max and the office drifted away on a tide of memories. Val had always been so damn eager for time with him. Her eyes shining, smile bright. She'd gone into a relationship with him with anticipation and enthusiasm. He'd taken it for granted, of course. Why wouldn't he? He'd known she loved him. That was only one of the reasons he'd been so sure that marrying her was the right move. How could he go wrong if his wife loved him?

More memories crowded his mind. Valerie, smiling at him. Val in France on the set of the movie, *Honor.* Val in their bed, giving him a wan smile after their disastrous wedding night. Damn it. Devlin actually squirmed in his chair at that memory.

But in his defense, he hadn't expected her to be a virgin. Hadn't thought for a minute that she'd be nervous, wound so tight every nerve was a live wire and a little toasted to boot.

Not his proudest moment, he admitted silently. He had wanted her badly and hadn't bothered with seduction. Sex that night had been a misery, and because of that, every attempt at lovemaking after that had been just as bad. Memories were a hard thing to defeat, and Dev hadn't been able to get past his own regrets and her burgeoning fears to make sex anything more than a disaster.

Pushing his dark thoughts aside, he focused on Max and said clearly, "It's none of the family's business."

"This is about Mom and Dad, isn't it? About their marriage."

Devlin speared a hard look at his brother. Since finding out that his own mother had cheated in her marriage to Dev's father, Devlin hadn't had a lot of faith in the sanctity of matrimony. Sure, it had colored his outlook a little. Why wouldn't it? The two people he'd always considered close to perfect had turned out to have feet of clay.

"Leave them out of this."

"Why? You're not." Max sighed. "You won't talk to Dad about this, won't hear Mom out and you're like the damn ice man around the rest of us."

"I've been working," Dev announced on a growl of irritation. "Maybe you haven't noticed but we've got a few films in postproduction, not to mention that little Academy Award nomination...."

"This isn't about work, Dev. This is about you. Your life. All you had to do was try, man." Max frowned at him. "Val loved you, and you blew it."

Regret stabbed at him again and Devlin didn't like the feel of it. He wasn't a man to look backward. He never had been one to think over past mistakes and try to figure out where he'd gone wrong. The past was past and there wasn't a damn thing you could do to change it.

Deliberately, Dev stood up and looked down at his brother. "I didn't blow a damn thing. And I should think you'd be better off spending time on your own love life instead of worrying about me and my wife."

"You don't have a wife, Dev," Max reminded him.

Funny, he'd said the same thing to Megan just awhile ago, but now, hearing Max say those words was enough to jumpstart a ball of fury in the pit of his stomach. But Megan was right. He *did* have a wife. He just didn't have her with him. Well, fine, he couldn't fix the past. But he could for damn sure do something about the future.

"Yeah, I do," he countered, realizing that he was sick

to death of fielding reporters' questions, dodging photographers and putting up with his own family's incessant prodding about Val. It was time he straightened this mess out.

After all, why the hell was *he* dealing with all of this?

He wasn't the one who'd walked out on their marriage. He wasn't the one who'd wanted to wander around an empty suite of rooms and listen to the silence. She'd put them through all of this, and he was damned tired of living with the situation she'd created.

"That'll be news to Val," Max said, pushing himself out of his chair.

"You let me worry about Val." The more he thought about this, the better he felt. Riding a surge of righteous anger, Dev stalked across the room, threw open the closet door and grabbed his suit jacket off a hanger.

"Where're you going?" Max demanded.

"I'm going to have a long talk with my wife," Dev said. And as the thought of seeing her again fixated in his mind, he realized just how much he'd missed her, damn it. "Time I reminded Val that we're still married."

"You think it's going to be that easy?"

Dev looked at his younger brother. For the past few days, he'd been surrounded by googly-eyed secretaries, assistants and family members. It seemed every time he turned around there was a box of candy or a bouquet of flowers being delivered to the office.

The hearts and flowers of Valentine's Day had only served to remind him over the past few days just how alone he really was. The emptiness he faced when he went home nagged at him. Watching his brothers and sister revel in their own romances was bothering him on a level he wouldn't have thought possible before now.

Why that was, he didn't really want to think about. After all, he'd been alone most of his life. By choice.

And maybe that was the real motivator here. He hadn't chosen to be alone. He'd been forced into it by a decision Valerie had made all by herself. Well, she'd had her say. She'd walked out. Gotten all the "space" anyone could possibly want. But that was over. It was time she came home. Lived up to the marriage vows they'd made. Nobody had said anything about *until you feel like leaving*. No. It had been *until death do you part*. When Dev took an oath, he kept it. He expected no less from his wife.

And it was past time he told her that.

Smiling grimly at Max, he said, "Easy or not, it's going to be done."

Valerie Shelton Hudson had her own condo over-looking the hills and trees and mansions of Beverly Hills. It was plush, luxurious, tastefully decorated and so damned empty she wanted to scream just to hear some noise.

She rarely turned on the television or the radio, though—she didn't want to hear anything about Hudson Pictures or the upcoming Academy Awards. Every time she heard Devlin's name, her heart ached and the lone-liness that had become such a part of her threatened to swallow her whole.

So instead of thinking about what she'd lost, she'd devoted herself to as little thinking as possible. She went to lunch with her friends, volunteered at her favorite charities, did some shopping and tried to ignore the paparazzi who tended to leap out at her, cameras clicking, every time she left her home.

She managed to fill her days, but her nights were empty, quiet, lonely. She wasn't interested in dating and couldn't bring herself to hit any of the trendy nightspots with her friends. So nights were long and days were crowded and still she found time to miss her husband. Miss the very man who had ignored her so completely that her only option had been to leave him.

"This is not the way I want to live," she muttered and stepped out onto the secluded, private patio off her living room.

A jumble of plants greeted her. There were ferns in hanging pots, flowers spilling out of ceramic tubs, neatly trimmed bushes and even a small lemon tree in the corner. There was a chrome-and-tile table and four decorative café chairs pulled up to it. There was also a patio swing boasting a bright red and yellow awning and it was to that spot she headed. Curled up on the swing, she could listen to the distant hum of traffic fifteen stories below her and know that in at least *this* place, she had privacy.

A place to think. Unfortunately, the minute she started thinking, her thoughts turned to Devlin. Scowling to herself, she pushed aside the image of him that raced into her mind: the stunned look on his face when she'd told him she was leaving. She hated remembering that she had turned tail and run away. She hated that she hadn't dug her heels in and fought for the marriage she'd wanted.

Oh, at first, she'd blamed Devlin for the inglorious

end to their marriage. But now, she was forced to admit that there was enough blame to go around for both of them. She hadn't ever spoken up for herself. Hadn't made him *see* her. Instead, she'd waited quietly—like a big idiot—for him to feel the same sparks she had the moment she'd met him.

She picked up a throw pillow, hugged it to her chest and leaned her head against the back of the swing. Closing her eyes, she allowed Dev's image to rise up in her mind again and in an instant everything in her body went into a slow burn.

God, she wished she could do it all over again. She'd do so many things differently.

"First off, I wouldn't be so damned accommodating," she muttered, eyes still closed as she studied the mental image of Dev. "I'd speak up for myself. Spend less time trying to be the perfect little wife and more time being myself." She choked on that last sentence.

Perfect little wife.

"Good God, no wonder he was bored. Could anything be more horrifying?" Groaning, she hugged that pillow tighter to her midsection and felt frustration bubbling up inside her. It was a familiar feeling these days.

"Ms. Hudson?"

Valerie sighed at her housekeeper's interruption, but didn't lift her head or open her eyes. "Yes, Teresa?"

"There's someone to see you," the other woman said quietly, almost apologetically. "I told him you didn't want to be disturbed, but—"

"I wouldn't take no for an answer."

Valerie's head shot up, her eyes flew open and her gaze locked on the one person she'd never expected to see again.

Her husband.

Two

Two

"Surprised?" Dev walked past the housekeeper, strolled out onto the patio and, with his hands in the pockets of his slacks, looked completely at ease.

"Yeah, I'm surprised." She stared at him as if he were an apparition and Dev couldn't tell if that meant she was happy to see him or not.

"I need to talk to you." Dev's gaze slipped from her to the housekeeper and back again.

Val took a deep breath, braced herself and glanced at the woman waiting in the doorway. "It's all right, Teresa. I'll be fine."

The older woman didn't look convinced. As she turned to go, she said plainly, "If you need me, Ms. Hudson, just call."

When she was gone, Dev actually laughed. "Your own private dragon?"

"I don't need a dragon at the gates, Dev. I can take care of myself."

One dark eyebrow rose as he watched her, then slowly, he nodded. "I expect you could."

"So, we're alone now. Why don't you tell me what this is about?"

She didn't sound exactly welcoming, but it didn't really matter. He'd come on a mission, damn it, and he was going to see it through. He'd thought about this all the way over here and he knew precisely the tack he was going to take with Val. He'd simply point out to her that this separation was ridiculous. They were married. They should be together. And, he'd remind her that the Oscars were fast approaching and that he wanted the Hudson family to show a united front.

All reasonable.

He was sure he'd convince her.

"Why are you here?"

Surprised himself now, Dev looked at her and watched as she tossed the throw pillow to one side and stood up. When she faced him, her chin was raised and her eyes were staring directly into his. All right, that was different. The Val he knew—the one he'd expected to find—was nowhere to be seen. She would have stayed curled up on the swing, hidden behind a pillow and keeping her gaze averted.

Still, a little backbone was a good thing.

"I've come to bring you home."

"I am home," she countered and walked to the table and chairs. She pulled out one of the tiny, more decorative than useful seats and sat down, staring up at him.

"I meant," he said, keeping his voice even, "our home. The family mansion."

"I don't live there anymore," she told him.

A flicker of temper flashed inside him, but he quickly tamped it down. He'd been in enough negotiations to know that an even keel was necessary to accomplish your goals. Pulling out the chair closest to him, Dev sat down beside her, braced his elbows on his knees and looked into her eyes.

"Yeah, you left. I remember."

"Then why—"

He held up one hand to cut her off. "It's been a couple of months now, Val. I think you've made your point."

"My point?" Her big eyes went even wider.

"You wanted to let me know you were unhappy. I get that. And I'm willing to talk this out and do whatever's necessary to get you back where you belong."

There was a long pause while she considered the speech he'd worked out on the drive to her house. He'd been logical, thoughtful and thorough. No one could ask for more.

"Why?"

He blinked at her. "What?"

"Not what," she countered. "Why. Why do you want me back?"

"You're my wife."

She blew out a breath before saying, "Okay then, why now? Why not a month ago? Why not a month from now? Why are you here today, Dev?"

He sat up, leaned one arm on the table and felt the cool, knobby glass beneath his hand. He hadn't expected questions. The Val he was used to would have simply agreed and gone along with his plan. *That* Val would have made this much easier.

Thinking fast, he told her, "Tomorrow's Valentine's Day."

"So?"

He should have brought flowers. Or candy. Or as Megan had suggested, *both*. Since he hadn't, he dropped the reference to the most romantic day on the calendar and went in another direction.

"It made me realize how much time has gone by," he said. Reasonable again. "The Academy Awards will be here soon, and I think it's important for the Hudson family to be together when we win for Best Picture."

"I see."

Not a flicker of emotion on her face. Dev couldn't tell what she was thinking and that bothered him more than he wanted to admit. Something else was bothering him as well, though. Something more disconcerting than trying to discover who this new, mysterious Val was.

One look at her and his body had gone tight and hard and eager. Damn it. Even remembering how disastrous the sex had been between them, he couldn't deny that he still wanted her. Badly enough that simply sitting, at the moment, was uncomfortable.

So he stood up. He took two steps, stopped, then whirled around to face her. "Look, my point is, we're married. We both knew what we were doing when we went into this marriage. We agreed when we first got together that there would be no divorce."

They'd both seen firsthand how out of control the cycle of marriage and divorce could get—especially in this town. And neither of them had wanted any part of that.

"True," she agreed.

"Good," he said, smiling now. His point made, he could afford to be magnanimous. "So you'll come home."

She stood up slowly, unfolding herself from the chair with a fluid sort of grace that gave her a suppleness that fed the flames already crouched inside Dev. He bit back a groan as she faced him.

"*If* I come home," she said, capturing his attention immediately, "there are a couple of conditions."

"Excuse me?" He hadn't expected *this*.

Valerie really enjoyed the expression of stunned disbelief on his face. Oh God, why hadn't she been more herself from the beginning? If she'd only shown him the real Valerie, so much heartache and misery could have been avoided. On both sides.

Well, she told herself, feeling a rush of excitement build within, she was getting a second chance. Devlin still didn't love her, she knew that. But he wanted her back. Had come to her home to get her to return to him. That was a huge plus for her side. And if he was willing to go that far, then surely he'd go a little further.

"If we do this," she said, meeting and holding his gaze, "then we do it differently this time."

"What do you mean, differently?" His expression was guarded now.

"I mean, I want a *real* marriage, Dev. Not the polite, distant merger we had before."

"Meaning?"

His eyes narrowed on her, but Val stood her ground. She wasn't the spineless, shy little Stepford Wife he thought her to be. She was a woman with her own mind and enough courage to face down the man she loved and tell him that she'd rather leave than have only half of him. If she'd had the strength to walk out on him, then she had the strength to fight for him.

"I want you to spend time with me. I want a partnership."

"Valerie—"

"Oh, no. Don't take that oh-so-patient tone with me, either, Dev," she said, cutting him off neatly before he could give her the figurative pat on the head he so clearly wanted to do.

His features went tight and hard, but she wasn't going to be dissuaded from saying exactly what she thought. Not this time. If they were going to try again, then Val wanted the brass ring this time around.

"You always use that specific tone of voice when you want to politely tell me to back off."

"No, I don't—"

"You did, too, but not anymore, okay?" She walked in closer, which wasn't easy because her knees were a little wobbly and the slow burn she'd felt the moment he walked onto her patio had become an inferno, spreading through her veins.

"Is that right?"

"Yep." She smiled up at him and watched, pleased, as his eyes flashed. "I'm your wife, Dev. And if we're going to do this marriage right, then I want more of your attention. There's something else, too. I know we didn't start off right, but I want you in my bed."

He nodded. "Good—"

"I want children."

"Children?"

"Doesn't have to be today," she amended when he got that deer-in-the-headlights look in his eyes. "But someday soon. I want a family, Dev. And for this to work, that means that I'll need you to devote to me at least a *quarter* of the energies you show to Hudson Pictures."

"That's quite the list of conditions."

"It is," she said and folded her arms across her chest to hide the nerves beginning to shake through her. She'd done the right thing, speaking up, letting him know she wouldn't go back to being his own private doormat. But now that she'd made her play and placed her bet, she was forced to wait to see if Dev was willing to start their marriage over again—the right way.

His gaze fixed on her, Dev scraped one hand across his jaw. Seconds ticked past and the nerves quaking inside her began to rattle like dice in a cup. Though Dev looked irritated, he, as always, had a tight grip on that control of his. He never let his emotions rule him.

That legendary control of his was the first thing Valerie had to break through. If she could just get him to open up, to let himself go, they might just stand a chance of making this work.

And the minute that thought flashed through her mind, she knew exactly what she was going to have to do to accomplish it. She would have to use sex to break down the walls he'd built up around himself. She knew it instinctively. Despite the fact that their lovemaking so far had been awkward and restrained, she knew that he wanted her as badly as she did him. All she had to do was seduce him into losing his self-control.

Sure, she told herself wryly, no problem.

"Say I agree…"

She stopped thinking and held her breath.

"What's to stop you from walking out again the next time you feel…unappreciated?"

"My word," she said, meeting that cold, hard gaze of his steadily. It was a fair question and he had no way of knowing that she'd been kicking herself silly ever since she'd left him. No, if she went back to him, it was for good. No more running. No more backing off. This time she was in it to win her husband or die trying.

"I give you my word," she said, "that if we start over, I won't leave unless you *want* me to."

"That won't happen," he said softly, his gaze dropping now to sweep over her body like a caress. She felt heat racing across her skin and her body nearly hummed with a sense of anticipation.

"Then we have nothing to worry about, do we?" God, was she doing the right thing? Yes, she answered that question immediately. She still loved Dev. She wanted a marriage with him. And if she could just make him see what they could have together, it would all be worth it.

"Well, then," he said, stepping in closer, cupping her shoulders with his big, warm hands, "looks like we have a deal, Mrs. Hudson."

"Looks like we do, Mr. Hudson," she said and silently congratulated herself on speaking at all. Her throat was tight and the heat rushing through her felt like magma, thick in her veins.

He was wearing that cologne she loved on him, with the mingled scents of spice and citrus. This close to her husband, Val could hardly breathe and she wondered just how she'd managed to live through the last couple of months without seeing him.

Touching him.

As he was now touching her. His hands moved up and down her arms, creating a friction on her bare skin that felt almost electrical with the buzz it created. She took a breath, held it for a second, then let it go as she stared up into his startlingly blue eyes.

"You surprised me today, Val," he said, his voice a hush of sound she had to strain to hear. "You were always so quiet. So…"

She frowned a bit. "Accommodating?"

He smiled. "Maybe."

"Disappointed?" she asked as his hands swept up her arms to cup her face.

"What do you think?" He lowered his head and kissed her.

His mouth claimed hers, his tongue parted her lips and swept inside her warmth, stealing away what breath she had left. She melted into the hard, broad wall of his chest and gave herself up to incredible sensations as they crested and peaked one after another inside her.

His lips, his tongue, made love to her mouth as he shifted his hands to slide down her spine to the curve of her behind. Then he held her, pressed her tightly to the hard, thickness of his body until she knew exactly just how much he wanted her.

The kiss went on and on and Val lost all track of time. Nothing else mattered. Nothing else was as important as this moment, here with him, when her life was starting over, when she felt the first stirrings of hope that one day she would have the marriage and the *man* she'd always dreamed of.

Then he broke the kiss, raised his head and looked down at her through dark, desire-filled eyes. "Let's get your stuff and go home."

"Right."

He took her hand and led her back into the condo and Val could only think that maybe the seduction of Devlin Hudson wasn't going to be as difficult as she'd thought.

Three

Moving her things to the mansion wasn't as difficult as Val would have imagined. Dev had a way of getting things done when it was something he wanted.

Almost before she knew it, her bags were packed, Teresa was given an enormous severance package and Val was back in Dev's suite of rooms at the Hudson family estate.

As she unpacked, she couldn't help remembering the last time she'd been there: the afternoon of Christmas Eve when she'd faced Dev and told him she was leaving him. She could still remember the look of stunned disbelief on his face as he'd heard her out. And she'd known then that he'd been more shocked by someone actually defying him than he had been by her leaving.

Devlin Hudson never lost. At anything.

And as if to prove that out, here she was, back again.

"But I'm not the same Val," she reassured herself. "Things will be different this time. I'm not going to be the convenient wife again. No more appearing when he wants me and disappearing when he doesn't. I'm here and he's just going to have to learn to live with it."

Of course, she'd been back at the mansion for an hour and so far, nothing had changed. Dev had dropped her off and gone back to work to "clear up a few things."

A bad start to their fresh beginning? she wondered. But as soon as that thought slid through her mind, she banished it. She wasn't going to start off resenting him. Valerie already knew that it would take her some time to win Dev's affections. Breaking down a wall he'd spent his entire life building wasn't going to be done overnight.

When her last blouse had been hung and the last sweater tucked away, she turned to look around Dev's— *their*—bedroom. She smiled to herself. No more of this his-and-hers bedroom stuff anymore, either. When they first got married, Dev had insisted that she choose one of the extra rooms in the suite as her own sanctuary. But as things between them had become more and more strained, she'd found herself, more often than not, retreating to the room that had become more of a hideout than sanctuary.

This time, she wasn't going to give herself a chance to hide away and lick her wounds. She wasn't going to give either one of them a chance to go back to the awkward behavior that had so ruined their sex life—and their marriage—before. Nope. If they were going to be married, then she was going to be right here.

In his bed.

Where he couldn't ignore her.

She wanted to share his bed every night and wake up beside him every morning. She wanted to become such a part of his life that he couldn't imagine a world without her in it. And this bed would be her battle-ground.

Okay, yes, she was a little nervous. But she'd spent the last several weeks thinking of everything that had gone wrong between her and Dev. Telling herself what she could have done differently.

Now was her chance.

She looked at the extra-wide, king-size mattress covered by a black duvet and mounded with pillows. Soft, late afternoon light crept through the opened drapes and lay across the bed as if in invitation. Thankfully, she thought, their wedding night had not been spent in this bed, so there were no lingering, uncomfortable memories associated with it. This was a new start and, as she looked at the bed, Val's mind filled with erotic images, all flashing through her brain in a dizzying sort of slide show.

Dev looming over her. Dev taking her in the shower. His hands stroking her skin even as she reached to touch him everywhere. Her heart pounded and her blood ran suddenly thick in her veins.

"Whoa." She swallowed hard and slapped one hand to her abdomen in a futile attempt to still the swarms of butterflies racing around inside. Then she shook her head at her own uneasiness. "You're not the same wimpy little virgin you were before, Val. You know you want him—so go get him already."

Monologue pep talks.

"Great. Not only am I talking to myself, I'm cheering myself up. Can't be a good sign."

Blowing out a breath, she left the bedroom, walked down a short hall and into the massive family room/den.

A stone fireplace crouched against one wall and its mantel was filled with framed family photos. On the beige walls, paintings by artists both famous and unknown were hung side by side. Brown leather couches and chairs were drawn up in conversational groups and heavy oak tables held stacks of books and scripts along with shaded Tiffany lamps. There was a wet bar in one corner and a 52-inch plasma TV on the far wall.

The room was beautiful, but it was also completely male. When she'd lived here before, she'd been too timid to try to put her stamp on Dev's place, so instead she'd left herself to feel like a temporary roommate in his home.

"Well, that ship has sailed," she promised the empty room, already planning some shopping and redecorating excursions.

Being here was both familiar and strange all at the same time. In the months they lived there together, Valerie had tried to fit into Dev's life rather than convincing him to build a new life for both of them. She'd put her own wants and desires aside, foolishly believing that if she was everything he needed, he would want her.

Now she knew that he could never really want *her* if he never knew who she actually was.

So, until her marriage was on solid ground and she could talk him into buying their own home, then she would have to find a way to make this place her home, as well as his. It might not be easy living here, but she could do it.

She laughed suddenly, appalled at her own thoughts. "Such a hardship, Val. Being *forced* to live in an entire wing of a palatial mansion in Beverly Hills. You poor baby."

Stupid to feel sorry for yourself while standing in what was practically a castle. But until she'd carved out a slice of this place for herself, she was just going to feel unsettled.

Smiling a little wistfully, she walked across the big area to the second-story balcony that overlooked the sweep of lawn to the side of the house. She opened the French doors, stepped onto the stone patio and lifted her face to the breeze sighing through the ancient trees surrounding the estate.

When she opened her eyes again, she noticed it was close to sunset. Already, brilliant shades of crimson and violet were staining the sky. Soon, Dev would be coming home. Nerves she was all too familiar with fluttered to life again in the pit of her stomach.

But this time, she deliberately fought them down. She wouldn't let her own sense of uneasiness ruin this before it had even begun. She was a wife who wanted her husband. A wife who had finally decided to steer her marriage down the path she wanted it to take. So, nerves or not, she was going through with her plan.

And, she thought firmly as she headed back inside, when he walked in the door, Devlin was going to have quite the surprise waiting for him.

Dev would have agreed to any of Val's terms—in theory. He wanted his wife back where she belonged. And once she was settled in the mansion again, she'd forget about her "conditions." Their marriage would return to the way it had been. With, he thought, remembering that kiss on her patio, one exception.

She wanted him in her bed? He wanted the same damn thing. They'd been too caught up in the disaster that had been their wedding night to ever overcome it. But it was past time they let that miserable night go.

He wanted his wife, damn it. As that thought registered, he admitted silently that he actually wanted her more than he'd ever expected to. Just looking at her this afternoon had fired every ounce of need and hunger locked inside him. And kissing her had pushed him closer to the edge than he had been in far too long.

Dev prided himself on his control. He kept a tight rein on all of his emotions at all times. He wasn't one to be led around by his desire and he wasn't one to open himself up to feelings that could potentially turn around and bite him.

But he wasn't prepared to live the life of a guilt-ridden monk, either. Yes, their wedding night had been bad and the few times they'd made love after that, he'd held back because he could still see the misery in her eyes. That time was past, though. She wanted a fresh start and he could ensure they had it.

This time, he was prepared to give her the seduction she needed to get past the fears that were no doubt still crowding her mind.

If he'd simply done this from the beginning, she never would have left, he reminded himself. This time, he was determined to get things right.

Hence the giant bouquet of flowers and the huge box of Godiva chocolates lying on the passenger seat of his sports car. He hated like hell that he was buying into the whole Valentine's Day thing, but this was a special occasion. His wife was home where she belonged and he wanted to catch her off guard. And if the flowers and candy didn't do it for him, then the slow seduction he had planned would turn the trick.

A candlelight dinner on the patio of their suite. Soft music playing on the stereo. A dance in the moonlight. By the time he was through with her, she'd be melting into his arms.

Smiling to himself, Dev steered the car into the circular drive in front of the mansion. He'd produced enough movies with sappy love stories in them to know exactly how to set a scene for sex.

Grabbing up the flowers and candy, Dev opened the car door, got out, then slammed it behind him. Instead of going for the front door of the house, he walked around to the side to his private entrance. No point in letting the whole house see him carrying roses and candy like some lovesick puppy.

Besides, what went on between him and his wife was their business.

The outside lights were on, tossing pale shadows of white into the encroaching darkness. Wind rustled the leaves in the trees and he heard the cheerful splash of water in the nearby fountain. He glanced to the second-story patio and caught a glimpse of white linen. Good—that meant the housekeeper had seen to the setting of the table. All he'd have to do was call down to the kitchen when they were ready to eat.

He smiled to himself as he stepped inside, ignored the family living room and took the stairs to his apartment on the second floor. He was willing to bet that Valerie had been surprised as hell to discover that he'd arranged for a candlelit dinner for the two of them.

Which meant, she was already primed for seduction. The flowers and candy would be as big a surprise and probably just enough to push her over the edge.

"The secret," Dev told himself as he hit the landing and strode down the hall to his den, "is to keep her off-balance. So that she never knows what's coming next." His fist tightened around the bouquet of roses and baby's breath as he stepped into the room.

"Surprise. That's the key," he told himself.

"Welcome home, Dev."

Dev dropped the bouquet at his feet. The box of candy followed. His jaw dropped and something deep inside him lurched unsteadily.

His wife, the woman he'd been so determined to surprise, the one who'd been so shy and awkward their first night together, was draped languidly across his favorite chair, wearing nothing but a string of pearls and her wedding ring.

She smiled, lifted the pearls to her mouth and idly nibbled at the soft, white gems. Glancing at the floor, she then lifted her gaze to his and asked, "Are those for me?"

"What?" His brain was fogged.

Dev shook his head, trying to get his mind jump-started, but all the blood in his body had drained to a spot much farther south. "You—I wasn't expecting—uh…"

She smiled and leaned her head against the arm of the chair. "What's the matter, Dev? Aren't you happy to see me?"

"Yeah." Idiot, he called himself as he stepped into the room and closed the door behind him. He'd thought to surprise *her?* Hell, his mouth was dry, his heart was pounding and his body was so tight and hard he thought he just might explode if she moved the slightest bit. "I'm…surprised—" damn it "—that's all."

"Well, good." She swung her legs off the arm of the chair and stood up slowly. Her long, lean body was even better than he remembered. High, firm breasts, narrow waist and trim legs. Her skin was the color of ripe peaches and her hair was loose and wavy about her face.

She was a temptress.

He'd never seen this side of his wife and he had to say he approved.

"I think it's time we surprised each other a little, don't you?" She was walking toward him—God help him. Each step brought her a little closer and his gaze moved over her body eagerly; he was loving the way the soft lights in the room drifted over her skin.

"That was my idea, too," he admitted and remembered that he'd dropped the gifts he'd brought home for her. Bending over, he scooped them up and held them out to her as she came closer.

"They're lovely," she murmured and buried her face in the luxurious bouquet of pale lavender roses. She lifted her gaze to his. "Chocolate, too? That's so thoughtful, Dev. Thank you."

She turned to set the flowers and candy down on the nearest table and Dev's gaze dropped to the curve of her truly luscious behind. His hands itched to touch her. His body craved hers. He wanted to toss her onto the floor and bury himself inside her.

But, he warned himself, that's just the kind of thinking that had made their wedding night so grim. No finesse. Just hunger. No seduction. Just need. He wouldn't repeat that mistake. So, though it might kill him to take it slowly, he was going to do just that.

She turned back to him, smiled into his eyes and said softly, "I want you, Dev. Now."

Something in his brain exploded.

That was the only answer.

Because he heard himself say, "Thank God," just before he grabbed her and pulled her close.

Val felt the strength in his arms and gave herself up to the wonder of knowing that his desire matched her own. What a fool she'd been when she first married him. She'd come to him too nervous to allow her own need free rein and she'd cheated herself out of these swamping waves of hunger.

His mouth came down on hers; his tongue danced with hers in a tangled web of passion that stole what little breath she had left. It had taken every ounce of her nerve to meet him naked as he walked in the door, but, oh, it had been so worth it. The look on his face when he'd first seen her would stay with her forever.

Devlin Hudson didn't know it, but Val had already won the first battle for his heart.

Then her thoughts dissolved under an onslaught of sensations that threatened to drown her. He tore his mouth from hers, buried his face in the curve of her neck and nibbled at her throat, tasting the pulse point at the base. His tongue swept over her heated skin and sent shivers of anticipation rocketing through her system.

Here was the magic she'd hoped to find on their

wedding night. What he did to her dissolved all thought and erased any of the lingering traces of anxiety she might have been feeling.

Valerie moaned softly, turned her head to give him greater access and arched into him, silently urging him on. His hands slid up and down her back, defining her spine, exploring her skin, cupping her bottom with a grip both firm and gentle. His fingers held on to her, pulling her in tightly enough that she couldn't miss feeling the hard, solid length of him pressed against her.

Her core went molten and liquid, every cell tingling and alive with expectation. Her breasts rubbed against his suit jacket and linen shirt, the fine material scraping sensuously against her sensitive skin. It was good. All good. But she wanted more. Wanted to feel his flesh against hers. Feel the heat of him sliding into her.

As if he heard her silent wish, he pulled away from her and tore his jacket and shirt off, tossing them onto the floor with no more thought than she gave them. Then he was holding her again, molding her to his broad, muscular chest, and Val sighed with contentment.

God, how she'd missed the feel of him against her. Even when things were bad between them, she'd loved the slide of his skin on hers. Loved the sensation of stroking her fingers through the mat of dark hair in the middle of his chest. For weeks, she'd thought about nothing else but getting back into Dev's bed.

And now she didn't want to wait another minute.

"Take me now, Dev," she whispered, going up on her toes as he bent his head to taste her breast. "I need you so much...."

He raised his head, looking down at her through blue eyes glazed with a passion she'd spent weeks dreaming of seeing. "This isn't how I planned tonight," he admitted, his voice rough with a tightly controlled need.

"Does it matter?" she asked and lifted one hand to let her fingertips trail from his collarbone down to his flat abdomen.

He shivered, closed his eyes, then opened them again to stare directly into hers. "No. It doesn't."

"I want you," she said softly, watching his eyes, gauging his reaction to her words. "I want you inside me. I want to feel you, hard and deep."

His eyes flashed and Val took a deep breath, luxuriating in the knowledge that her husband, the man she loved, could be so hungry for her. He might not love her yet, but desire was a good place to start. If he felt only half of what she was feeling, then she knew she could win his love. Knew she'd convince him that what had begun as a marriage of convenience on his side could become what all marriages should be. A match of love.

"Hold on," he muttered, then bent, scooped her into his arms and carried her across the wide room, down the short hall and into his bedroom. He paused on the threshold and Valerie turned to see the room as he was seeing it.

She'd prepared for this night in here, too. Dozens of candles flickered around the room, their dancing flames casting shadows of light and movement on the walls. The patio doors were open to the night and the soft song of the cool wind slid into the room, caressing heated skin.

The duvet was turned back, displaying dark red sheets, and the pillows were plumped in invitation.

He turned his gaze down to hers and smiled briefly, one corner of his mouth tipping up. "You've been busy."

"Yes," she said, lifting one hand to trace that slight smile with the tip of her finger. "And I've been waiting for you for hours."

"Waiting's over," he told her. "For both of us."

Then he carried her into the room, eased her down onto the mattress and stood back long enough to strip the rest of his clothes off. Val's breath caught in her chest as she stared up at the man who had claimed so much of her heart and mind for months.

His chest was sculpted and tanned. His legs were powerful, muscular, and his erection was immense. Before, she'd been terrified by the size of him. Now, she took another breath and fought down the first signs of trepidation to rear their ugly heads that night. She remembered the pain of their first joining and couldn't help wincing at the memory. But that was then, she told herself as he leaned over her. This is now. And tonight would be different, because *she* was different.

She wasn't going to lie back and be made love to. She was going to be an active participant.

Dev's gaze was locked on hers and Val saw the hesitation there even before he asked, "Are you sure?"

"Yes," she said, making her voice firm enough to convince not only him, but herself. Nerves were willed into the background and passion was given complete control. This wasn't the time for thinking. Here, in his arms, she wanted only to feel.

"Good," he said and took her mouth with his even as his left hand swept down her body to cup her heat.

Valerie nearly came off the mattress as his fingers and

thumb stroked her inner core, driving her closer and closer to a ragged edge of sanity. Sensation after sensation crowded into her system as she felt herself tightening into a coiled spring that was sure to explode any second.

Magic, she thought again, her mind fogging over as Dev's tongue tangled with hers, his breath sliding into her lungs. Here was what she'd dreamed of.

Her hips arched off the bed as she moved into his hand, again and again, rocking against him, whimpering from the back of her throat as he pushed first one finger, then two, into her depths. It felt so good. So right. So…amazing.

His thumb brushed over the most sensitive spot on her body, sending electrical-like jolts of something incredible spinning off through her system only to slide back and build into another crescendo. He tore his mouth from hers, shifted position slightly and took first one of her nipples and then the other into his mouth.

His lips and tongue and teeth tormented her while his magic fingers continued to push her higher and faster than she'd ever been before. With so many feelings trapped inside, Val could hardly breathe.

She opened her eyes and watched candle-flame shadows dance on the ceiling until Dev raised his head and moved to block her view. Then all she could see were his eyes. The passion. The hunger, staring back down at her. His jaw tight, his breath hissing from his lungs, he was a man so tightly strung she couldn't imagine the control he was wielding.

But she didn't want him controlled. She wanted him as wild as she. Wanted him to feel what she felt. To experience the raging pulse of sensation that he was providing her.

Val tried to tell him that, tried to speak, but words wouldn't come as her body exploded under the frantic ministrations of his hand. Sparks of brilliant color flashed in her mind as her hips rocked and she mindlessly moved into what he offered, seeking more.

She'd had no idea. None. She'd expected that sex could be great, though her experience up until tonight hadn't been fabulous. But this was something else. Something she couldn't have been prepared for. This was *everything*.

"Now," he whispered in her ear as he shifted position, kneeling between her legs, pushing his hard, thick body into hers inch by delectable inch.

She felt the pressure of his gentle invasion and this time instead of fighting it, she welcomed it, spreading her thighs wider, lifting her hips to take him deeper. And when he was settled completely within her, she took one moment to relish the sense of rightness that rushed through her.

This is what she'd been missing. What they'd *both* missed.

Val looked up into his eyes as he rocked his hips against her and she saw his dark blue gaze go even darker as passion claimed him and drew him into the same vortex that held her so tightly in its grasp. They moved together—finally, together—in an ancient dance performed by lovers for centuries.

Here was the magic.

Here was the hunger.

Here was where she belonged.

In his arms.

Val locked her legs around his hips and held him tighter, deeper, as his pulse raced, his breath came short and fast. Amazingly enough, she felt her own body's climb to release again. It started deep within her and mounted every time Dev moved inside her. Stroking, caressing, claiming.

And this time, when her climax slammed into her, Dev was there with her. He called her name out low as he followed her into that mind-numbing world where sensation is king.

Four

Stunned, Dev fought for breath, looked down into Val's eyes and felt himself getting lost in those wild, violet depths. She smiled up at him and ran her fingers down the side of his face, and he could have sworn he felt that gentle touch right down to his bones.

She'd shaken him, loathe as he was to admit it.

To avoid those thoughts, Dev rolled to one side of her and lay staring blankly up at the ceiling. Heart pounding, body still humming, he had to admit that she'd shocked him completely. He couldn't even remember the last time anyone had taken him unawares.

Turning his head, he looked at her and, in the candlelight, her skin looked like gold, her eyes were soft and her mouth—her incredible mouth—was curved into a self-satisfied smile.

Proud of herself, was she?

Well, damn, she had a right to be. Never in his life had he come so close to losing himself so completely in a woman. Always before, there'd been that silent presence in his mind, warning him to maintain control. Tonight, he'd had to *fight* for that control. Tonight, the woman who was his wife had nearly brought him to his knees.

This was *not* the Valerie Shelton Hudson he had married. He'd known something had changed that afternoon, when she'd faced him down in her condo and delivered her list of conditions before agreeing to come home. The woman he'd known before had been shy; timid, really. Never venturing an opinion, never opening herself up to confrontation.

She'd changed in the time they'd been apart. Somehow, she'd come into her own, found a backbone and a sense of self. Or had she always possessed those attributes and had simply been hiding them? But why would she have done that? That didn't make sense.

God, his brain was too fractured to figure any of this out tonight. His body was still reeling from spectacular sex and his lungs were busy trying to draw in enough air to sustain him.

She'd blindsided him.

Seeing her waiting for him—naked—Dev hadn't been able to think beyond his own needs. He doubted he'd be able to get that image of her out of his mind anytime soon, either. But having her match the needs pounding through his body with a desire he'd never experienced from her before had only fed the fires consuming him.

This, Devlin hadn't counted on.

He'd optimistically hoped that he and Val could find a way to live together with some semblance of a decent sex life. He'd thought that he'd spend the next few weeks easing her past her fears and awakening her to her sensuous side.

He'd never considered that what he might find with Val could leave him shaken.

But even as that thought shot through his mind again, Dev dismissed it. He wasn't really shocked. Just surprised, he reassured himself. Happily surprised.

But this tenuous new connection he had with Val was not going to intrude on his life. He'd asked her to marry him for sensible, logical reasons that were still valid. He wouldn't allow his heart to be involved. Better to stay as remote as possible. Yet…

"What are you thinking?"

"What? Oh. Nothing."

Val turned into him, pillowed her head on his chest and wriggled in until she was comfortable. Dragging the tips of her fingers across his chest, she sighed. "That was incredible, Dev. Didn't you feel it?"

God, he thought. Why did women always want to *talk* after sex? What was it that drove them to dissect whatever had happened, talk about their feelings and then ask about *his*?

"Sure," he said in as noncommittal a fashion as he could before tipping his head down to look at her. She was staring at him with stars in her eyes, and Dev could almost feel the ground beneath him lurch and tremble.

Her cheeks were flushed; her deep, violet eyes were shining and her mouth was still puffy from his kisses. She looked absolutely edible. And as he felt his body stir, he knew he hadn't had enough of this surprising woman.

"I had no idea it could be like that," she said, still a little breathless.

"Neither did I." The words were out before he could censor them.

"So you did feel something special—"

Through talking, Dev found a way to distract both of them. He cupped one of her breasts in his palm and lazily stroked the tip of her nipple. She sucked in a gulp of air, closed her eyes and released that breath on a sigh.

"That feels so…"

"Yes, it does," he finished for her. And suddenly, ending a conversation was the last thing on his mind. He wanted to taste her again. To take his time and explore his wife's tempting body. So he stopped any further questions by taking her mouth with his.

Instantly, a rush of heat rose up inside him and staggered Dev with the force of his reaction to her. Only moments ago, he'd been finished, damn near destroyed by the power of their lovemaking—and now he couldn't wait to be inside her again.

Passion roared more ferociously than before and Dev surrendered to it. His tongue parted her lips and as he tasted her warmth, she wrapped her arms around his neck and held his head to her, giving as good as she got. When she sighed, he felt a twinge of something he didn't want to identify. So he ignored it and concentrated on the woman in his arms.

He might be keeping his heart out of this, but that didn't mean he couldn't revel in the pleasure they found together. Dev dragged Val over him until she was sprawled on top of him. Her hair fell on either side of her face like a soft, sweet-smelling brown curtain.

She smiled down at him as he ran his hands up and down her back and Dev felt again that nudge of something inside. But he closed it off, barricaded it behind the wall of control he'd spent years building and instead concentrated solely on the feel of her in his arms. Her eager response was open and trusting and made him even more grateful that she'd somehow found a way to overcome her shyness.

"You amaze me," he said before he could stop himself.

She grinned suddenly and braced herself on his chest, looking down at him as if she'd discovered some glorious secret that she was keeping to herself.

"I'm glad, Dev," she said softly just before she leaned in to brush another kiss against his lips. "I'm so very glad."

Then she went up on her knees and slowly, incredibly slowly, lowered herself onto him. Where the hell was she finding all of this sensual bravado? And why did he care? Devlin grabbed her hips, hissed in a breath and his gaze locked on hers, forgot everything but what she was doing to him.

His shy little wife was gone and in her place was the kind of woman who could haunt a man's dreams.

Nothing mattered more than the next moment, the next slide of her body onto his. She arched her back, moaned his name, and he was caught in the glory of her.

She swayed and the candlelight caressed her skin. The pearls at her throat gleamed with what looked like a soft, inner light. She moved on him, her body taking his deeper, higher, until Dev couldn't form a single thought that wasn't about her.

And as she shuddered over him, riding the crest of her release, he let himself go, the ragged edges of his control nearly sliding from his grasp.

By the next morning, though, his blood had cooled and his brain was back in charge. Now, Dev was ready to consider what might be motivating Val's complete personality turnaround. Who was this new version of his wife? Was this who she really was, or was it all an act designed to snare him into sexual submission?

As that thought shot through his mind, Dev snorted at his own wild imaginings. He was making her sound Machiavellian. She wasn't, he assured himself, though doubts still clanged in his mind like warning bells. If she did have an ulterior motive for this sexy new persona, what could it possibly be?

He glanced at her sleeping in his bed and fought the urge to join her there. He'd never spent a night like the one he'd just lived through and a part of him hadn't wanted it to end.

Valerie had shown him a side of her he hadn't known existed. Now that he knew, now that he'd experienced something he'd never found with anyone else, he wasn't sure what to do about it. Of course, the only real option was to continue on as he'd always been. Cool. In control. There was no reason he couldn't enjoy the nights in his wife's arms and still maintain the distance he required in a relationship.

She sighed in her sleep and rolled over, dragging the red sheet up higher on her shoulder. The contrast of the rich, silky material against her pale, smooth skin jolted something inside him. Something he didn't care to explore.

Frowning, he told himself it was enough that she was back here. Where she belonged. Soon, they'd ease into a routine. A calm, organized marriage of mutual respect and shared pleasures. Just the way it should be.

As long as he remembered who was in control.

"No problem," he whispered. Smiling to himself, and already thinking about the night to come, Dev headed out, quietly closing the bedroom door behind him. He glanced toward the balcony where the remnants of their dinner remained on the table and told himself not to remember how they'd eaten dessert.

If he allowed himself to think about the chocolate raspberry mousse and just how good it had tasted when licked from Val's abdomen, he wouldn't be able to walk. Blowing out a breath, he shook his head and strode to the door.

Rather than taking the private entrance from his suite, he went down the double-wide staircase. He wanted to talk to his father before leaving for work, which meant hunting Markus down at breakfast.

Dev's shoes clicked against the marble floor and echoed weirdly with the fifteen-foot ceilings as he hit the bottom of the stairs and stepped into the foyer.

"Morning, Mr. Hudson." One of the maids was already at work, polishing the hall tables.

"Good morning, Ellen." He kept walking, moving down the long, marble-tiled hallway. Dev barely noticed anymore the hand-painted wallpaper or the antiquities his parents had collected during their travels over the years. The Hudson family home was old, stately and elegant, from the formal dining room to the front salon where guests were lavishly entertained. Not exactly kid-friendly, though he and his brothers and sister had run wild through the place when they were young.

But as refined as the public areas of the house were, the back half of the house was for family.

There was, of course, a private screening room, where the Hudsons could gather to watch films—both the ones made by their company and others, to keep up on the competition. But the family room was filled with bookshelves, a pool table and a bar where they could all relax. The kitchen was huge and airy, with a connected breakfast room, where the family usually tried to have Sunday brunch together. A chance for all of them to catch up on the latest news, which lately, he thought grimly, hadn't been worth talking about.

With the bombshells that had landed in the middle of the Hudson clan in the last couple of months, the family was mostly in defense mode. Circling the wagons. Holding together as a united front.

Which was one of the main reasons Dev had wanted Val to come back to him. Especially with the Academy Awards coming up in just a couple of short weeks. The more the newspapers and tabloids saw that the Hudson family were together in this, the better.

Of course, it was hard to look united, he thought, when his own mother had slipped out of the family mansion to hole up in the penthouse suite at the Chateau Marmont.

He pushed that thought out of his mind because if he started thinking about everything his mother had done to sink this family, he'd need a drink and it was way too early for that.

Dev found Markus Hudson in the family breakfast room, reading the morning paper. A pale wash of early morning sunlight sifted in through the wide windows and lay across the pale oak table.

"Anything interesting, Dad?" he asked and moved to the sideboard where a pot of coffee waited. He poured himself a cup and carried it to the table.

"The usual," Markus said with a smile as he set the paper aside. His dark brown hair was liberally streaked with silver, and his brown eyes were shrewd. As the CEO of Hudson Pictures, Markus had his finger on the pulse of the studio and didn't miss much. "You're up early."

He *was* early. Even for him. But Devlin hadn't wanted to risk having to "talk" to Val before having a chance to do some thinking. But no way was he going to say that to his father. So he shrugged. "A few things I want to check on at the studio."

"Problems?" his father asked, leaning back in his chair, all attention focused on his son.

The last thing he wanted to do was give his father more to worry about. "No, not really, but I wanted to tell you before I handle the situation."

Instantly, Markus went on alert and Dev admired that ability. Most of his life, he'd striven to be as much like his father as he could.

"What's going on?"

Dev smiled, enjoying this quiet time with his father. "The usual. Harrow's gone way over budget on location and I'm going to tell him to pull it back or I'll pull the plug on the film."

Markus laughed, clearly enjoying that image. "That will make you popular."

Wryly, Dev nodded. As the chief money man of Hudson Pictures, he was often the target of bitter directors and furious actors. But what none of them seemed to remember was that making movies was a *business* first. Sure, the art of the thing was important. But if he wasn't controlling the financial aspect of everything, then there wouldn't be any art, would there?

"Do what you have to do, Dev," his father said, reaching for his coffee cup. "I trust you."

"Thanks." That trust was something Dev worked hard to honor. In fact, trust was everything. Without it...well, they already knew what happened when *faith* was broken. Sabrina Hudson had broken faith with everything the Hudson family had stood for. She'd betrayed Markus and just thinking about it made everything inside Dev cold and hard and filled with resentment.

His own mother had cheated on his father. The "perfect" marriage he and his siblings had always held up as the measuring stick of all relationships had been fractured years ago and then covered up in secrecy. It was amazing that the truth hadn't been revealed long ago. But what if it had been, he wondered. Would Markus and Sabrina have divorced? Would Dev and the others have grown up shuttling between parents as so many other children in Hollywood did?

He hated this. Dev looked at his father and realized the man looked older than he had just a month or so ago. Treachery, and grief over Lillian's death wasn't good for the soul, apparently. Plus, Dev's grandmother had died recently and his father was still reeling from it. And another tide of resentment toward his mother washed through Dev. His father hadn't spoken against his wife and Dev hadn't brought the subject up, not wanting to make things even harder on the older man.

But though he was furious with his mother for her betrayal, there was a part of Dev that wanted to go to her. Talk to her. Ask her how in the hell she could have done something so hideous to all of them.

It wasn't just her husband she'd betrayed. She'd lied to *all* of them for years, simply by pretending nothing had happened. That everything was as it should be. And she'd lied about his sister Bella's parentage. Hell, Bella was only just now recovering from the shock of discovering that the man she'd considered her uncle was, in fact, her father.

David Hudson, Markus's brother, had made himself scarce since the scandal had broken, but that was hardly surprising. Any bastard who would sleep with his brother's wife wouldn't be man enough to stick around after he'd caused so much pain.

"Dev," his father said tightly, "you've got to let the anger go."

"What?" He blinked, shook his head and stared at his father.

"I can see by the look on your face what you're thinking about." Markus held his coffee cup and tapped one finger against the porcelain edge.

"I don't know what you're—"

"Save it," Markus said. "You don't have a poker face, Dev. I've always been able to read you like a book."

True. But it had nothing to do with a poker face. The reason Markus could read Dev was because they were so much alike. And maybe that was why his mother's cheating had hit Dev especially hard. He was like his father. So in choosing to step away from her husband, Sabrina had also chosen to step back from her oldest son. And that cut dug deep whether he wanted to admit it or not.

"Sorry," he muttered, taking a sip of the too-hot coffee and burning his tongue for his trouble.

"Don't be." Markus sat forward, leaned his elbows on the glossy, mahogany dining table and looked at his son. "Do you think I don't know you're in pain, too? That all of you haven't been affected by this?"

"It's not about us," Devlin tried to say.

"The hell it's not," Markus countered. "I don't want any of you being angry at your mother over this."

Dev snorted. "A little late for that, Dad."

"Well, get over it."

"I'm sorry?"

"You heard me." Markus set his cup down onto the saucer with a quiet clatter. "Yes, this has upset the whole family and you're all involved…especially Bella." He paused, swallowed hard and shook his head as if to push away disturbing thoughts. "But Sabrina's your mother and you owe her respect."

"Respect."

"That's right." His father's eyebrows lowered over narrowed eyes. "You four are her children. You don't have the right to sit in judgment of her."

Dev snorted.

His father glared at him. "What's between me and my wife, we'll settle ourselves. You don't know everything, Dev. You couldn't. None of you can. Your mother and I have things to resolve and we will. In our own time. Our children don't get a vote in any of it no matter how much we both love you all."

A little stunned, Dev looked at his father. He hadn't expected Markus to defend Sabrina, though he should have. His whole life his parents had been, seemingly, happy. Sure, his father had been devoted to his work, as Dev was, but a child can tell when his parents love each other. That had never been in doubt. Which was why all of this had been such a blow to the family. "You've spoken to Mom?"

Markus sighed. "Of course I've spoken to her, and that's my point, Dev. Whatever happens between your mother and me is between your mother and me."

He understood that. On a purely rational, logical level. But the truth was, what he was feeling had nothing to do with logic or rationality.

This was about lies.

Lies she'd told.

Lies she'd lived.

And the pain of realizing his mother was not the woman he'd always thought her to be was something Dev was having a hard time accepting. But he wasn't going to cause his father even more grief by arguing with the man.

"You're right, Dad," he said, draining what was left of his cooling coffee.

"Glad that's settled. Now, was there anything else you needed to talk to me about?"

Dev thought about it for a moment, then decided there was no point in keeping Val's return a secret. "Yeah, there is. Not work-related, though. Val's back in the mansion."

"Really?" Markus smiled, reached out and slapped his oldest son on the shoulder. "That's wonderful news. I'm glad you two worked things out. Your mother will be…"

His voice trailed off, and Devlin scowled. Everything came back to Sabrina and the rift her actions had caused in the family. By rights his mother should be here. At the house. Instead, she was staying in a hotel, leaving her husband here alone.

God, how had this happened to them?

The Hudsons had always been the anti-Hollywood family. Strong. United. Untouched by the scandals and the troubles that seemed to fester in this city. He'd always thought they'd been blessed, somehow. Apparently though, the warranty on "blessed" had run out.

Dropping all mention of his mother, Dev said, "Look, I've got to get hold of Harrow and stop him before he spends another week on the location shoot. He should be able to do interiors at the studio and he can CG whatever else he needs in postproduction."

"Harrow won't like that," Markus warned with a knowing smile. "He's an 'artist.' Just ask him, he'll tell you."

Glad to be back on safer ground, Dev smiled at his father. "He may be an artist, but I'm the man with his hands on the money. So Harrow will listen. He won't like it but he'll listen."

Standing up, he buttoned his suit jacket and headed for the door. His personal life might be filled with questions at the moment, Dev told himself, but at least he could still lose himself in work.

Five

Valerie woke up alone. Somehow, after the night before, she'd expected to be awakened by a husband who wanted to rekindle the fires they'd discovered. A tiny twist of worry settled in her stomach as she wondered if Dev had already dismissed her from his mind. But she quickly resolved that if he *had* put last night behind him already, she would soon remind him of everything.

She wasn't going to be ignored this time around.

And in that spirit, she spent the morning figuring out how she could change things up in their wing of the mansion. If she wasn't going to get a home of her own just yet, then she was going to make sure Dev realized that he was now *sharing* this apartment.

There wasn't much she could do about the big stuff

until she'd had time to see a decorator and go shopping. But she wanted to get a jump on as much as she could. Really all she was trying to do at the moment was make a statement. Something subtle, to let Dev know that this was a brand-new day. That she was his wife and she was a part of his life, not just an incidental appendage.

Then naturally, her mind drifted to the night before. She slid her gaze to the balcony beyond the open French doors. The housekeeping staff had already been through, clearing away the remnants of their late-night dinner. But the memories were with Val for life. Just thinking about the cold chill of chocolate raspberry mousse hitting her heated skin made her shiver all over again. Her husband could be very…inventive. She smiled to herself, delighted so far with her second chance at marriage.

"But sex is just the beginning," she whispered, reassuring herself that she would have more than a mattress as the basis of her life. "All I have to do is show him how much he needs me. And he *does* need me. He's too alone. Too shut off." She frowned a little, then added, "But not for long."

Now if only she had a touch more muscle.

The chairs in the main room were heavier than they looked and thumped heavily against the floor when she shoved at them. Well, moving them an inch at a time was going to take a year at least.

Out of breath and getting seriously irritated, she was grateful when a knock sounded on the door outside Dev's room. She whipped her hair back out of her eyes, glared at the ugly brown chair that was fighting to hold its ground and then yanked open the door.

"Val! You *are* back! This is great! Dad told me you were, but I just had to see it for myself. And I'm so glad!" Bella Hudson sailed into the apartment, her expensive perfume trailing in her wake. Her auburn hair hung in thick, lush waves around her shoulders and her blue eyes were sparkling with humor. She wore a dark green silk shirt, skintight blue jeans and a pair of gold sandals.

To complete the package, tucked into the curve of her arm was Bella's favorite accessory, her dog, Muffin. With tangled, wiry hair, a pushed-in face and crooked teeth, the fifteen-pound dog was friendly, but possibly the ugliest canine in the known universe. Today, Muffin was wearing a T-shirt the very same color as Bella's blouse.

Val hid a smile and closed the door behind Dev's sister. "It's so good to see you."

Over the last couple of months, her sister-in-law had been through some pretty ugly times. Every paper in the country had been blaring the long-kept secret that Bella Hudson was not Markus's daughter after all, but the result of an affair between her mother and Markus's brother, David. And though Val's heart had hurt for Bella, she hadn't been able to talk to her, offer support.

Mainly because the moment the story broke, Bella had run to France, trying to distance herself from nosy reporters and photographers. No doubt she'd also been trying to come to grips with the news herself.

It didn't help the situation any that Val had left Dev just after Bella's world dissolved. Now they were both back at Hudson Manor and both trying to rebuild their lives. Of course, Bella was ahead of Val on that score.

She was madly in love with her fiancé, Sam Garrison, and lucky for her, Sam felt the same way.

Briefly, Val sighed inwardly, hoping that one day, she'd know how it felt to love and be loved in return.

Then Bella wrapped Val in a tight, one-armed hug, stepped back and gave her a good looking over. "You look different." She tipped her head to one side. "What is it?"

Did good sex actually show on your face? Val wondered, just a little embarrassed to think that might be true. It was one thing to discover your sexy side and quite another to have the whole world clued in.

So she shrugged and said, as casually as she could, "Nothing different, you're just looking through happy eyes."

"So true. I *really* am." Bella set Muffin down onto the hardwood floor so the dog could wander around and sniff everything in reach. Standing up again, Bella did a quick spin in place. "It's amazing, Val, but a couple of months ago, I was sure my life was over, and now…"

"Better?" Val asked.

"Oh you wouldn't even *believe* how much better."

"How is Sam?" Sam Garrison had clearly made a wonderful difference in the woman's life. She was practically glowing.

"Fabulous." Bella grinned, both eyebrows rising into high arches as she teased, "Been reading the papers, have you?"

"Yes." Valerie dragged her friend over to the closest sofa and once they were seated, she said, "How else could I keep up with my friends?"

Instantly, Bella's smile faded and a guilty expression

flashed across her face. "Oh, honey, I so should have called you, but everything's been so nuts and—"

"No," Val brushed away her friend's concern. She more than anyone else could understand how things could pile up around you until you felt as though you couldn't see straight anymore. "Don't worry about it. I know just what you mean, anyway. I wanted to call you after—"

Bella frowned and chewed at her bottom lip, clearly remembering how crazy things had been when the scandal concerning her parentage broke. "It's probably better that you didn't. I wasn't really good company."

"I know. But you're here now, at the house, so you've made up with—"

Bella shook her head. "I came to see my *father*." She emphasized the word as if making sure Val knew that she still considered Markus her real father.

And who could blame her? Markus was the one who'd loved her, raised her, worried over her. If that wasn't a father, what was? David Hudson might have contributed the DNA to Bella's makeup, but Markus would always be her father.

"And your mom?" Val leaned forward, laid her hand over Bella's and squeezed.

"We haven't talked yet, but we will soon. We have to. It's just that I don't even know what to feel, you know? I mean, I love Mom, that doesn't change. But how could she have kept this a secret from me? I know I have to talk to her, hear her side of this," she admitted. "I'm still so confused over all of it and I'm not sure if talking to Mom is the best thing to do right now, so…" She glanced around to check on her dog. "Baby, don't chew Uncle Dev's shoe."

Valerie glanced over the back of the sofa and winced. Too late. The Ferragamo loafer was already toast. Shrugging, she thought it served Dev right for leaving them out.

"You know," Bella said brightly, obviously ready for a change in subject, "I'm so tired of talking and thinking about my own weird problems. Tell me about you instead. What brought you back to the Fortress of Solitude?"

Good description of Dev's suite, Val thought, and only a sister would have nailed it so completely. "Your brother."

Bella blinked. "Seriously? He came and got you?"

"Is that so surprising?"

"Are you kidding?" Bella curled her legs up under her, laughed and called out, "Muffin, baby, Uncle Dev won't like it if you tear that book." Then she turned back to Val, still laughing. "The great Devlin Hudson went out of his way to chase down the wife who walked out on him?"

Valerie cringed a little. "Isn't there a nicer way to put that?"

"Nope and don't you dare try," Bella told her with a grin. "It's just what Dev needed. A good solid kick in the pants. And clearly it worked! He went after you! It's historic, that's what it is."

"Bella..." Val couldn't help smiling.

"I mean it! Dev has *never* gone after *any* woman." She shook her head and sounded disgusted with her entire gender as she added, "Women have been throwing themselves at Dev since he was a kid. So the fact that he went after you—why, it's amazing, really."

Thinking about the legions of women who would gladly change places with her didn't fill Val's heart with glee, but at the same time, maybe Bella had a point. He *had* come to her. He *had* been the one to suggest giving their marriage another chance. Maybe she had a better shot at winning her husband's love than she'd thought.

"And thank heaven you agreed to come back to him," Bella said. "He's been the most awful bear of a person to be around since you left."

"Really?" Oh, that made her feel better. She'd hate to think she had been the only one miserable when they were apart.

"Oh, totally. He was so mad when you left, nobody wanted to talk to him. Even his assistant walked a wide berth around him and Megan Carey's not afraid of anybody."

That small spark of pleasure inside her quickly sputtered out of existence. She'd been hoping to hear that Dev had been lonely, missing her, even maybe heartbroken. Instead, he'd simply been angry. "So he wasn't miserable; he was pissed."

"He was both, trust me. Dev's not used to losing. At anything. When you left, he was so stunned, all he could handle was anger for a few weeks. Then the misery kicked in." Bella gloated for a second, then frowned, clucked her tongue and said, "Muffin, sweetie pie, you shouldn't sleep on that pillow, I think it's silk."

Valerie glanced over her shoulder and almost applauded as Muffin settled in on one of Dev's hideous brown pillows. When the ugly little dog started nibbling at the corner of the pillow, Valerie could have hugged her.

"Anyway," Bella was saying, "Honestly, Val, I've never seen my brother so…down. I mean he's never been Mr. Sunshine, God knows, but this was a new level of low. You know Dev, always on the even keel. Nothing gets to him. Nothing pushes him over that icy edge of control. Well, until *you*. I think you really shocked the hell out of him when you walked out."

"That's not why I left." Though it was a small comfort to know that she'd finally reached him. Yet how ironic was it that being *with* Dev hadn't melted his reserve—only leaving him had done the trick?

"Honey, I know that." Bella gave her an understanding smile. "Remember, I grew up with the Hudsons. And as much as I love them, that doesn't mean I don't see their faults. And Dev's got more than his share."

Funny, but Valerie felt like defending her husband. Which was just silly, since she basically agreed with his sister's opinion. But even with those faults, Devlin was more of a man than any other Val had ever known. And the only man she'd ever loved.

Which told her he was worth fighting for.

"Oh, I know he's stubborn and arrogant and too closed off," Val said. "But underneath all that, I think he's an amazing man. I really do. All I have to do is convince him how much he needs me."

"You're right, you know," Bella said, smiling, "he *does* need you. Desperately. But just like every other man in the world, he can't see what's right in front of his face. I have faith in you, though. If anyone can get to my stubborn brother, it's you. I think you're perfect for him. Especially now," she added, tilting her head and studying Val carefully. "You seem more…sure of yourself than you were before. Sort of more self-confident."

"Good, I'm glad it shows." Val leaned back into the

sofa. "Before, I was so in love with Dev, I just wanted everything to be perfect, you know?"

"Oh yeah."

"I didn't argue with him, didn't venture an opinion, didn't even stand my ground when he tried to roll right over me."

"He does do that," Bella said with an understanding nod.

"Exactly," Val said and looked around the clearly masculine room, pausing to admire the crystal vase full of the sterling roses Dev had brought her the night before. Then she shifted her gaze back to Bella. "The first time I moved in here, I was so busy trying to be Dev's *wife,* I forgot to be *Val.* But that's not going to happen again."

"Yay, you!"

Valerie grinned and enjoyed the feeling of solidarity with Bella. It was good to have a friend who understood what you were talking about. Who was on your side.

"You know, when we got married, I'm not even sure I knew what I wanted, besides Dev, of course. But now…" She shifted her gaze back to her friend and her husband's sister, "Now I want it all."

"No point in going for half," Bella agreed. "God knows I wouldn't settle for less than all of Sam, so you've got my vote."

"Thanks. I appreciate that."

Bella smiled. "So, what were you up to in here when I showed up?"

"Well, I *was* trying to move this furniture around. You know, just shake things up a little. But it's so darn heavy, I can't really budge it."

"Wondered what that thumping I heard was about," Bella mused, glancing around the big room with the sunlight spilling through the French doors. "Hmm. You're right. This room *is* frozen in time. Dev probably hasn't moved a thing since he moved into this wing years ago."

Just what Val had suspected. Well then, it was way past time for a change, wasn't it? "You know, if I had a little help, I could probably move this furniture. So, do you have some time? Can you help me shift things around?"

Bella laughed. "You *do* know we could call downstairs and get plenty of help in an instant."

"Yeah…" Val said, not wanting to do that. If she was going to show Dev that she was a brand-new woman, then she was going to do this by herself. Well, with Bella, if she'd help.

"You want to do it," the other woman said softly.

"Yes, I do."

"Then we'd better get started," Bella told her, pushing up from the sofa. "Oh, Muffin, honey, do you have to go potty?" Then a moment later, she glanced at Val with an apologetic shrug. "You were going to get rid of that ugly pillow anyway, right?"

"Definitely," Val told her, looking at the spot where Muffin had apparently lost the fight to control her bladder.

"Okay, then, no loss." Bella grinned. "Where do we start?"

Val stood up, looked around and sighed. "For right now, let's just shake up the furniture arrangement. These deliberate little conversation areas give me chills."

Bella laughed. "Really. If you have to *tell* people to have conversations, what's the point?"

"This is gonna be fun," Val said. "Let's start by sliding this sofa over there by the fireplace."

"Excellent." Bella positioned herself at one end of the big couch. "Good thing there are hardwood floors. We can slide these monsters around."

Val thought briefly about the condition of the gleaming floors, then dismissed the notion of scrapes and scratches. She'd just have them redone. Or buy colorful rugs. Or maybe carpet…God, the possibilities were endless.

"I can see you imagining all sorts of different things," Bella mused.

"Am I that obvious?"

"Only to me and that's only because I care about you. And Dev. So my fingers are crossed for you." Bella smiled at her and Val felt a rush of warmth for the sister-in-law who had become a friend.

With support like this, Val thought her chances of winning Dev over were much improved. She knew how close the Hudson siblings were. When the scandal about Bella's birth had been leaked to the press, the woman's brothers had figuratively circled the wagons to protect her from as much hurt as they could.

"Thanks, Bella. I appreciate it. Because frankly, I think I'm going to need all the help I can get."

"Oh, I don't know." Bella straightened up, gave a knowing look to the roses and smiled. "Seems to me you've got his attention already."

"True. It's *keeping* it that's got me worried."

"Not going to be a problem. I think you're perfect for Dev. Just don't give up on him. He's going to be a lot of work, but he's so worth it. He's a good man, Val. Keep reminding yourself of that," Bella said.

"Don't worry," Val told her and bent over to get a good grip on her end of the sofa. "I'm not leaving again. This time, I'm staying."

"Atta girl." Bella blew out a breath. "So, you ready to push this monstrosity into position?"

"More than ready," Val said, knowing she was talking about much more than rearranging furniture. She was up to the challenge of rebuilding her life and dragging Dev right along with her.

"You can't do this to me," Dave Harrow shouted and tore at his already sparse gray hair. "I need another three days, at least, on location. I can't be expected to shoot this movie completely in studio."

Dev wasn't moved by the histrionics. If there was one thing Hollywood directors were good at, it was drama. Hell, there should be an Academy Award category for drama-queen directors who had more of a lock on acting than the young actors who caused so many young women to dream happy dreams.

"Look, Harrow," Dev told him, drawing the man away from the crowd so clearly interested in their conversation. "You're already over budget and you know it. I've bent the rules as far as they're gonna go. So dial it back or see the film shelved."

Harrow's frantic brown eyes slid from side to side, as if looking for someone to come to his rescue. But there was no one. The older man had been doing this long enough to know that Devlin Hudson didn't bluff.

"Fine," he finally grumbled. "We'll wrap the shoot tomorrow and do the rest in studio."

"Today."

Harrow's features flushed a brilliant red and he kicked at the dirt at his feet. "Tomorrow and that's my last offer."

Dev thought about it, hid a smile and let the director think he was winning this round. When the truth was, Dev had already decided on the drive to the location to give the man one more day to wrap things up.

"Fine," he finally said, as if he'd been considering options. "Tomorrow. Then you're done."

"Agreed, you tightfisted, penny-counting bastard."

At that, Dev actually grinned. "Coming from an arrogant, egotistic spendthrift, I take that as a compliment."

"As you should," Harrow grudgingly admitted. "You're a hard man to deal with, but you don't stick your nose in too much, I suppose."

"Harrow," Dev asked with a smile, "does this mean you really, really like me?"

The older man snorted derisively. "That joke's almost as old as you are. Besides, I don't like anybody and you damn well know it." He nodded at the craft services table. "Feel like a cup of coffee before you get the hell out of my hair?"

"You keep yanking at that wild mane and you won't have any left." Dev checked the gold Rolex on his wrist. "Why not? You can complain some more."

Harrow led the way to the catering trucks, set up under a bank of trees near the cliff's edge overlooking Laguna Beach.

A pretty city in Orange County about forty miles outside L.A., it was the perfect location for the outdoor shoot, but that didn't mean that Dev was going to keep authorizing money spent on dragging actors, sets, lights and catering trucks all the way out here.

"You guys in the office don't understand what we have to put up with," Harrow was saying as he stalked toward the promised coffee.

"And you guys behind the cameras always say that," Dev shot back, enjoying himself now. Truth was, Harrow was a damn good director and this movie was sure to be a hit for Hudson Pictures. With its bright young stars, beach location and the best writer in Hollywood, Dev was already calculating a runaway blockbuster.

They'd almost reached the catering trucks when Harrow was sidetracked by an assistant director, so Dev wandered a bit. The sea wind pushed at him as he strolled to the edge of the cliff and looked down on the waves crashing against jagged rocks. It was February, but that didn't stop dozens of surfers from sitting on their boards in the cold, gray Pacific.

There were only a few people strolling the sand and one golden retriever splashed into the water chasing a bright red ball. When his cell phone rang, Dev grumbled. "Take a damn second to relax and see how long it lasts."

He glanced at the screen and everything in him fisted as he recognized a number he hadn't seen on his phone in more than two months. Flipping it open, he said, "Valerie?"

"Hi, Dev, yes, it's me. I wanted to know if you were going to be here for dinner."

The question took him completely by surprise. She'd never before called to ask when he'd be home. Or even *if* he'd be home. She'd actually pretty much tiptoed around him, as if afraid to open her mouth.

Those days, apparently, were gone.

"What?" He shook his head and stared unseeing out at the choppy waves pummeling the beach.

Silence for a moment, then she said, "You know. *Dinner?* The last meal of the day?"

He scowled a bit and absently watched a surfer ride his chosen wave into shore where it dissolved into foam. "I know what it is, I'm just not sure why you—"

"I picked up some amazing scallops at the Farmers Market earlier and I thought I'd make dinner but I wanted to make sure you'd be here on time, otherwise—"

"You're *making* dinner?" he interrupted her and pulled the phone away from his ear briefly to check again on just who was calling him. But it was Valerie. No mistake.

Still, this was a different Val than he remembered. She hadn't once cooked for him since they'd been married. Most often, they'd had meals with the family in the first-floor dining room. Easier all around and frankly, he hadn't been looking for alone time with his too shy and quiet wife.

What in the hell would they have talked about?

Clearly though, those days were long gone. Then memories of the night before swam in his brain and he reminded himself that she was different in a *lot* of areas.

"Yes, I'm cooking. I'm pretty good, too," she argued hotly.

"I didn't say you weren't."

"You were thinking it."

"You read minds now, too?"

"It wasn't hard," she said softly.

Did she sound disappointed, or was that just his imagination?

"So will you be home or not?"

Now she sounded exasperated, and that he was sure he wasn't imagining.

"Yes." He checked his watch, glanced over his shoulder to see the director waiting for him and said, "I'll be there. Should be home by six."

"Excellent."

He could almost *hear* the smile in her voice and he caught himself smiling in response. Then he frowned to himself and wondered why the hell it pleased him to make her happy all of a sudden. But the answer to that question wasn't something he wanted to consider.

"Okay then," Val said, her voice a lot chirpier now, "I'll see you later. Have a good day, Dev."

Then she was gone and he was standing in the windswept sunshine, staring down at his phone as if he'd just lost a connection to Mars.

What in the hell was going on with his wife?

That question stayed buried in the back of his mind even as he walked to meet Harrow and talk movies.

Six

Valerie was lighting pale pink taper candles when she heard Dev's key in the lock. Her breath caught in her chest and instantly, a swarm of bumblebees started doing doughnuts in the pit of her stomach. Stupid, really, to be nervous. But she couldn't help it. She was so determined to win her husband's love that every move she made, she worried if it was the right one.

But she'd already decided on this course, and heaven knew she was prepared for it, so she might as well enjoy the scene she'd set. The candles were flickering lazily in the soft wind dancing across the balcony. Cool jazz was drifting from the stereo. Appetizers were arrayed on the table for two and she was wearing the dress Bella had talked her into buying.

She was as ready as she was going to be.

As the door opened, she hurried into the room to meet him, but before she could call out a greeting, Val heard a sharp thud followed by Dev's yelp.

"Dev?" Hurrying across the shadow-filled room, her high heels sounded out at a fast clip on the hardwood floor. "Are you okay?"

He dropped his keys on the table she'd moved into position that morning then limped toward her. "Once the throbbing stops I'll be fine."

"What did you do?" she asked.

"I nearly killed myself on the damn table that wasn't there when I left for work," he told her, then stopped dead and looked around the room. Dozens of candles threw soft light into a shadowy cavern of a room, but provided just enough illumination for him to see the changes she'd made. "What happened in here? Who moved the furniture?"

"I did."

His gaze slid to hers. *"Why?"*

His blue eyes were narrowed in suspicion and his dark hair was rumpled, as if he'd been dragging his hands through it. His tie was loose at his neck and the collar button of his shirt undone. He looked absolutely incredible. Val's body seemed to light up like a Christmas tree, but she fought the delicious sensations into submission. There'd be time enough later for everything she wanted to do with him.

Right now, he was still waiting for an answer to his question. Valerie gave him a nonchalant shrug, defying the still-swarming bumblebees in her stomach. She'd wanted everything to be perfect when he got home, which just sounded so 1950s TV wifish. Of course, she hadn't considered that Dev would stroll into what he thought was a familiar room and break a leg. Well, she had wondered what his reaction to all her changes might be.

Now she knew. Apparently Dev didn't do well with change. He'd get used to it, she told herself.

"Because we *both* live here now, Dev. And I wanted to shake things up a little."

"A little?" he echoed, then half bent to rub his shin. "I almost killed myself on the table you left by the door."

"Gee," she said with a smile, "you look healthy enough to me."

He shook his head, glancing around the room again, and Valerie followed that movement with her own gaze, loving the layout of the living room now. She'd like it even more once she replaced this ugly brown man-furniture with some nice, overstuffed cozy pieces.

"Looks good, doesn't it?" She pointed. "See, I moved that sofa to face the big-screen TV, but I wanted the other one facing the fireplace. Good for snuggling."

He looked at her. *"Snuggling?"*

She smiled. "And I raided your mom's garden for some fresh flowers. I hope she won't mind...."

"Mom's not here."

"I know, but she'll be back."

He sighed. "Valerie…"

Fine, clearly he didn't want to talk about his mother. She didn't, either. Not at the moment, anyway. "I think you'll like this a lot once you get used to it."

"If the room doesn't kill me first," he muttered. "How did you do all this in one day?"

"Bella helped me."

"Bella was here?"

"This morning," Val said, enjoying the fact that she could surprise him so easily. Tucking her arm through his, she led him farther into the room. "We had a great time."

"I can see that," he muttered, and Valerie's heart sank a little. Was he going to fight her on everything? Was he going to keep making this harder?

Even if he did, she told herself, she wasn't going to stop. She had known going in that this wouldn't be easy. But she was a determined woman. She wanted her husband and she was willing to fight for him—even if that meant making him miserable in the short term.

"So how much do you hate it?" she asked, stopping beside the small, elegantly set table on the balcony. She was becoming very fond of this oh-so-private little patio area. After what she'd experienced there the night before, she'd almost like to see the table bronzed. Heat washed through her at the memories flooding her mind, so to distract herself, she picked up the bottle of cold Chardonnay, poured each of them a glass and handed one to Dev.

In the moonlight, his eyes were shadowed and the emotions she might have seen there were much harder to read.

He took a sip of the wine, blew out a breath and looked at her. "I don't *hate* it. I was just…surprised."

He sort of grimaced on that last word and Val had to wonder why. But then she let that thought go as she noticed his gaze fixed on her. Straightening slightly, Val raised her chin and looked into his eyes. Her skin sizzled with heat as he looked her up and down with a quick, hungry stare. Heartbeat thudding in her chest, she was suddenly very glad she'd gone shopping with Bella that afternoon.

The black dress she wore had a neckline so low, it stopped just short of exposing her nipples. The hem ended right beneath her behind and the narrow shoulder straps were merely a suggestion of black silk. The dress clung to her body like a second skin, so tight in fact, she hadn't been able to wear even a thong because the lines would have shown through. Bella had talked her into buying the dress and Val had been damn near embarrassed just putting it on this afternoon.

But now…with Dev's gaze fixed on her as if he were a starving man and she was the last steak in the world, she felt…powerful.

He took another long sip of wine. "You look—that dress is—"

"You like it?" she asked, doing a slow turn for his benefit. She heard his quick intake of breath as he admired the plunging back and tiny skirt.

"Yeah," he said tightly. "You could say I like it."

"I'm glad."

Her smile was brilliant and Dev felt something inside him lurch, hard and painfully. What the hell was she up to? Was she trying to make him insane? Because if that was the plan, she was doing fine.

Rearranging the furniture, cooking dinner, wearing a dress that made a man want to tear it from her body with his teeth. Lust roared through his system like an out-of-control freight train. He'd done nothing but think about her all day and now there she stood, and he was praying she'd take a breath deep enough to have her breasts pop free of that dress.

God. She'd been home less than forty-eight hours and already she'd tossed his world into complete disorder.

This had *not* been his plan when he'd gone to her condo to bring her home. He was supposed to be the one setting the rules. He was supposed to be the one surprising *her*. Instead, he had the weird sensation of having walked onto a movie set halfway through filming. He didn't know his lines, the plot or any of the twists that Val kept throwing at him.

"Why don't we sit and talk for a while before dinner?" she asked. "When we're ready it'll only take ten minutes for me to cook up the scallops."

Oh, he was ready to eat all right, but dinner was the last thing on his mind. Damn, he was sinking fast here.

"Yeah. That's a good idea." Maybe if he got her talking, he'd be able to figure out just what in the hell she was up to.

"Let's sit on the snuggle sofa, why don't we? Would you mind carrying the wine over while I get these snacks?"

The *snuggle* sofa, for God's sake.

She picked up a silver tray dotted with what looked like delicious appetizers and headed for the couch she'd planted in front of the fireplace that now held only six or seven flickering candles. If he didn't know better, Dev would swear she was deliberately trying to seduce him.

What was she up to?

Devlin's gaze dropped to her behind as she walked away from him and he had to admire the curve of her body caressed in that tight, black material. Then he shook his head to wake himself up and grabbed the bottle of wine. Before he followed her, Devlin glanced at the scene she'd set on the very balcony where they'd made love so frantically the night before.

Candles, fine china, silver ice bucket holding the chilled bottle of wine. The late afternoon breeze was soft and the first stars were just beginning to shine in the dark violet sky.

Funny, but he'd never noticed that the evening sky was the exact color of her eyes.

The minute that thought presented itself, Dev groaned inwardly. Not a good sign, he told himself. Waxing poetic about his wife's eyes, even silently, was a danger sign.

Grumbling to himself, he wondered if she was trying to keep him in such a sexually charged mood that he wouldn't have time to think.

If that was her plan, it was working. Damn it.

His body was tight and hard and uncomfortable and he had the distinct feeling that he'd better get used to it. He carried the wine to the sofa, where she sat waiting for him, legs crossed, eyes shining, welcoming smile on her face.

"Isn't this nicer?" She asked as he sat down beside her. "I love being able to stare into a fire."

"Uh-huh." He slid a glance at her, his gaze dropping to the swell of her breasts, and took an immediate drink of the icy wine, hoping it would help. It didn't.

"Of course, it's too warm tonight for an actual fire, but the candles are good."

"Very nice," he said and heard the tightness in his own voice.

"I think you'll like the furniture arrangement once you get used to it."

"I suppose." He leaned back into the couch, stretched his legs out in front of him and crossed them at the ankle. The scent of her perfume drifted toward him and he instinctively dragged it deep into his lungs.

She was making him crazy.

"Of course, there are a few things I'd like to replace."

"Sure." He paused, thought about it and turned his head to look at her. "What?"

"Well, leather couches aren't really all that comfortable, are they?" She leaned back into the sofa and rested her head on his shoulder.

Her hair was soft and felt cool against his jaw and smelled of flowers and sunshine. Dev took another sip of wine.

"Just don't buy pink, whatever you do," he said. "Bella redid the guest cottage once and there was so much pink it felt like you were walking into cotton candy."

She laughed and he liked the sound of it.

"No pink, I swear."

He smiled, too. It felt…good, sitting here like this, with her, in the shadows, with only the dancing candle flames for light, with the slow slide of jazz whispering into the air. Devlin took another sip of his wine and felt the ragged edges of his hurried day sort of untangle and relax.

Of course, other parts of his body were so far from relaxed he couldn't get comfortable.

"It's a nice night."

"Yeah," he said brusquely. "It is."

She sighed and rubbed her head against his shoulder. "I thought it would be nice to have dinner out on the balcony again. Hope you don't mind…."

"No," he said, quickly shutting down the mental images of their "meal" the night before. "Why would I mind?"

"Good. That's good." He felt her smiling against him. "How was work?"

"How was *work?*"

"Yes," she said and slid her crossed legs against each other in a slow, fluid motion that tore at the edges of Dev's control.

"What are you doing, Val?" He took a big gulp of wine and hardly tasted it as the dry wine slid down his throat.

She sat up straight, raising her head to look directly at him. "What do you mean?"

He waved one arm, encompassing everything she'd done in preparation for his return home. "The wine, the intimate dinner, the questions about my work…what's going on?"

She blinked up at him in wide-eyed innocence. "I don't know what you mean."

Oh, she was good. Much better than he'd given her credit for. They both knew she was playing at something here—and that it was working. So what was the point of denying it? "Yeah, you do."

She sighed, reached down for the bottle of wine and topped off both their glasses. "Dev, I went shopping and wanted to make dinner for you. I bought a new dress I thought you'd like, so I wore it. The weather's gorgeous, so I set the table on the balcony—which you did last night—"

Yes, he thought, but he'd had an ulterior motive for that little dinner.

"And you're my husband," she continued, "so I asked how your day went. If you don't want to talk about it, that's fine, but don't pretend that this is some sort of conspiracy designed to entrap you in some evil plot."

"I didn't mean that," he hedged, knowing he'd meant exactly that.

"Good." She smiled again and used the toe of her high-heeled pump to nudge his left calf. "So why don't you tell me about today."

Oddly defensive now, Dev grabbed at his loosened tie, tore it free and tossed it onto the arm of the sofa. He sat up, handed her his glass and then shrugged out of his suit jacket. Tossing it aside, too, he took his wine from her, had another sip and tried not to notice that in candlelight, her eyes looked like purple velvet. Soft, inviting.

"What do you want to know?"

"Everything," she said, reaching out to lay one hand over his. "What'd you do today?"

Sullenly, he surrendered to the inevitable. Dragging his gaze away from his wife, he leaned back, stared at the candle flames in the hearth and started talking. "I had to go to a location shoot to have a confrontation with a director."

"Mmm. Harrow?"

He shot her a look. "How'd you know that?"

She laughed. "I'm not an idiot, Dev. When we were apart, I didn't stop keeping up with the news. I know Harrow's working on *The Christmas Wish*. I also know that he's legendary for going over budget. It only makes sense that you'd have to go and rein him in."

"Oh." Frowning, he took another sip of wine and felt the cold slide through his system.

"So how did it go?"

Before he knew it, Dev was telling her all about his meeting with the Oscar-winning director. She laughed at his description of the man's temper and then grinned at how easily Dev had defanged the other man.

Encouraged by her interest, he kept talking, telling

her about the rest of his day. She asked intelligent questions, made suggestions for solving problems in ways he wouldn't have considered, and Dev found himself actually relaxing.

He was enjoying this, he realized. He'd never really had anyone but his father or his brothers to bounce ideas off. Bella was too much an artist to want to talk about the nuts and bolts of picture making. And the women he'd dated in the past had been more interested in the glamour of the movie industry than the business of making it run.

But Val, he discovered, had an objective point of view he found refreshing. Something else he'd never expected. She was continuing to surprise him.

But even as he felt himself warming up to her, relaxing in her presence, Devlin heard a warning bell ring in his mind. He couldn't allow himself to be drawn too tightly into her web. He wasn't going to fall in love. Wouldn't make the same mistake his father had.

Look what love had done to *him*. Women couldn't be trusted, he reminded himself. Markus was miserable without Sabrina, despite how he'd defended his wife only that morning—Dev could see that clearly. But how was he supposed to forgive betrayal?

No, Dev would be smarter than his father had been. He'd protect his heart. Keep it safely behind the defensive walls he'd built so well.

"Daddy says you've got a series of ads planned to celebrate *Honor*'s Oscar nominations."

"Yeah," he said tightly, his newly reaffirmed vow fresh in his mind.

"I've been thinking about it and have an idea you might not have considered."

Warily, he asked, "What?"

She smiled and leaned toward him. Dev half expected her breasts to spill out of that dress and couldn't help the pang of disappointment when they didn't.

"I was thinking, every studio in town is running ads touting their movies, but *Honor* is different," she said thoughtfully. "It's a true story."

"Yes, and everyone knows that...."

"Of course people know the basics, but why not remind everyone that this movie is about your family?"

Intrigued, Dev asked, "What did you have in mind?"

She set her glass of wine on the low table in front of them and looked into his eyes. "When you do the ads, promote the reason behind the movie. Remind people—and the Academy voters—that this story is about the Hudsons. Showcase the real story about your grandparents in the ad. Use their photos alongside shots from the movie. Something about the WWII soldier falling in love with the lovely French woman."

While she talked, Dev's mind was racing, seeing possibilities.

"The romance of the story is powerful," Val said, her voice a whisper coated with romance. "Charles and Lillian working together in Nazi-occupied France. His getting wounded, her nursing him back to health. Show their painful separation when he was forced to leave her and their joy when he returned at the war's end."

Dev watched her eyes shine as she spoke and suddenly understood how his grandfather could have been so captivated by a woman that he'd risked everything for her. Valerie was so much more than he'd known. So much more than he'd expected. Her voice, her smile, her scent; she was an assault on the senses from which he might not recover. She made him want. Made him hunger for the touch of her.

"The romance of this story is immense, Dev," she was saying. "It's not just make-believe. It's real. It's the triumph of love during a time of war. It's the real happily ever after that people long for. Remind everyone of just how special their story was."

When she stopped speaking, Dev was still caught in the spell she'd woven and despite the warning bells in his mind, he felt himself falling. There was a breathless silence as she waited for a response from him.

He waited to get a grip on the rushing feelings pouring through him. Finally, hand tight about the stem of the wineglass, he took a long drink, forced the liquid past the knot in his throat and risked another glance at her expectant expression.

"It's a good idea," he admitted, and one he hadn't considered before. She was right. To put *Honor* in a class by itself, separate it from its competition, they had to point out that this movie wasn't just Hollywood doing its magic. This was life.

At its most difficult.

At its most triumphant.

She smiled at him, clearly pleased.

And Dev felt the walls around his heart trembling.

Is this what Charles had felt those long years ago? Is this what his parents had once had?

It felt as though Dev's brain was racing in circles. As Val leaned in closer to him, though, wrapping one arm around his middle, his mind shut down. No thought necessary for what he wanted now. What he *needed* now.

"Do you want dinner?" she asked, tilting her head up to kiss the underside of his jaw.

Instantly, heat swamped him and with his body hard and ready, food was the absolute last thing on his mind. He was willing to bet she knew that, too. Damn, she was good.

"Not really hungry for scallops at the moment," he said, shifting so that he could wrap his arms around her, slide his hands over the incredibly soft, silky material covering her lush body.

"Good," she said smiling. "Neither am I."

Staring down into her eyes, Dev watched as passion ignited in those violet pools. He reached for the hem of her dress, slid one hand beneath the material and up the length of her thigh.

She sighed and turned in his arms, offering herself up for his touch.

He moved his hand up, up, to the curve of her behind and then he stilled. Heartbeat thundering in his ears, he fought for breath and said, "No underwear?"

She gave a half shrug. "It would have ruined the lines of the dress."

"Let's hear it for fashion then," he muttered and took her mouth in a hungry kiss designed to send them both careening into the blaze already engulfing them.

His last coherent thought as he lost himself in her was that he was a walking dead man. His wife had somehow snapped a trap shut around him and God help him, he didn't even *want* to escape.

Seven

A week later, Dev was no closer to figuring out how he'd lost control of the situation between him and Val.

Oh, it wasn't a total loss, of course. During the day, he managed to retreat behind his wall of control enough that he felt as though he had some semblance of power. But at night, the rules changed. In their home, in their bed, Valerie was a siren he couldn't resist.

The woman he'd once considered to be too shy and timid to ever capture his attention was slowly but surely driving him to distraction. And he couldn't figure out why.

There had to be a reason behind her transformation.

She had to have some sort of scheme in mind.

All he had to do was figure out what it was.

The problem in that was that he had too much work

to do to spend enough time trying to decipher the reasons behind Valerie's complete turnaround.

But at least he had the satisfaction of knowing that at work he was in charge. In control. At the office he knew where he stood. Knew what was expected of him. Knew what to demand from everyone around him.

At home, things were different.

It wasn't just his wife that was new and improved. She'd made so many changes around his house, he could hardly keep up with them all.

In the last few days alone, he'd arrived home to find new furniture in the living room, a new bed in his bedroom and a new stove in the small kitchen he'd hardly used before bringing Val back where she belonged.

Now, not only was she cooking nearly every night, she had him *helping* her. Val had him making dinner with her every night. He was slicing onions, marinating steaks… and he was *enjoying* all of it. Not just the cooking, but spending time with her, listening to her laughter, watching her eyes shine when she was having fun.

Shaking his head, he turned his back on his office, on the stacks of correspondence and financial papers he still had to deal with, and stared instead out the windows at the bustling studio going about its business.

Not many people could see what he did at work every day. Extras walked around in full costume, everything from the carolers working on *The Christmas Wish* to what looked like a space alien sucking down a trendy coffee drink through a straw so he wouldn't mess up his dripping fangs.

It was a weird world Dev lived in and he loved it. Knew it. Appreciated it for what it was.

It was his home life that had him half crazed.

"That's a hell of a thing," he muttered, still not quite sure how she'd managed to turn his whole damn life upside down over the course of one short week.

Shaking his head, he let his mind wander back over the last several days. He found himself hurrying home from work now rather than looking for an excuse to stay late at the office. And every time he walked through the doors of their suite, he found something new waiting for him.

Hell, he hardly recognized his own place now, what with all the overstuffed furniture and throw pillows and brightly colored rugs she had scattered all over the floors. There were flowers in vases, music was always playing and the whole damn place smelled like her perfume.

But she'd changed more than his house, Dev thought, she'd changed *him* and he wasn't entirely sure he was comfortable with that.

What he had to do was retake control of the situation. Stop being so passive about all this. Remind her just who the hell he was. No more letting Valerie make all the moves, set up all the surprises.

If he wanted this marriage to work out the way he'd planned—and he did—then he needed to be the one calling the shots.

He was going to stop being dragged around by desire. No matter how much he was enjoying it.

"Hey, Boss?"

He tossed a glance over his shoulder as the door to his office opened. "What is it, Megan?"

"Your wife's here."

"What?"

One of Megan's eyebrows rose. "You know? Your *wife?*"

"Funny. What the hell is Val doing here?" He came around the edge of his desk and wondered if just thinking about the woman could conjure her up. She'd never been to the studio before. But then, she was big into surprises these days, wasn't she?

Val slipped into the office, smiled at Megan and said, "Thanks. I won't keep him long. I promise."

"Oh, you keep him just as long as you like, honey."

Megan closed the door behind her. Val locked it, which had Dev wondering what she was up to and then she laughed. "Well, your assistant's just how I pictured her from your description."

His gaze locked on the upturned corner of her mouth and he felt his body fist in need. He didn't want to be glad to see her, but he was. He didn't want to remember that the door was now locked, but he did. To hide those truths from her—and from himself—Dev spoke more sharply than he'd intended. "What're you doing here, Val?"

She blinked at him. Seemed he could surprise her after all. Well, what did she expect? he wondered. Open arms? A happy little late-morning tryst on his desk? He muffled a groan as that thought settled in his brain and took root. It was all he could do not to go to her, grab her up and have her. Here.

Now.

Damn, he was as horny as a teenager with his first crush. All he could think about was sex and looking at Val now wasn't helping the situation any.

Dev couldn't take his gaze off her. She was wearing a sleek gray suit with a skirt that hit her knees, but had a slit up the side of her right thigh. Her tight gray jacket was worn over a white blouse with a deep V neckline and the sky-high heels she wore were black, to match the bag she had tucked under her arm. Her hair looked windblown, her violet eyes were shining and her mouth looked ready to be kissed.

So he didn't.

"Well," she said softly, "aren't you the crabby one?"

"Not crabby," he countered stiffly. "Busy."

This was his office. Here, he made the rules. Here, he was in charge. Completely. Home and office didn't mix. She might as well find that out now.

"What's up, Val?" He kept his voice cool deliberately.

She tipped her head to one side and a gold earring winked at him. "Is there a problem?"

"No problem," he said, walking back to his desk and sitting down behind it. He'd use the broad expanse of solid walnut like a shield. Maybe it would be enough to keep him from stripping her down and doing what he really wanted to do at the moment. "Just busy, like I said, that's all. Something you needed?"

Her expression was a blend of hurt and confusion, but he steeled himself against any guilt that might be trying to wrap itself around him. He hadn't invited her to the studio. And maybe it was time she found out that not all her surprises were going to be welcome.

"Nothing very important," she said.

"In that case…" He waved one hand at the stacks of papers in front of him.

"I did want to show you this, though," she said and opened her purse as she walked across the room toward him.

Carefully, Dev kept his gaze fixed on hers, refusing to notice how great her legs looked or how the soft gray of her jacket made her eyes look even more purple than usual. Damn it.

"What?" He leaned back in his chair, folded his hands across his abdomen, and looked up at her.

"Here, see for yourself." She handed him a sheet of paper.

It only took a moment to scan what it said, then he looked up at her again. "Not important?" he asked, using the words she had only a moment ago. "Your father's holding the center page of every one of his papers for three straight weeks for the ads we want to run for *Honor*?"

She smiled, looking pretty damn pleased with herself. "That's right. Daddy was happy to do it."

Well, hell, Dev thought as he glanced down at the handwritten note from Val's father. This was one of the main reasons Devlin had wanted to marry Valerie in the first place. The Shelton newspaper dynasty had tentacles that spread across the entire nation. With promotional material in the Shelton papers, Dev could guarantee that the ads for *Honor* would be seen by millions. It was a hell of a thing.

His publicity department would be doing backflips over this. With every studio in Hollywood out to arrange promotional space in the media, this was a gift from the heavens. Or more precisely, from his wife.

What was she up to?

"Whose idea was this?" he asked. "Your dad just suddenly decided to be generous?"

Val set her purse down onto his desk, shrugged, then

walked around his office, looking at the posters on the walls, the plaques and certificates displayed in a glass case and the magazines stacked messily on one corner of a table. Bending down, she straightened them and Dev felt a tightness in his chest as his gaze locked on the firm, round curve of her behind.

The woman was making him nuts.

Was she trying to tempt him? Or was she just doing to his office what she'd done to his home? What was next? Redecorating the place?

But the moment that thought hit him, he called himself a fool. Straightening some magazines hardly qualified as taking over.

"It was my idea," she said, glancing at him over her shoulder. "I told Daddy that I thought it would be good business for him *and* for Hudson Pictures to show a united front. You know, one big happy family?"

The very reason he'd convinced Val to give their marriage another shot, he reminded himself. Coincidence? Hell, who knew? The important thing here was, she'd arranged for publicity space with no fuss at all.

"It was a good idea," he said grudgingly.

She straightened up, slowly walked to his desk and, setting both hands on the edge, leaned into him. "Thanks." Her smile was quick, and beautiful. "How about you take me to lunch to thank me properly?"

Or, he thought, his gaze dropping to the creamy valley of skin between her breasts, he could just take her right here. On the desk. Right now. His body was hard and tight and hot, despite his every effort to keep a tight rein on the reactions she inevitably stirred in him.

She licked her lips and Dev smothered a groan. The

woman was tying him up in knots and the hell of it was, she was doing it so effortlessly.

"I don't think so," he told her, before he could change his mind. "I've got a meeting in an hour, and there's plenty of paperwork to catch up on before then."

"Oh." She sounded disappointed.

Well, hell. So was he. But he had to draw a line somewhere, didn't he? "Come on. I'll walk you to your car."

He stood up and came around the desk. He took her hand and she instantly wrapped her fingers around his and squeezed. She looked up at him through her lashes and said, "How about a quick tour of the studio before I leave then? I've never really seen this place before and I'd like to know more about what you do."

Dev stood there, hot and eager for her, and when she moved the tips of her fingers against his palm, everything in him went even harder than it had been a moment ago.

Voice tight and low with a need that was just barely being kept in check, he asked, "Val, what're you doing? Why're you really here?" His hand on hers tightened, stilling the touch of her fingers. "You could have given me that note from your father at home. So why come here?"

"I just wanted to see you," she said, her voice a caressing whisper of sound. "Is that so hard to believe?" She moved in closer and laid one hand over his heart. When she felt the rapid slam of it against her palm, she added, "I wanted to find out if you missed me as much as I miss you during the day."

He groaned, let his head fall back, then straightened again to stare down at her. "This isn't the time," he said and each word sounded as if it had cost him a terrible price to utter. "Isn't the place."

"Why not?"

She had a point. Why the hell not?

She smiled again. "The door's locked. We're here. Alone. And I want you, Dev. So much."

Screw control. A man could only hold out for so long, he told himself as he grabbed her, yanked her in close and took her mouth in a hard, frantic kiss. Her tongue met his in a clash of desperate need and Dev knew this battle was lost. He had to have her. Now. This minute. He didn't care if half the studio was waiting for him outside his door. All he cared about was here in this room.

Val slipped her arms around his neck and held on. She had her answer. He did miss her. He did think about her while they were apart. And her coming here to the office, imprinting herself on his brain while he was at work, had been the best idea she'd had yet. Now he wouldn't be able to put her out of his mind even when he was locked away working.

Her mouth fused to his, she tasted his heat, swallowed his breath and gave him hers. Every inch of her body was humming wildly with need, with passion that seemed never to be quieted. It didn't matter how many times they came together. She always wanted more. Always wanted *him*.

He tore his mouth from hers, buried his face in the curve of her neck and nibbled at the base of her throat. How was it possible that he could make her feel so much? How had she managed to *not* feel this the first time they had come together?

She'd reentered her marriage with the notion of seducing Dev and holding him to her with the silky strands of sexual heat. But she hadn't expected to like sex this much herself. Every time he touched her, she felt something new. Something more vital. Something more compelling.

Val fought for air as electricity seemed to explode inside her. Her body was hot and wet and so ready for him she thought if he didn't take her that moment, she might fragment into a million jagged pieces from the stress of wanting so deeply.

Then his hands were at her waist and he was turning her around to face the desk. "Dev?"

"Bend forward," he ordered, "and hold on to the desk."

Instinctively, she did as he said, her gaze locked on the scene beyond the windows. Only then did she realize that the entire world could be watching them. It was one thing to seduce her husband. It was another to perform for an audience. "Dev. Quick. Shut the blinds."

"No need," he told her, his voice a rough rasp of sound. "The windows are tinted. No one can see in."

At those words, a swirl of something wickedly exciting lit up inside Val as she felt Dev's hands at the hem of her skirt. Outside this office, the world went on. She could see them, but they had no idea what was happening right in front of them. And somehow, that knowledge made what was happening between her and Dev that much more thrilling.

Slowly, he slid the material up her legs, inch by luscious inch. She wiggled in place at the touch of his fingers against her heated skin. The cool air of the room brushed over her bare thighs and her own internal heat spiked in response. This was magic, she told herself, biting down on her bottom lip as she reminded herself to breathe.

She heard him open the zipper of his slacks and then her skirt was hiked all the way to her waist. She knew he was seeing the dark red lace thong she'd worn for his benefit, just in case. And she wondered what his expression was like. But she didn't want to look. She wanted only to feel. To stare out that window at an unsuspecting world and let Dev take her to the heights only he could.

"Beautiful," he whispered, and she felt him bend over her. Then his lips and teeth worked at the sensitive flesh at the small of her back and she groaned softly, moving against him, into him.

"But," he added, snapping the fragile elastic of her panties and pulling them off her, "we're going to have to get these out of the way."

"Dev…"

"Shh…" he whispered and fitted his palms to the curve of her bottom. Long, strong fingers massaged her skin and she tightened her grip on the edge of the desk, hoping she wouldn't fall over and ruin this spectacular moment.

"Open your blouse," he said, his tone brooking no argument.

Wobbly, a little off-balance, she did as he wanted, quickly undoing the tiny buttons that lined the front of her tidy white blouse. The lace of her bra felt unbearably scratchy against her sensitive skin and when Devlin reached one hand around her to cup one breast in his palm, she actually whimpered at the contact. His thumb and forefinger played with her nipple through the fragile material of her bra and the sensations were incredible.

"Devlin," she whispered and heard the break in her voice, "please…"

He pulled her hair away from her neck and nibbled at her skin as he shifted his free hand from her breast to the aching center of her need. Instantly, heat exploded within her and she nearly purred with contentment as he stroked her intimately with the tips of his fingers. She widened her stance, giving him access, silently asking him to touch her more deeply, more fully. To enter her and end the sweet torment he was causing.

But he was clearly in no rush to end this encounter. Again and again, he touched her, smoothing over her swollen folds, teasing the tiny bud at the core of her, making her want more and more until her body vibrated with a pulsing hunger that hammered at her for release.

"Now, Devlin. Please, *now*."

"Yes," he said on a groan. "Now."

He thrust deep, one swift stroke from behind that had Val gasping for air. She bent over farther, pushing back against him, wanting to feel him even deeper inside. His neatly stacked papers were knocked from the desk and neither of them noticed. He rocked his hips against her, caressed her backside and slid his hands up and down her spine as he took her over and over again, pushing her higher, racing with her toward the precipice that waited just out of reach.

Val's vision blurred and the scene beyond the windows became nothing more than a wild blend of colors and movement. All she felt, all she cared about was what Dev was doing to her. His body pressed into hers, his body claiming hers, his hot breath on her neck as he leaned over her, whispering erotic, wicked suggestions as he laid siege to her body with hot, hard thrusts.

And when she felt as though she couldn't stand any more pleasure without shattering, the end grabbed her and held on. She bit down hard on her bottom lip to keep from screaming out his name as wave after wave of pulsing satisfaction rippled through her. Before the last of those tremors died away, she felt him tense and then heard his groan as a moment later, his body emptied itself into hers.

As he groaned her name, his arm came around her middle and held her tightly to him, as though he was cushioning her fall from a truly dizzying height.

Moments—maybe *hours* later, who knew for sure?—Val heard Devlin ask, "Are you okay?"

"I'm way better than okay," she assured him and almost protested when he withdrew from her body and carefully tugged her skirt into place.

Slowly, she straightened up and leaned one hip against the desk to keep from toppling over. Her knees were weak and it felt as if every muscle in her body had gone as limp as cooked spaghetti.

She looked at Dev and watched as he closed up his slacks. He looked as shaken as she felt, and that was good, Val thought. She'd hate to be the only one reacting to whatever it was that lay between them.

Buttoning up her blouse, Val kept her gaze locked with his and smiled. "That was much nicer than lunch."

"Yeah," Dev said, but he scowled rather than smiled as he said it. "Yeah, it was."

"Your frown really sells that," she told him, tipping her head to one side and studying him carefully. She knew he'd felt what she had. She'd experienced his hunger, his release almost as completely as she had her own. So why would he retreat now? Why would he pull away even though they were standing right beside each other?

"Sorry," he muttered, moving around her to gather up the papers they'd pushed off the desk. He set them down in a neat pile again, bent down to pick up her discarded panties and tucked them into his pocket before he turned to face her. Reaching out, he cupped the back of her neck, pulled her in for a fast, hard kiss and then gave her a forced smile that didn't come close to reaching his eyes. "It was great. Really. But I *do* have that meeting coming up and—"

"Fine." Val cut him off and took a breath. She'd known going in that this was going to take some time. Winning her husband, making him fall in love with her, wasn't going to happen overnight. So there was no point in becoming disappointed or in letting him see that she was discouraged by the way he could shut himself off so completely.

"Maybe you could come back next week? I'll give you that tour of the studio and we can have lunch at the commissary."

It was her turn to plaster a less-than-sincere smile on her face, so Valerie did just that. "I'd like that. And maybe we could do this again, too…" She stroked the edge of his desk with her fingertip.

His blue eyes flashed and Valerie felt better. He might be able to pretend that what they shared meant nothing more than a good orgasm. But there was more. She knew it. All she had to do was make him believe it.

He cleared his throat, grabbed his suit jacket off the

back of his desk chair and slipped it on. Then he came around his desk, took her hand in his and said, "Come on. This time I *will* walk you to your car."

When he unlocked the office door, he said, "I'll be back in a few minutes, Megan."

As he led her across the reception area, Valerie caught Megan Carey's eye and grinned when the older woman gave her a wink and a thumb's up.

Seemed she had allies.

She also, Val told herself an hour later, had a few enemies.

"Come on, Valerie. One statement for our readers."

She'd stopped at an organic grocery store on Melrose to pick up a few things and now, Valerie was regretting the impulse. After a little afternoon loving with her husband, the last thing she wanted to do was face down a reporter.

Especially this one.

Carrie Soker, a too-tall, too-thin, gossip tabloid reporter had been sitting on the hood of Val's car waiting for her and clearly had no intention of getting off the car until she got her quote. The overhead sun threw Carrie's face into shadow and seemed to define its sharp planes harshly.

"Carrie," Val asked in a tired, oh-so-patient voice, "don't you ever get tired of Hudson hunting?"

The woman had the nerve to grin. Not a good look. Her face was skeletally thin. She wore dark red lipstick, green eye shadow on the lids of her brown eyes, and had her brown hair pulled back from her face with an alligator clip. She wore blue jeans, a black, long-sleeved

T-shirt and running shoes—no doubt so she could chase her quarry down if they tried to escape.

"Why would I get tired of it?" she asked. "There are so many of you that there's always variety."

"Good," Val told her, loading her groceries from the cart into the trunk of her small SUV. "Go find variety. Go bother someone else. Luc. Or Max."

"Please. Luc's in Montana and Max is on studio grounds," Carrie snapped with a frown. "I can't get past the guard. Yet, anyway."

Finished unloading her purchases, Val slammed the trunk shut, pushed the cart out of the way, then walked to the driver's side door, glaring at Carrie, still perched cozily on her hood. "What is it you want?"

"I'm just trying to make a living, you know?" Carrie laid one hand against her chest and tried to look innocent. It was as convincing as a barracuda masquerading as a goldfish. "You Hudsons are news, you know? And now that you and Devlin seem to have patched everything up, you're even bigger news."

"Our marriage is our business," Val said.

"That's where you're wrong." Carrie scooted off the hood, took two steps and stopped on the other side of the driver's side door that Val had opened and slipped behind. "You're news. All of you. Hell, your own father's a newspaperman. You know how this works."

"Yes," Val pointed out, "but my father's papers don't report on aliens driving school buses."

Carrie grinned again and wiggled two straggly brown brows. "That wasn't my piece, but it was a good one. Now, how about you give me a good quote that we can run tomorrow?"

"Fine, here's one."

"Excellent." Carrie hit her tape-recorder button, held it out and waited.

"Valerie Hudson claimed to have no comment when pestered by annoying reporter."

Carrie scowled at her and shut the recorder off. "Real funny. But you know I'm not going away, right?"

"Just like death and taxes," Val muttered, sliding into her car. She tried to close the door, but Carrie grabbed it first.

"Just answer me this. Did you and Devlin get back together just for the Oscars? Want to make everything look happy and rosy before the big night?"

Val flushed. Instantly, the memory of Devlin saying almost those exact words the day he'd come to bring her home filled her mind. But that wasn't the only reason, was it? No. She knew he felt more for her now than he had then. He couldn't be faking his responses to her. The passion. The hunger...

"Oooh," Carrie murmured with a cagey smile, "looks like I hit a nerve."

Valerie shook her head, cleared her mind and focused on the woman staring at her with shark's eyes. "What you *hit*," she said coolly, "is the end of my patience. Go bother someone else, all right?"

Then she jerked the car door free of the woman's greedy fingers and slammed it closed. Firing up the engine, she put the car in reverse, turned to look behind her and bulleted out of the parking place. She drove away without looking back, so Val missed seeing Carrie Soker doing a happy little dance in place.

Eight

"Next time you talk to that damned woman, tell me about it. I don't *like* surprises," Dev shouted the next morning.

"All I told her was to go away."

"You shouldn't have talked to her at all." Devlin waved the paper in one tight fist and squeezed as if he could make the damn thing disappear with a little effort.

"It wasn't as if I could avoid her," Val pointed out in her own defense. "The woman was planted on my car like a hood ornament."

"Next time, run her over. It'll be easier to deal with." Dev's gaze dropped to the headline of the trashy grocery-store rag he'd picked up when he went out for muffins and coffee.

Another Hudson Marriage in Trouble? His blood

boiled as he looked at the computer-generated image of him and Val facing away from each other. And underneath those bold black letters and the picture was, *Devlin and Valerie Together for the Sake of Oscar. True Love Not in Hudson's cards.*

"She's making it up," Val told him for the fifth time.

"Of course she's making it up," Dev ranted and tossed the damn paper down onto the closest table. "That's not the point. By talking to her, you've given her an edge toward believability."

"So this is all my fault?" Val came up out of her chair and stalked across the room to grab up the paper he'd tossed down.

And even through his frustrated fury, a part of Dev was watching his wife and admiring the fire in her. If asked, he'd have had to say he much preferred this new Val to the one he'd known months ago.

Then she was yelling at him and he decided it'd be safer to pay attention.

"Some crazy woman stalks me, I tell her to get lost and I'm the bad guy because she writes some delusional article for this piece of trash paper she works for?"

"You're right. I know you're right. I'm just...so pissed I can't see straight."

"Fine. Be mad. At *her.*"

Frustrated and irritated beyond belief, Devlin shoved one hand through his hair and stalked across the room to the fireplace. Setting both hands on the mantel, he stared into the mirror above the hearth and looked at his wife watching him.

It was Sunday morning. He'd planned on spending

it leisurely exploring his wife's luscious curves, delighting both of them with new and inventive methods of making love. And if he hadn't volunteered to go out for coffee and muffins, that's exactly what they'd be doing at the moment.

But no. Now he had to worry about that idiot reporter slamming his family. Again.

"This isn't about just us, is it?" Val asked, her voice quieter, her expression thoughtful.

He kept his gaze locked on her reflection as he shook his head. "No. Read it. You'll see she spares plenty of room to toast my parents' breakup and to bring up the scandal about Bella again."

He waited while she read the short, vicious article, then when she lifted her gaze to look at him, Dev turned around to face her.

"I'm sorry about that, Dev, but honestly, I didn't tell her anything."

Disgusted with himself, he blew out a breath. "I know that. It's just, Bella's past the hurt now. She's got Sam and she's happy. And my parents' business is just that—their business. I hate seeing it all played out in the paper again."

She folded the gossip sheet and tossed it to the floor before walking toward him. Her soft blue robe was belted loosely at her waist and he caught tantalizing glimpses of her bare legs as she came toward him.

When she was no more than an arm's reach from him, she stopped, lifted one hand and cupped his cheek. Giving him a wry smile, she said, "If it helps, Carrie's story on us is running right beneath the article on a woman in Colorado who's in contact with Saturn."

He snorted a laugh.

She smiled. "No one's going to pay any attention to it, Dev. No one who matters, anyway."

"I suppose."

"And we know that the Oscars wasn't the only reason you came to get me, don't we?" She looked up into his eyes and waited for his response.

The Academy Awards was the reason he'd given himself for going to her. But even then, he'd known it wasn't the whole truth. And now? Now he wanted her here too much. He admired her almost as much as he desired her. It worried him just how much she was coming to mean to him. But he wouldn't love her. He'd never let it go that far. Because if he let her in too deeply, he'd be giving her the very ammunition she needed to devastate him.

But he couldn't tell her any of that, so he smiled instead and reached for her. Wrapping his arms around her, he tucked his face into the curve of her neck and whispered, "Yeah, baby. We know the truth."

"So what is the truth?"

"Good question," Dev muttered and leaned back in his desk chair. He spun the thing around so he could watch the activity on the back lot while he talked to his younger brother Luc on the phone.

He'd told Luc all about the article Carrie Soker had written and about the argument he and Val had had over it the day before. "Val says she didn't talk to Carrie and she probably didn't. But the fact is, she did see the reporter and didn't bother to mention it until I saw the damned article in the paper myself. Why wouldn't she tell me? Why keep that a secret?"

"Maybe she didn't think it was important enough to mention," Luc suggested. "After all, the Hudsons have been hounded into the ground by reporters for years. Hell, I chased Leslie Shay off the ranch last week. And good ol' Leslie bothered Gwen, too."

But Dev was focused on the fact that Val hadn't even mentioned the confrontation to him. "She's always asking me about *my* day, why the hell didn't she tell me about hers?"

"Are you actually *looking* for problems?"

"Don't have to look," Dev muttered. "I opened my eyes and there they are."

"Damn, Dev," Luc said, his voice sounding as strong as though he were in the same room, not out on the Montana ranch he shared with his wife, Gwen, and their son, Chaz. "Haven't you wised up yet?"

Dev lifted his legs to the windowsill and crossed his feet at the ankles. "What do you mean?"

"I mean, Val's not the enemy. She's not out to submarine you. She's your wife."

"I know who the hell she is."

"Yeah, but you don't act like it."

"Excuse me?" Dev frowned as though his younger brother could see the expression. "You're in Montana, for God's sake, how do you know how I'm acting?"

"Because, I know *you*," Luc said with a laugh. "You've always been the one to back off anytime somebody got close."

"Look who's talking," Dev told him. "I didn't see you and Gwen having a happy, shiny time of it."

There was a long pause, then Luc muttered, "That's different."

"Yeah, because it's you. Well, this is me and I can handle my own life, thanks."

"Sure," Luc muttered. "Because you've done a bang-up job so far."

"Did you call just to give me a headache?" Devlin frowned again and watched as a space alien and an eighteenth-century woman walked hand in hand toward the commissary.

"No, that's just a bonus," Luc admitted, laughing. "I'm actually calling to tell you Gwen and I will be there for Oscar night."

"That's great, Luc." He smiled to himself. The whole family together. That's what they needed. To show Hollywood, to show the world, that the Hudsons were a unit that wouldn't be divided.

Of course, as soon as that thought registered, he remembered that his parents were still separated and that he had no cure for his mother's betrayal or his father's pain. And he was no closer to trusting the woman who was his wife. How the hell could he? She'd already left him once. Why would he let himself care only to watch her walk out again? What would be the point?

"Dad'll be pleased," Dev said.

"And Mom?" Luc said softly.

"Don't."

"She's our mother, damn it."

"I know that. You think this is easy on me?" Dev asked.

"I think you're making it harder than it has to be," Luc said. "What happened with Mom was so long ago...."

"Yeah, but it's here now, isn't it?" Dev felt a stab of pain in the middle of his chest. The anger at his mother was mostly gone, but the sense of betrayal was something he couldn't get past. "Look at what happened to Bella because of it."

"Bella's putting it behind her. Maybe you should think about trying it, too."

"Let it go, Luc." Dev didn't want to talk about this with Luc, with anyone. The sting of his mother's betrayal still resonated too deeply with him. And he wasn't going to "get past it" by talking it over with his siblings.

"Fine," Luc said after a long, silent moment. "You always were the most stubborn of us. So why don't you just tell me what's going on at the studio."

Grateful for the shift in subject, Devlin shook his thoughts away and concentrated on the sound of his brother's voice. "Regretting your decision to move and become a full-time cowboy?"

"Hell no," Luc said with a laugh. "I just want to hear how crazy you Hollywood types are. Remind me how good I have it out here."

Dev was happy for his brother. Hell, for all his siblings. They'd all managed to find that one person who seemed to complete them. If he resented the fact that his life was less settled than the rest of them, well, that would just continue to be his little secret. He was the oldest. It was up to him to make sure the family stayed strong. And if ensuring that meant keeping his wife at a safe distance from his heart, then that's what he'd do.

The ties holding the Hudson family together were already being tested, thanks to what had happened between his parents. He wouldn't add to the stress by trusting his heart to the wrong woman only to have her smash it.

"Fine, let me tell you what Max is up to first. He's always the most entertaining," Dev said and settled in for a long talk with his brother.

Malibu was more than a beach. It was Hollywood West.

Years ago, this stretch of sand had been crowded with tidy bungalows, cottages used by owners who came out on summer weekends. Now those cottages were mostly gone, replaced by mini-mansions that hugged the shore and were threatened by high tides almost annually.

Now, at the end of February, the ocean was slate gray, reflecting the cloud cover overhead and only a few hardy surfers dared the frigid water. The wind was cold and harsh, the beach mostly empty and the cries of the seagulls wheeling in the air sounded like screams.

Val loved it. She loved standing at the edge of Jack Hudson's property with the laughter and shouts of the Hudsons behind her and the great sweep of sand and sea in front of her. The back of Jack's house was mainly glass, allowing them an unobstructed view of the water, while cliffs behind the house were filled with brush and a few twisted cypress trees. At the shore's edge, a black lab raced through the frothy water chasing a stick thrown by its owner.

Still smiling, she turned to look at the group crowded together on Jack Hudson's patio. The whole Hudson family—save for Luc and Gwen who were in Montana, and Jack's sister, Charlotte, and her husband, who were at their home in France—were gathered here for a barbecue. Even Sabrina and Markus had both attended, though Val hadn't seen them speak to each other yet. Despite that bit of tension, the day was going well.

Almost three-year-old Theo Hudson was giggling on his grandmother's lap as Sabrina tickled and teased him. The adults were gathered around the smoking barbecue or lounging on the deck chairs scattered across the wide patio. Another burst of laughter rose into the air and Val sighed in response.

This was one of the things she'd dreamed of when she had married Dev. This whole loud, confusing, wonderful gathering of an extended family. As the only child of a workaholic widower, Val had never really been a part of anything like this before. And she meant to make the most of it.

She pushed wind-blown hair out of her eyes as her gaze quite naturally slid across the crowd until she found Dev. In his worn blue jeans, black T-shirt and dark green sweater, he looked more like an adventurer than an executive. And she realized she liked him in both of his personas. Though this Dev seemed more approachable. More relaxed somehow.

"Don't look now, but you're drooling."

"What?" Val jumped, startled and turned to look at her sister-in-law. Shaking her head, she demanded, "Bella. Are you *trying* to scare me to death?"

"No," the other woman said with a smile. "Sorry. I was just noticing how you were noticing Dev."

"Obvious again?" Just what she needed, Val thought. She knew that every one of the Hudson family had been very aware before how crazy she was about Dev and how little he'd returned that affection. She so didn't want to go through that again.

"I know what you're thinking," Bella told her and leaned back against the weathered red fence surrounding Jack's property. "But you're wrong. Nobody thought less of you back then, Val. We were all mad at Devlin."

"Oh, thanks," she said wryly. "That makes it all better."

"I'm just saying, we were on your side then and we're on your side now."

"What happened to Hudson solidarity?" She glanced at Bella then shifted her gaze back to where Dev stood talking to his brother Max. Seriously, how did one family produce so many gorgeous men?

"Oh, there's solidarity all right. We're solidly behind *you*." Bella dropped one arm around her shoulders and said, "I told you, you're the best thing that ever happened to Dev. And I'm not the only one here who thinks so."

As good as it made her feel to know that her husband's family were being supportive, it didn't matter to her as much as what Dev was thinking. "Thanks, but it only matters if *Dev* thinks so."

"He does." Bella gave her a squeeze, then let go. "But he's a man, honey. They learn slow."

"I hope that's all it is," Val said a little wistfully. Nothing had really changed between her and Dev.

They'd been back together more than two weeks and she was no closer to breaking down his emotional walls than she had been the first night she'd seduced him.

Oh, the sex was amazing. At night, when they were locked together, she felt closer to him than to anyone she'd ever known and she knew that he felt the same thing. But once the sun was up, everything shifted again, with Devlin becoming more remote, more the man she remembered from the first time she'd tried to build a marriage all by herself.

Why was he so determined to keep her at arm's length? Why wouldn't he let her in? Didn't he know that they couldn't go on this way forever? Frowning, Val watched her husband scowl at Max and felt something give her heart a hard squeeze. As much as she loved him, she wouldn't settle for being his partner only in the darkness. She wanted all of him. And this time, she wasn't going to settle for less.

"Did you talk to Mom?" Max asked as he handed Dev another beer.

"No." Dev's gaze slid to where Sabrina Hudson sat on a deck chair, Theo on her lap. She was still a beautiful woman, he thought, though for the first time, he noticed a strain of unhappiness around her eyes. "Not yet."

"I'm glad she came. I know it meant a lot to Cece and Jack to have her and Dad here."

Dev took a long drink of his beer. "Yeah, but did they ask Dad how *he'd* feel about it?"

"Why would they?" Max frowned at him. "This is a family thing. Everyone's invited, you know that. Besides, does it look like Dad minds?"

Dev followed Max's pointing finger to find his father, seated not far from his wife, watching her through shadowed eyes. Despite the whirl of laughter and conversation surrounding them, Markus and Sabrina looked to be on their own private, hellish islands. He could almost feel his father's pain from there.

"He doesn't look happy."

"Neither does Mom," Max pointed out.

"And whose fault is that?" Dev snapped.

"Damn, Dev." Max shook his head and stared at him. "Are you really so perfect you can't forgive anyone else for being human? You're wasting your time running a movie studio. You should be a saint."

"Didn't say I was perfect," Dev muttered darkly and took another swallow of icy cold beer.

"Yeah? It's how you act. What? Nobody makes mistakes in your little world?"

He stiffened, glared at his younger brother and shifted another look across the patio at his mother, still holding a squirming Theo on her lap. As he watched, his mother raised her chin to smile at Dana, then accepted a glass of iced tea that she shared with little Theo.

And just watching her made Dev realize that he'd really missed having his mother around the mansion. Sabrina had always been the one to laugh the loudest and love the hardest. Hell, he could remember dozens of times when he was a kid that he had gone without seeing his father—busy at the studio. But Sabrina had always been there for her children.

Funny, he hadn't thought of that in a long time.

Shaking his head, he took another drink of his beer and said, as much for his own benefit as for Max's, "Sure, people make mistakes, but then they've got to pay for them."

"With what?" his brother demanded, moving to block Dev's view of his mother. "A public flogging?"

"Don't be stupid."

"I'm not the idiot in this conversation," Max told him. "You keep holding Mom's mistakes against her, but how about looking at it from her side?"

"What *is* her side then, Mister Tuned In To His Feminine Side?"

Max scowled at him. "How about a mistake she made thirty years ago came back to bite her publicly? How about her daughter was tortured by the press? Her marriage was dissected in sound bytes? How about her own damn oldest son won't talk to her and give her a chance to tell him what she's feeling?"

Irritated, Dev shifted uncomfortably. Fine. So he'd had a case of tunnel vision where this thing with his parents had been concerned. But what the hell else was he supposed to think? His mother wasn't the woman he'd thought she was and how the hell was he supposed to reconcile that now?

"Damn, you really are the most stubborn human being on the planet," Max mused. "Bella always said so, but I completely get it now."

"I'm not stubborn," Dev said, "I'm—"

"Rigid? Inflexible?" Max provided

"Consistent," Dev said uncomfortably, then added, "either change the subject or go away."

Max blew out a breath, shrugged and said, "Fine. How's this? The wedding plans are getting way out of hand."

"What?" Dev stared at his brother and waited for more of an explanation.

"It's like planning an invasion."

And Max looked more happy about that than Dev had seen him in a long time. How was it, he wondered, that what had happened to his parents' marriage didn't seem to affect how any of his siblings thought about the whole married thing? Was he the only one to be bitten by the caution bug? Didn't anyone else see the inherent risks in trusting someone so much?

"Nothing to say?" Max nudged.

"Just that you're a lucky man," Dev said and slapped his brother on the back. He was glad Max was happy again. And the whole family already liked and accepted Dana, so that was a plus. It was his own confusion that had Dev's head spinning.

"I know," Max said.

A ping of envy resonated inside Dev briefly and he almost wished he could be as unconcernedly happy as his brother. But someone in this family had to keep thinking straight, didn't they?

Dev glanced their way and noticed that his mother did look happy, though her eyes still held a shadow of pain. Guilt reared its ugly head for a moment, but Dev squashed it mercilessly.

"And," Max added, pointing with his beer bottle, "looks like Bella and Val are having a great time, too."

Dev glanced across the yard at his wife, laughing and talking quietly with his sister. He frowned.

Max said warily, "Always makes me nervous when women get together to whisper."

"Yeah," Devlin murmured. "Me, too."

He caught Val's gaze and when she smiled, his chest felt lighter, as if he'd somehow shrugged off an invisible weight he hadn't even realized he was carrying. How'd she do that? he wondered absently. How did she manage to make him feel as if he wasn't the loner he'd always been at these gatherings?

Before Val, he would watch his brothers and sisters with their dates or their mates and be the extra wheel.

The one who kept his heart locked away. The one who stayed on the fringes and watched everyone else live their lives.

Now with Val here, he felt more of a part of the festivities than he ever had. And he wondered when the hell that had happened. His gaze moved over his wife, dressed in blue jeans, tennis shoes and a long, tunic style deep lavender sweater that made her eyes look as dark and mysterious as twilight.

His body tightened and something inside him shifted, making air a little harder to come by. Frowning to himself, he worked hard to avoid his body's automatic response to Val and told himself it meant nothing. Nothing. But even he didn't believe him.

"Wonder what they're talking about," he murmured.

"Probably best if we don't know," Max told him just before he wandered off to find Dana.

"Probably," Dev whispered to himself, his gaze still locked on his wife. As Bella walked off toward Sam, Val strolled toward the crowd of Hudsons by the main table. She made her way to Sabrina, bent down and kissed the older woman's cheek in greeting. Dev saw his mother's eyes light up and for a second or two, he felt tension bleed from him. Val. She knew his family, obviously cared for them, and they felt the same, that was plain enough to see.

She fit in well with everyone, he thought and realized that Val had carved out a niche for herself in the family. Seeing her with his mother made him want to go over there himself. Maybe Max was right. Maybe there was more to all of this than he'd thought. Maybe he owed it to Sabrina to hear her out.

But even as he considered it, he knew that whatever his mother's reasons, she'd betrayed a trust and he just couldn't find a way around that. So instead, he focused on Val, though his feelings for her were just as confusing.

He'd watched her earlier, playing with Theo, laughing with his father, chatting with Jack's wife, Cece. And now, there she was, sitting on the patio beside Sabrina's chair, playing with Theo, chatting with his mom. Val fit in so seamlessly it was as if she'd always been there.

And that worried him, too. Hell, he told himself as that thought settled in, maybe he was as crazy as Luc had suggested. Maybe he was making trouble where there wasn't any. Why couldn't he just relax and enjoy his wife?

Because, he thought, taking a sip of the cold beer and lifting his face into the slap of the sea wind, it was safer to be on guard. To remember that he'd married Val for her newspaper connections. For the fact that she was intelligent and beautiful and would make an excellent hostess.

The fact that she damn near set his sheets on fire was just a bonus.

The unmistakable clink of a knife against crystal sounded out and the Hudson clan quieted for an announcement.

Jack Hudson grinned once he had everyone's attention. Then he held out one hand toward his wife and Cece slipped up next to him, wrapped her arms around his middle and smiled up at him.

Jack gave her a quick, hard kiss, then looked out at his family. "I guess you're wondering why we called you all here today...."

"To play with *me!*" Theo shouted, then dissolved into giggles as his grandmother kissed his neck.

A few laughs burst into the air at the little boy's shout, but Dev just stood there, waiting. Apparently, more than one family member had something to say today.

"Well, sure, that's part of the reason," Jack told his son, then spoke up even louder as he said, "Cece and I have an announcement." His voice carried easily over the wind and the surge of the sea. Then he paused for dramatic effect and shouted, "We're going to have another baby!"

Cheers erupted from the family as everyone there rushed to hug and congratulate Dev's cousin and his wife. Even Theo was excited, shouting something about baby brothers and puppies. But Dev hardly heard any of it.

He was too caught up in the look Valerie was sending him. It clearly said that she would love to be pregnant. To be announcing that *they* were having a baby. Devlin stilled. He felt as though time had stopped and he and Val were caught in a bubble, separate from everyone else as their locked gazes linked them together.

A baby?

Was he ready for that? He'd better be, he thought suddenly, since as far as he knew, they hadn't been doing anything to prevent conception. And why hadn't he thought about that before right now? A father? Him? Hell, he wasn't really ready for the wife Val had become.

Before the cheers for Jack and Cece had died away, Max was on his feet, holding on to Dana as if half expecting her to try to escape him. Then he announced,

"As long as we're all celebrating… Don't forget about our wedding!"

Another round of happy shouts and laughter rose up and as the Hudsons celebrated, Dev looked at his wife and tried to come to terms with a marriage he hadn't expected and a woman he wanted far too much.

Nine

Three days later, Val and Sabrina were lounging in the pedicure chairs while heated jets of water massaged their feet.

"This is wonderful," Sabrina whispered on a half moan. "Thank you for suggesting it, Valerie."

"My pleasure," Val assured her, leaning her head back and closing her eyes.

The spa day had been a spontaneous suggestion the day of the picnic. Despite the family's happy news, her mother-in-law had seemed so sad, so…lost, that Val had wanted desperately to somehow ease the discomfort she was feeling. So she'd suggested a day of leisure at the best day spa in Beverly Hills.

So far, she'd have to call it a resounding success.

All she needed to make it completely perfect was to

not be worried about Dev. He'd been more withdrawn than ever since the picnic and the news from Jack and Cece. Val couldn't understand why he was so determined to keep her at bay. Why he refused to allow her all the way inside. The other members of his family seemed to have no trouble connecting with those they loved. Why did Dev?

Maybe talking with his mother was the way to gather some clues.

While they sat in silence, with piped-in classical music vying with the rush and swirl of the water in the pedicure tubs, she and Sabrina sipped cold glasses of chardonnay. They'd already had manicures, facials and body wraps, with the pedicure being the finale of their pamper day.

Val sighed into the quiet, grateful that the attendants had left her and Sabrina alone to relax for a while in private. But the moment she had too much time to think, her thoughts filled with images of Dev and her heart ached because she was no closer to winning her husband's heart.

"You're thinking about him again," Sabrina whispered, head back, eyes closed.

Val looked at the older woman beside her and could only hope that when she reached her fifties, she'd be as gorgeous. Smiling, she asked, "How did you know?"

"You were far too quiet. Which means you're thinking." Sabrina gave a casual shrug. "And, since you're married to my son—a man who is legendary for being…difficult—the direction of your thoughts wasn't hard to decipher. You love him and he's making you crazy."

Val choked out a laugh. "You could say that."

"You could also use much harsher words," Sabrina said, smiling, "but he is my son and I love him, too."

"I know." Val sat up, glanced down at her buffed and polished fingernails and said softly, "And I know that Devlin is making all of this so much harder for you."

Sighing, Sabrina sat up straight, too, and looked at her. "It's not entirely his fault. The only one to blame here is me," she admitted and looked as though she wanted to cry. But a moment later, she blinked, stiffened her chin and said, "It was such a long time ago, but the echoes of what I did just won't stop."

"Can I ask—" Val stopped, thought about it and then changed her mind. Whatever had happened all those years ago between Sabrina and her brother-in-law wasn't really her business. Though a part of her thought that the long-ago affair was at the heart of her problem with Dev, how could she ask Sabrina to talk about something that was so clearly painful?

The other woman smiled sadly. "You want to know why I did it," she said softly. "Why I slept with David."

Val nodded. "I'm sorry. I shouldn't have said anything."

"Oh, don't be sorry," Sabrina said quickly, reaching over from her chair to pat Val's hand. "I'm actually grateful. Since this whole thing came out, you're the first one to actually ask me that question. No one else wants to hear about it—though how can I blame them? My poor Bella, especially."

"I saw you talking to her at the picnic last weekend," Val said quietly.

"Yes," Sabrina said. Her smile was a little wobbly, but it was there. "It wasn't easy, but I had to try. She's my daughter and I love her."

"Of course you do," Val said hotly.

Another smile from her mother-in-law. "You don't have to defend me, Val, though I thank you for the effort." She paused, looked down at the frothing water in the pedicure tub and said, "Bella's hurt, of course. And she's very protective of her father—Markus, I mean. Because no matter what else happened so long ago, Markus *is* her father. He's a kind man. A good man. He deserved better. I think," she added thoughtfully, "Bella knows that I still love him. But she also knows that I can't regret what happened because that would mean I regret her birth. Which I don't."

"I know that, too. And yes, Markus is her father. In every way that matters," Val offered. "But if it helps any, I know that Bella misses you. She loves you very much."

Sabrina sniffled, wiped a single, stray tear from the corner of her eye and gave her a smile. "Yes, it does help. I have some hope that she'll eventually forgive me and we'll find our way back to each other. Thank you for that."

"So," Val asked, reluctant to say the words, but grateful that Sabrina had given her blessing, "if you loved Markus…why did you sleep with his brother?"

Easing back into the chair again, Sabrina looked around the small, private room. Val followed her gaze, idly noting the pale pink-wallpaper, the baskets of ferns, the reading lamps and the iced bottle of wine that sat between them.

"It seems like another lifetime ago sometimes," Sabrina whispered after a long moment of silence. "Markus was so busy at the studio back then. He was hardly home. It felt as though I was a single mother most of the time," she added wistfully. "And I suppose, the reality of the situation was, I was lonely."

"Sabrina—"

"No, no sympathy, Val. I don't deserve it. Not really. I was sorry for myself, feeling neglected by my husband and worn to the bone by my very active sons." She smiled at the memories crowding her mind, though the smile didn't last very long. "David was…attentive. His wife, Ava, was always complaining of some malady or other. The woman loved a good illness," she said, almost to herself.

Val could almost see the scenes as Sabrina told her story. A young mother, alone most of the time, her busy husband so buried in work that he didn't notice the woman he loved slipping away from him.

Actually, there were too many likenesses between her story and Sabrina's for Val's taste. But for the fact that she wasn't a mother, she could really understand how left out and alone Sabrina must have felt. And she wondered if Markus had shut his wife out of his thoughts as Dev seemed to do so easily.

"It's an old, sad story," Sabrina said. "Practically a cliché. I listened to and believed David's flattery. I craved the affection that Markus was too busy to give me and I allowed myself to believe that David really wanted me. Loved me."

"He didn't?"

"No." Sabrina turned her gaze on Val then and didn't try to hide a thing as she said, "I slept with him willingly enough, but the moment the deed was done, I regretted it. I felt horribly guilty. I'd betrayed my marriage, my husband, my family. In that blinding moment of clarity, I knew I'd risked everything that was important for one instant of selfishness. I tried to explain to David that it was all a mistake, that I loved Markus and would never do something like that again."

A chill swept along Val's spine as she asked, "What did David say?"

"He laughed." Sabrina swallowed hard and her eyes went cool and distant. "He told me that he didn't love me, that now that he'd had me, he was finished with me. And that his only reason for bedding me was to get back at Markus."

"Oh, God...." Val couldn't even imagine what Sabrina had gone through. To be used so horribly. "But he didn't tell Markus."

"No, he didn't. I suppose that knowing the truth was enough for him."

"I...don't even know what to say."

Sabrina gave her a sad smile. "No reason why you should. Even I can't believe at times that I actually was so foolish. That I almost ruined my marr—"

She broke off, obviously remembering that her marriage was now crumbling under the weight of a twenty-five-year-old secret.

"Sabrina—what about Markus?" Val asked quickly, diverting her to the past so that the future wouldn't hover quite so closely. "How did you keep the truth hidden for so long? Didn't he suspect?"

Now that she'd gotten everything off her chest, Sabrina took a long, deep breath and sighed heavily. "It nearly killed me, keeping that secret. But confession would have been for my sake, not his. The truth could only have hurt him. So I accepted the secrecy as part of my punishment.

"I couldn't bear the thought of telling him. Watching his heart break. Seeing the betrayal in his eyes." She shook her head as if wiping away all the memories. "I devoted myself to him, to the boys, and when I found out I was pregnant with Bella, I took that as a sign that I was exactly where I was meant to be. Where my heart already was. That baby would be mine and Markus's.

"I never said anything to Markus, of course, which is why this is all so devastating now...." She paused, tipped her head to one side and seemed to be considering something carefully before she said, "Sometimes, though, I suspected that Markus knew. That he had somehow guessed what I'd done. He never said anything outright," she added hastily. "But after that time with David, things changed. Markus again became the man I'd loved and married. It was as if with neither of us saying a word about it, we had both decided to devote ourselves to our family. And when Bella was born, Markus couldn't have loved her more."

Another sad smile curved her mouth as her lovely eyes brimmed with tears she refused to shed. "Now, everything is such a mess."

"I understand," Val said. "I really do."

Something in her voice must have alerted Sabrina to the fact that Val understood all too clearly.

"Oh, Valerie." She reached out one hand toward her again. "Are you and Devlin having more problems?"

Now it was Val's turn to share a sad smile. "I love him so much—"

"I know you do."

"—but it's not enough," Val finished, clutching her

mother-in-law's hand tightly. "I think he…*cares* for me, but—"

"He holds himself back."

"Yes. Exactly."

Sabrina sighed. "He was always like that, you know. Too much like his father in that way. As if letting anyone get too close was a danger signal. And, since the truth of my…indiscretion broke—well, he's only closed himself off even more. I'm sorry to say that my past mistakes are probably coloring your marriage."

Val threaded her fingers through Sabrina's and held on. Two women, in love with their husbands and seeing no real hope for rebuilding their marriages. Weren't they a sad pair?

"I don't know what to do about this, Sabrina," Val confessed. "Dev is doing to me what Markus did to you so long ago. Shutting me out. Ignoring me except in the bed—" Good God, she thought, shutting up fast. She couldn't talk to Dev's *mother* about their sex life!

But Sabrina laughed, obviously delighted. "That's good to know, Val. Trust me on this, if Dev is attentive in the bedroom, then you're on his mind. It's just going to take patience. Do you have enough patience to deal with a man as stubborn as he is?"

"I thought I did," she admitted, then realized that she was more downhearted than she had thought.

"Try, Val," Sabrina urged. "He's a good man, my son. I believe he's worth the effort."

"But it's been nearly three weeks that we've been back together and he seems no closer to letting me into his heart than he ever was."

"Three weeks isn't so very long."

"No, but how long is too long? Do I stay and risk that he'll never feel for me what I want him to?" Val asked, her voice low and filled with misery. "Or do I leave while I still can and try to make myself forget him?"

"Only you can answer that, dear," Sabrina said gently. "I can only tell you that once your heart is given, you won't find happiness anywhere else. Believe me, that is the one lesson I learned."

Before Val could say anything else, the door opened and one of the spa attendants walked in, smiling. "How are you two? All ready for your pedicure pampering?"

"Yes, thank you," Sabrina said, with a smile for Val.

"Great," the tall brunette answered. "I'll just go and get Monica and we'll be right back to take care of everything."

As she left, she allowed the door to stay open, so Val and Sabrina made a silent pact to keep quiet. No more chatting about private matters while a door into the rest of the salon stood open. Hollywood gossip spread quickly enough without *inviting* it.

Voices drifted into the room and Valerie tuned them out until she heard the name *Hudson*. Then she couldn't help but listen in.

"I'm telling you," a woman on the other side of the door was saying, "it's criminal that a man like Devlin Hudson is being wasted on that nothing-much wife of his. Please. Could she do something with her hair at least?"

Val's hand reached to smooth down her hair even as Sabrina shot her a sympathetic look. "Pay no attention," she mouthed.

But Val was listening to every word.

"It'll never last," another woman answered smugly.

"They've broken up once already and they've been married what? Four months? Devlin's going to get tired of her really soon. Heck, his own father's dumped his mother."

Sabrina inhaled sharply and Val's back teeth ground together.

"Yes, but their marriage lasted thirty years."

"That's Hollywood years, honey," the other woman told her friend. "They've probably been boffing everybody in town and managing to keep it quiet."

"In this town? It's a miracle," the first woman said on a laugh. "I'll tell you what. As soon as Markus divorces his wife, I'll swoop in and claim him. You can have Devlin when Little Miss Mousy finally splits."

"Oooh. That'd be great. You know I'm reading for a part in the next Hudson picture. I could probably find a way to 'accidentally' bump into Devlin while I'm on the lot."

"If you can't," her friend said with a chuckle, "nobody can."

"That's it," Val muttered, standing up in her pedicure footbath.

"Valerie, just let it go," Sabrina advised. "I've been around long enough to know that people talk. You can't stop it. You can't do anything about it at all."

"I can stop *them*," Val said tightly and grabbed a lush pink towel to dry her feet as she stepped out of the tub. So much for a day of pampering. She'd just have to leave the spa with naked toes because once she was finished with these two women, she wouldn't want to stick around.

"Val, don't—"

She started for the door, then stopped and looked at the mother of her husband. Hadn't Sabrina suffered enough? Was she really expected to listen to vicious cats sharpening their claws on her name? No.

"No, Sabrina. I'm finished. I'm not going to be the passive little observer standing around doe-eyed while the world does whatever it likes to me. Not again."

"Oh, my…" Sabrina was already levering herself out of the pedicure chair when Val left the room, turned a corner and glared at the two women sitting in the manicure chairs.

It was some consolation to see the looks of pure shock on their nearly-identical-Hollywood-perfect faces as she stared at them. But not nearly enough.

"How dare you sit there and spout off about me and my family," Valerie started. "Who do you think you are, anyway? Do you really presume to know what goes on in a private home? Or is the word 'private' a new one for you?"

"Now just a minute," one of them said.

"No, you had your say and we heard every word."

"We?" the other woman asked with a cringe.

Sabrina appeared in the open doorway and both women groaned.

But Valerie wasn't finished. She was on a roll now and completely enjoying herself. The fact that half the salon was now listening to every word didn't matter to her. She didn't care who else was there. It was time the world listened to Valerie so she might as well start there.

"You two think you can guess what someone's marriage is like? You think you can gossip about someone and never be called on it?"

"We didn't say anything that isn't in the papers," the first woman explained.

"Really? Which paper did the word 'mousy' appear in?" Val tapped her bare foot against the floor, planted both hands on her hips and leaned in, shooting first one of the women, then the other, looks harsh enough to melt steel. "Let me tell you something, you wanna-be-starlets. I'm not mousy. My mother-in-law's marriage is just dandy and her husband doesn't need to look to someone like *you* for comfort. As for *my* marriage, you should be so lucky as to have what I have."

"Just a min—" one of them tried to interrupt.

"And as for your 'audition'?" Val said, her voice dropping to a low growl, "one word from me and the closest either of you will get to a movie role is selling tickets in the lobby."

"Look, we're really sorry, we didn't know—"

"No, you didn't *think*," Val corrected for her. "Maybe next time you will. Now why don't you both get out of here before you find out how really 'mousy' I can be."

"Good idea," one of them said, giving her friend a hard nudge. "C'mon, Dani, let's jet."

"Right behind you," her friend said as they gathered up their purses and headed for the door.

Once they were gone, a smattering of applause broke out in the salon. Val's temper was still spiking so hotly she hardly noticed.

Sabrina stepped up, wrapped her in a tight hug and said, "Brava!" Then she leaned back, looked her in the eyes and said, "I couldn't ask for a finer daughter-in-law."

Val grinned and felt a surge of triumph she'd never

known before. Who would have guessed that standing up for herself could feel so…wonderful? At the moment, she even felt as if she could face down Dev and come out the winner.

"Thanks. What do you say we blow off the pedicures and go have a late lunch?"

Devlin walked in the door, tossed his keys onto the table in the entryway and walked into the main room of his suite. He was used to the changes in his home now and actually liked them, though he hadn't told Val that. The overstuffed furniture was more comfortable than his old leather pieces and he had to say, he thought with a smile, that he definitely approved of Val's "snuggle sofa" idea.

Just remembering their first night on that couch in front of a candlelit hearth had him going hard and ready for her. Amazing just how easily he was aroused with thoughts of Valerie. Even more amazing that he was somehow able to block thoughts of her during the day only to lose himself in her once he got home.

Shaking his head, he looked around the room and when he didn't see her or hear her, called out, "Val?"

"I'm in here," she shouted back and he smiled, already headed for the kitchen.

It was quickly becoming his favorite room in the house. Who would have guessed that cooking together every night could be so much fun? Although, he had to admit that sex on the table last night had added to the allure of the room. Maybe he could talk her into a fast, sweaty bout of sex before dinner tonight, too.

He pulled off his jacket, tossed it to a chair and was

pulling his tie off as he walked into the kitchen. Val was at the butcher block table in the center of the room, slicing onions, and the smile she gave him told him that she'd be open to anything he might suggest. But first, something smelled great and he made straight for the bubbling pot on the back of the stove. "What've you got going here?"

"Spaghetti sauce."

He looked at her. "From scratch?"

She grinned and tossed her hair back out of her eyes. "Is there any other kind?"

Until Valerie had entered his life, he thought, he would have made do with jarred sauce and a table for one. Or, he would have gone down to the family dining room to eat whatever they were serving.

Shaking his head, he lifted the lid off the pot and took a deep breath of the incredible scents drifting up in a tower of steam. "Smells great."

"Tastes even better," she assured him. "Want to help slice onions?"

"It's what I live for," he told her and walked around to stand directly behind her. Laying his hands over hers, he leaned in close, making sure she could feel his body, hard and eager for her. He wanted her to know without a doubt that slicing vegetables wasn't what he had in mind.

She sucked in a gulp of air. "Dev, if you do that, I'm liable to chop both of our hands off."

"Maybe you'd better set the knife down, then."

"But dinner—"

"Not what I'm hungry for," he told her and, when she dropped the knife onto the cutting surface, turned her around in his arms. Deftly then, he undid the buttons of her blouse and just as handily unhooked the front snaps of her bra.

"This is what I need, right here," he murmured, freeing her breasts and palming their weight.

Her head fell back, her eyes closed and she sighed heavily. "That shouldn't feel so good. It should be illegal."

"Call me criminal then," he whispered and slowly dropped to his knees in front of her. "Are you ready for me?"

"Aren't I always?" she teased, looking down into his eyes.

Yes, he thought, his body leaping into life, his heartbeat hammering in his chest. It was a little game they'd been playing over the last week. No matter what clothes she happened to be wearing when he came home, she made sure she wasn't wearing underwear. After he'd torn through three of her favorite lacy thongs, they'd both decided it would be cheaper—and faster—for her to go without.

All the way home, he'd been imagining this. Thinking about it until he'd nearly driven himself off the road. When had she become so important to him? When had she become the center of his thoughts, the image of his fantasies? And what did it matter now that they were here, together?

"Dev…what're you going to—"

Her words trailed off as he showed her exactly what he'd been thinking about for the last half hour. Thankfully, she was wearing a soft, cotton skirt, which made this all the more easy. Kneeling in front of her, he lifted the flimsy material, dragged it up her thighs and leaned in close enough to taste her.

"Oh! My! Devlin…"

His tongue and lips teased her core. Flicked wildly over the sensitive bud at the heart of her passion and drove them both a little crazed. Her scent, her taste, inflamed him, made him crave more and more of her. Her gasping breaths, her fingers threading through his hair, holding him to her only made him more desperate to push her screaming over the edge.

She twisted against the cooking island, holding on with one hand as she used her free hand to hold his head to her. He glanced up and saw her watching him taste her and that only fed the fires clamoring within. Again and again, he licked and caressed and nibbled. He pushed her higher, faster than he ever had before and could hardly catch his own breath by the time she shrieked his name, trembled violently in his grasp and then slumped bonelessly against him.

"That was—oh my—Devlin, you—" She couldn't even complete a sentence. And he wasn't finished. Not by a long shot. There was more to this fantasy and he wanted it fulfilled now.

Rising, he grabbed her close, kissed her mindless, then lifted her, swung her around and planted her behind down onto the cold, granite counter. She yelped a little, but an instant later, she was lost in their kiss, just as he wanted her.

She was more and more to him every day. Every time he lost himself in her, it only made him want her again. There was no end to this clawing, burning passion. There was only *again*. Fires burned brighter, heat was more explosive and desire fed the need inside him until Devlin could think of nothing but her. How had this happened? How had she slipped so far into his heart, his soul? And how would he ever be able to keep her at a safe distance when everything in him clamored for him to draw her in closer?

She looked at him then and her twilight eyes were dazed with satisfaction and tinged with renewed hunger. She was amazing. She was incredible. And she was his. For now, she was his.

"Devlin," she said on a whisper, "I want you inside me, right this minute."

"That's the plan," he muttered. He opened his zipper, freed himself and moved in close enough to take her there, in their favorite room. He entered her with one long, hard thrust and she gasped at the invasion.

She was tight and hot and welcoming and Devlin let his mind go blank as emotions, *need,* demanded precedence over coherent thought. Rocking his hips, setting a rhythm that she matched eagerly, he pushed them both along that dazzling road to completion until Val groaned, arching into him. Her body flexed, she trembled and in seconds, Dev called out her name and held her tightly as they tumbled into a star-filled chasm.

A few minutes later, Val recovered first, raising her head from his shoulder and smiling at him with so much love it nearly made him breathless. God knew, it made him nervous.

Yes, Dev knew she loved him. She always had. And he…cared for her. God, that was a weak word and he knew it. But he couldn't give her love. Wouldn't allow it of himself. So what he felt for her now, this growing emotion, had to be enough. For both of them.

Disentangling them, Devlin rearranged his clothes,

closed up his zipper, then lifted her off the counter as she smoothed her skirt into place.

"That was quite the greeting," she said, still grinning.

"I like surprises," he told her, already mentally backing away from what he was feeling for her. *Surprises*. Amazing how often that word had come up in the last few weeks. Val's newly discovered self-confidence, the incredible chemistry they shared, his own sense of…affection toward her. He'd been prepared for none of it and that was probably why he was having so damned much trouble dealing with the situation.

Valerie must have picked up on his deepening confusion because her smile faded as she walked back to the cooking island to resume her task.

"Well, I had a surprise today, too."

"Yeah, I was there," he said, leaning back against the counter as he idly considered having the damn thing bronzed.

"Not *that* surprise," she said, tossing him a quick look over her shoulder. "Your mom and I went to a spa today and—"

He came away from the counter, walked to her side and turned her to face him. "You and Mom?"

"Yes," she said, clearly confused by his reaction. "Last weekend at the picnic, we arranged to spend the day together."

He scrubbed one hand across the back of his neck and wondered just how many ways this could be trouble. What had his mother said to her? Had she confessed all her reasons for shattering her family? Did Val sympathize? "That's the surprise?"

"No," Val said, clearly oblivious to his racing

thoughts. "Actually, we had a great time. We had a chance to talk and she…told me about what happened."

Everything in Devlin went from warm to cold in an instant. He stiffened and he felt himself pulling away from her. So Sabrina had talked to her about everything.

"I could tell you—"

"No, thanks." He cut her off fast. He didn't want to hear his mother's secondhand confession. There couldn't be an explanation and an apology was about twenty-five years too late. What was done was done and nothing could be changed.

"Dev, if you'd just let her talk to you—"

He waved one hand and scowled at her. "Never mind about that. What's the surprise you were talking about?"

She sighed, clearly disappointed, but set the knife down, turned to face him and forced a smile. "Well, we were nearly finished at the spa and then we heard these two women—cats, really. They were saying the most horrible things about your mom and about you and me."

Dev gritted his teeth and waited her out. Gossip was nothing new to this town, but the idea of Val and his mother being subjected to actually overhearing the talk about them didn't set well with him. The fact that he was feeling defensive on their behalf didn't really occur to him.

Val kept talking and the more she said, the more Dev's head pounded. This was more than mere gossip. Didn't she see what she'd done? Didn't she get it?

"Anyway," she was saying, "after I finished telling them off, those two took off so fast, I swear you could see sparks flying up from their oh-so-trendy sandals. I was so proud of myself for setting them straight, your mom and I went out to lunch to celebrate."

He stared at her as if he'd never seen her before. "*Celebrate?* Are you nuts?"

"Dev—"

"Damn it, Val, don't you see you've only made this *worse?*"

Ten

Sabrina opened the front door of the Hudson family mansion, stepped inside and paused on the threshold as if she half expected the butler or Hannah, the housekeeper, to come rushing at her to toss her out. But that wouldn't happen. Markus hadn't asked her to leave. She'd gone of her own free will, knowing they both had needed time to deal with the exposure of such a hurtful secret.

But watching Val facing down those malicious gossips at the spa that afternoon had given Sabrina the nudge of courage she'd needed to do a little confronting of her own. She couldn't remain at a hotel for the rest of her life. Not while her heart lived here. In this place. With Markus.

Whether or not it was the right thing to do, she'd had to come home. Had to find out if she still had a marriage to fight for.

Quietly, she moved into the house and, just as quietly, closed the door behind her. She took a long breath to steady herself, then turned around to face the familiar home she'd missed so much. It was so silent, she thought. In the early years, she'd have given any amount of money to find some peace and quiet for an hour or two.

Now, what she wouldn't give to hear her children running through this place. To hear the sounds of their laughter and shouts. To be back in the body of that young wife she'd once been, with the knowledge she now had. But even as she considered that, she knew she couldn't really have changed how her past had played out. Because to do that, she'd have to give up her daughter. And that she couldn't do. Especially now that it looked as though she and Bella were going to be all right.

She'd spoken to Bella on the phone just an hour ago and though the bond between them was fragile, Sabrina knew that the love between them was strong enough to conquer even mortal failings.

After talking with Bella, though, Sabrina had known that she'd have to come here, to this place, to resolve everything else in her life. She'd loved in this house. Raised her children here. This house was as much a part of her as her arms, her legs.

But the man who lived here meant more. So much more.

"God, I was such an idiot," she whispered to no one, her words a hush of sound in the silence.

"No."

She jumped, startled to find she wasn't alone. Markus stepped out of the formal living room to her left and stopped in a slash of lamplight. His features looked strained, but his eyes—the eyes she knew so well—were filled with regret. And seeing that emotion on her husband's face tore at Sabrina with such force, a silent sob wracked her.

And she'd convinced herself she was ready to see him. But how could she? Knowing how hurt he must be? Knowing that her betrayal had cost them both so much?

Covering her mouth with her hand, she turned blindly for the doorknob again. Barely able to speak, she muttered, "I'm sorry, Markus. I shouldn't have come."

He stopped her, laying one hand on her arm. "No, you should never have left."

Slowly, Sabrina raised her gaze to his. "What?"

He smiled. The man she still loved so fiercely, smiled at her and Sabrina's heart settled into a hopeful beat. "I'm so sorry, Sabrina," he said.

Stunned by the one thing she'd never expected to hear from him, she whispered, "Markus, no. I'm the one who should apologize. I never meant to hurt you. Never meant to—"

He took hold of her shoulders, his hands bleeding a welcome warmth into her body after weeks of feeling a bone-deep cold. Sabrina's eyes filled with tears she didn't dare shed for fear of not being able to stop them.

"You don't owe me an explanation, Sabrina," Markus told her and leaned in to kiss her forehead. "I remember what I was like back then. I remember how often I left you alone. How determined I was to keep you at a distance."

True, she thought, all of it true. And why she'd

turned to another man for the attention she'd wanted from her husband.

"Why?" she asked, finally asking the question she should have asked so long ago. "I know you loved me, so why would you want to keep me at bay?"

"*Because* I loved you," he confessed, with a wry smile. "I thought I loved you too much. Thought that if I told you how much I needed you, you would have all the power in our relationship."

"Oh, Markus...."

"I was the fool," he said and shifted one hand to tip her chin up so that he could look directly into her eyes. "I felt you slipping away and did nothing to stop it. I saw David maneuvering you and convinced myself that nothing would happen. I felt your heartache and ignored it."

A single tear traced its way down her cheek and Sabrina didn't bother to wipe it away. Markus did, though. His thumb caught that one stray drop of moisture and his gaze dropped to it. "I didn't mean to hurt you, either, Sabrina," he whispered.

Her heart cracked a little and the pain she'd been clinging to for so long began to seep out and dissolve. Being here with him where she belonged felt so right. How could she ever have risked losing this? Losing him?

Hope filled her, hope that she might regain what she'd lost through selfishness and shortsightedness. But before anything else was said, she had to know something. "Bella. Did you suspect back then that David was her biological father?"

Pain flashed briefly across his features, then was gone an instant later. "Yes," he said softly. "I knew. But it didn't matter. Bella's *mine*. She's *ours*. She always has been."

Her secret, guarded so carefully over the years, had never really been a secret. Ironic? Or was it justice? That she suffered alone and so had Markus, each of them blaming themselves for what had happened and neither of them willing to risk a confession.

"Oh, Markus, I do love you. I've always loved you." She finally raised one hand to wipe away the other tears now raining down her face. "I only got…lost for a while."

"Getting lost isn't important," he said softly. "It only matters that you find your way home. That we *both* found our way home."

"I've missed you so much," she admitted.

He pulled her in close, wrapping his arms around her, and Sabrina drew her first easy breath in weeks. The scent of him, the warm, solid strength of him, so familiar, so very necessary, let her know that she had, finally, come home. Because as much as she loved this house, this *man* was the only home she'd ever really need.

"Never leave me again, Sabrina," he murmured, kissing the top of her head, holding her even more tightly. "I can't live without you."

"Never," she swore, then raised her head so that she could look into his eyes. Smiling, she promised, "I'll always be with you. Always."

His mouth curved, his eyes warmed and he turned her toward the stairs without releasing her. "Let's go upstairs and I'll show you just how much I missed you."

Leaning her head on her husband's shoulder, Sabrina sighed gratefully and wished for her daughter-in-law the same kind of happiness she herself was feeling.

* * *

"Worse?" Val looked at him as if he was out of his mind and that's exactly how Dev felt. "What do you mean? How does standing up for myself and your mother make anything worse?"

Dev cursed under his breath. Man, things could turn to crap in a heartbeat. A few minutes ago, he'd been buried inside his wife, feeling better than he had all day and now...

"Damn it, Val, of *course* you've made things worse."

He shoved both hands through his hair and stalked around the kitchen. He wanted something to kick, but there was nothing in his way. He'd just have to settle for the urge, he supposed. "What the hell were you thinking?"

She was turning in a circle, following him on his mad pace around the room. Violet eyes wide, hands at her hips, she argued, "I was *thinking* about defending myself. And your mother. Protecting this *family*."

He snorted an unamused laugh. "Nice job."

"What is wrong with you? It was a situation in a salon with a couple of women nobody cares about."

"Right." He stopped dead, looked at her as if he'd never seen her before and said, "In case no one ever told you, this is Hollywood. Those two women will shoot their mouths off all over town. You think they're going to keep quiet about you using your connections at the studio to see they never get an acting job? There's no such thing as a well-kept secret in this town—" As soon as he said those words, though, he realized that his mother had managed to keep her secrets locked away for thirty years, so he added, "usually."

"Dev, I couldn't just sit there while they insulted your mother."

"You damn well should have," he snapped, already seeing imaginary headlines in the morning papers…Hudson Wife Threatens Actress. Perfect. Just perfect.

"Why?"

"Hell, hasn't there been enough bad press about the family? And when those two spread what you said all over town? How's that going to look? My wife telling actresses she can ruin them in this town? Yeah," he muttered, "thanks very much for your help."

She scowled at him, clearly still not seeing the problem here. "You're making too much of this, for heaven's sake."

"And you should mind your own business."

She looked as if he'd slapped her. Her head jerked back, her eyes went wild and wide and she clenched her jaw so tightly, he wouldn't have been surprised to find out she'd ground her teeth to powder.

Finally, though, she took a breath, and said calmly and quietly, "The Hudson family *is* my business. I'm one of you now, whether you want to admit that to yourself or not."

"What the hell does *that* mean?" he shouted and felt the urge to kick something again.

"If you're going to shout, I'm not going to talk to you."

"The hell you're not," he shouted, "we're in the middle of an argument!"

"No, I'm having an argument," she told him flatly. "You're having a tantrum."

"Tantrum." He threw both hands in the air and looked

toward the ceiling and heaven beyond as if searching for help he knew damned well wasn't coming.

"Fine." His voice was tight, but lower now. "What the hell did you mean when you said whether or not I want to admit that you're part of the damned family?"

She blew out a breath, raised her chin and glared at him. "It means, that as long as we're in bed together, you're happy as a clam to have me around. But the minute the sun comes up, you expect me to disappear."

"That's ridiculous." But her words were far too close to the truth for his comfort.

"Is it?" She walked toward him, mouth tight, eyes flashing fire, and Dev backed up a step. He might be furious but he wasn't an idiot.

"This isn't about us," he countered, despite the fury raging in her eyes. "This is about my family's business being talked about all over town and *you* encouraging these morons by threatening them in public!"

"*Our* family is being attacked, Dev. And I defended *your* mother. Something you haven't been able to bring yourself to do."

"Don't start," he warned.

"I didn't start it," she told him hotly, "*You* did. You blame your mother for what happened twenty-five years ago. Well, she blames herself, too."

"As she should—"

"Not finished," Val snapped. "Did it ever occur to you that it takes *two* people to make a good marriage or a bad one?"

"So this is my father's fault?" He shook his head and laughed in her face. "That's great. Perfect. Is that what

Mom told you? That she was *forced* to sleep with my uncle because my father wanted her to?"

"Now you're just being stupid," she said and turned away. "Obviously, you don't want to hear what I'm saying."

He grabbed her forearm, though, and spun her back around to look at him again. "No, finish this. You want it out. Fine. Let's talk about it. My mother betrayed my father. Betrayed *all* of us."

Valerie sighed. "Don't you think she knows that? Don't you think she's sorry?"

"Does being sorry change a damn thing?" he demanded and released her because he felt the need to pace again. To move. So much energy and anger was pumping through him, Dev couldn't have stood still if it meant his life.

"If she changed things, you wouldn't have Bella," Valerie reminded him softly.

He stopped, turned and glared at her. "A low blow."

"Just the truth, Dev," Valerie said and gave another sigh. "I'm not saying your mom didn't make a mistake. What I am saying is that she didn't make that mistake alone. Have you ever considered that maybe if your father hadn't been too busy with his work to even notice he *had* a wife, that none of this might have happened?"

He scowled at her, wanting to push her argument aside, but hadn't he just been thinking something along those lines a few days ago? At the picnic at Jack's house? He'd remembered then how rarely he'd seen his father when he was a kid. Looking back now, with the perspective of an adult, he could see that his mother had been alone most of the time. But even as he admitted that, he heard himself say, "That doesn't give her an excuse to do what she did."

"No, it's not an excuse, but it's a reason," Val said, not letting up on this at all. "Maybe Sabrina needed to feel needed. Needed to know she was loved."

"And sleeping with her brother-in-law did that for her?" He smirked at her. "Nice."

"No, you big jerk, what David did was humiliate her. Use her."

He stared at her, disbelieving. "What?"

"You heard me," Val said and walked toward him again, her eyes still glinting dangerously. "Sabrina was taken advantage of. Her own husband ignored her and the man who seduced her into an affair was really only using her to hurt her husband. So just who was the really injured party here?"

Val's words slapped at him, forced him to realize a few things he'd rather have ignored. For instance, that his mother had feelings in this, too. That maybe his parents' "perfect" marriage had had trouble long before his mother's affair. But he didn't want to acknowledge Val's point, because if he did, he'd have to admit that both his parents were fallible. Not something easily done.

"Don't you see, Dev? There're two sides to every marriage. And if only one person loves, it's doomed to disaster."

He looked into her eyes and realized she was talking about more than his parents' marriage, now. She was talking about them. But they weren't his parents. They understood each other. They had a great sex life. They laughed together. And for God's sake, he damn near raced home every night.

"Our situation is different."

"Is it?"

Irritated beyond measure now, he asked, "It is unless *you're* sleeping with my uncle."

"That's not funny."

"Neither is any of this," he muttered, shoving one hand through his hair as if he could massage away the headache bursting into life behind his eyes.

He looked at Val and tried to find the distance he needed from her. God, he needed it more tonight than ever before. But his own heart was working against him. She was getting to him, reaching some part of him that had been closed off for years.

And the hell of it was, a part of him welcomed it. Thankfully, though, his mind was still in control. Even if everything she'd said about his parents was true, it didn't change the fact that betrayal had torn them apart. His father had trusted his wife and she'd broken faith with him.

How the hell was a man supposed to live with that?

"Dev—"

"Just let it go, Val, okay? For tonight, just let it go." Then he walked past her, needing the outside air, needing to move, to think, away from those violet eyes that saw too much.

"Where are you going?" she called after him.

"Just out back. I need a walk. Clear my head." Then he left, striding into the lamp-lit darkness of the estate.

He stalked to the edge of the garden and looked back at the house where he'd grown up. The argument with Val still buzzing in his brain, Dev let his gaze drift over the old house, until he spotted something at his father's suite. Shadows moving in the lamplight.

Two silhouettes moving toward each other in silence.

He had no trouble recognizing the people—his parents. Clearly, Markus and Sabrina were working out their problems. Shock registered first, then surprise. But then, he thought in disgust, there were plenty of surprises lately in that house.

Turning away, Dev stared out into the night and listened with half an ear to the sounds of the neighborhood. From the end of the street, a yapping dog made itself heard and a car with a powerful engine growled off toward the city.

How in the hell could he not forgive his mother when his father obviously had? And how could he convince himself to forget betrayal and bring himself to trust *anyone* with the power to destroy him?

Disgusted with his parents, his wife and mostly himself, Dev headed off down the greenbelt stretching along the length of the mansions crowding the street.

Looked like he needed that walk more than he'd thought he did.

A few days later, nothing had been settled between Dev and Val, but other problems in the Hudson family were smoothing themselves out.

Val smiled as she walked down the curved staircase toward the family part of the mansion. Sabrina was practically glowing, now that she and Markus had resolved their differences and she had moved back home permanently.

Sabrina had even reconnected with her daughter, though things were still a little fragile at the moment. But Bella was on her way over right now to join Val and

Sabrina for tea and to talk about the upcoming wedding. It seemed that Bella had changed her mind about a quick, uncomplicated ceremony now that she and her mom were speaking again. So the plans would probably take on the scope of the war room at the Defense Department.

Which was good, Val told herself. Anything was good if it kept her mind off her own troubles with Dev. Since their fight in the kitchen the other night, the temperature between them had been cool at best. Yes, their lovemaking retained all the heat and combustion it had before—because neither of them was willing to give up that part of their relationship—but the distance between them otherwise was beginning to broaden.

It was as if even knowing that his parents had made up their differences, Dev was still determined to keep himself locked behind the walls Val had almost given up on smashing.

She stepped onto the marble entryway and turned toward the kitchen and family room. When the phone rang, though, she automatically stepped up to answer it.

"Hello."

"Hi!" A woman's voice, a little hesitant. "Um, who's this?"

Val almost smiled. She recognized the voice easily enough. "Hello, Charlotte, it's Val."

"Val, hi!" The other woman's voice was high, excited and loud enough that she probably could have been heard from her home in France even without the telephone connection.

"I was calling to talk to Aunt Sabrina," she said quickly. "I called the hotel, but they said she'd checked out, so I was sort of hoping she'd gone home and everything was okay now and—"

Now Val did laugh a little. In spite of her own miseries, it was nice to hear someone else so happy. "You were right," she said, interrupting Dev's cousin, "Sabrina did move home a few days ago. I'll go get her for you."

"That'd be great, but wait a sec. I swear I just can't stand not telling somebody, Val, so you get to hear first, just don't tell Aunt Sabrina until I do, okay, because I really want to surprise her and—"

"I promise," Val said, lifting her head as the sound of heels on marble reached her. She smiled at Sabrina as the older woman approached and said, "She's right here, Charlotte—"

"I'm so excited about the baby!" Charlotte gave a delighted laugh.

Val's heart twisted and a pang of envy rattled around inside her even while Charlotte kept talking.

"Honestly, Val, everything is so good here. I never thought I could be this happy, it's just so wonderful...."

"That is great," Val managed to say as Sabrina came up to her, a worried look in her eye.

"And I didn't tell you the best part," Charlotte said quickly, as if sensing that Val was getting ready to hand off the phone. "The baby's a *girl,* and we're going to name her Lillian, after my grandmother."

Another sharp pang jolted Val, despite her best efforts. Family. Connections. Traditions. The Hudsons were moving on, building lives, rebuilding them when necessary and she and Dev were stuck in neutral.

With the frothy sound of Charlotte's happiness ringing

in her ears, and the concerned look on Sabrina's face directly in front of her, Valerie had to acknowledge that she'd made a huge mistake in coming back to Dev. She'd thought she could win his love, but it was obvious to her now that he wasn't interested in what she could give him.

He didn't want to love or be loved. He wanted to be alone while having a sexual partner handy should he require her.

Misery rose up to tangle at the back of her throat and nearly choke her. But somehow, Val managed to say, "Look, Charlotte, your aunt's here, so why don't you tell Sabrina the news about the baby? I've um, got something, to um…"

"Sure, sure. That'd be great. Thanks for listening, Val, and give your husband a big kiss from me!"

"I will. Hold on." Val took the phone from her ear and held it out to Sabrina.

The older woman took it, covered the mouthpiece with her hand and said softly, "Val? Is everything all right?"

"Fine," she said and forced a smile that must have looked as hideous as it felt. "But I don't think I can join you and Bella after all, Sabrina. I've got a few things to take care of today and—"

"It's okay, sweetie," Sabrina said, reaching out to stroke one hand up and down Val's arm in comfort. "But if you need to talk…"

"Thanks," she whispered, already turning back to the stairs. If she didn't leave quickly, the tears building up inside would explode and rain down all over everyone. "I'll see you later, Sabrina."

She couldn't talk to her mother-in-law. Couldn't talk

to anyone about this. The sorrow was just too deep. Too overwhelming. She couldn't live her life watching the people around her grow and be happy and have all the things she wanted so badly for herself. If that made her selfish, then she'd just have to live with it.

Her heels clattered on the marble steps and when she closed herself off in their suite, Val finally gave in to the tears and let them fall, knowing there was no one there to notice.

The moment Dev got home, he instantly knew something was wrong.

No music played.

No tantalizing scents drifted in the air.

Frowning, he walked into the main room, and spotted Val, curled up on a chair by the window, staring out at the garden. She looked beautiful and somehow haunted. "Val?"

She turned her head to look at him and he realized she'd been crying. "What is it? What's wrong?"

"Us," she said softly. "We're what's wrong. Or maybe it's just me. I'm not really sure."

Something cold settled in the middle of his chest as he walked toward her. Sure, things had been a little strained since their last argument, but he'd thought they'd put it behind them. After all, his parents had worked their problems out and he'd even spoken to his mother that morning. So what the hell was wrong now?

"What're you trying to say?" he asked, taking a seat in the chair opposite her.

"I'm saying I want a divorce."

Eleven

Shocked, Dev just stared at her. This he hadn't been expecting. "Where the hell did that come from?"

"Don't sound so stunned," she told him wryly. "Dev, you know this isn't working. We're not happy."

"*I'm* happy and I thought you were, too," he countered, his temper starting to edge past the cold knot of tension in his chest. He was blindsided and trying to make sense of what he was hearing.

"I tried to be." She wrapped her arms around her knees as if for comfort and said, "I really tried this time, Dev. I did. But I'm obviously not the woman you want. You see, I *love* you. I thought I could make you love me, too. But clearly I can't. And since I can't settle for less than love, I can't stay."

"But we're getting along great," he pointed out,

jumping to his feet. "Our sex life is perfect, the family's troubles are winding down, hell, I even talked to Mom this morning because I knew you'd want me to."

She smiled sadly and that tiny expression was enough to shake him to the bone. "I'm glad you're talking to your mom, but don't you see? This isn't about the family. It's about us. And what we don't have. Your cousin Charlotte called to talk about the baby."

"What?"

"Charlotte. She called today from France. The baby's a girl they're naming Lillian."

"Good for her," Dev said, "but what's—"

"She's building a family." She sniffled, wiped her eyes and firmed her mouth. "Jack and Cece have moved on. Max and Dana are engaged. Bella's planning her wedding. Luc and Gwen are nestled in at their ranch. Everyone but *us* is having the kind of life I want. The kind of family I want. The kind we can never have."

"Of course we can."

She shook her head slowly, sadly. "Not without love on both sides, Dev."

"Love?" He snorted the word, shook his head and took two fast steps away from her only to spin around and come right back. "This is about love? Love is over-rated, Val. Look what happened to my parents. *Love* nearly did them in. Their supposedly rock-solid marriage nearly shattered because it was based on love. Is that what you want? Isn't it better to have a relationship based on friendship and honest lust?"

She unfolded herself from the chair and stood up to face him. Her mouth trembled but she made a deliberate effort to firm it up. "But it's not just lust on my side, Dev. I love you. And as for your parents' marriage…don't you get it? It's because they love each other that it's going to work out. Love makes every high higher and every low lower. It's what makes life worth living."

"You're wrong," he muttered. "Love's dangerous. Not to be trusted."

"And as long as you feel that way, we won't have anything real." She sighed and crossed her arms, her hands rubbing up and down her upper arms as if for warmth. "I'll stay with you until after the Oscars, Dev. I know how important it is for you to have the family together for that night. But when it's done, I'm leaving. This time for good."

Fear grabbed the base of his throat and he didn't like the taste of it. She seemed so broken. So…sad. She was going to leave. He was going to lose her. And this time there would be no bringing her back. He sensed it instinctively. This was the end. Permanently.

Isn't it better though, his mind taunted, to lose her now, rather than in thirty years? She would have left you eventually. Isn't this way easier?

No. Nothing about this was easy. And no way was he going to let her get away.

"You gave me your word. That day on your patio at your condo…when I went to bring you back home, you swore you wouldn't leave unless I wanted you to," he reminded her. "Well, I don't."

"Yes, you do," she said sadly. "You just don't want to admit it."

"That makes no sense at all."

"None of this does," she agreed. "I'm telling the man

I love that I want a divorce. How is that in any way logical?"

"I'll fight you on the divorce."

"Why?" she asked, one quick flash of hope sparkling in her eyes.

He was breathing heavy, as if he'd run a long race and was only now crossing the finish line, dead last. "Because you're mine. I don't let go of what's mine."

She sighed. "So you don't love me, but you don't want me to leave."

"I *care* about you," Dev said tightly, staring down into twilight eyes glittering with unshed tears. "Can't that be enough?"

"No," she told him. "No, it's not enough. I deserve better. *We* deserve better." Raising one hand, she touched his cheek then reluctantly let her hand fall again. "I'm so sorry, Dev. Sorry for what we could have had. For what we've missed."

When she walked away from him, Dev damn near chased her down. She was making him crazy. Couldn't she see that he was doing this for both their sakes? Love was an unstable emotion. They couldn't risk building a life on something that was so intangible. Couldn't she see that his way was the right way?

He stared after her long after their bedroom door had quietly closed behind her. Emptiness rose up in the shadow-filled room and threatened to swallow him whole. If she left again… No. He wouldn't allow it. Would find a way to stop it. He couldn't lose her. Not now.

He still had some time. She wouldn't leave before the Oscars, so that gave him at least ten or twelve days to change her mind. All he needed were the right words.

Shaking his head, Dev pushed that thought aside as he headed for the door that would take him downstairs into the Hudson family room. What he needed was some of his father's best brandy.

"You look like hell, boy."

Dev stopped in the open doorway of his father's study and looked at the older man seated across the room from him. Markus held an open book in his lap and a tumbler of brandy in his right hand. He could have been an actor on a movie set. The man of leisure at home, surrounded by walls of books, Tiffany-shaded lamps and a crystal carafe of brandy close at hand. Dev had never been more glad to see anyone.

"I've had better days," Dev admitted, then pointed at the brandy. "Got another one of those?"

"Help yourself."

He hadn't counted on seeing his father at the moment, but he realized that this was what he needed. He'd pretty much patterned his life after his father's. Who better to understand the way he felt about his marriage?

Dev poured himself a healthy draught of the French brandy, then took a chair near his father. Staring down into the amber liquid, he searched the surface for the answers to his questions and found nothing.

"So," Markus offered quietly, "you want to talk about whatever's bothering you?"

Snorting a broken laugh, Dev said, "Not really." Then he took a sip of the liquor and felt the fire of it burn right past the knot of cold in his chest. "But I think I need to."

Markus closed the book, set it aside and faced his son. "Shoot."

He should just start talking, Devlin told himself. But where should he start? How to begin?

"You and Mom," he said abruptly. "You've...worked things out?"

Markus frowned a little, took a sip of his own drink and nodded. "We have. I've convinced her to forgive me."

That had Dev's head snapping up and his gaze locking on to his father. "You asked for forgiveness? For *what?*"

"Damn, you really are like me, aren't you?" Markus shook his head and said, "Not everything's black and white, Dev. I made plenty of mistakes early in my marriage. As much as I loved your mother—*do*—love her, I never really allowed her into my heart."

Dev's throat closed up, but he forced another swallow of brandy down anyway.

His father continued, though, as if he hadn't noticed Dev's start of surprise. "I kept a distance between me and your mother. I spent too much time at the studio and not enough with the woman I loved so madly." He chuckled a bit and the sound was soft and sad. "I was so sure I was doing the right thing by holding myself back from her. So positive that was the way to ensure my marriage never overtook my life. Hell, I drove your mother into searching for the affection I denied her."

"She didn't have to betray you," Dev muttered, clutching the brandy snifter as if it were a life raft tossed into a churning sea.

"I betrayed her first," Markus said, leaning forward, bracing his elbows on his knees. "I cut her out of my heart and told myself it was necessary. When the only *really* important thing in the world is love. And the ability to give it as well as receive it."

Dev shook his head. He never would have expected his father to be saying these things and every word the older man said resonated in Dev's heart like a clanging bell echoing over and over again. What the hell was he supposed to think? Do?

"Dev, let me tell you something else," Markus said softly, "when you're an old man, looking back at your life, it'll be nice to remember the awards and things— but if you're looking back alone, it will mean your life was a failure."

Silence dropped over the room until the only sound was Dev's own breathing and the soft muffled tick of the clock on the wall. His mind was racing, his heart was pounding and one thought after another chased themselves through his brain. And every thought had one thing in common. Valerie.

"How? How do you do it?" he asked, slanting a glance at his father. The man he'd loved and admired his entire life. "How do you let yourself trust?"

"You find the right woman, like I did. Like *you* did. Cut yourself a break, son. Open yourself up before you miss everything worthwhile. Don't be the man I was. Be a better man. A wiser man."

Wiser. He'd thought he was wise in keeping himself cut off from his wife. But what kind of wisdom was that when it felt as though he was cutting his own heart out of his chest to be without her?

Markus shifted his gaze to the doorway and smiled broadly. "Sabrina."

Dev shot to his feet, turned around and watched his

mother's hesitation as she looked at him. Was she expecting to be shunned? For him to turn away from her? Well, why the hell wouldn't she? He'd been a roaring jerk for weeks, why would his mother have guessed that he'd finally come to his senses?

Setting his brandy snifter down on the table, he walked across the room, his gaze locked on his mother's. And when he was close enough, he wrapped his arms around her, pulled her in tight and held on as though he were a child again and needed the comfort only she could offer. "Mom, I'm so sorry."

She cried. One short, sharp sob, then she was holding him back, murmuring his name and rubbing her hands up and down his back just the way she used to. "Oh, Dev, honey, me, too."

"I know." He straightened up, smiled at her and said, "I've been a jerk for weeks. Hell, years. But I think I'm finally catching on."

She tilted her head to one side, gave him a knowing smile and asked, "Does Val know about this epiphany?"

"She's about to find out," he told her, already headed for the stairs that led to his suite. "Wish me luck."

"Luck," Sabrina whispered as her husband came up behind her and enfolded her in a tender embrace.

Val couldn't breathe.

She opened the windows in the bedroom she shared with Dev and lifted her face into the wind, and still it didn't help. She couldn't seem to draw air into her lungs and she guessed it was because her heart had shattered in her chest and the airways were blocked.

She couldn't believe it had come to this. She'd had

so much hope, so many plans. And she loved Devlin Hudson so very much. How could it all have dissolved so quickly, so painfully?

"Val!"

"Oh, God…" She swiped her hands under her eyes and steeled herself for whatever argument he might have come up with in the last half hour. But it didn't matter what he said. She couldn't stay with him, loving and never knowing what it felt like to be loved in return.

Val heard him rushing from room to room in the apartment, but didn't say a word, not anxious to once again have her heart stepped on. Finally, though, he came into the room behind her and she was forced to turn and face him.

"I thought you'd left," he said.

"I told you I'd stay until after the Oscars."

"Right. Of course you did. Look, Val…"

She held up one hand. "Please, Dev. If you don't mind, I'd rather not have the same argument again tonight. I'm just too…"

"No argument," he said and walked toward her with several long determined steps. "Just an apology."

She blinked at him, not really sure she'd heard him correctly. "An apology? For what?"

"Being a jerk," he blurted. "Not being what you needed. What we *both* needed."

Valerie felt a little dizzy all of a sudden and was forced to lock her knees in place to keep from falling over. Her heart gave a quick, hard thump in her chest. "What're you saying?"

"I'm saying I love you."

She swayed and he reached out to steady her. His

hands hard and firm on her upper arms, she felt the heat of his touch sliding down inside to ease the pain and erase the emptiness. "You what?"

"Love you. Wildly. Passionately. Desperately. I love the way you think. Your laugh. Your sighs. I love how your eyes look like the sky at twilight just when the stars first come out."

"Dev—" Oh, God, could this be happening? Could she really be hearing what she'd dreamed of hearing from him?

"You're smart, you're funny and you make me think. You make me a better man." He pulled her in closer, stared down into her eyes and smiled as he'd never smiled before. "I thought I could keep you at arm's length. Protect my heart. But you *are* my heart."

"Oh, Devlin, I love you so much."

"Good," he said, grinning now. "That's very good. I want us to go away together," he added. "Now. We'll take that honeymoon we never really had. We'll go to Bali or Europe or…wherever the hell you want to go."

"Now?" she said, laughing, hope rising up inside her like the most brilliant sunrise she could have imagined. "We can't go now, the Oscars."

He cupped her face in his hands and said softly, "Doesn't mean a thing to me. Screw Hollywood. All I need is you."

It was like waking up on Christmas morning and finding just what you'd wished for waiting for you. Val threw her arms around his neck and held on for all she was worth. "You don't know how much I love hearing you say that."

"I mean it, Val. All of it."

"I know you do. And not that I'm not enjoying this, but what happened? What's changed?"

"Me. I've changed. Being with you, loving you has changed me completely. I just didn't want to admit it. But those days are over."

"I can see that," she whispered, "and I'll take you up on your honeymoon offer the minute the Oscars are over."

"Deal," he said quickly. "And there's something else, too. We're moving out of the manor."

"What?" She drew her head back to look up into the eyes she loved so much.

"We're going to get our own place. Anywhere you want." He paused, then said, "Hey, the place two doors down from Jack's in Malibu was for sale. How about that?"

"The beach?" Her heart was racing, her skin was humming and her mind was filled with so much happiness, she didn't think she could take much more. She remembered the house he was talking about. Very Cape Cod. Very homey. Very perfect. "That would be wonderful."

"Done," he announced. "We'll buy it tomorrow. You can redecorate it every week, so I can break my legs on tables that shouldn't be there."

Valerie laughed giddily.

"And it has to have a great kitchen," he added, kissing her quickly, once, twice.

"With granite counters," she suggested.

"Oh, definitely," Dev agreed. "You'll see, Val. We'll build our own family. Our own place. Our own memories and traditions."

"With love," she promised.

"With more love than I ever thought possible," he

admitted, sounding like a man who'd finally found the road home.

"Oh, Devlin," Val whispered, looking up at him with stars in her eyes and love swamping her heart. The man she loved, loved her back and that was all she'd ever really needed. "Stop talking now and kiss me."

"Your wish," he said with a grin, "is my command."

Epilogue

The Hudson table at the after-Oscar party was loud and celebrational. *Honor* had not only taken Best Picture of the year, but awards for Best Director, Best Actress, set design, and so many others, Dev could hardly keep them all straight.

And it didn't matter anyway.

Dev had already won the most important thing in his life. The Oscars were just the frosting on the cake.

"To the Hudsons," he proposed, lifting his champagne glass and looking around the table at the family gathered there. His parents, his brothers and sister, his cousins and most especially, his beautiful wife. "We did it. We honored Charles and Lillian. We made the world see them as we knew them. And we did it with a hell of a lot of style."

Lots of applause, cheers and laughter followed that statement.

But Dev wasn't finished. "It's been a full year. For all of us." His gaze shifted from one familiar face to the next and love for his family overwhelmed him.

Val had given him this, he told himself and counted his blessings again. She'd opened him up to the possibilities surrounding him and he'd never again be the closed-off man he was when he'd first met her.

He sent a silent thanks to the fates that had guided him to her and he'd never stop being grateful to her for not giving up on him.

But his family was watching him, waiting.

So he smiled, reached down for Val's hand and closed his fingers around hers. Still holding his glass high, he ignored the roar of noise from the surrounding partiers and the music blasting down from the overhead speakers.

"We came through. All of us. The Hudsons are a family and that's where our strength comes from. It's what we draw on, what we lean on, what we depend on."

Smiles and nods greeted him and he felt like a damn king as he added, "To the family. To the heart of us. And next year…we win it *all*."

While their table erupted in cheers and laughter and kisses, Dev sat down, looked at Val and smiled. "I love you."

She grinned back at him, leaned in and kissed him hard and long, silently promising all sorts of private celebrations when they got home. "I'll never get tired of hearing that, you know."

"Thank God," he said softly.

Then as his parents left the table to dance, Val leaned in close again and whispered in his ear, "Are you up for another surprise?"

"With you? Always."

"I think I'm pregnant."

He jerked back, looked at her in stunned surprise and then laughed, loud and long. Standing up, he dragged her to her feet, then wrapped his arms around her and swung her in a tight circle. She held on tight and her laughter sounded like music to him.

"Make me a promise," he whispered.

"Anything."

"Never stop surprising me."

* * * * *

A sneaky peek at next month...

By Request

RELIVE THE ROMANCE WITH THE BEST OF THE BEST

My wish list for next month's titles...

In stores from 19th July 2013:

❑ Bedded for His Pleasure — Heidi Rice, Kate Hardy & Trish Wylie

❑ What Happens In Vegas... — Katherine Garbera

3 stories in each book - only £5.99!

In stores from 2nd August 2013:

❑ Claimed by the Rebel — Cara Colter, Michelle Douglas & Jackie Braun

❑ Princes of Castaldini — Olivia Gates

Available at WHSmith, Tesco, Asda, Eason, Amazon and Apple

Just can't wait?

Visit us Online

You can buy our books online a month before they hit the shops! **www.millsandboon.co.uk**

0713/05

Special Offers

Every month we put together collections and longer reads written by your favourite authors.

Here are some of next month's highlights— and don't miss our fabulous discount online!

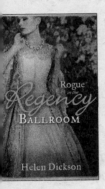

On sale 2nd August

On sale 2nd August

On sale 19th July

Save 20%
on all Special Releases

Find out more at
www.millsandboon.co.uk/specialreleases

Visit us Online

0813/ST/MB428

The World of Mills & Boon®

There's a Mills & Boon® series that's perfect for you. We publish ten series and, with new titles every month, you never have to wait long for your favourite to come along.

Blaze.
Scorching hot, sexy reads
4 new stories every month

By Request
Relive the romance with the best of the best
9 new stories every month

Cherish™
Romance to melt the heart every time
12 new stories every month

Desire™
Passionate and dramatic love stories
8 new stories every month

Visit us Online

Try something new with our Book Club offer
www.millsandboon.co.uk/freebookoffer

M&B/WORLD2

What will you treat yourself to next?

*Ignite your imagination,
step into the past...*
6 new stories every month

INTRIGUE... *Breathtaking romantic suspense*
Up to 8 new stories every month

*Captivating medical drama –
with heart*
6 new stories every month

MODERN™ *International affairs,
seduction & passion guaranteed*
9 new stories every month

n o c t u r n e™ *Deliciously wicked
paranormal romance*
Up to 4 new stories every month

RIVA™ *Live life to the full –
give in to temptation*
3 new stories every month available
exclusively via our Book Club

You can also buy Mills & Boon eBooks at
www.millsandboon.co.uk

*Visit us
Online*

M&B/WORLD2

Where will *you* read this summer?

#TeamSun

Join your team this summer.

www.millsandboon.co.uk/sunvshade

SUNSHADEa

Where will *you* read
this summer?

#TeamShade

Join your team this summer.

www.millsandboon.co.uk/sunvshade

SUNSHADEb

Mills & Boon® Online

Discover more romance at
www.millsandboon.co.uk

- 🌹 **FREE** online reads
- 🌹 **Books** up to one
  month before shops
- 🌹 **Browse our books**
  before you buy

...and much more!

For exclusive competitions and instant updates:

 Like us on **facebook.com/millsandboon**

 Follow us on **twitter.com/millsandboon**

 Join us on **community.millsandboon.co.uk**

Visit us Online | Sign up for our FREE eNewsletter at
www.millsandboon.co.uk

WEB/M&B/RTL5